DEALING WITH DISCIPLINE

BOOK 2 IN THE DOMESTIC DISCIPLINE SERIES

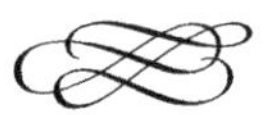

GOLDEN ANGEL

Printed in the United States of America

Cover art by DesignRans
Edited by MJ Edits
Formatted by Raisa Greywood

~

Thank you so much for picking up my book!

Would you like to receive a free story from me as well? Join the Angel Legion and sign up for my newsletter! You'll immediately receive a free story from the Stronghold series in a welcome message, and as part of the Angel Legion you'll also receive one newsletter a month with teasers, sneak peeks, and news about upcoming releases, as well as what I'm reading now!

ACKNOWLEDGMENTS

Thank you so much to Queenie and Fifi who have helped me throughout the writing process of this book and to all of you who are constantly motivating me to keep writing.

Thank you Lee Savino, my author sensei!

As always, thank you to my husband for his love and support.

CHAPTER 1

St. George's Church was packed with wedding guests, decorated with pink roses and white lilies, while the Rector, Viscount Petersham, Lord Hyde, and the Earl of Spencer waited patiently at the altar. Only the occasional shifting of Viscount Petersham's weight indicated his nervousness on his wedding day. The various ladies of the *ton* in attendance fanned themselves, whispering to each other as best they could without being overheard by their men.

The matrons with unmarried daughters were disgruntled, although they'd known for months about the arrangement between the Earl of Harrington and Baron Standish for their children. The missish daughters sighed over the loss of two of the *tons* most eligible, and handsome, bachelors, as Lord Hyde had recently been married to Viscount Petersham's sister. They were eyeing Wesley, the Earl of Spencer, with acquisitive determination. The more brazen widows and unhappily married young women eyed Hugh and Edwin with speculation, wondering if they would remain faithful to their brides and for how long. London was already abuzz with gossip about Lord Hyde's almost nauseating devotion to his bride; word of their behavior in Paris during their honeymoon had followed them home, and the ladies in London were finding no better luck in their flirtations than the ladies of Paris had. Then again, considering the close relationship between Lord Hyde and his wife's brother, perhaps he found it wise to cleave unto his wife and no other.

Reformed rakes made the best husbands of course, but how did anyone know if he was truly reformed? Most of the women, remembering the rumors of the passionate prowess when the men were bachelors, thought it wouldn't hurt to try their chances with any of the young lords standing at the altar.

The gentlemen in the crowd ignored the feminine titters and whispered remarks, their minds on their various wagers and businesses, and a few with an eye towards comforting those disappointed ladies of the *ton* who were sighing over the loss of Harrington's son and Lord Hyde. Not that either Hugh or Edwin had been particularly indiscreet or even overly generous with their affections, but those ladies whose beds they had graced had been well satisfied and their reputations were such that there had been plenty more who would have enjoyed their attentions.

Standing next to each other, outfitted in their finest clothing, it was no wonder they set the ladies' hearts racing. Hugh was the golden boy, his blonde hair glinting in the sunlight coming in through the windows, looking like every woman's idea of the perfect storybook hero. More than one lady whose bed he had graced had called him an "Adonis," further enhancing his reputation. Standing next to him, and looking like a dark angel compared to Hugh's lighter features, was Edwin, Lord Hyde. They were the extremes; it would have been easy for any man but Wesley to fade into the background next to such elegant gentleman.

Wesley was pure rogue, his roving hazel eyes filled with amusement and invitation, the waving, sun-streaked mahogany brown hair tied back into a queue. His tanned face and hands stood out starkly against the crisp linen of his shirt and cravat, making him look all the more dangerous. As a recent returnee to London, from exotic India, and newly come into his title of Earl, he was in obvious need of a wife and an heir. Obvious, that is, to the calculating matrons and their daughters, although gossip said there was no sign of him courting any respectable woman since his return. Surely with the example of his two closest friends he couldn't be far from the matrimonial way, the ladies reasoned.

Lady Hyde sat next to her father and mother in the front pew, the Earl of Harrington and his wife. Strange to think how one day Hugh would be the Earl and, as Edwin's wife, she would be a Marchesse. Unwillingly, her bright blue eyes flitted to the forbiddingly attractive figure of her husband standing next to her brother. Her heart fluttered every time she looked at him and she hated it.

When they'd returned from their honeymoon, she'd had the awful revelation that she'd fallen in love with her husband. Awful, because she had never intended to fall in love and, worse, she had no sign he returned any such strong emotions. Oh he cared for her, to be sure... but he always had, in the way a young man might care for a friend's little sister. She had no idea if his feelings had changed or grown from the affection he'd always held her in. He did desire her, of that she was certain.

Although now they were back from their honeymoon, the hinting questions of the other ladies of the *ton* had her wondering if his desire would continue once she provided him with an heir or if it might wane even before that. It seemed to her that far too many of the ladies were interested in her 'health' because they wanted to know when Edwin might give up his place in her bed and occupy another's. Far too many gentlemen of the *ton* were only faithful for as long as it took to beget the heir, if even that long, since many began to stray the moment they managed to get their wife with child.

Would Edwin be one of those? Would she even know if he was? Considering his close friendship with her brother she was sure he would be discreet, but her heart ached at even the idea. She was torn between wanting to have his child and the fear the passion between them would end the moment her monthly courses did.

Sometimes he looked at her in such a way she felt surely he must reciprocate her feelings. Yet how could she know for certain? He certainly never said so and she didn't have the experience to know if he treated her like a man in love would, or just a man who was fond of his bride. This was exactly why she'd never wanted to fall in love.

Once they'd returned home she'd resolved to discover what his feelings towards her might be, but every attempt had confused her further. She'd realized almost immediately she had absolutely no way to judge whether or not a man was in love with her. There were not many love matches among the *ton* for her to observe or compare her own marriage with and the one shining example she had of love within a marriage were her mother's feelings for her father. But even in her wildest imaginings she couldn't picture Edwin acting like her mother; she'd never fooled herself into thinking he was the kind of man who would shower her with affection, presents, and sonnets. Well, presents perhaps, he did like to give her things, but all men gave jewelry and flowers. In fact, many men gave them in lieu of apologies. Affection... if that went hand in hand with passion then he gave her that as well, but men were wont to show passion in the bedchamber, especially with a new wife. And Eleanor knew she was attractive.

At first she'd tried to be more affectionate than usual with him to see how he would respond, thinking perhaps a show of her own would spur him into admitting to some finer feelings. Instead he'd seemed pleased by her affections and responded by taking her to bed immediately.

His reaction seemed rather inconclusive since she wanted to know his emotions and not his passions.

That had led to her pouting and doing her best to give him the cold shoulder, wondering how he would react and thinking his response might give her further insight.

Which had gotten her a spanking—and not a pleasant one, like on their honeymoon—although not nearly as harsh as any of the ones she'd received before the honeymoon either. It had been more of a reprimand than a punishment for being disrespectful to him. Apparently Edwin did *not* like to be ignored when he asked her a question.

Would a man spank the woman he loved?

It was humiliating and painful, and yet it aroused Edwin like nothing else. So if passion was an indication of feeling then perhaps.

But Eleanor wasn't convinced that it was. Of course, she couldn't imagine being intimate with anyone other than Edwin, but that was because she was in love. Edwin, of course, had already been intimate with other women before their marriage—many women, she thought darkly. But he'd never been in love that she knew of.

Not that she had any experience with love herself, but she couldn't think of any other explanation for the warmth which fluttered through her whenever she saw him, the constant desire to be in his company, the piercing pain that lanced through her at the thought of him with another woman or the fact she constantly felt herself wanting to bow to his wishes and give him whatever he desired.

She fought the latter. Not just from pride but from self-preservation.

If he were to know she loved him then he could use her emotions to control her, whether or not he loved her in return. Exile her to the country, knowing she would do as he wished in order to make him happy. The same way her mother had always followed her father's edicts. And she couldn't live with that, she couldn't bear the idea of being so ill-used. She wouldn't allow herself to be.

If only she could be certain he loved her the way she loved him, life would be wonderful.

"Stop fidgeting," her mother hissed under her breath.

Eleanor sighed. "I can't help it," she whispered back. "When does this start?"

"The ceremony should have started already, but that's to be expected," her mother hissed back. "There are guests still seating themselves in the rear. Now stop fidgeting and be *silent.*"

Rolling her eyes, Eleanor leaned back against the pew. Nervous movement was a family trait, one that she shared with her father but she noticed her mother wasn't scolding him, even though he was twisting around in his seat as if taking note of who had dared arrived late to his son and heir's wedding.

"Sit up straight!" hissed her mother. The whisper strangled in her throat as she coughed delicately into her hand, covering it.

Stifling a retort, Eleanor straightened her spine. She'd always thought being a married woman would mean her parents would no longer try to mold her into the perfect Society lady. Obviously they hadn't thought the same.

~

"STOP FIDGETING," Edwin whispered out of the corner of his mouth to Hugh. Behind him he could hear Wesley chuckle. Fortunately everyone else was far away enough they couldn't hear anything the men said, although he was sure they could all see Hugh had begun shifting impatiently back and forth on his feet.

"Sod off," Hugh muttered back. "You have no idea what this is like, you didn't have to wait like this for Nell."

No he hadn't. Edwin hadn't had to wait at all, not for a courtship nor for a long wedding service. His beautiful lady wife was easy to find, sitting a mere fifteen feet from his position besides Hugh. Dressed in one of her new gowns from Paris, the soft peach and rose accentuating the peaches and cream of her skin and the pink of her lips, she looked much sweeter and more innocent than he knew her to be.

In fact, his wife was on the verge of sending him straight into madness.

Their honeymoon had been blissful, he thought they'd managed to come to an accord within their relationship during their time away. She had been the sweet yet spirited, joyful, passionate, and wonderfully creative young woman he'd known her to be. But it was as if she'd left that woman behind on the Continent. Since their return to London, Eleanor had blown hot and cold to the point where Edwin never knew what he would be facing in the morning.

The only place she was consistently pleasantly hot was in his bed.

No complaints about that.

But she was running him ragged outside of the bedroom. He had the most uncomfortable feeling his every word, his every action, was being observed and judged by his wife, and mostly found wanting. At first he'd thought perhaps she was still overwhelmed from her new position within the household, especially as she had finally taken up the reigns of responsibility she had originally neglected before their honeymoon. Then he thought perhaps the grandiosity and pomp of her brother's wedding was stirring her envy and possibly her resentment towards Edwin, as he knew she had not been entirely happy with the simple, private ceremony in which they'd been married.

He'd tried to be patient, although he'd taken her over his knee when she'd outright ignored his conversation. While he hadn't wanted to stir her resentment, if that was what she was feeling, that didn't mean he would tolerate disrespect. Still, she hadn't seemed resentful at all afterwards, he thought smugly. In fact she hadn't even tried to protest when he'd stripped the rest of her clothes off and taken her right there, immediately afterwards. It was amazing the effect she had on him, whether her skin was creamy or a bright, hot red…

"Stop that," Hugh whispered, nudging him in the side with his elbow.

"Stop what?"

"You're looking at my sister like you're about to devour her. Everyone can see you."

Edwin realized Eleanor was staring back at him, her eyes wide as if she was able to see exactly what he was thinking about. Other guests in the crowd were eyeing him as well and he realized his thoughts must have been practically painted on his face. Most of the men looked amused, most of the women disapproving, and more than one rather envious.

"You don't have to stay for the reception if you'd like to take your wife home afterwards," Wesley whispered, nudging Edwin from the other side.

"Shh," said Edwin, turning his head to look back up to the end of the aisle after catching Lord Harrington's eye. Hugh and Eleanor's father managed to look both amused and disapproving at the same time.

A rustle went through the crowd as the doors at the back of the sanctuary began to open, the stir of excitement as they all turned to see the bride.

~

SHE WAS SMILING SO HARD her face felt broken. Just like her heart.

Wife. She was a wife. And not to the man she loved. Hungrily she stared across the room at him, only to feel a stab of guilt like lightening through her chest. Quickly she turned back to look at her husband, catching her mother's eye on the way. She was Viscountess Petersham and she had to remember that. The hard look her mother gave her only heightened the anxious butterflies in her stomach.

Not butterflies. Pigeons. Nasty dirty pigeons pecking and scratching and clawing at the inside of her belly.

She deserved to be pecked from the inside out. Looking up at her husband she was consumed with guilt. Hugh was a perfectly wonderful man; incredibly handsome, unfailingly kind, generous, and with a sunny disposition (her mother would have added titled and wealthy to the list of desirable traits). He had a bit of a rakish reputation, but he also had a reputation for being discreet and there had been no rumor of any woman within the past year. Certainly not since he'd begun courting her. London gossip was a nasty business and she knew someone would have told her if there had been the slightest hint of impropriety on her groom's part. Despite the fact everyone knew this was an arranged match.

Any other woman would have thought herself to be marvelously lucky in Irene's position. Not only had she found a man to marry her, despite her family's financial situation and her measly dowry of land (although the location of that land was exactly why Hugh was marrying her), but he was young and handsome. Extremely handsome. In fact, going by the gossip, he was one of the most desirable of the unmarried men available.

But she hadn't grown up with him, he hadn't kissed her skinned knee or taught her to dance or ride. He hadn't brought her violets on her sixteenth birthday. He hadn't been her first kiss.

Unfortunately she'd given her heart away long before she'd ever met him.

Perhaps her guilt was misplaced. Her mother had reassured her over and over again that among the *ton* it was understood husbands and wives had certain... arrangements. Certainly she'd seen the evidence of that since she'd come to London. There were a few love matches however; in fact she was fairly certain Hugh's sister had one.

How she envied Eleanor that. There was no mistaking the affection in Lord Hyde's eyes when he looked at his wife, or the way Eleanor practically glowed when in his presence. Irene didn't feel glow-y at all. She felt rather wilt-y. And like a big fat liar. Because hadn't she just pledged to love, honor, and obey? Yet she did not love her husband. She had gone into the marriage already planning to be unfaithful as soon as she had provided him with his heir... but theirs was an arranged marriage and that was how such things were done, were they not? She's seen so many other marriages like that since arriving in London and her mother certainly espoused the notion, although Irene didn't like to think about what it might mean about her parents' marriage.

She did not expect fidelity from him, had not even before her mother had convinced her she should acquiesce to the arrangement, and so he should not expect it from her. At least, according to her mother's explanations. Yet it didn't sit right with her at all. Shouldn't she be expected to cleave to her vows?

"Are you alright sweetheart?" Hugh's voice skated across her nerves, his warm breath tingling against her ear. His breath smelled of mint and Irene found herself instinctively turning towards him, feeling a strange urge to be closer. There was no denying Hugh was a very attractive man, even to her. "You look pale."

"I'm fine," she said, giving him her best social smile. The concern in his bright blue eyes only made her feel even worse. Sometimes she wondered if he had feelings for her beyond affection, although her mother had shaken her head over and over during the courtship and said Irene was reading far too much into Hugh's solicitousness and gifts. "Just tired."

Something foreign and hungry looking glittered in Hugh's eyes for a moment, freezing her breathless to be on the end of such a look. She'd never had a man look at her quite like that, but it was becoming a regular occurrence with him. What did it mean?

"We'll be on our way soon enough," he said, taking her hand in his and giving it a kiss. The expression on his face made her think of a child being presented with a plate of sweets... and she was the plate. There seemed to be something more beneath his words than just a reassurance that soon they would be done doing the pretty, but she didn't understand what.

The warmth of his hand wrapped around her much smaller one seemed to sear her through the thin fabric of her kid gloves, the press of his lips hotter than ever and she felt a strange tingle sweep through her body as his eyes drifted down to the small amount of bosom exposed by her wedding gown. Edged with lace and gold threads, the bodice of her white gown hugged her body tightly, much more tightly than she'd realized before this moment when she felt like she might suddenly run out of breath.

"Now, now, time enough for that after your guests have left," Hugh's mother said chidingly as she stepped to Irene's side, beaming at her new daughter-in-law. Irene had never been more grateful for an interruption; she didn't understand what had just happened between her and her new husband but she had found it incredibly unnerving. Air suddenly filled her lungs again as the intense expression on Hugh's face slipped behind his usual social mask of complacency. "Come Irene, I want to introduce you to my cousin."

Obediently Irene allowed Hugh's mother to lead her away, sparing him a small glance over her shoulder, looking both intrigued and hesitant. He grinned at her before turning and striding to the nearest group of well-wishers, immersing himself back into his social duties.

"NICE WEDDING BRUNCH," said Wesley. He and Hugh had scouted out an alcove from which they could watch the activities without having to engage in them. Hugh hated doing the pretty and currently his mother was involved in showing off her new daughter-in-law so she wasn't there to badger him into it. "Very entertaining."

They were watching Eleanor lead Edwin on a merry chase around the room. For whatever reason she seemed quite determined not to spend very much time by his side, and he was just as determined to have her there. Unfortunately for him she was quite adept at starting just the right conversation which would mean the person she was talking to would want to engage Edwin in it, allowing her to slip away and join another group of guests. It would take him several minutes to untangle himself without giving offense, and then he'd be off after her again, his face becoming grimmer and harder with every stride he took.

Hugh and Wesley found it hilarious.

"Son!"

They turned to see Baron Standish approaching, a wide-grin on his face. Hugh rather liked the Baron; he was a family man, a good country man, who'd done the best he could for his family and Hugh respected that. Unfortunately the Baron's father had not been so responsible and by the time the title and lands had come to Irene's father they'd also come riddled with debt and neglect. The man had recouped such losses as well as he could, but a year of flooding followed by a disease running rampant through his sheep flock had set him back grossly. Hugh's desire to marry Irene had come at a crucial moment for the family and they all knew it. Although the Baroness seemed to resent the gratitude she had to feel towards Hugh, the Baron treated him as another son. Both being country men at heart they'd found they had quite a bit in common and had already talked about cross-breeding some of their dogs.

Standish was not a very tall man, almost an entire head shorter than Wesley and Hugh—who were admittedly blessed with long, lean bodies—but he was in very good shape since he spent most of his time outdoors, often on horseback. He was still a fine figure of a man, other than the loss of most of his hair. What was left ringed the crown of his head; despite the hints of gold and red it was obvious

Irene's coloring came from her mother. Fortunately, in Hugh's opinion, her personality had much more of her father in it.

"I hope you don't mind me calling you that," the older man chuckled. "I can't tell you what a relief, and a pleasure, it is to welcome you to the family." That honest forthrightness was one of the things Hugh liked best about the man; many amongst the *ton* would never had admitted to their financial straits, much less expressed gratitude in public for it. Wesley knew all the particulars anyway, being such a close friend of Hugh's, but many men would have too much pride to say such a thing at all.

"A pleasure for myself as well," said Hugh, grinning back at him. "And I don't mind at all. Have you met the Earl of Spencer here?" He gestured at Wesley.

"No, I hadn't," said the Baron, giving Wesley a little bow. "Spencer, my condolences on your father, I was sorry to read of his passing."

"Thank you," said Wesley, bowing back. "It was a hard time for my family." He didn't mention that he and his father had been estranged at the time or that the hardship, in Wesley's opinion, was not over the loss but over the responsibilities which came with assuming the title.

"You were in India, at the time, were you not?"

"I was," said Wesley, seeming surprised the Baron knew, considering the families were not previously acquainted.

Standish smiled disarmingly. "You came up fairly often in conversation with Hugh here," he said, by way of explanation. "Did you enjoy your travels? I always wanted to see more of the world, but with one thing and another... not that Caroline was ever interested in going farther than London." He chuckled indulgently.

Personally, Hugh didn't see how the amiable and personable Standish could bear to spend any time with his social climbing, judgmental, and icy wife, but to each his own. On the outside Irene might seem all closed up like her mother, especially when she was first introduced to someone, but she warmed up quite quickly and he was more than a little aware of the hot passion buried just beneath the surface. Just a touch was enough to set her simmering, although he was quite sure she didn't entirely understand her responses. He hoped with a little coaxing her passion would flare as brightly as her vibrant hair.

The conversation between Standish and Wesley flowed past him as he looked around the room, searching for the bright red hair of his new bride. Since she was the eldest and tallest of her sisters, and the only one dressed in shimmering white and gold, he found her almost immediately. She was facing Hugh and talking to another man, laughing actually, and Hugh felt a violent fission of jealousy lance through him. If she was talking so freely with the man she must know him well enough to feel comfortable; she was not the type to be so relaxed around a mere acquaintance. Unfortunately he couldn't see who it was because the man's back was to him, but he looked well dressed and his hair was a dark auburn, almost brown. Perhaps he was a relation.

Not wanting to look like the jealous bridegroom he was, especially if the man turned out to be a cousin, Hugh turned to his new father-in-law and waited for a break in the conversation.

As soon as it came, he pounced. "Excuse me gentlemen, Standish, I was wondering, who is that talking to Irene over there?" He nodded his head in their direction. "A cousin? I didn't recognize him."

Standish craned his neck, not having the advantage of height, as Wesley turned to look as well.

"Ah… oh, Alex. Lord Brooke, that is, Warwick's heir, and our neighbor on the other side. His mother is quite close with Caroline, so he and Irene practically grew up together. He's been like a big brother to her since she was born, looked out for her while they were growing up and such; I'm sure she's quite relieved he managed to come into town for the wedding, he hasn't been in London for a while."

As soon as he heard Brooke's name, Hugh relaxed a trifle. They were acquainted. Not well acquainted, but they'd met and he knew Brooke was a good man despite the… ah… circumstances with his wife. Well that explained why Eleanor's friend Grace wasn't here at least, he'd been wondering about that because he knew she'd been invited. Grace's mother was here, being bosom friends with his own mother, but Lady Grace would never deign to step foot in the same event as her husband if she could help it.

Brooke was a rake, true, but he never dallied with other men's wives. Widows, actresses, a few select members of the demimonde, but perhaps his own marital circumstances had soured him on accepting another man's wife into his bed.

Besides, the way Standish made it sound, they were like Wesley and Eleanor. Of course, Edwin and Eleanor had turned out rather differently. Controlling himself, Hugh turned back to his father-in-law, determined not to become a jealous bridegroom. It was good Irene's *almost brother* could come to their wedding.

CHAPTER 2

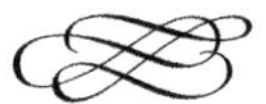

"You make a beautiful bride," Alex said, smiling down at her. Irene loved the way his eyes glowed when he looked at her, the special smile he reserved for her. He didn't smile nearly enough, but he always smiled at her. So what if he didn't look at her hungrily like Hugh did? She wasn't sure she liked the way Hugh looked at her anyway. It rather unnerved her.

"Thank you," she said earnestly, truly smiling herself for the first time that day. When Alex looked at her she could almost forget everything else in the world. Like the fact he was married to someone else and now so was she.

Alex had always been her knight in shining armor, her hero. She had no doubt if he'd known of their family's financial situation he would have waited to marry her. Her whole life Alex had always been everything good and kind, he had not only tolerated her following him around, he'd included her in whatever he was doing. Tall, handsome with his dark reddish hair and dancing, warm brown eyes, she'd been in love with him since she was a little girl. How could she not have been?

Then he'd gone away to school when she was sixteen, before she'd really grown into a young woman even though at the time she'd felt like one, and by the time she'd seen him again, he'd already married Lady Grace. Look how that turned out. The smiling young man she'd known had disappeared, replaced by a cold stranger… except for when he was with her, talking to her. Then he turned back into Alex. Irene was good for him, she knew she was. Who else did he always have a smile for? Who else could make him laugh? Since his marriage she had seen no one else who was able to do so.

If only he'd waited for her, she would have made him the perfect wife. After all he was the perfect man and he deserved nothing less.

But she would try to be a good wife to Hugh, she truly would… but in her heart she knew she would be waiting for the day when she had given Hugh his heir and his spare and then she could follow her heart's desire. Although she'd been wary of her mother's insistence that this arrangement would work, now, looking at Alex, she felt in her heart it would turn out fine. More than fine. Wonderfully. They could not be together as man and wife but they would be together in another way eventually.

"I'm so glad you could come today," she said feelingly. "It means so much to me that you're here to support me." What she really meant was it meant so much to her to be able to see him at all, to know he cared.

"Of course, pet," he said with a chuckle, reaching out to take her hand in his. Warmth suffused her, a burst of love and affection as he touched her. When they were younger he'd called her 'pet' because some of the other boys had teased her for following him around like a puppy dog. Alex had been the one to show her how to take the sting out of their taunts by embracing the idea, making it a special joke between them, turning it into a good thing. He didn't call anyone else in the world 'pet,' it was her own special nickname—and since coming to London she knew it was occasionally used by other men as an endearment. Actually she hadn't heard him call anyone else by any other kind of nickname or endearment either. It thrilled her to hear Alex call her that now, reassuring her she hadn't lost his affection just because she was now married. Obviously her mother had been right! "I wouldn't have missed it for the world. Although I doubt you need much support, your new husband seems like a good man."

"You've met him before?"

"On occasion, usually outside of London. He's a bruising rider. You two have a lot in common."

Such an observation surprised Irene, although most of her conversations with Hugh had included some discussion of life in the country. Still, she hadn't realized Alex would be considering her compatibility with another man.

"Alex." The woman's voice was low, husky, and seductive, cutting across what would have been Irene's reply. The kind of voice Irene couldn't imitate even if she practiced it. "What a surprise." Alex stiffened immediately, a dark look crossing his face.

Irene felt herself withdrawing, sinking into herself, as Alex turned his head to look down his nose at the elegant woman standing beside them. She was older than Irene, obviously closer to Alex's age, and a raving beauty. Long black hair, creamy skin, and a shocking expanse of bosom showing for a morning wedding; in fact, she looked quite a bit like Alex's wife in a superficial manner. From her time in Society Irene recognized Lady Winifred March, a widow whom she only knew of because she was rumored to be Alex's latest mistress. Here, at *her* wedding.

For a moment she felt outraged and hurt, betrayed, but that was nothing compared to the storminess now darkening Alex's face.

"It shouldn't be, as I told you I informed you I would be here when I saw you last week," he said in a low angry voice, one Irene had only heard him use rarely. It made her shiver, but Lady March just stood there provocatively, leaning forward as if to give him a glimpse further down her ample bosom. "I believe I recall asking you not to come."

Lady March pouted at him. Did the woman not realize how displeased Alex was by her presence? Did she think he was playing a game? Obviously, no matter how… *intimate* their relationship, Lady March didn't know him as well as Irene did. That thought filled her heart with a small surge of warmth, bolstering her despite the situation. She watched, fascinated by this display between the two of them. Never before had she been so close to a man having any kind of interaction with his rumored mistress—rumors which were obviously true —much less between Alex and his paramour.

"I didn't think you meant it," the lady purred, leaning closer to brush her chest against his arm.

Half disgusted, half fascinated, Irene couldn't tear her eyes away from the sight. Was this what men wanted? Despite Alex's icy demeanor he was still looking at the woman's bosom. By comparison Irene's own bosom felt very modestly covered and not nearly ample enough.

"I did. You received your *conge*, madam, and I have no further need of you."

With that, he turned his back deliberately and stalked away. Lady March sniffed in affront before turning and stalking in the other direction leaving Irene standing alone. Both of them seemed to have forgotten her presence, which might have upset Irene more if she hadn't known how very angry Alex had been made by his ex-mistress' presumption.

"What are you doing?" her mother's voice hissed into her ear, fingers suddenly digging into the soft flesh of her upper arm hard enough to make her squeal. "Why did you stand there like a ninny?! Bad enough you were flaunting yourself in front of Lord Brooke, looking at him like you're a lost little lamb, but to continue standing here *that* woman… with her reputation…" Mother was practically sputtering she was so upset but looking around the room no one else seemed to have noticed the altercation. Only Hugh was looking her way and he gave her a supportive little smile, making her heart beat a little faster. The man truly was too good looking for his own good, and she couldn't help but feel a little surge of pleasure that he was looking at her when there were beautiful women like Lady March about.

If only he could save her from her mother.

"Do not embarrass us." The fingers dug in and Irene bit her lip. There would be bruises tomorrow. Despite her pale skin she actually didn't bruise very easily, but her mother's digging nails and bony fingers would surely leave a mark. The fabric of her dress wasn't nearly strong enough to guard her skin against the sharp pinch. "Stay away from Lord Brooke. When you have given Hugh his heir and spare, *then* you can act the whore for Brooke, but not before."

The words stung and Irene gasped at being called a whore by her own mother, but there was nothing she could do. She knew from past experience that trying to deny her mother's accusations or defend herself would only result in further unpleasantness. Practically dragging her, her mother sat her down in a chair next to Eleanor who was looking rather sulky and glaring across the room at her husband. Unsurprisingly, he was now standing with Hugh and their friend the Earl of Spencer enjoying their conversation, but she could see his eyes continuously roaming over to land on his wife. Who glared all the harder every time he did so.

"La, my daughter is feeling a bit overwhelmed by all the excitement," her mother trilled with false cheeriness. "Would you mind if she joined you, Lady Hyde?" Without waiting for an answer she deposited Irene in the chair beside Eleanor, turned and floated off to find her friends again. Eleanor and Irene looked at each other.

"I'm sorry," said Irene, rubbing her forehead as she fought down the tears burning at the backs of her eyes. Sometimes she wondered if her mother meant to be cruel or if she was ignorant of how damaging her words could be. "If you don't wish for company I can sit elsewhere."

"No, join me," Eleanor said, her eyes returning to her husband for a moment. They couldn't keep their eyes off of each other apparently, although Eleanor didn't look entirely pleased at the moment. Actually she looked rather wary. "Was that Lord Brooke I saw you talking to?"

"Yes," said Irene absently, rubbing her arm where her mother had pinched the skin. "We grew up together." She found her gaze following Eleanor's to the three men across the room. They really were quite breathtaking as a group. Hugh looked up and their eyes met, a tingle went down her skin and she shivered and looked away.

He was looking at her *that way* again. The way that made her feel hot and strange, making it hard for her to breathe. She much preferred the way Alex looked at her, warm and comforting. Never setting her nerves on edge or disorienting her. Alex made her feel safe and secure. Hugh, for all his gentleness with her, always scared her a little even though he wasn't very scary in and of himself; but sometimes the way he looked at her made her feel almost itchy inside of her own skin. Of course she hadn't known him as long as she'd known Alex. She'd also known almost from the moment she'd met Hugh that he was going to be her husband and she'd unfairly resented him a bit, so it wasn't truly his fault, but she couldn't help it if she preferred Alex's settled company to Hugh's unnerving presence.

"What did Lady March have to say to him?" Although Eleanor wasn't looking at Irene and her attention seemed to be entirely on the men across the room, Irene couldn't help but remember Eleanor was friends with Lady Grace. Good friends. Was she asking to make conversation, because she was truly curious or because she wanted information to tell Grace?

Unfortunately Irene wasn't sure what Alex would want her to say so she just spoke the truth. He'd seemed quite intent on cutting Lady March, and if anyone else *had* been watching they'd know that much at least.

"She was flirting. He wasn't interested. He reminded her that she'd received her *conge*." Suddenly her breath caught in her throat and her eyes jerked away from Hugh's laughing face (why had she been watching him anyway?) and sought out Alex's familiar head of auburn hair as the significance of that remark finally dawned on her.

Of course she'd known Alex had mistresses. How could he not, what with the way things were with his wife? It had always made Irene's heart ache with jealousy, to know other women were having a part of him, a piece of him. But if he'd given Lady March her *conge*, it must have been recently; he was too angry about being approached and she was too eager to speak to him for there to have been any real time. How long would it take him to find another mistress?

Would she return from her honeymoon, finally knowing what

passed between a man and a woman, only to have to watch him indulge in *that* with yet another woman?

Or would it take him longer to replace Lady March?

Perhaps she could use her honeymoon to learn… to learn everything a man might want. Everything that pleased a man. Surely her husband would enjoy having a wife who knew what he desired, and when he tired of her and she'd given him his heir they could go their separate ways and she could show Alex how well she could please him. Of course, she wasn't entirely sure what being a mistress to a man entailed, but she knew it had something to do with the activities of the marriage bed. Whatever it was she was sure she could learn to do it for Alex. Learn to do it better than any woman he'd ever done it with before.

"My dear?"

Her heart seemed to leap into her throat as she looked up into Hugh's glowing blue eyes. Guilt swamped her as she realized she was yet again thinking adulterous thoughts on her wedding day. The way he was looking at her was almost tender, although there was still a hint of that strange hunger as well. Barely married for three hours and already she was thinking about the day when she would betray those vows. She was truly an awful person.

"Yes my lord?"

"I think you can call me Hugh now, sweetheart," he said, laughing a little as he reached out for her hand. Instinctively Irene placed her fingers in his, allowing him to help her to her feet as she blushed, feeling rather silly.

"Of course. I'm sorry."

"Don't be sorry," he murmured, stepping close enough to her she could feel his body heat, his hand searing her as he placed it against the small of her back. His other hand still gripped her fingers and she found herself staring up at him, feeling like a trapped bird, her heart pounding inside of her chest. The smile spreading across his face was rather wicked and her face heated as his eyes traveled back down to sweep across her bosom. Beneath her dress her breasts seemed to tighten in the strangest manner. "You can call me whatever you wish, sweetheart, but I prefer Hugh."

"Hugh." She repeated, and then nearly gasped as his eyes actually seemed to darken, like the sky when it was going to storm. The strangest expression ran across his face and suddenly it was almost as if they were the only two people in the world. Her breath caught in her throat and she found she couldn't speak another word, not that she could think of one to say.

Someone cleared their throat, loudly and closely, and she and Hugh both jumped and then turned their heads to stare at Edwin. Who was staring back at them, grinning. He shook his head and turned to his wife.

"Nell, can you help Miss—uh, Lady Petersham to her room."

"Right, yes." Hugh suddenly came to life again, as debonair and smooth as always as he looked down at her. The intensity of his gaze had lessened again; the moment, whatever it was, had passed. "My dear, as soon as you're ready to travel we may leave."

"Oh..." Irene said in sudden understanding as she looked down at her dress. Of course. She'd had her maid set aside a dress this morning for her to wear when it was time to go. The dress she'd been married in was far too fine to travel a long distance in a carriage, not to mention not as comfortable as the dress she'd set aside. A feeling of almost panic sparked inside of her. It was time to go so soon?

But there was nothing to be done. At least Eleanor would be with her and hopefully her mother would stay downstairs to entertain the guests. She was currently across the room and not even looking Irene's way so perhaps it was time to make good an escape. Turning to her sister-in-law she smiled tremulously.

"You don't mind going with me?"

"No, I'd be happy to go upstairs with you and spend some time with some worthwhile company," Eleanor said with a sniff and a pointed look at her husband. Irene bit her lip as Edwin raised his brow at his wife. She had always found Edwin a little frightening, with his dark good looks he managed to look rather dangerous, the way she'd always pictured a fallen angel to look (and she'd heard she wasn't the only lady of the *ton* to make that comparison). Although Hugh looked just like a true angel and yet she still found his presence disturbing, but she didn't truly find *him* frightening. Just her reaction to him.

~

SIGHING, Hugh watched his new bride and his sister walk away. Irene seemed quite skittish at the moment, although he chalked that up to wedding nerves. Especially now they were going to be alone in a carriage for hours, and it would be the first time they would be alone and completely unchaperoned together, but as long as they made good time then they should be to the first of his family's estates by sundown. Understandably she also might be a bit nervous about the wedding night.

He could only imagine what her icicle of a mother had told her to expect.

"What is the matter with Nell?" he asked, wondering why she'd been so sharp with Edwin.

"I have no idea," Edwin replied, staring daggers after his wife as she left the room with her arm linked through Irene's. They made an attractive pair with their contrasting hair of gold and red copper. "But I certainly intend to find out."

With a wry smile, Hugh gave his friend a sidelong look, thankful he'd ended up with a sweet bride like Irene and not a termagant like his sister. Not that he wanted to hear any details about why Edwin enjoyed disciplining his sister so much, but he had to admit he found himself curious as to what discipline might have to do with bedroom activities. It was certainly not something he'd ever thought to combine, despite the fact he'd been raised to wield the cane when necessary, whereas Edwin certainly had not. But it was only a mild curiosity and he was quite content to have it go unsatisfied. With a docile, sweet wife like Irene he was quite sure he would never need to use any kind of strict discipline.

"Excuse me, Viscount Petersham?"

Now that was a sentence he'd heard more than enough of this morning, and the masculine voice was completely unfamiliar, as quite a few of them had been. Stifling a groan he put on his best social smile and turned to find himself facing Lord Brooke.

"Ah, Lord Brooke, thank you for coming today," he said with a smile, holding out his hand for the other man to grip. He felt rather relieved he didn't need to search the other man out to speak with him, it also boded well that Brooke had approached him first.

"Brooke," said Edwin, offering his hand in turn.

"Hyde."

"Standish tells me you and Irene grew up together," Hugh said once they'd gotten past the pleasantries. "I confess I'm glad she had a long-time friend to attend the wedding today, although she's made some acquaintances in London, I could tell she feels much more comfortable with you." Hugh did his best to sound nonchalant, although truly he was waiting to see the other man's reaction to his words. Wondering whether Standish's depiction of Irene and Brooke's relationship was correct.

Brooke's smile seemed to almost split open his face, like a crack in a rock. The expression looked strange on him. Then again, considering the state of his marriage and his lack of heir, he didn't have much to smile about.

"She was the little sister I never had," Brooke said, shaking his head at the mental vision he had of a little girl with red pigtails done up in clashing pink ribbon. It had been a shock for him to see Irene all grown up, every time he'd returned to visit after leaving for school. Seeing her on her wedding day had been double that. "Still is. I hope you don't mind, but I felt it was my brotherly duty to speak with you."

Hugh raised an eyebrow, a little surprised but not offended. In fact he was feeling quite relaxed now that he'd heard Brooke's own declaration. "You waited until now?"

"Ah, I just came back to town recently," Brooke said, his face hardening again. "I've had some business to attend to at my estates." Apparently not very pleasant business. Or perhaps it was just the necessary business of making enough money to cover his wife's outrageous expenses. The woman did seem to enjoy spending his money even if she avoided his company. A small smile broke through again as he refocused on why he was speaking with Hugh. "I wouldn't have missed Irene's wedding for the world."

"That's good of you," said Hugh, smiling back. There was still a small twinge of jealousy that this man had known his wife for so much longer, but it was obvious from the way Brooke spoke of her, not to mention Standish' attitude, that there was nothing romantic between the two of them. While Hugh had to admit to himself he would prefer his new wife's friends be female, if she was going to have a close male friend at least it was one like Lord Brooke who obviously saw her in a familial light. "She seems to be quite shy, although I've quite enjoyed the time we've spent together."

"She and Eleanor seem to get along well," Edwin offered. "Nell likes her quite a bit, so I'm sure she'll make certain Viscountess Petersham is never left out at social events. My wife can be quite the champion for her friends." It felt strange to call a woman by his friend's title, but the obvious masculine smugness which settled onto Hugh's expression had Edwin and Brooke exchange an amused look. From his relaxed demeanor, every moment with Hugh was helping to ease Brooke's potential qualms about how well Irene would be cared for.

"I'm sure she'd be a wallflower if her mother would let her," Brooke said dryly, with a little twitch at the corner of his mouth. He shook his head. "Every time I see her in a ballroom it's a bit of a shock, she's much more at home out in the country."

"So she and her father have told me. I'll admit, I was relieved to hear she prefers the countryside although we'll have to come to London for at least part of the Season, of course. My parents would have pushed for the match anyway, for the land she brings with her, but I couldn't imagine myself with a wife who wanted to spend all her time in London."

"Yes... I'd heard it was an arranged match." Brooke hesitated, unsure of his right to say his next words and yet determined to do his duty by Irene anyway. "Do you... care for her at all?"

"Quite a bit," said Hugh honestly, unaware of the smile spreading across his face as he thought of Irene's sweet smile and beautiful face. "Otherwise I wouldn't have offered for her, land or no land. The more I've come to know her, the more I appreciate her company."

"You'll probably enjoy her company even more in the country," said Alex, looking rather relieved. More so at the change in Hugh's expression than his reassuring words, anyone paying attention could tell he was sincere in his affection for his new wife. "She blossoms out there." His voice lowered to a mutter. "Especially once she's away from her mother."

Edwin murmured his agreement and Hugh made a small expression of distaste. Obviously none of the men were enamored of the Baroness. It hadn't taken Hugh or Edwin long to realize Irene quickly clammed up in the presence of her mother and barely dared to breathe when the woman was watching.

"We'll be touring my estates for our honeymoon, I'm hoping she'll enjoy that. She didn't seem interested in going further afield, although Edwin and my sister just returned from their honeymoon in Paris." He nodded at his friend, acknowledging the trip.

Brooke raised an eyebrow. "That surprises me, I always thought Irene wanted to travel more than she was able to. But I'm sure she feels it's more important to see her new home."

"Hmm, perhaps," said Hugh, slightly perplexed but not wanting to show it. Irene had been rather adamant about not wanting to travel. Then again, perhaps Brooke didn't know her as well as he thought he did. He rather liked that interpretation.

A flurry of activity at the bottom of the staircase drew the men's attention and they turned to see Eleanor and Irene descending. Irene had changed into a dress more suited for travel, made of muslin which had been dyed forest green; the clever cut showed off her neat figure quite nicely, although the tempting expanse of bosom her wedding gown had displayed was no longer visible. The vivid color went beautifully with her coloring, much more so than her previous gown which had made her pale cheeks seem even paler even if her hair had flamed by contrast.

Hugh drew in a little breath at the sight of her, already picturing peeling the dress off of her and revealing all the delightful sights it was modestly covering. Beside him Brooke stirred and gave him an amused look, content at seeing the expression of near—infatuation on Hugh's face. With a quick word of farewell, Hugh was striding eagerly across the room to claim his wife, leaving Edwin and Brooke to amuse themselves at his expense.

THE CARRIAGE CARRYING Hugh and Irene away disappeared down the street and most of the guests began calling for their own carriages. As the weather was rather mild, some of the younger set chose to saunter down the street, ostensibly headed for Hyde Park which was only two blocks away. Eleanor watched them all rather enviously; unfortunately she was not able to leave until her husband chose to.

Her husband who was obviously not entirely happy with her at the moment.

If asked, she couldn't have explained why she'd spent most of the morning avoiding him. They hadn't been seated near each other at the meal, as it was their duty to help host the brunch, and after she had found herself playing a game of cat and mouse with him. Part of her wanted to see how long he would follow. Part of her wanted to watch him interact with other women while she wasn't standing by his side. And part of her just wanted to run.

Eventually her father had caught up with her, sat her down in a chair and told her not to move because she was making him dizzy with her constant rotations round the room. Edwin, seeing the exchange, had grinned triumphantly at her (and that burned as badly as when he'd bested her during their childhood) and then allowed himself to be drawn into conversation with his friends while she sat in her chair and sulked.

Considering she'd finally been given strict orders to stay in one place she had thought he would finally, definitively, catch up with her, not ignore her! It rankled and made her even more out of temper with him.

Once she'd returned to the festivities, after helping a rather nervous Irene change into her traveling gown, Edwin had reappeared at her side and she hadn't been able to get away since. Her hand was tucked into his elbow, his other hand covering hers to keep her securely connected to him. A few experimental tugs had produced nothing more than a scowl in her direction before he'd pulled her even closer to him, pressing her hand between his arm and side.

"What a lovely wedding," her mother sighed, as Edwin and Eleanor approached. She was standing next to Eleanor's father, who was chatting with Wesley. Lady Harrington was practically glowing with happiness despite the almost translucent quality to her skin and the bags and dark circles under her eyes. Edwin wondered if she was quite well, and then remembered that planning this wedding had probably taken a bit of a toll on her. "I can't believe we managed to get both of you married off, to such wonderful matches, all in one Season." Beaming at Edwin, Eleanor's mother looked practically blissful. Inwardly Eleanor sighed, but she didn't have it in her heart to dampen her mother's spirits by making any tart remarks about her own marriage. Besides which, she was under the distinct impression Edwin was at the end of his patience with her for the day.

"Which means you'll be able to return to Bath soon," Lord Harrington said, joining the conversation and smiling down gently as his wife as he took her hand and looped it around her arm.

Edwin could feel his own wife stiffen at his side and he looked down at her, wondering at the reaction, but her face was completely void of expression. Very blank in fact, which was rather unusual for her.

"Will you join me there soon?" Lady Harrington asked rather wistfully.

"For a bit, my dear," Lord Harrington replied, patting her hand. "I've completed most of my business in town for the moment." The smile that spread across Lady Harrington's face was nothing short of brilliant, quite similar to the genuine smiles which would flash across Eleanor's when the situation warranted it.

Not that it had today. Edwin was eager to get his wife home where he could question her as to her odd behavior, but it wouldn't do to be rude and leave too hastily. After all there were still a few guests mingling in the foray as they awaited their carriages, but he kept her firmly planted at his side as they circulated. He'd had quite enough chasing her around during the previous hours.

She looked beautiful today, in a dark rose colored gown displaying her splendid bosom to advantage without being overly revealing. Apparently, that lesson had been well learned—forcibly planted into her bottom really. The wisps of honey blonde hair that had escaped her pins curled and caressed the delicate length of her neck and it was all Edwin could do not to wrap the strands around his fingers. Eleanor entranced him, enchanted him… that is when she wasn't driving him completely mad. As she was wont to do.

It seemed to take hours, although it couldn't have been more than forty-five minutes, before they were able to take their leave from her parents. The carriage ride back to their home a few streets away was quiet as Edwin gathered his thoughts, knowing his silence was unnerving Eleanor. She pretended to be engrossed in staring out the window but she kept darting little glances his way, her cheeks alternatively blushing and paling. Edwin just stared straight ahead, which meant he was looking slightly over her head. Not quite at her.

When the carriage stopped he exited first and waved the footman off. He would help his wife down himself.

Nell nibbled at her plump lower lip when she saw him standing there waiting with one hand outstretched, but she delicately placed hers in it and stepped down. Unwilling to look at him, she kept her eyes downcast, pretending to be adjusting her skirts as he curled her hand around his arm again, and led her towards the house. There was just the slightest amount of resistance from her, as if she wanted to pull away but didn't dare to.

Good. At least she wasn't so willfully stupid as to make a scene in the street. It had been bad enough wondering whether or not anyone other than Hugh, Wesley, and her father had noticed him pursuing her around her parents' house this morning. His friends had because he'd been complaining of her odd behavior to them before the ceremony and so they'd been watching afterwards. Otherwise he might have escaped the embarrassment of providing them with some entertainment.

The tugging of her hand to get away from his grip increased once they stepped through the front door of course. Edwin nodded at Banks before turning his head to speak low into Eleanor's ear.

"Let's go to the library, I'd like to speak with you."

CHAPTER 3

Although Edwin's words had the sound of a request, Eleanor knew they were an order and she felt both more anxious and slightly calmer. At least it wasn't his study, with that awful chair, the one which seemed like it had been made to bend her over for discipline. It was far too like the one she'd grown up bending over in her father's study. Not that she'd done anything which truly merited a punishment this morning, although she was sure Edwin was quite frustrated with how elusive she'd been during the wedding celebrations.

Reluctantly she nodded and allowed him to lead her to the library. She swept in, ignoring the chairs in favor of freedom of movement, standing as far away from him as she could get as he closed the heavy doors behind them. They stood across the room from each other, he by the doors studying her, and her by the windows facing to the side so she could see out of the window while still keeping an eye on him.

He crossed over to the desk, which was behind her, forcing her to turn to face him if she wanted to keep him within her line of vision. Despite the fact that he was several meters away, she felt rather crowded just by the sheer force of his presence. It struck her again what an incredibly attractively dangerous man her husband was, and she could feel herself weakening towards him, wanting to touch him, kiss him, *be* with him. And yet she couldn't allow herself to do that. Be like her mother? Who was already being exiled to Bath now that Hugh's wedding was over?

Who knew when her father would let his wife return to London once he had her safely ensconced away from the capital; yet her mother would accept it, make the best of it and pretend to be happy even as she was sighing with longing for her husband. It didn't matter her father was going to accompany her now, eventually he would leave her mother there and, without Eleanor, she'd be lonelier than ever.

Well Eleanor would never find herself in that trap. If Edwin didn't have the same feelings for her as she did for him, then she would wall her own feelings away and never let them see the light of day.

Yet part of her still hoped perhaps there was something more to his emotions than just absentminded affection or the care a man might have for a woman he'd grown up with. More than the passion that flared up between them on a regular basis.

"Would you like to explain your behavior this morning?" Edwin asked, his voice deceptively calm. She could feel every one of her muscles tense, the skin on the back of her neck crawling. A casual observer, one who had not grown up with Edwin, wouldn't have heard the danger in his tone. Wouldn't see the stubborn set of his shoulders, the authoritative tilt of his head. It was the same voice she'd heard him use when he was twelve and had confronted the son of one of his father's tenants about putting a frog down the back of Eleanor's dress.

"I'm sure I don't know what you're talking about," she said airily as she swept to the other side of the room, keeping the desk between them and lengthening the amount of space. Part of her knew she shouldn't needle him like this, that she should at least acknowledge she'd been making him chase her all around Hugh and Irene's wedding brunch. At the very least she should ask him what he was talking about, but no, she had to phrase it in such a way that made it clear she was avoiding the issue. That she was baiting him.

There had to be something wrong with her, because intellectually she knew what the best course of action was and yet she poked at him instead. It was like poking a tiger with a stick. All fun and games, until the tiger realized the door to its cage was open.

"I'm sure you do," Edwin said, his voice taking on a darker, more dangerous edge, no longer quite so placid or calm. The war going on inside of Eleanor made her feel particularly testy as she battled her desire for him, fighting against her feelings for him by fighting against *him.* "You certainly led me a merry dance around your parents' until your father took you in hand."

Eleanor sniffed. "I was just being sociable. A good hostess. I don't understand what that has to do with you. Whatever you imagined I was doing, you shouldn't take it so personally." *Stop it,* she wanted to yell at herself. At the same time she was too fascinated by toying with him. Angling for a reaction that was something other than controlled and dignified.

Wondering if perhaps pushing him to a place beyond his control would reveal something of his true feelings for her.

Her husband took a step towards her and Eleanor eyed him warily, her clenched fists hidden in her skirts. She didn't want him to see what an effort maintaining this indifferent and careless pose was for her.

"I took it personally, *madam,* because you spent the entire morning avoiding me while I wanted to spend it with my wife on my arm." The taut anger in his voice was more than a warning sign and yet she found herself recklessly enjoying it. Nearly as much as she enjoyed hearing him admit he wanted to spend time with her, although she would have preferred if he'd said 'you.' Would he have wanted any wife of his on his arm, or was it only because she was his wife?

Shrugging one shoulder elegantly, she tipped up her nose at him. "Perhaps your wife was not so interested in spending the morning with you."

Now Edwin began walking around the desk and Eleanor swiftly began walking in the other direction, keeping the distance between them. He stopped immediately, scowling. He even looked attractive doing that. Attractive and foreboding. Her heart was starting to beat faster, a prelude to passion… or a warning of imminent danger.

"And why might that be?" he asked. Eleanor noted the fists clenched at his sides, the way the tendons stood out in his neck above his cravat. It sounded like his teeth were actually grinding together and yet he did not continue to chase her, he just stood there and asked questions as if he expected her to behave illogically, expected her to be a brat.

So she threw all caution to the wind and put her hands on her hips, rolling her eyes as if in exasperation. His own lack of reaction, his self-control, was feeding her impulsiveness, making her reckless.

"Why must we always be arm in arm? Other couples amongst the *ton* aren't like that. Grace didn't even come to the wedding today because Lord Brooke was there. Why must you always follow me around?"

"It seemed to me that originally you wanted a husband who would follow you around," he accused in a silky voice, his eyes hard as he began to circle around the desk again. Staring back at him, heart fluttering in her throat, Eleanor was unsure whether she felt fear or arousal as she began to move, doing her best to keep the desk between them. "A husband who would beg for your attention. Is that what you're doing Eleanor? Trying to make me into your puppy dog, to follow and beg for you? You think to teach me to do tricks?"

"N-n-o," she stuttered. She certainly had never thought she'd be able to make Edwin into the kind of husband she'd originally wanted, that her other suitors would have made. Or had she? Was that what she had been trying to prove today? There had been something immensely satisfying about making Edwin follow her all around the room, something she would have never expected to be able to force her confident, elegant husband to do. Even if he had stopped the chase once her father had sat her down. She was suddenly confused, wondering if she'd truly thought through her tactics.

Now he was chasing her again, but in closed quarters with no one around. A much more volatile situation, one almost guaranteed not to go her way. And yet… she felt almost excited by it. Excited and frightened. This, like so many of her other plans, was not going her way. She could see this little game of cat and mouse was rousing Edwin's passions, he was looking at her the same way he did before he undressed her at night, but she already knew he desired her. The goal had been to discover what softer feelings he might have for her.

Frustrated, Edwin stopped stalking her and planted his hands on the desk. "Come here, Nell."

"No." She backed further away, feeling even more contrary now that this plan—like so many others—had been frustrated. They'd rotated around the room so she was now closer to the door and Edwin was behind the desk with his back to the windows. Her backwards momentum was stymied when she ran into one of the bookshelves and she put out a hand to steady herself.

His voice lowered, almost coaxing, although no less dangerous for its gentleness. "Come here, Eleanor."

"No." Frustrated she practically threw the word at him. She didn't want passion, or she did, but it wasn't her goal at the moment and she didn't want to be distracted. Her emotions were chaotic, frustrated, and she was acting out of sheer instinct at this point.

"Eleanor I'm tired of this game." Edwin's dark eyes skewered her, accusing, almost hurt and it ripped at her, but she couldn't make herself go to him. She couldn't give in. That's what her mother would do, wanting to soothe the man she loved, whatever the cost to herself. But Eleanor wasn't her mother and if Edwin knew how much she cared, the way her father did, and still discarded her or sent her off to live in the country without him, like her father did with her mother, she could not bear it. Better he not know. Better she keep something back from him until she knew if she could trust him with her heart. *"Come here."*

"Why can't you just leave me alone?" she practically wailed, a sentiment straight from her heart. She didn't mean she wanted him to leave her alone really, just that she couldn't take much more of this uncertainty about his feelings towards her. That right at this moment, she couldn't bear to have him force her to reveal her feelings by coming to him when she had no idea whether they were returned. It felt as if she was standing on a precipice and he was urging her to jump, without promising he would be there to catch her.

He jerked as if she'd slapped him, looking incredibly startled. Who knew what would have happened then, how he might have reacted, if Eleanor hadn't been so far gone in her own torrent of emotions that she did something monumentally stupid.

Grasping the first thing that came to hand, an ornamental bookend on the shelf she'd been grasping, she threw it at him. Right at his stubborn, incomprehensible, unreadable head.

Her aim had always been good and it was only his quick reflexes which allowed him to duck out of the way. Watching in horror as the heavy wooden decoration flew across the room, Eleanor's hands covered her mouth as she stared in shock. Edwin whirled back around to stare at her as the bookend clattered to the floor behind him. She didn't think, she just whirled around and ran.

BEING on the opposite side of the room from his wife, with the desk in his way, had not been the best positioning, Edwin thought grimly as he stalked after his fleeing wife. She'd managed to get out the door and partway down the hall before he was able to come barreling out of the room after her. But he refused to run. Already there was a maid standing in the hall, staring open-mouthed after her mistress. He would not run after her… besides, his long strides, unhampered by skirts, made him move fast enough to keep her in his sights.

What on earth had possessed her?

His heart clenched as he wondered why she wanted him to leave her alone. What was wrong? Was it her monthlies? No… that had happened while they were still in Paris, it wasn't time yet. Was it resentment over the lavishness of Hugh's wedding in comparison to their own small ceremony?

The idea she was more interested in the trappings of a wedding celebration than in their union as husband and wife bothered him more than he wished to admit.

Whatever her reasons, he wished she had just talked to him instead of making her chase him. Not once, not twice, but *three* times now today. This time with their staff staring after them. His muscles burned as he stretched his legs as much as possible, doing his best to keep up with her without actually running. Damned if he was going to give up the last bit of dignity left to him.

Where the devil was she heading? She was going towards the back of the house, turning corners, almost as if she was trying to trip him up and lose him.

Edwin began to pick up the pace, jogging after her, cursing under his breath. At this point it didn't matter the reason, when he got his hands on her he was going to blister her bottom. Not just for her attitude towards him or her lack of communication, as frustrating as that was, but he couldn't allow her to actually throw things at him and then run without there being some kind of repercussion for such behavior. Although thinking about disciplining her was not assisting his pursuit of his wife, because of his inevitable reaction to thinking about turning her creamy little bottom a dark, hot red.

He'd already been somewhat aroused in the library, almost enjoying the contest of wills between them. So had she, despite the way things had ended. He was able to read her body language enough to know she had been fighting her rising desire.

Ignoring his amorous thoughts, Edwin abandoned his dignity and began to run, determined to end the chase. Hearing his pounding footsteps approaching, Eleanor glanced over her shoulder and squeaked, blue eyes big with anxiety, and darted to one of the servants' staircases. The one leading to the kitchens.

He caught her about five running steps into the kitchen, startling Cook and her assistants as they were washing and peeling vegetables for dinner that night. The staff stared at their master and mistress, shocked to see them disheveled, red-faced, and out of breath.

"Everyone out," Edwin said, his tone flat, tight. Still in command, no matter the situation.

Eleanor whimpered, a barely audible sound under the sudden rush of footsteps hurrying from the room. Fortunately it was too early in the afternoon for anything to actually be cooking, so the temperature of the room was fairly reasonable. He kept one firm arm around her waist as the staff fled, enjoying the feel of his wife pressed up against him, her soft bottom snug against his groin, her every breath panted against his restraining arm. Trying to distract himself from his desire to bend her over the table in front of them and sink into her immediately, his eyes wandered around the room, landing on a large wooden spoon and he grinned, hit by sudden inspiration.

Quickly he wiped the expression off of his face. No matter how much he might enjoy punishing his wife, the truth was she very much deserved it and it would not do for her to think anything otherwise. He truly was quite angry with her, but he was relieved he could also find something to smile about in the situation. While he had every right to be angry, he would not punish Eleanor unless he was in control of himself and his emotions.

Which, thanks to the minute it took for the kitchen to empty and his male interest to completely rouse, he was able to reign in his temper.

"Edwin," she said in a shaky voice, practically trembling in his grip. If she hadn't just thrown something rather heavy at his head, unprovoked, less than ten minutes before he might have felt some pity for her. "I-I—"

"Bend over the counter Eleanor," he said in a cold voice as he released her and put his hand in the small of her back, pushing her forward. She stumbled and he moved to catch her but she righted herself quickly enough. Still, she turned around fast enough to see he had positioned himself to help her, before he snapped himself back into place and looked down at her. Those big blue eyes were filled with what looked like true remorse and a few tears. She took in the expression on his face, the determination, and silently, slowly turned back around, facing away from him.

Placing her hands on the counter, she lowered her upper body onto it, biting her lip. This was going to be her first real punishment since their honeymoon and she knew it was going to hurt... so why was her heart thumping with excitement? Why did the area between her legs feel swollen and wet? What kind of woman was Edwin turning her into?

"Very good," Edwin murmured, pleased Eleanor hadn't protested or tried to talk her way out of being disciplined. Although, of course, she'd already tried to run and been caught so perhaps he shouldn't be too impressed with her current obedience, but it did give him a thrill how she'd meekly bent herself over the counter before him. "Now reach across and hold onto the other side."

It was at just the right height she had to go up on her tip toes to truly be able to put her weight onto the surface. By obeying his order for her to reach across, she was actually placing the full weight of her body on the counter, her legs dangling down so her toes were barely brushing the floor.

"Edwin, I'm sorry," she said, quite truthfully. The chase had worn down her chaotic emotions and now all she felt was guilt and regret. "I don't know what came over me. I didn't mean to lose my temper that way, I'll never throw anything at you ever again."

"No, no you won't," he said softly as he tucked up her skirts around her hips. He laughed softly at what he discovered. "No drawers, Nell? Are you sure you didn't anticipate this?" Eleanor whimpered but didn't answer as she felt the air of the kitchen on her bare thighs and bottom, unsure if she was whimpering from fright or arousal. She could practically feel the heat of her husband's gaze on her private areas, knowing they were basically in a public room where anyone could walk in at any minute, adding to the illicitness of the situation. "Is that all you're sorry for?"

Her fingers tightened around the edge of the countertop. Of course, he wanted an apology for her behavior at the wedding that morning.

"No," she said. "I'm also very sorry for making you chase me around the wedding brunch this morning. And around the house just now."

"Hmm," he said as he picked up the wooden spoon, knowing she couldn't see what he was doing. "You don't sound very sorry about this morning. But I believe I know how to fix that."

THWACK!

Eleanor shrieked. That wasn't his hand! The impact area was far too small, far too stinging to be his hand. It bit into her tender skin much more harshly than the blow she'd been anticipating. Her head swiveled around to see Edwin standing behind her, large wooden spoon in his hand, holding it up for another strike.

"Stop!" she cried out.

THWACK!

"You attempted to injure me with a wooden object," Edwin said calmly as he rubbed his hand over the two dark pink imprints on her creamy bottom as Eleanor gasped and half-choked on a cry. "It seems only fitting you now be spanked with one."

THWACK! He made a third imprint, admiring the way the spoon almost immediately turned the areas of impact a dark pink, but he'd lightened his blows a little as he could also see the effect was much greater on Eleanor than his hand would have been.

"It hurts!"

"It's supposed to. Now don't let go of the counter or we'll have to start all over again."

Tears burning in her eyes at the indignation and stinging pain, Eleanor clung to the countertop and swallowed back a howl as the spoon bit into her tender bottom again. Even worse, the pulsing burn had an answering throb from her core. The realization that some part of her body was enjoying this, even if it was out of her control, only made her angrier.

THWACK! THWACK! THWACK!

Edwin peppered her bottom with spoon marks, slowly increasing his pace and the force as her bottom began to twitch and heave up and down, her gasping breaths coming faster and harder. His cock felt like it might burst out of his breeches he was so aroused from seeing the crimson splotches which were blooming all over her arse, it was a good thing the garment had sturdy seams or he actually might have split one.

"Edwin, stop! I'm sorry, I'm sorry!"

TWHACK! THWACK!

"*Edwin*! You bastard, I said I'm *sorry*!" The plea and insult was accompanied by a loud sob.

He rested one hand heavily on her lower back, holding her in place as her legs began to kick and she squirmed and bucked against the counter top, filling in all of the ivory skin of her cheeks with a darkening red. Why had she insulted him, she wondered almost mournfully. Did she *want* him to spank her harder with the blasted spoon? The focused impacts were incredibly painful and yet Eleanor felt almost a lightening of her heart as they continued, as if the guilt over throwing something at Edwin was slowly dissipating, pushed out by the pain of her punishment. She was strangely aware of the heat of Edwin's hand against her back and the heaviness of his breathing, despite her own sobbing breaths and hot bottom.

"Two more," Edwin said, slowing to examine his handiwork. His wife was squirming relentlessly, unable to hold still, her bottom a patchwork of varying shades of pink. For a moment he was tempted to count and identify each shade... salmon, coral, magenta, fuchsia...

Examining the smooth back of the spoon and looking down at Eleanor's poor, punished bottom, Edwin was struck with sudden inspiration.

SMACK! SMACK!

She screamed bloody murder as the most incredible pain exploded through her body. The fire in her bottom was nothing, *nothing* compared to what rippled through her when Edwin landed the last two blows directly on her tiny anus. Although she'd occasionally had a birch lash at that tender spot, she'd never experienced a focused assault on the crinkled hole, and it more than burned, it stung like all fury.

With her legs kicking high in the air, her hands were clenched so hard around the edge of the counter that her fingertips tingled when she finally managed to relax them. The wooden spoon clattered to the floor as Edwin put both hands on her bottom, holding her in place and rubbing her abused cheeks.

"Shh, it's okay, it's over now," he murmured comfortingly as Eleanor's body shook with slowly subsiding sobs. When he slipped two fingers down to her quim, Eleanor moaned and shook her head as if to deny the evidence of her body. Edwin nearly groaned as he found her sopping folds, hot and swollen and soaking wet to the touch.

Why?

Eleanor didn't know. She hated the reaction, it was humiliating and it only served to encourage her husband. While she hadn't minded becoming aroused when he'd given her a rather pleasurable spanking in Paris, this situation was completely different. It was certainly nothing that had occurred when her father had disciplined her. But when it was her husband doling out punishment it didn't seem to matter how much it hurt, her pussy creamed itself as if the burning of her skin somehow translated itself directly to the warmth at her core.

Perhaps it was just Edwin's presence which made the difference. He was certainly more creative than her father had ever been, constantly changing the type of punishment and amount of strokes she received. And doing so with an erotic enthusiasm that couldn't help but translate itself to her, especially when she saw his eyes darken with passion and his manhood swelling with need. She wanted him inside of her.

"God, Eleanor," he said with a groan, pulling her up from the counter and flush against him, turning her to face him, his hands gripping her bottom hard as he plundered her mouth with his tongue. The back of her skirts were still rucked up and Eleanor cried out as his hands dug into her hot flesh, the stinging pain magnified by the kneading motions of his fingers. The hard ridge of his erection pressed against her body, nestling into the V of her legs as much as he could with her skirts in the way. He kissed her as if he was drowning and she was air itself, desperately, passionately, and she opened herself to him, inviting him into her mouth and body.

Her fingers felt practically numb from the time spent gripping the counter, the softness of Edwin's coat strange against the pads of her fingers, his hard chest tense beneath it. When he pulled away her lips felt swollen from the force of his kisses and both of them were breathing hard.

"Edwin!" she screeched as he flipped her over his shoulder, pulling down her skirts to decently cover her bottom and legs. Her head hung down on one side, her legs on the other, one of his hands around her legs and the other wrapped upwards around her waist with his hand resting on one buttock. Even through the layers of her skirt he could feel the heat emanating from her red hot bottom.

"Quiet," he growled, giving her a sharp smack on one upturned cheek, hard enough to make her squeal again.

Eleanor covered her face with her hands, both mortified and somewhat excited as he paraded her like that out into the hallway, ordering the staff back into the kitchen before heading towards their bedroom. No one dared comment of course, but her face heated almost as red as her arse as she thought about what they must be saying once they were back in the safety of the kitchen, knowing the master and mistress of the house would be busily ensconced in the bedroom.

She couldn't bear to look up to see who else of their household might be watching as Edwin paraded her though the house on his shoulder.

"Edwin, set me down!"

His only response was another sharp slap against her rump that made her shift and bite her lip to muffle her squeal. Edwin was behaving like a complete barbarian! And yet... it made the hot aching need between her legs increase as if he'd put his mouth to it.

CHAPTER 4

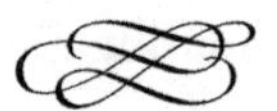

The need to get his wife alone and naked had completely overridden any veneer of class or decorum that had been ingrained into him, awakening his most primitive instincts. It was only some small part of his brain insisting he didn't want anyone else walking in and seeing his wife *dishabille* that had him carrying her to their bedroom rather than taking her in the kitchen the way he wanted to. That and he found himself rather enjoying hauling Eleanor around over his shoulder; there was something wonderfully proprietary about it, almost as disturbingly arousing as his reaction to punishing her beautiful bottom.

When he finally put her down in their room, after kicking the door closed behind him, Eleanor's face was flushed pink from embarrassment as well as the blood which had rushed to her head when she was upside down, her perfect hair was half undone with the pins falling out of it, and she looked alluringly disheveled despite her obvious humiliated outrage.

"Edwin how could you?" she cried out as he pressed her backwards until she was trapped between the bed and his thighs, their lower bodies almost fused together. Edwin kissed her jaw when she turned her lips away, his hands already behind her, undoing the buttons going down her back. Eleanor wriggled against him, trying to find a more comfortable position as her flaming backside was squashed against the hard frame of their bed, causing her hips to jerk forward as the hard bulge of his erection nestled against her soft belly.

"How could I what?" he asked, kissing his way down Eleanor's neck. His wife let out a little moan as he scraped his teeth along a spot he knew her to be particularly sensitive, her hands clutching at his jacket now rather than pushing at his chest. Feeling her resistance melt only inflamed him further, driving his need to claim and conquer her.

"Carry me through the house!" she practically wailed. The way she responded to him was humiliating, even when she should have been furious she could feel herself on fire for him. And not because of the smoldering state of her poor bottom.

Edwin laughed, tugging her dress away from her body, moving away far enough to push it down over her hips so she was standing in nothing but her chemise and corset. All day she'd been without her drawers, he realized as his eyes roved over the glint of golden hair beneath the sheer fabric of her chemise, that small patch denoting where her womanhood was. It was enough to make a man's blood boil, thinking about her lack of proper undergarments. Did she do such a thing often?

"I thought you would be protesting your spanking first," he teased, pulling at the laces on her corset, desperate to get her undressed. Eleanor's face blazed hotter and she looked away, no longer able to meet his eyes. "Does this mean you enjoyed that?"

"No," she said stubbornly, although she still couldn't look at him. Then her eyelashes flicked as the corset was tossed away and he took her breasts in his hands, squeezing them through the silky material of her chemise.

"Well I enjoyed it," he said, watching her face as he fondled her breasts and pressed his lower body to hers. With her weight supported by the bed it was easy for him to slide between her thighs, his cock nestled against the hot snugness of her body. His voice lowered to a verbal caress, seductive and hungry. "I enjoyed seeing you bent over the counter, your gorgeous arse up in the air, turning dark pink with every slap of the spoon. I enjoyed hearing you cry out my name, hearing you beg me, hearing you moan." Eleanor let out another little moan, her eyelashes fluttering as her nipples turned to hard little pebbles he pinched and rolled with his fingers. The pulse in her neck throbbed and he leaned forward so he could lick the fluttering spot before whispering directly in her ear. "I enjoyed seeing how wet you became while I spanked you, knowing some part of you wanted it."

One hand slid between their bodies and pulled up the front of her chemise so he could cup her womanhood with his palm, one finger slowly sliding inside of her as Eleanor gasped and clung to his coat. She was now straddling one broad thigh, which was supporting his hand as the heel of his palm pressed against her swollen pearl, his finger swirling inside of her tight tunnel.

"No..." she whispered, a useless denial.

"Don't lie to me, Eleanor," he whispered into her ear, nibbling on the sensitive lobe, feeling her body riding his hand and thigh, her sheath tightening around his probing finger. "We both know you enjoy it when I punish that sweet arse of yours and then fuck you hard afterwards."

Eleanor moaned, a guttural sound of pure erotic need, arching against him. Placing his mouth over hers, Edwin kissed her deeply, drinking in the sounds of her passion. They rocked back and forth, his finger fucking her until he felt her begin to quiver and then he pulled away, leaving her leaning against the bed, shaken and unsatisfied.

"Take off the chemise," he ordered as he began to untie his cravat.

Licking her lips, Eleanor stared at him, her sapphire eyes dark with lust, the swollen tips of her breasts pressing against the thin fabric, sensual need obvious in every line of her body. For a moment he thought she might protest, continue to fight, but then she pressed her thighs together and a small shudder ran through her. The needs of her body conquered her desire to rebel and she submitted to him, grasping the hem of her chemise and pulling it over her head as he dropped his cravat to the floor, pulled off his jacket and began unbuttoning his waistcoat.

"Up onto the bed," he said softly. "On your hands and knees, facing away from me."

Again he thought she might refuse, but then she turned, tendrils of golden hair caressing her shoulders, and climbed up onto the bed. The sunrise colors of her creamy cheeks had deepened and merged to become a brilliant overall dark pink, with a few darker tinges scattered across the landscape. He nearly tore the front of his breeches in his haste to get them undone.

Feeling even more vulnerable than usual, Eleanor glanced worriedly over her shoulder. She truly felt as if she was putting something more than just her body on the line, giving in to Edwin the way she was. Yet it felt so natural, so right. But frightening as well.

"Edwin?" she asked, craning her neck to try and see where he was and what he was doing, feeling a sudden need for reassurance.

"Stay just like that, Nell," he rasped, his voice heavy with passionate urgency. "God you're beautiful."

The mattress dipped and then she felt him behind her, caressing the curve of her bottom and making her whimper a little as his hands brought back little flickers of flame across the sensitive surface. She'd almost become used to the low burn until he'd touched her cheeks and it flared up again, his fingers felt rough against the sensitive surface of her skin. Then the head of his cock brushed up and down the wet crease of her quim and she moaned as the burning shifted, spreading from the surface of her body to deep inside of her.

Why did this feel so good?

They both groaned as he pushed inside of her, her snug passageway gripping the length of his cock in a way that pleasured both of them as her muscles stretched. Two rocking thrusts and then he was buried completely inside of her, staring down at her gloriously red ass which was flush against his groin, the creamy skin of her unmarked back a stark contrast to her buttocks. Eleanor's head tipped backwards and he reached forward, wrapping his hand around her jaw and thrusting his finger between her lips. She mewed like a cat, her sheath squeezing him and releasing as her tongue licked against his fingertip like it was a small cock.

He pumped his finger into her mouth and then pulled it away to trail down her back and grip her hips before he began to withdraw from her body, feeling her shudder beneath his palms. Leaving just the head of his cock inside of her wet heat, he paused.

"Tell me you want me, Nell."

"Edwin…" Her head dropped forward, thrusting her bottom upwards even further and he knew she was trying to hide her flushing face, even though he couldn't see it anyway.

"Tell me, Nell." Running his fingers over the heart-shaped flaming red of her bottom, he pushed in and out slightly with his cock, teasing her swollen folds. "I want to hear you say it."

She was burning for him, her entire body on fire for him, of course she wanted him… she just didn't want to say it. But the stark desire in his voice called to her too, the idea that he wanted her just as badly as she wanted him. Perhaps in more than one way.

"I want you," she whispered into the sheets.

"I can't hear you."

"I want you, Edwin," she said, practically moaning his name and she felt his cock jerk inside of her as it surged forward, heard the urgent need in his voice as he groaned her name and plowed into her. Her back arched as he bottomed out. "Edwin, I want you."

The rough thrusts of his body as his hands pulled at her hips were enough to send flaring pain through her already punished cheeks, his body slapping against them and causing them to jiggle and ripple with every shove of his cock into her juicy tunnel. Eleanor moaned and her fingers dug into the sheets, her body bowed down before him like a worshipper as she lowered herself to her forearms to brace herself against his rough thrusts. And yet… he found himself wanting to see her face more than he wanted to see her red bottom bounce and quiver.

Pulling himself out of her, Edwin flipped her onto her back before she realized her body was empty, shoving himself back in between her spread thighs with a force that took her breath away. Her face was flushed, her pink lips open as she moaned almost without taking time to draw in new breath, eyes bright blue and unfocused as her lashes fluttered over them. Beautiful. Erotic. A woman in passionate heat, freshly punished and writhing in sexual need.

"Edwin!" she cried out in surprise, her hands coming up to rake across his chest. Nails bit into his skin and he groaned, the shock of her sharp attack almost making him lose control. It felt good, too good. He grabbed at her wrists and held them down above her head as he lowered his mouth to hers, giving her the fleeting image of an avenging dark angel looming over her before he began to plunder her lips.

With her hands trapped in his, Eleanor felt so incredibly small and vulnerable beneath his hard body. It reminded her of when they'd been in Paris and she'd fulfilled one of his fantasies, which had involved tying her to their bed while he'd pleasured and filled her. Only this was far more intimate than a cravat, far more dominating to feel the strength of his fingers wrapped around her delicate wrists, holding her securely in place. Pain in her bottom flared as it rubbed against the fabric of their covers with his thrusts slamming her into the bed, her legs wrapped around his with her ankles digging into the backs of his thighs as she tried to draw him deeper into her. His cock seemed to fill her completely, over and over again, her helplessness against his hard hands, the complete surrender of her body to his as he held her down, had her screaming his name as she climaxed in a burst of heat and light.

He felt his wife shatter beneath him, encouraging his strokes to become harder, more ruthless as his own release came upon him. The pump of his hips surged as his ecstasy rose and he burst, sending jet after jet of frothing seed deep into her body. The convulsions of her climax throbbed around his cock as it pumped its offering into her womb. They cried out together, lost in a sea of sensual bliss, their bodies jerking with the force of their passions.

Collapsing on top of her, Edwin rocked his hips more gently, savoring Eleanor's breathy cries as her climax slowed and softened, her body beginning to relax beneath his. He propped himself up on his elbows and brushed the tendrils of hair from her forehead, staring into her blue eyes as they slowly came back into focus. Red-rimmed eyes, from the crying she'd done when he'd taken the spoon to her bottom. If not for those eyes he could have almost forgotten he'd just punished her, quite thoroughly.

With a small sigh Edwin kissed the tip of her nose. "My beautiful, rebellious Nell. Why did you run from me this morning, sweetheart?"

"I don't know," she said rather miserably, pouting as she closed her eyes to him.

Knowing he wasn't going to get any better answer than that for the moment, Edwin let out a little chuckle and withdrew from her body, turning her on her side so he could curl himself around her and hold her close in his arms. She was so soft and warm, and right now it was as if he'd beaten all the snippiness out of her and had been left with his sweet Eleanor. Holding her tight, he wallowed in the moment.

More confused than ever, both at her reaction to being spanked with a spoon followed by Edwin's obvious need for her and tenderness towards her, Eleanor wondered what kind of marriage she'd gotten herself into. Would Edwin ever say the words she wanted to hear? At moments like this she was sure he must feel something more for her than mere affection. Or was she reading too much into his actions?

Was she putting too much emphasis because that's what she *wanted* to believe? Was she already dooming herself to be her mother?

She had a moment of pure envy for Irene. If Hugh wasn't in love with his wife already, he was more than halfway there and she knew her brother wouldn't hesitate to express his feelings for the woman he loved. He'd probably never spank her either, she thought sourly as the press of Edwin's hard stomach against her poor, abused bottom made her wince. But not because Hugh didn't know how to be a disciplinarian, she just couldn't imagine Irene ever transgressing so badly he would feel the need to.

Of course she could do the same thing. If she chose to. Still if she ever behaved badly enough that Edwin sent her away, the way she'd originally planned, then his feelings towards her would be rather clear. While he obviously wished she wouldn't need discipline, there was no denying the effect it had on him. She thought wistfully back to the rather playfully pleasurable spanking he'd given her in Paris.

Somehow she just didn't think it was in her to behave well enough to only ever receive that kind of punishment to her poor bottom. Besides, being spanked and kept close rather than banished from his presence... well, strangely, it made her feel loved.

HUGH STUDIED his bride from across the carriage where she was looking out the window as if the scenery outside was the most fascinating thing in the world. That had seemed somewhat plausible while they were in London and perhaps a bit plausible for the first hour in the countryside, but they'd literally been riding past the same scenery of meadows for close to an hour and a half now. The silence had lengthened throughout the ride and was now beginning to make him uncomfortable. After all, he could have chosen to ride beside the carriage out in the open air—which he would have preferred—but he'd thought it would be more considerate to ride in the carriage with his bride.

"Well... Irene," he said, reaching across to take her hand, deciding she'd had long enough to gaze out the window. She started in surprise, those wide green eyes finding his and blinking rapidly as if she'd truly expected to ride in silence the entire trip. Then again, thinking about her mother, it wouldn't surprise him at all if Irene was used to riding in silence—it was probably better than starting a conversation with that harpy. He gave his new wife his most charming grin and had the pleasure of seeing her flush in response, her fingers fluttering against the palm of his hand the way a frightened baby bird might. "Are you looking forward to seeing Stonehaven?"

Stonehaven, the great house located in Harrington, center of his father's Earldom. Irene swallowed, trying to focus on the conversation rather than on the way Viscount Peter- *Hugh*'s fingers were caressing her palm. It was his family seat and their first stop on their honeymoon. Although he'd asked if she wanted to travel abroad, Irene had insisted they stay in England. Secretly she'd always wanted to see more of the world, but that was when she'd had hopes of marrying Alex. Now she preferred to stay in England, close to her family and her childhood love, the white knight she could always count on to protect her when the situation called for it.

So she'd informed Hugh she'd like to stay in England for their honeymoon and he'd suggested she see her new lands. He'd told her they'd visit two other estates, the last one being his primary seat in Westingdon until he inherited the entirety of it upon his father's death. Westingdon's lands were the ones which abutted her family's, although she'd never visited the great house there, known to the locals as the Petersham Seat. Named after the heir's title of course. The house was called Stanley House. Now it was her home. How very, very strange.

"Oh yes," she said, a little breathlessly and she told herself it was at the thought of suddenly becoming such an important lady and not because of the warmth of his hand on hers. It truly was strange how her body always reacted to Hugh's gentle touch in such an odd manner. "I do love to be out in the country. It will be such a relief after all the bustle of London."

"Ah, but I did see you enjoying yourself at some of the balls," he teased gently and she looked up into his sparkling blue eyes before her glance skittered away as if frightened by what she saw there.

"I do love to dance," she confessed. "But the socializing was a bit… overwhelming. And the crush of people! Sometimes I thought I might be squeezed to a tiny sliver of nothing in the press."

"I certainly won't miss it," he said with a chuckle, and her breath caught as he turned her hand over in his and stroked his thumb along the center of her palm. Even through the glove she was wearing, she felt the caress like a hot brand across her flesh. "I look forward to showing you around your new home."

The warmth in his voice should have increased her guilt over her love for Alex when she was married to Hugh, would have at any other time, but she was too distracted by his touch and the nearness of his body as he leaned forward. His eyes caught hers again and held, the way she imagined a snake's might hold a mouse, as he undid the buttons of her glove one by one. Had such an act ever been so strangely exciting? The baring of the skin on her arm made her feel vulnerable, anxious… The jerking carriage seemed to disappear as her heart pounded in her chest, her mouth suddenly dry. Her corset was too tight and yet she couldn't ask him to stop even if she wanted to.

Cool air brushed over her wrist as he flicked back the fabric and began to gently tug it from her hand. Irene was ensnared, captivated, by the hungry look in his blue eyes, the feel of her glove slowly being tugged away. She gasped when he touched her hand without that thin covering, the pads of his fingers almost harsh against her softer palm.

Very slowly, watching her very carefully as if he was afraid she might bolt, Hugh lifted her hand to his lips and pressed them to the center of her palm. Irene's heart felt like it might actually burst out of her chest it was thumping so hard, her breasts heaving against her corset as if she'd just run through a field or galloped on a horse. Soft... his lips were soft... but his eyes were hard as sapphires and that caused just as much consternation in her body as the warm press of his lips against her skin.

Then he was lowering her hand and she was surprised to feel a pang of disappointment, although he kept her hand in his.

For himself, Hugh was all too aware of the need to hold onto his self-control. Irene was a complete innocent, although obviously attracted to him. Her passionate nature was hidden but present, and while he looked forward to undoing her inhibitions he had not meant to finish his quest in a moving carriage. Only to begin his seduction. Her flushed cheeks and quickened breath indicated he'd awakened some of her senses, and he needed to get his own back under control before he ended up ravishing his bride along a country road.

"I hope you will like Stonehaven and the Stanley House," he said, his voice somewhat rougher than normal as he shifted in his seat, trying to relieve the pressure on his groin without her seeing what he was doing. If she'd even realize the significance of the bulge at the front of his breeches. "Especially Stanley House, as I spend at least half the year there and I'd like you to be there with me."

Irene smiled somewhat tremulously, surprised at her reaction, which was pleasure at the thought. Surely she couldn't enjoy the idea of spending her time with Hugh over being with Alex in London? Even if the time with Hugh would be out in the country. Goodness... she'd almost forgotten Alex completely when Hugh had begun to touch her! Guilt from the other side suffused her. What kind of flighty woman was she, to forget her one true love just because another man was touching her?

True, no man had ever touched her bare skin the way her husband just had, but that was certainly no excuse.

Confused, Irene pushed her feelings to the side and concentrated on what Hugh was telling her about the estates. At least she could appreciate his obvious love for the country. She was rather enjoying his conversation, something else she hadn't entirely expected. Irene had become rather used to keeping to herself ever since Alex had gone to school; it was nice to have someone interested in what she was thinking, to ask her questions and want to converse.

"I haven't had the pleasure of seeing you truly ride," Hugh was saying, smiling at her with that almost devilishly attractive smile of his. If she hadn't been in love with Alex, and if Hugh's touch didn't do such disturbing things to her body, she might have been able to fall in love with him for his smile alone. He truly looked like an angel when he smiled like that. "I'm looking forward to doing so once we're in the country."

Her returning smile was one of pure pleasure and anticipation. "I do love to ride. I enjoyed exercising your horses through Hyde Park, but you're right, they were not nearly as enjoyable as being in the country where I can gallop."

"Well then we will have to make sure we get our fill of riding before we must return to town," Hugh said with a laugh, squeezing her hand—and, it felt like, the air out of her lungs again.

~

STONEHAVEN WAS MUCH LARGER than any residence Irene had ever been to, even out in the country when she'd attended a few house parties with her mother. It fairly took her breath away, even if Hugh hadn't been doing that on a regular basis throughout the entire carriage ride. He'd helped her put her glove back on as they'd driven down the lane, but even so his touch still burned when he helped to hand her down from the coach. The small smile on his face indicated his pleasure at her delighted and amazed reaction to his family home.

Indeed, the carriage ride had served to make Irene look almost deliciously disheveled; softer, with wisps of hair around her face that had escaped from her coiffure. The wrinkles in her dress only made him wish he'd been responsible for some of them. While she looked less sophisticated, she also looked much more approachable… less like a model of what a proper young lady should look like and more like a flushed, happy young woman. He'd like to make her look even more flushed and happy.

But he would not descend on his wife like a ravening beast, even if he felt like one after torturing himself the entire carriage ride by touching her the soft skin of her hand, watching her soft, pink, tempting lips as she spoke, and smelling the sweetness of her skin as it permeated the small confines of the carriage. Irene smelled like a dream and he couldn't wait to bury his face in her hair and breasts.

"Welcome to Stonehaven, dearest," he said, lifting her gloved hand to his lips. For once she didn't blush at the contact, she was too busy examining the house with something akin to awe.

It was beautiful, larger than any house she'd ever been to before, and yet somehow as welcoming as it was imposing. While she'd known the reputation of the house as being made entirely of stone, she hadn't expected the dappled appearance of the walls. Most buildings she had seen that were made of stone were done so in rocks of the same color.

"Is it really all made of stone?" she asked, blinking as she stared up at the impressive four stories and the many windows set in rows.

Curtains were visible through all of them, although she couldn't tell the exact color of the highest row.

"Hence the name," Hugh said with a grin, wrapping her hand around his arm as he began to lead her towards the entrance.

"I always wondered which came first," she admitted, looking up at the monstrosity. "The name or the house."

Hugh laughed. "The house, although the stone was taken from the quarries around the land here so I can see how you might have thought otherwise. If the area *had* been known as Stonehaven already, it would have only made sense to build the house with it. Although, of course, inside there's wood paneling on the floors and walls. It's only the outside of the house that's made with stone."

"It's beautiful," she said honestly. She rather liked the uniqueness of its structure, although by modern standards it was rather mundane, without the more decorative baroque elements which were currently all the rage. Irene thought the simplicity of Stonehaven's lines were very appealing and the various hues of black, white, and grey more than enough decoration.

Her husband seemed pleased by her appreciation of the house, although her admiration was nothing but the truth. For herself, Irene enjoyed the tour although she was quite sure she wouldn't remember the location of every room he showed her. Fortunately they would spend most of their time in the public rooms and the East wing, which is where the family's rooms were, so that was what she concentrated on trying to memorize.

"This is my room," Hugh said and Irene felt a vivid blush rising in her cheeks as he led her into one of the bedrooms along the second floor hall.

"Oh..." she said as he crossed over to open the drapes a bit more and let more light in. The room was furnished with heavy wood and moss green drapes and cushions, without the slightest hint of a woman's touch. The heavy bed was huge, larger than any she'd seen before and she walked forward in amazement to examine it more closely. The four posts were carved with nothing more than a few swirls around their lengths, the coverlet on the bed a slightly lighter shade of green than the curtains and cushions of the chairs.

Suddenly she was aware Hugh had moved and he was standing behind her. Standing very closely behind her, his hot breath on the back of her neck making the little hairs all over her body rise. The infernally strange reaction she seemed to have every time he was near had slowly dissolved somewhat during the long carriage ride as she'd become accustomed to his presence, but now it had returned more intensely than ever. Turning to face him she took a step back, discomfited by the gleam in his eye, only to run into the bed.

The gleam seemed to shine brighter as he took a step forward, effectively trapping her between himself and the very large piece of furniture.

She could barely breathe as her husband looked down at her, one lock of blonde hair falling across his forehead. For some strange reason she wanted to reach up and brush it back, but she was too frozen to move.

"Well, our room really," he said, the smile on his face softening and he stepped back as if he was aware he'd startled her. "I hope, if you agree."

"Our room?" she echoed, her mind struggling to catch up with what he was saying.

"Yes, our room," he said, stepping toward her and reaching to grasp her hand. The very closeness of his body set her heart thumping madly, her body thrumming with a strange kind of physical awareness she'd never experienced before. It was similar to the disquiet he usually stirred within but much more intense. "I know it's not the usual thing, but I would prefer to share a room with you, if you do not object."

"Oh..." she said, unsure of how she should react. But she did want to be a good and obedient wife to Hugh, even if her heart was with another man, and her husband obviously wanted her to say yes. Irene was good at doing what other people wanted. "That would be nice."

The smile that lit up his face told her she had made the right decision and he brought her hand up to his lips, turning it so he could lay a kiss on the inside of her wrist. The touch of his lips against that bare patch of skin was so intimate, so shocking to her as a young woman who had been quite sheltered by her parents even by the standards of the *ton* for unwed virgins, that she quite thought her knees might give way beneath her. What was this strange power Hugh had over her, that he might make her so discombobulated?

"Good," he said, and then, before she quite understood what he was about, he pressed his lips against hers.

This was nothing like their kiss at the church, Irene realized that immediately. The long hard line of Hugh's body moved against hers, trapping her between him and the bed, and she let out an involuntary moan. He took advantage of the parting of her lips to thrust his tongue in, claiming her mouth. Irene was shocked by the blatant indecency; her mother hadn't mentioned such a thing at all. Was this the marriage act? Or part of it?

It couldn't be though... it wasn't night time and they weren't in the bed... and it was nothing like the descriptions her mother had given her. Irene felt breathless pleasure, a strange sense of rising excitement in her breast as her heart fluttered and she found her mind melting away into a sodden heap of sensation. Little thoughts flitted through the back of her head, warnings about Hugh's physical effect on her, alarm at her reaction, and fleeting thoughts about Alex... all of which seemed very far away in comparison to the reality of her husband's hard body, his caressing hands, and the taste of him in her mouth.

Irene's innocently passionate response to his kiss had Hugh going up in flames, his self-control rapidly unraveling. He felt quite certain she had no idea she was whimpering in the back of her throat, the sound completely innocent and yet wildly erotic. The movement of her body against his thigh seemed completely reactionary, instinctive, and not at all aware. With her soft, supple body trapped between him and the bed, he was able to caress her through her dress, internally cursing the corset which kept him from feeling the softness of her breasts. Instead he placed his hands against her bottom, cupping a handful of each mound and pressing the v of her legs more firmly against him.

The gasp against his lips as he touched her so intimately reminded him he was dealing with a virgin. His pure, untouched wife, and with a groan he pulled his mouth from hers and let his hands drop back by his sides. Irene stared up at him, her red hair in minor disarray, green eyes wide with shock and so dark they almost looked like jade rather than emeralds. Her usually creamy pale skin was flushed bright pink, her lips swollen and dark from his kiss. Leaning her weight against the bed, she looked ready to crumble to the floor and it was all he could do not to lift her in her arms, lay her down on the bed, and consummate their nuptials immediately.

But, by the same token, he didn't want to frighten his new wife with his appetite for her. At the moment she was looking up at him with confusion, lust, and wariness. He would not have her think him a savage, to take her so quickly and without proper ceremony.

"Well... shall we continue?" he asked smoothly, reaching to take her hand and kiss it. Even the one small touch had his groin aching, but he controlled himself.

"Continue?" Irene asked, feeling more than a little dazed from the assault on her senses and its sudden removal.

"With the tour of the house," Hugh said, although a purely masculine smile wreathed his face. He'd never made love to a virgin before and he found Irene's innocent and untutored responses, not to mention her obvious passion, to be more appealing than he would have thought possible. It was the way she fell into her actions, as though she couldn't help or stop herself, rather than being controlled and purposefully seductive. Although he'd desired her almost since he'd seen her and had felt the attraction flare between them on more than one occasion, he hadn't been sure how she would actually respond to her wifely duties. Any doubts he'd had were now erased and he was more than eager to introduce her to the pleasures of the flesh.

"Oh... yes..."

Hugh kept his hold on her hand as they continued onward.

CHAPTER 5

As her maid, Flora, helped Irene into the scandalous filmy nightrail that had been provided as part of her trousseau, Irene couldn't stop trembling. Dinner that evening had been pure torment. All she could do was wonder what the night would bring, her first night as Lady Stanley, and what the marital act might involve. Hugh had always been gentle with her so she couldn't imagine him hurting her deliberately. Perhaps he wouldn't indulge in the act at all?

But it was her understanding the marital act was what would ensure an heir. And he needed one of those. Biting her full lower lip, Irene gave her maid a side long look and wondered if she dared ask her for some womanly advice.

She had not been brought up to be familiar with the servants, but at the moment she was feeling a dire need for some kind of feminine reassurance and it didn't matter the social class of the giver. A small gurgle of laughter nearly bubbled out of her chest as she wondered what her mother would think of Irene contemplating begging a maid for advice.

"You look beautiful, my lady," Flora said as she tied the gown at Irene's neck. It would have taken a completely unobservant person to not see Irene's distress; it was clear from the tremors shaking her body, the gnawing of her soft pink lip, the frightened eyes and the pale cheeks that not all was right with the lady of the house. Flora's heart had gone out to this wane looking creature with her soft voice and polite manners when she'd first been hired by the Baroness and had been thrilled Irene had asked her to continue her position after Irene became a Viscountess; Irene might not be the warmest mistress but she was certainly not a cruel or haughty one either. "Your husband will be very pleased."

"Thank you, Flora," Irene said, her voice barely higher than a whisper.

That little bit of reassurance helped bring some of the color back to Irene's cheeks as she remembered her goal. A goal she seemed to have forgotten ever since Hugh had kissed her in his—*their*—bedroom during the tour. She needed to learn how to please her husband; she needed to learn everything about pleasing a man so she could become Alex's next mistress. Since she had no idea what being a mistress would entail she would be her husband's student and she would have his babies quickly and efficiently and then she would be free to pursue the man she'd loved all her life. That was how things were done in the *ton*, she reminded herself, repeating her mother's words. There was no need to feel guilty she was already planning to break her marriage vows.

After all, this was an arranged match with no love on either side. According to her mother, Hugh would have his own mistresses. Strange how the thought made her stomach curdle a bit. Surely it was only because she disliked the idea there was no love at all within their marriage and she was no longer free to wed the man who held her heart. She wondered if Hugh had a woman he loved but could not be with. But she didn't enjoy dwelling on that thought any more than she did on his hypothetical mistresses. Only because she didn't like the idea of unrequited love, such as hers. Of course that was the reason she felt strange at the thought.

"My lady?" Flora's soft voice broke through her reverie. "Are you ready?"

No. That was what Irene wanted to scream. No, she was not ready to face this irrevocable future, to learn what the dreaded marriage act was, to lie back and allow a man who frightened her to touch her and do... something to her. Was the act really so unspeakable her mother could not have given her any further instruction?

But she had no choice. It was not as if she could stand in her dressing room all night, although thank goodness she and Hugh had separate dressing rooms even though they were sharing a bed chamber.

"Yes," she whispered, steeling herself for... well for whatever was going to happen next.

The marital act.

After all, she reminded herself, she had to learn how to do this if she was going to eventually be Alex's mistress. Men enjoyed it, wanted it. Whatever *it* was.

Flora ushered Irene into the room. Her wide green eyes darted around the corners until she located her husband, standing in a dark blue dressing gown in front of the fireplace. In the flickering light of the fire Hugh looked even more angelic, especially as the velvety blue of his robe set off his blond good looks. His hair shone like a star against the night sky and Irene had to catch her breath as those strange reactions his presence elicited rippled through her.

For his part, Hugh could only stare at Irene. The gauzy white nightrail she was wearing did very little to hide her charms. He could see her little pink nipples poking at the material, the faintest blush of color behind the fabric, and the darker thatch of coppery color glinting between her legs. His mouth felt dry with absolute raging lust and he had to remind himself she was inexperienced. That he would need to go slowly with her.

"Wife," he said, his voice imbued with all the desire he had for her, all the hope for their future. Holding out his hand, he forced himself to stand still so she would come to him. Despite her obvious trembling, Irene tilted her chin up with determination and stepped towards him. The thin fabric of her nightrail whispered around her, caressing her body, and she felt the strangest throbbing in her lower belly as she reached out and met her husband's hand with her own. The smile he gave her was nothing short of wicked and her breath caught in her throat as he pulled her into his body the same way he had when they'd last been in this room.

Except there was no bed behind her, instead his arms had wrapped around her like iron bands, holding her in place as his mouth came down on hers. The kiss was gentle, coaxing, surprising her with its tenderness and she found her mouth automatically opening to receive his tongue. This time she kissed him back. Shyly. Hesitantly. Daring to dart her tongue out and explore his mouth as well, causing Hugh to groan and press against her, tightening his grip on her soft body and nearly lifting her off her feet in his passion.

Irene was already lost in the heady sensations ricocheting through her body. She felt consumed by the strange throbbings, the hunger erupting inside of her. It was almost frightening how out of control she was, and yet her fear was lost in the maelstrom of other, more powerful sensations. The gentleness of Hugh's kiss shredded and his mouth claimed her, his hands pulling her tightly against him. Irene's pulse pounded as she moaned, allowing him deeper into her mouth.

Sweeping her up in his arms, able to wait no longer and reassured by her passionate response that she wouldn't panic, Hugh headed for the bed.

Too lost in the heat engulfing her, in these new sensations as Hugh stroked her body and plundered her mouth, Irene didn't even notice where they were going until her new husband was tossing her onto the bed. Then she had a moment to stiffen in fear as she remembered what they were there for, a panicked expression crossing her beautiful face as her mother's words and advice seemed to echo in her ears. Yet when she looked up at Hugh as he stripped off his robe, those words seemed very quiet and very small.

It was her first time seeing a naked man, after all, and she was both shocked and curious about the differences between their bodies. Hugh was muscular, hard where she was soft, with long flat planes of skin dusted with wiry golden hairs, slightly darker than the ones upon his head. Rising from his groin was a thick, long staff of flesh that was nothing like Irene had ever seen or imagined before. It was strange looking, with a reddish-plummy head, reminding her of a dome. The entire appendage was slightly darker than the rest of his skin, and darkest at the tip where a bead of moisture had gathered around a small slit in its end. Completely fascinated, Irene stared at him, watching as the strange appendage jerked upwards before her eyes.

"Did your mother explain what happens tonight?" Hugh asked as he crawled onto the bed, his cock bobbing beneath him. He wanted to hold it in his hand but he didn't dare touch himself; he was so randy at finally having Irene for himself that he didn't trust himself not to spend his seed immediately. When he did, he wanted to be deep inside of her.

"She... ah... yes..." Irene's pale face heated to a bright pink which clashed adorably with her flaming hair. Leaning back against the pillows with her legs firmly together, as he approached she pulled her knees up to tuck against her chest and wrap her hands around herself. Her wariness returned now that he was no longer kissing her.

Hugh smiled reassuringly, laying himself down on his side next to her, close but not quite touching her. "It's all right, sweetheart," he murmured as he stroked his hand down her arm. She looked at it as if it were a snake, his reminder of the talk she'd had with her mother bringing back her fear. So far everything had been quite delightful, which meant they weren't to the bleeding, painful part yet or the boring part. "We'll take this slow."

He reached up to cup his hand around the back of her head and pull her mouth back down to his. He'd already seen how she melted into his kisses and considering her obvious anxiety over the marital act, he decided it was best to slowly seduce her body until she was past the point of thinking. Past the point of worrying. It might just kill him to take things so slowly, but it would be worth it in the end if he could convince her that making love was wonderful rather than fearful.

Slowly he shifted until she was beneath him, although he didn't rest his weight on her. Irene was lost in his kiss, in his gentle caress as he stroked the side of her stomach with one hand. It wasn't until she felt the brush of fabric against her thigh that she realized he was slowly pulling the hem of her nightrail upwards, to expose her body to him.

Putting her hands up, she was shocked when her fingers encountered bare skin. She'd almost forgotten he was nude. Hugh pulled away to look down at her as she stared at her fingers, splayed across his chest. Her skin was so much lighter than his, he looked almost golden next to her pale ivory. Curious, she stroked the wiry hair she encountered there, reaching down to explore the flat pink nipple until she heard him hiss and she snatched her hands away, remembering where she was and who she was with and what they were doing.

"Don't stop," Hugh husked, grabbing her hand and bringing it up to touch his chest again, lowering his mouth to hers. The skin of his nipple was baby soft with a hard little nubbin in the center, and she felt, more than heard, him groan as her fingertip ran over it. Suddenly the length of his hard body was pressing against her side and she realized her touch must have some kind of effect on him. Perhaps the same disturbing effect he had on her?

Experimentally she rubbed her fingers over the little nub again and his kiss suddenly intensified, his tongue thrusting deep into her mouth as his body pressed against hers. Perhaps his weight should have frightened her, but instead she found herself turning towards him, eager to press herself against him as well. Despite the fire burning through her, she found she craved the heat of his body. Her fingers stroked through the hair on his chest, returning to his nipples over and over again as he flexed his hips against the side of her thigh.

When his hand touched the bare skin of her thigh she cried out in surprise. Her nightrail was ankle length when she stood, how had he pulled the skirt up so high without her noticing? Now he was trying to pull it higher still, to expose her body to him.

"Wait," Irene cried out, tearing her mouth from his. Her pink lips were swollen from his kisses but her eyes were wide with confusion, desire and more than a touch of fear.

"What's wrong sweetheart?" Hugh asked, nuzzling his mouth over her ear and licking at the soft lobe. Irene moaned, unable to stop herself, as a shudder went through her body. Her hands clutched at the bunched fabric of her gown, trying to pull it downwards, but Hugh didn't let her. "I want to see you."

"No, please..." she begged, looking up at him and Hugh sighed as he looked at her and saw the consternation in her expression. "I can't... it's so immodest!"

He laughed, but he also stopped trying to tug up the rest of her gown. "Very well sweetheart, you may leave the gown right here. I will push it no higher and you will push it no lower."

Irene might have protested, but then Hugh pressed his hot, wet, open mouth to her neck, licking at the sensitive skin there and she found herself moaning and writhing, her hands automatically coming up again to press against his chest as he shifted more of his weight atop her. Almost feverishly, she wondered at his compromise when he obviously wanted her to be as nude as he was; she had half-anticipated he would force the issue. Instead he was letting her retain a bit of her modesty and she was grateful for it.

She needed the thin shield between them, because she was fast losing herself to the mindless pleasure that his hands and mouth were igniting within her. Only she found it wasn't enough to protect her. Hugh's hands cupped her breasts through the gossamer material, squeezing gently and her insides spasmed in response. Nothing had ever felt so good... at least, not until he lowered his mouth to her nipple and sucked it into his mouth, his tongue laving over the fabric and rubbing it against her sensitive nub. Crying out, Irene found herself clutching Hugh's head to her bosom, her back arching as she thrust her breasts up towards him.

What was happening to her? She'd had no idea the force of her strange reactions to Hugh could ever turn into something like *this*. Completely out of control, she couldn't stop the sounds coming from her mouth or her legs from spreading as he settled his weight between them. It felt good to have him there, right somehow, and she found her hips lifting and rubbing against him as his mouth attended to her other nipple. Looking down she could see the outline of her hard nipple clearly through the wet fabric, just as his fingers closed around it, his mouth already suckling at its twin.

In that moment she gave up and gave herself over to the vortex sucking her under. It was useless to fight and she no longer had the strength. Sinking into the pleasure Hugh was creating inside of her body, Irene clung to him as she felt his fingers stroke intimately between her legs. The fire inside of her leaped in response. Her hips moved up and down as his fingers touched her in ways he shouldn't, but that felt so good she couldn't bring herself to protest.

Then something hot and hard nudged her where his fingers were and Irene moaned, thrusting her hips upwards, seeking more.

"I'm sorry," Hugh whispered in her ear, and before she could ask what for his own hips were thrusting forward and something stung her had between her legs. She cried out in pain, blinking tears from her eyes as she felt something rip, clinging to her husband in shock. Hugh murmured comforting words into her ear, soothing her with his hands. "It's over now... that's the only time it will hurt, I promise."

Moaning, Irene shifted beneath him, trying to get away from the hard rod pressing slowly inside of her. The sharp pain had subsided almost immediately but it was replaced by this strange ache as something pushed into her. Looking down, Irene realized Hugh was pushing that strange appendage into her body. Her eyes widened.

"Hugh, no, it's too big!" she cried out. Surely something so large couldn't fit inside of her. If only she hadn't seen him before, she wouldn't be so frightened now.

"Shhh, sweetheart, it's alright," he said soothingly, lowering his head to kiss her.

She wanted to tell him it wasn't alright, that he was wrong and his *thing* couldn't possibly fit inside of her body, but his mouth muffled her protest.

Lifting his body slightly from hers he slipped a hand down between them to rub her wetness along her pleasure bud. He could feel the stiffness of her body beneath his and he knew she needed to relax if she was going to find any enjoyment from their coupling. It would also give him time to gather his control as the wet heat of her body clasped him so tightly. Although he regretted the necessary pain of divesting his wife of her maidenhead, the surge of masculine triumph he'd felt in breaking that barrier had been both unexpected and extremely erotic.

Now her sheath rippled around him, squeezing him in a way he'd never experienced before and it was all he could do to hold himself still inside of her. Giving her time to adjust before he fully breached her body.

As he rubbed the pads of his fingers over her clit, his mouth devouring hers, he could feel her begin to respond to him again. Her inner muscles relaxed, the stiffness of her limbs softening, and her fingers stopped pushing at his chest and began to move in small circles through his wiry hairs again. A woman's soft submission, everything he could desire and more as she began to move her hips slightly, rubbing herself against his insistent fingers.

Hugh hadn't lied to her; the pain had receded almost completely, especially once he'd begun to use his fingers on her again. While some small part of her insisted she shouldn't enjoy him touching her *there*, the pleasure was far too great for her to heed that voice. When he began to push into her, deeper, joining them further, she could feel her body welcoming him in.

To her utter surprise, he truly did fit inside of her. She could feel it when his body met hers, fused together at their centers, and her insides squeezed around him. It felt as if he was so deeply inside of her she shouldn't have been able to hold him, and yet magically she did.

"Irene..." Hugh breathed her name into her ear, his arms holding her, almost cradling her now that he was fully sheathed inside of her. "God... Irene... you feel so good around my cock... you have no idea how good you feel, sweetheart."

He kissed her again, drinking her in, and she wrapped his arms around her neck as she dazedly took in the new word. A cock... Hugh's cock was inside of her.

And it felt very, very good.

Then he began to move and everything Irene had already experienced was downgraded by the sheer intimacy of it, the heady pleasure lurching through her. Now his body was pressing against the same sensitive spot his fingers had rubbed, a fizzing need burgeoning every time their flesh connected. Irene whimpered and cried out, spreading her legs to take him deeper, harder, clinging to him as he moved above her. His own masculine groans seemed to vibrate through her, urging her onward to something hovering just out of reach... something she desperately desired without even knowing what it was.

Feeling Irene coming alive in his arms, her throaty cries, the erotic undulating of her body against his, and the snug haven of her quim was almost more than Hugh could bear. He was the first man to touch her in this way, to teach her passion and pleasure, and he would be the only man to do so if he had anything to say about it. Their marriage might have been brokered by their parents, but he'd desired her from the very beginning and now he had her in his arms, now that he was buried as deeply inside of her as he could go, he knew he would never be completely sated. Irene set him on fire and he was thrilled beyond measure she had accepted their sleeping situation because he was determined to have her in his bed every night and every morning.

Thrusting deeply into her welcoming body, he slid his hands behind her back, lifting her hips so he could press himself into her completely. Her splayed legs wrapped around him, urging him to greater heights of effort, and he used one hand to press against her coppery mound and rub his thumb over her clit. Her response was electric.

She writhed before him, hands clutching at the pillows as she came. A hot flush spread over her face and chest, her upturned nipples puckered and bouncing as her breasts jiggled. He rubbed her little pearl hard and fast, feeling her insides spasming around him in ecstatic convulsion.

Irene had no idea what was happening to her, she only knew she was shattering apart into a million pieces, but in a good way, in a wonderful way. Her body was bursting with sensation, her core full and tingling as her journey towards that indefinable need was finally completed and Hugh's clever fingers satisfied her completely.

Then he was on top of her again, thrusting, his weight pressing her down into the bed. Her sensitive feminine folds were ablaze with sensation, still burning from the heights of rapture he'd brought her to, and so she continued to ripple around him as he took his pleasure in her soft wetness. A particularly hard thrust had her crying out again, her body tightening around the length of him, and she felt something inside of her throb. Holding himself completely sheathed inside of her, Hugh groaned with ecstasy as he spilled his seed, filling her womb with the frothy liquid.

For a moment his weight rested fully atop her as Irene slowly came back to her senses; crushing her, but in a way she almost enjoyed. Never in her life had she felt so intimately connected to someone, as if she *belonged there.* Her arms remained around Hugh's neck as he pulled back gently, looking down at her with his stunning blue eyes and kissing her lips, her cheeks, her forehead. Warmth spread through her at the tenderness of his touch and for once the disturbing reactions he always stirred in her body were absent. She was able to just enjoy his obvious appreciation and gestures of affection, clinging to him a bit as she kissed him back.

The strangest feeling was of him slipping away from inside of her and she found herself feeling rather disappointed as he pulled his body away, disrupting their connection.

"Beautiful, Irene..." Hugh murmured, kissing her again. "You were perfect."

"Was that... was that the marriage act?" Irene asked shyly. She didn't want him to laugh at her, but she wanted to know. Hugh didn't laugh, although he certainly looked amused as he peered down at her.

"Yes sweetheart, that was the marriage act." There was a hint of laughter in his voice but it wasn't cruel laughter and it didn't feel as though he was mocking her, so Irene relaxed. Then her brow wrinkled. Hugh smoothed a finger over it. "Is something wrong?"

"It wasn't at all what I thought it would be." There had been the pain, but it had been swift and not nearly as bad as she thought, and after that there had been quite a bit of pleasure. She hadn't been bored once.

This time he did laugh and Irene blushed. His weight shifted on top of her and a little shiver of pleasure slid through her, causing her eyes to blink rapidly. When she looked up at Hugh again he was smiling rather smugly.

"What did you think it was going to be?"

"Awful."

She said the first thing that came to her mind. Somehow this intimacy, being in his arms, made it easier for her to be herself. Especially now she wasn't becoming dizzy or breathless or anxious just because of his presence. Plus, she wanted to make him laugh again, and he seemed to enjoy her honesty.

The shaking laugh he gave this time vibrated through her and she smiled up at him. He was so handsome when he laughed, not quite so angelic or predatory looking, instead he looked carefree and rather boyish. Not nearly as intimidating.

"Then I am glad to defy your expectations," he said teasingly, landing another kiss on her mouth. Irene opened her lips for him, kissing him back as she was learning to do, and she felt Hugh's body rock against hers and she moaned.

He pulled away reluctantly, shaking his head. "You're going to be too sore to do it all over again, sweetheart."

"We can perform the marital act more than once?" she asked, rather shocked.

Hugh laughed again. He was not at all used to virginal pillow talk, certainly not the way Irene did it. Although her questions were quite a bit more brazen than he was accustomed to hearing from her, he rather enjoyed she obviously felt comfortable enough with him to ask them. He was going to thoroughly enjoy educating her on the pleasures of engaging in said act.

"We can make love as many times as we wish," he informed her. "But you will be sore tonight and I want you to enjoy our couplings."

"I did enjoy it..." Irene hesitated for a moment but her natural curiosity overcame her reticence. "Is that what it's called? Making love or coupling?"

"It's called many things," Hugh said, pulling his lower body away from hers and sliding off to his side. The look of disappointment on her face had him pulling her body into his—although he would have done so anyway. To his delight she snuggled into him, her head resting on his shoulder. "Making love, coupling, bedding, fucking, sex... but we make love."

"Oh." Irene thought about it and she decided she liked that term. Making love. The other terms didn't seem nearly as intimate or as important, and 'marital act' felt rather clinical and removed, compared to what she had just experienced.

Kissing her on her forehead, Hugh decided to let her think that over for a moment. "Stay right here sweetheart, I'm going to get a cloth to clean you up."

It was only as he pulled away and went to the washstand that Irene realized there was a damp stickiness between her legs and her nigh-trail was still hiked up around her waist. Blushing furiously she pulled the flimsy material down, although Hugh just pushed it back up again to gently wash off the fluids from her most intimate areas. Closing her eyes, Irene was too embarrassed to look at him as he did so, especially after the brief glimpse she caught of his enthralled expression. It made her feel all quivery inside all over again.

When he went back to the washstand she took the opportunity to peek at his backside. She didn't know what constituted a nice backside, but she rather thought Hugh's must be one. It certainly looked nice to her, although she looked away quickly enough when he turned back around again. The appendage between his legs—his cock—had shrunk to a much smaller size. It hung in front of him, swaying gently as he walked.

Crawling back into bed beside her, Hugh gathered her into his arms and Irene found herself curling back against him. It felt nice to be held, to be wanted. Something about the way Hugh handled her made her feel rather cherished and she soaked up the affection the way a sponge soaked up water.

Considering the rather full day she'd had it was no surprise that almost as soon as Irene closed her eyes, sleep sucked her under.

Rather bemused at the intensity of their love-making and Irene's reaction to it, Hugh lay stroking his new wife's hair as she slept. She felt so small and sweet next to him and her hidden passion was everything he could have hoped for and more. From talk in the clubs he knew a wedding night was not always a great experience, not just for the lady but for the gentleman as well. He was relieved not to have had to suffer through pleas, tears, or any kind of resistance. Indeed, Irene had rather melted into his arms and now she was curled so trustingly within them that it made his heart ache. He smiled happily, secure in the knowledge that he'd married a woman more like his mother than his sister.

Yes, he could quite easily fall in love with his new wife.

WHEN IRENE WOKE in the middle of the night it took her a moment to orient herself. She was almost frightened for a moment, realizing immediately she wasn't in her own bed, before she remembered she was in Hugh's—their—bedroom. Because she was a wife. A woman.

As evidenced by the slight dampness that remained between her legs and the soreness of her muscles as she moved. Muscles she hadn't even known existed until now.

But it had felt wonderful, she thought with a touch of awe, turning onto her side and cuddling a pillow to her chest. Hugh was not in bed with her and she dimly remembered him kissing her forehead and telling her to keep sleeping. A little smile wreathed her face at the memory of his affection although she wistfully thought she might have preferred him to stay in bed with her.

How strange to know yesterday she had been a bride and today she was a wife.

A sudden chill shot through her spine.

Not just *a* wife. *Hugh's* wife. She was Viscountess Petersham, not Lady Brooke as she'd always dreamed of being. For a moment she felt completely disoriented, as if she'd stepped into a dream world that had completely turned her world on its head.

Horrified, she realized last night she had not only forgotten her determination to learn about the marriage act in order to please Alex, she had forgotten about *Alex himself.* Not once had she thought about him after she'd entered the room and faced Hugh. Not once had he appeared in her thoughts.

Perhaps that was only right as she shouldn't be thinking of another man while making love with her husband... but she didn't actually *love* her husband, she loved Alex! How could she have forgotten that crucial fact last night? How could she have found such pleasure in the act with him, rather than the pain and indignities her mother had spoken of, when she was in love with another man?

And she'd woken up so happy, without a thought of Alex in her mind at all.

Sitting straight up in the bed, Irene stared down at her body as though it belonged to someone else, her heart thudding wildly in complete confusion.

What had Hugh done to her?

The soft noise beside her reminded her that she wasn't alone, at some point Hugh had returned to the bed and fallen back asleep with her. There wasn't enough light in the room for her to see Hugh, although when she tried to look at him she had a dim impression of golden hair and the outline of his profile. Biting her lip, she reached out and touched him. His skin was hot. Soft. It reminded her of how it had felt to have him on top of her, their skin rubbing against each other.

Sighing she laid back down on her back and tried to sort through her conflicting emotions. Hugh shifted and cuddled her closer, murmuring nonsensical nothings in his sleep as he curled around her. Surprisingly, it didn't take too long for her to nestle into him, her nose rubbing up against his chest hair, and fall asleep.

CHAPTER 6

Waking up next to his wife was even better than Hugh had ever expected. Irene was soft and sweet in his arms, snuggled up with her bottom pressing against his groin, the filmy material of her nightgown bunched up around her waist, strands of her red hair tickling his face. Her response to him on their wedding night had been innocently passionate, something he had found incredibly arousing.

Indeed, he was already lustfully hard, his cock wedged between the ample mounds of her buttocks, hard and aching to be firmly planted inside of her. He congratulated himself on securing her agreement to a single bedchamber. It was not the norm within the *ton*, but he'd always enjoyed having a woman beside him when he awoke in the morning, and to him having a wife just meant he would always enjoy that benefit.

And what a wonderful woman he'd chosen to wake beside every morning.

Rocking his hips slightly, Hugh moaned a little as he slid his hand up her smooth stomach to cup a breast. He'd been so amused by her insistence she keep her nightrail on last night; it had been another token of her innocence, as well as adding a kind of illicit thrill to the proceedings. One which was returning as he fondled her in her sleep, feeling her stir against him, her breath stuttering out as he squeezed her soft flesh.

With a grin on his face, Hugh decided to awaken his bride.

WHEN IRENE HAD FALLEN asleep after waking for the first time she had been rather troubled, unsure of what to do as Hugh had curled beside her, taking her into his arms. In many ways she felt as if her body had betrayed her—not just her body but her mind. She couldn't help but feel a certain tenderness towards Hugh, although she told herself it was only natural now that they were man and wife.

The relentless turmoil of her thoughts had kept her up far past the time when Hugh had fallen asleep beside her. It was strange to sleep in the same bad as another person, especially a man and she had found herself almost wishing there was light enough to see him by so she might examine him more closely. Curiosity had always been one of her besetting sins. She had to wonder, would Alex look the same? Would he touch her in the same way? Bring her to the same kind of pleasure? And of course she was still rather confused about the marital act—making love—itself. It was so unlike what her mother had described.

Eventually she had fallen into a troubled sleep that had become quite deep by the time Hugh awoke. She was completely unaware of her nightrail being pulled up to expose her breasts, of her husband's low groan at the unobscured sight of her strawberry nipples, although her body felt and responded to his mouth as he sucked one hardening bud between his lips. The dream she had been having about wandering through a maze abruptly shifted as a nameless man was suddenly fondling her intimately, bearing her down to the grassy floor of the maze.

Alex, she tried to say, thinking it must be him.

Her body caught on fire in a way she had never associated with him before and she gasped in shock as her legs were pressed apart.

Lips suckled at her breast, fingers plucking at her free nipple as she moaned and writhed, eager for the explosive climax she had only recently discovered.

For a moment her body shifted and she frowned. *Hugh.* She had discovered that bliss with Hugh, not with Alex. Alex had never made her blood run hot or her lungs collapse; Alex was safety and warmth, Hugh was sparking flame and a fluttering in her stomach. The man in the dream lifted his head from her breast and she saw his golden hair, his azure eyes blazing for her.

Hugh.

The most exquisite sensation speared through her core and she cried out, waking herself up to find her dream had become reality. Except Hugh's angelic countenance was not hovering over her the way he had been in the dream, it was buried between her legs with his mouth intimately connected to her body.

"Oh! Don't!" She gasped and her body jerked as his tongue probed her sensitive folds.

Her hands moved down to push him away but instead her fingers caught in his hair and she found herself pulling his head into her, as if urging him to continue in the unnatural act. Everything inside of her said he should not be kissing her *there.* Yet it felt so unbelievably good that she was melting underneath the skillful laving of his tongue, her body quivering like a harp string as he continued to lick and suck on her womanly parts.

"Huuuugh..." His name came out as a moan as her legs moved fitfully, her body screaming for the ecstasy that she'd experienced the night before.

But surely this wouldn't... surely she couldn't...

Before she could truly understand what was happening, she already was.

The heat and pleasure burst forth as Hugh sucked some incredibly sensitive part of her between his lips; the tingling ecstasy rippling outwards from that area between her legs.

Watching Irene come apart for him, her sweetness on his lips and her mostly bared body writhing, was the most incredible thing Hugh had ever seen. She had woken up so hot, so imbued with passion, that she hadn't even noticed her entire body was lying exposed to his eyes, her breasts free and jiggling with every movement she made. In the light of day she was even more beautiful and he found himself rather satisfied with his first sight of her naked body being the morning after their wedding day.

As her throaty cries of completion came to an end he pulled himself up onto his knees and wrapped his hand around his cock, jerking it roughly and quickly. It only took a few moments before his seed shot forth and landed on her coppery curls and the swollen pink lips of her cunt purse, decorating her with swathes of white fluid. Blinking up at him through confused and passion hazed green eyes, Irene almost looked like a virgin sacrifice—especially with the speckled red of her lost virginity staining the sheets beside her where she'd lost it the night before.

"Hugh?" she asked in an unsteady voice as he panted, his member slowly shrinking in his hand now that it had been spent. While he would have liked to have finished inside of her, he hadn't wanted to hurt her and he wasn't sure how sore she would be this morning.

He smiled at her gently. "Good morning, sweetheart."

"What just happened?" Looking down at herself, Irene was rather shocked by the stark white sticky fluid on the copper curls covering her mound. Blushing hot red all over again, she quickly tugged down her nightrail over her breasts and hips, sitting up as she drew her legs upwards.

Chuckling as this repeated show of modesty, Hugh went to dampen another cloth and brought it back to clean her with as he explained. "That was part of making love, sweetheart. At least it can be. It's a way a man can bring pleasure to a woman. I didn't want to really make love to you again because you're going to be a bit sore today after losing your maidenhead and you need time to recover but," he smiled ruefully. "I just can't seem to keep my hands off of you."

"And... what is that?" Irene pointed at the seed coating the curls of her mound without looking at it as Hugh pushed her nightrail up and her legs down. She didn't resist his ministrations even though they obviously embarrassed her, a fetching blush staining her cheeks again.

"That's my seed," he explained, marveling at Irene's complete innocence. Were young brides always this uninformed? Or perhaps her cold mother just didn't care to give Irene any more information than she had to. He could certainly believe it of the Baroness. "When it is released inside of you, that's what will eventually give us children."

"Oh." Irene blushed, glanced at it, and then turned away again, wrapping her arms around her upper body as if to shield her breasts from his gaze. Frankly that just made her look even more appealing, as hints of her breasts peeked out from between her arms... except... Hugh frowned.

"Sweetheart..." He ran his finger over the pattern of bruises on her upper arm, only visible to him now because of her position and the light coming into the room. Certainly he hadn't noticed it the day before, although he realized her dresses probably would have been covering it anyway. "Did I do this to you? Why didn't you tell me I was holding you too tightly?"

"What?" Irene twisted her head around to look, and then caught his eye, her blush fading as she paled and glanced away again. It was starting to bother him how often she avoided looking at him. "No, you didn't do that." Her normally soft voice was clipped and sharp and he didn't bother to ask who had.

The Baroness. Her own mother had left bruises on her arm, on her wedding day. Hugh would be willing to bet his title on it. And Irene protected her mother by showing it was not a topic for conversation. Not that he needed her to tell him. The Baron would never handle his daughter so roughly and no one else would have dared handle Hugh's wife that way.

"If she ever does anything like that again, tell me," Hugh said shortly, his voice tense with anger. Irene gave him a rather wild look, the way a half-feral cat might look at a human—hope combined with worry and a tinge of fear—before bowing her head and using her hand to cover up the marks as if she was ashamed. Bending his head, Hugh kissed her in reassurance. "I'll go get Flora, she can give you a bath to relax in before breakfast."

Then he had to leave the room before he lost his temper and Irene saw how infuriated he was with her mother.

Rather confused, Irene huddled on the bed. Hugh had been so gentle with her last night, but when his face was lined with anger he'd looked rather ferocious. Almost frightening, and not in the way he normally frightened her with her reactions to him. Nibbling her lower lip, she twisted her head around to look at her arm again. The bruises weren't particularly bad, they'd fade after a few days. She rather wondered at Hugh's reaction; no one else had ever really cared how she was treated in her mother's care. It seemed as if Hugh was angry with her mother, was that why he wanted to know if her mother bruised her again? Would he make her stop?

Something like hope rose up in Irene's chest. While she'd once told her father that her bruises came from her mother, he hadn't done anything about it once he'd known they'd been inflicted by his wife. She hadn't had a champion since Alex...

Alex!

How did she keep forgetting about him? Hugh's very presence was more than disturbing now that he had complete access to her body and her senses, he was actually driving the love of her life from her mind. Irene groaned as her lower body throbbed with the remembered ecstasy as she focused on it. Definitely a mistake.

Sternly she told herself she needed to keep her goals in mind. She must learn as much as she could about making love so Alex would take her as his mistress, so at least she could have some small part of him and pretend to be his wife the way she'd always wanted to be, and she must keep Hugh happy and satisfied so he would teach her.

And also, a tiny little part of her admitted, because some secret part of her heart wanted Hugh to be happy with her.

Ever since the incident with the spoon Eleanor had been on her best behavior. Who knew a small wooden implement could hurt so much? And, more humiliatingly, bring her such incredible ecstasy when her husband made love to her afterwards? The morning after the impromptu discipline and subsequent soreness of her bottom in the days following convinced her that prodding Edwin to constantly discipline her was perhaps not the most effective route to discerning his feelings towards her. Once she'd had time to think it over she had also realized if he did have any burgeoning feelings, acting a complete shrew could quite quickly kill them.

It hadn't helped that he'd obviously been quite taken with the sore, slightly bruised state of her chastised cheeks. They'd made love in a variety of places for the next few days afterwards, during all hours of the day, and it didn't take more than a slight squeeze of her bottom and her subsequent whimper to have Edwin's passion flare again. Hers too, for that matter. At least she was well assured he wanted her in *that* way, whatever deeper feelings he may or may not have for her.

"Nell? Are you ready?" Edwin entered her dressing room as if he had every right to be there. She supposed he did.

Raising her eyes from the mirror she was sitting in front of as Poppy worked on her hair, she could feel her heart squeezing as she took in his handsome personage. He was formally dressed as they would be attending the opera this evening, the snowy cravat as his throat tied in a complex knot and setting off his dark good looks splendidly. With the silvery gray of his waistcoat and the simple black and white of his shirt, slacks and jacket, he looked even more like a fallen angel in all those crisp colors. Many men preferred more decorative dress, but not Edwin. He had no need of extra decoration, they would only distract from his good looks rather than add to them, although she'd become aware that his valet was as responsible (perhaps more) for Edwin's style as her husband himself was.

"Nearly," she said, trying to cover her roiling emotions with a smile, glancing away from his penetrating eyes to look up at Poppy.

"There," said her maid smugly, pushing one last pin into the elaborate coiffure. Smiling, she turned and bobbed a curtsy to Edwin. "She's all yours, my Lord."

Truer words were never spoken, Eleanor thought a little dismally. She was all his, but was he all hers?

"You look delectable," Edwin said, his eyes dark and hot, drinking in the sight of her and she could feel the reaction throughout her body. The way he looked at her made her nipples bud, her lower lips plump and dampen, and her pulse quicken. "But you are unfinished."

"Unfinished?" Her voice wavered as she looked at herself in the mirror, Edwin's gloved fingers stroking over her bare shoulders and down to her collarbones. Immediately her breasts began to ache as she wished he would move his hands lower and dip them into the low décolletage of her dress. She was becoming quite wanton now that she was a wife, her experiences with her husband providing much more explicit material for her imagination.

"Quite," he whispered into her ear, and she turned her head to catch his lips but he was already moving away.

Then he reached into his pocket and pulled out a stream of glittering blue.

As Eleanor gasped at the sight of the sapphires he'd commissioned, picking out the stones himself to exactly match her eyes, Edwin could only grin with pride. She had turned in her chair, cooing over the beautiful gems, stroking their glittering faces with her fingers as if she couldn't quite believe they were real. They would look very well indeed with her navy gown and its silvery edging.

Wrapping the necklace around her slender throat, Edwin clasped it at the back. The stones were cold and heavy against her skin although they started to warm immediately.

"They match the color of your eyes perfectly," he murmured as she put up a hand to her throat, staring in wonderment at her reflection. "I thought they would. Although they are no match for the brightness and beauty of your eyes."

"They're lovely… Oh Edwin, thank you."

His wife's eyes were shining extremely brightly, perhaps with tears, but she didn't shed any as she twisted around in her seat and impetuously grabbed at his jacket, pulling him down for a kiss. That was his Eleanor, impulsive to her core. The eagerness of her mouth tugged at him and for a moment he seriously considered grabbing his wife and tossing her on the bed…

But the whole point of this evening was to reward her for her good behavior the past few days. And also to indulge in a pastime which they both enjoyed, as well as attend to their social duties. While Society could be fairly understanding about newlyweds indulging themselves, at some point they were expected to reemerge on a regular basis.

With an effort he pulled himself away, although he kept his hands on Nell, pulling her from her seat at the same time so she was standing beside him.

"Come, my dear," he said, pulling her arm through the crook of his. "You know I abhor being fashionably late to the opera." While he didn't mind it at all with balls, he cared more about watching the stage than watching the audience when they went to the theater. Smiling up at him with complete adoration, Eleanor fairly floated alongside him out of the house.

THROUGHOUT THE FIRST ACT, Eleanor stroked her necklace over and over again. They were sharing the Clarendon box with Wesley and the Dowager Countess of Lilienfield, a lovely widow in her thirties who had been married to a much older gentleman. She had never remarried, preferring to raise her son, the current Earl, under the guardianship of her brother as laid out by her late husband's will. It gave her quite a bit of freedom, including taking lovers amongst the *ton's* rakes, of which Wesley was most assuredly now a part of.

They sat in front of her and Edwin, flirting and touching each other, exchanging meaningful glances. It was a subtle dance Eleanor now recognized, knowing just how potent those small touches could be. Next to her Edwin was sitting close enough the hairs on her arms were standing up, but he wasn't touching her. Just sitting so close as to distract her. She wondered why they weren't exchanging the same touches and smoldering looks as the unmarried couple sitting in front of them. Was it because he was truly engrossed in the opera? Or was it an indication of his true feelings for her?

When she'd originally imagined a marriage, she'd thought about the jewels and presents her future husband would shower her with.

Now these jewels felt cold around her neck, just like when he'd first put them on her. Cold and not nearly as indicative as she would have liked. Had she truly thought such gifts would make her feel more loved? Instead she felt as if Edwin had spent money rather than time and affection on her, as if he'd gone the easier route of buying a token rather than giving her true emotion. Still, the sapphires *were* the exact color of her eyes and he'd made special note of that.

Interpreting every little gesture he made was exhausting and yet she couldn't seem to stop herself. She was so confused. At one point in her life she would have thought a trip to the opera accompanied by a fabulous necklace would show proof of a man's feelings. Now that she had those things she felt as though she was floundering more than ever. Money spent did not equate to love.

"Stop fidgeting, you look beautiful," Edwin murmured into her ear.

Eleanor's breath caught in her throat. She'd been so caught up in her thoughts she hadn't even felt him shifting closer to her. Immediately she dropped her hand onto her lap.

"I'm sorry," she said under her breath. To all appearances, she immediately turned her attention to the action on the stage.

Frowning, Edwin leaned back, feeling rather at a loss. She'd seemed so happy when they'd first left for the theater, but sometime during the first act she'd become closed off again.

No matter what he seemed to do, his wife was constantly running hot and cold. Well, except for at night when they were in their bed and she blazed with fiery passion in his arms. He'd thought the trip to the opera would please Eleanor, but instead she seemed distanced and distracted. Was she even paying attention? She'd been practically tugging at the necklace, as if she wanted it off, when she'd seemed so elated about it earlier in the evening.

For all the years they'd known each other, for all his knowledge of women, Eleanor continued to confound him.

Which, he had to admit, excited him as much as it frustrated him. Life with her would certainly never be boring. Studying her profile, he saw the high blush in her cheeks which said she knew he was looking at her, but she didn't turn her head to acknowledge him. Instead her eyes dropped to where Lady Lilienfield's hand was obviously in Wesley's lap.

Quirking his lips, Edwin wondered if Eleanor was watching their blatant courtship. Certainly she seemed more interested in it than in the opera. Or perhaps, the smile faded from his face, she was wondering if Wesley had the same unbrotherly affection for her that Edwin did. It wasn't beyond the realm of possibility, after all. Jealousy lanced through him before he could wrestle the unwelcome emotion away. She had done nothing to indicate her feelings for Wesley went beyond the friendship they had always had.

Reaching over to rest his arm on the back of her chair, Edwin let his fingers brush against the back of her neck. His wife jumped as his fingertips touch the tendrils of gold that were falling against her sensitive skin, and he hid a grin as he watched her gaze slant towards him. Not that she actually turned her head, but it was obvious she was no longer ignoring him.

Edwin shifted closer so he could examine the color in her cheeks and the rise and fall of her breasts as he brushed his fingers across the nape of her neck again.

Oh... why was he tormenting her so?!

She couldn't be in the same room as her husband without being aware of him, and now that he was touching her in these little ways she was so acutely attuned to him that she couldn't concentrate on the opera even if she wanted to. A moment ago she'd been yearning for such touches from him and now it was all she could do not to jump as his fingers brushed the back of her neck, played with the short hairs there, traveled along her shoulder blades...

Inside her corset her nipples were aching for his touch and she could feel her lower body heating, coiling. In the theater! Their private box was not very private, and this was not Paris, their friends and acquaintances were in the audience. Wesley was sitting in front of them, not even a foot away. Edwin wasn't doing anything completely scandalous, Wesley would see nothing but her hot red cheeks if he looked over his shoulder, but she felt incredibly exposed all the same. Maybe this was why Edwin hadn't been touching her before; but if so, why had he changed his mind?

"Edwin," she hissed under her breath, leaning towards him without turning her head.

"Yes sweetheart?" His lips came so close to her ear she could feel his breath against the sensitive appendage, and she almost lost her train of thought.

"Stop it!"

"Stop what?"

Fingertips brushed along her neck again and she couldn't suppress the shiver that went through her at his touch.

"That!"

"Stop touching you?" His voice was amused as he pressed his fingers more firmly to the top of her bare shoulder. "But I like touching you."

"It's distracting."

Edwin leaned closer, his lips right against her ear so she could feel them moving as he whispered so low it was barely a sound. "I think you like me touching you too."

She rapped his thigh with her fan, hard, and he jumped. Eleanor glared at him, even harder, when he grinned delightedly at her in response. What was wrong with the loon?

"Just stop it," she hissed.

Next to her Edwin settled back down in his seat but it was with a smug, insufferable kind of air. Eleanor seethed quietly for the rest of the performance, head held high and ignoring the occasional glint of an opera glass trained in their direction.

During the intermission more than one lady of the *ton* complimented Eleanor on her necklace. By the third time it happened her smile felt pasted on as the lady in question cooed over how *generous* and *thoughtful* Lord Hyde was, all the while fluttering their fans and eyelashes his way as if to indicate their receptiveness to being on the receiving end of such thoughtful generosity. It was enough to make Eleanor grind her teeth, although she felt Edwin's reproving fingers tighten about her waist every time she began to be a bit snappish with importuning ladies.

The small reminder from him was just enough to settle her down, warning her to behave unless she wanted a spanking when they returned home. Which she most assuredly did not.

Her husband played the thoughtful suitor by her side, much the way he had in Paris. In some respects it relived her greatly that he danced attendance on her, apparently oblivious to the flirtatious advances of some of the women; on the other hand it was a drain to keep herself from dragging him off to some dark corner as he continued to torment her with small touches and caresses. She knew she was being slightly unreasonable in her resentment towards him for heating her body in such a way, after all, she had been watching Wesley enviously with Lady Lilienfield and wishing for exactly that, but as soon as her wishes had been granted she'd realized just how awful it was to want intimacy with her husband and be denied for hours.

"Lady Grace!" Eleanor called out, relieved to see her friend in the crowd.

Immediately the head of ravens-wing hair turned and Grace's bright blue eyes flashed with pleasure as she saw who was hailing her. If Eleanor's mother had been there she would have chided her daughter for raising her voice like a fishwife at market, but Edwin just chuckled and continued chatting with one of his acquaintances as Grace made her way over to them on the arm of a new rake whom Eleanor vaguely recognized by reputation alone. Lord Benjamin Warpoole, son of the Marquess of Dean, whose dark good looks rivaled Edwin's. He looked rather bored, despite having a walking scandal like Grace on his arm. Apparently it didn't bother him to receive the cut direct from more than one person.

"Hello darling," Grace cooed, exchanging kisses with Eleanor. She introduced Lord Warpoole, who almost immediately joined in the male conversation, despite looking singularly uninterested in the topic. Perhaps that was just his default expression, and not a true indication of his feelings. "This is a surprise. I didn't know you'd be attending tonight."

"The tickets were a surprise from Edwin," Eleanor explained with a little smile.

For a moment an emotion which looked surprisingly like envy flashed across Grace's face and then it was gone, hidden behind her ravishing smile and bright eyes. "How sweet... and the necklace? That must be new, I've never seen it before."

Again Eleanor's fingers stroked across the piece, although the compliment from Grace felt remarkably different than from the other women's this evening. There were still undertones, but not the kind that said she was complimenting Edwin more than she was Eleanor. Something lurked beneath Grace's words but Eleanor wasn't quite certain what.

"A PRESENT FOR TONIGHT," Eleanor said. She smiled rather ruefully, wondering if Grace attached emotional importance to jewelry... she'd seen some of the pieces her friend had accepted from her various beaus. "They match my eyes."

"They do indeed," Grace murmured. She sidled closer, lowering her voice. "Are you with child?" Her tone indicated she thought there must be some significance to the jewelry. It also sounded rather envious.

"I don't think so..." Wonderingly, Eleanor splayed her hand across her abdomen. There had been so many things to think about, she hadn't thought about it since her last menses. Which would be due any day now.

Did she even want Edwin's child right now?

Part of her said no, another part of her emphatically said yes. So, as usual, she was confused. Delightful.

"What's it like?" Grace's low musical voice broke through Eleanor's thoughts. She had moved even closer, to ensure not even the men standing next to them would overhear what they were saying.

"What's what like?"

"Being in a marriage that's not a travesty."

Eleanor didn't know how to answer her friend. Indeed, she'd never seen Grace looking so completely vulnerable. Did this have something to do with Lord Brooke being in town? She had heard the gossip that neither the Lord or Lady were showing any signs of leaving London; she didn't think Grace would give in and bow out during the Season, so that left it up to Lord Brooke. Yet she couldn't really say whether or not her own marriage wasn't a travesty, it all depended on Edwin's feelings towards her.

Certainly, if she loved him and he did not return that affection than it would be a travesty for her. And so far she had no idea.

"It's time to return to our seats," Edwin said with a smile, turning back to the ladies before Eleanor could formulate a response. Immediately a smooth social mask shuttered Grace's eyes and she simpered up at Lord Warpoole as he held out his arm. Eleanor had never seen the like and she suddenly had to wonder how much of Grace's flirtations were an act. Edwin's hand pressed against the small of Eleanor's back, rather possessively. "Come, sweetheart."

Mulling over the mysterious implications of Grace's question, Eleanor allowed her husband to sweep her back to their seats.

WHEN THEY RETURNED HOME Edwin gave his wife a kiss before she went off to attend to her nightly toilette and he retreated to his study. He felt in dire need of a brandy. The rest of the opera hadn't gone any better than the first part, although the opera itself had been magnificent. Eleanor had been thoughtful and distracted after the first intermission and he wondered what Grace had said to her.

Although he did not want to try and dictate his wife's friendships, he didn't particularly think Grace was a good influence on her. The Lady had been rather wild since her marriage to Lord Brooke and most of the *ton* did not find her acceptable company. Indeed, sometimes it amazed him she was invited anywhere considering her utter disregard for the social conventions. Yet gossips loved scandal; inviting Lady Grace Brooke anywhere was sure to cause some minor flutter, whether due to her behavior or her latest amour. Especially since, for whatever reason, Lord Brooke didn't insist she be ostracized.

Definitely not the kind of influence he wanted his wife to have, and yet she'd been friends with Grace almost as long as she'd known him.

He wondered that Lord Brooke put up with it. After meeting the man at Hugh's wedding, he and Wesley had run into him several times at White's and had sat down to a drink and a meal with him. He didn't seem the kind of man to tolerate the behavior his wife indulged in, and yet nothing had ever been done to stop her.

It was a mystery, but when he'd queried Eleanor, he'd discovered she didn't know much more than he did. Only that Eleanor assumed it had something to do with Grace's father arranging the match. Eleanor claimed Lady Grace was a romantic although Edwin couldn't quite picture it.

Perhaps the two were completely incompatible. Not a problem he and Eleanor had, he thought with a small smirk as he readjusted himself in his chair. They proved their compatibility nightly. He sighed as he relaxed back into his seat. After a night of sitting at the theater it was a relief to be reclining on his favorite armchair with its well-worn cushions.

Still, he mused, it's not as if there weren't plenty of incompatible marriages within the *ton*. But the wives still managed to produce an heir for their husbands before embarking on their various extramarital activities. Grace was a rather glaring exception. Why did Lord Brooke allow things to go on as they had?

Perhaps once he and Edwin became better acquainted the other man would confide in him. Not that it was any of Edwin's business, but he couldn't help but be curious. Or perhaps Wesley would find out first; he had been spending a fair amount of time with Lord Brooke now that Hugh was on his honeymoon and Edwin was spending his evenings in with Nell.

Glancing at the clock, Edwin decided his wife had had enough time to ready herself for bed. Tossing back the last of his brandy he got to his feet, and then paused to open one of the draws on his desk, examining the contents with a thoughtful eye. Picking up a small glass bottle, he held it up to the light and then closed the drawer.

After all, it was rude not to utilize Wesley's wedding present at some point. Nell didn't even know what he'd given them.

Whistling happy, Edwin tucked the bottle into his pocket and went off in search of his wife.

CHAPTER 7

Standing in front of the full length mirror in their bedroom, Eleanor examined her body. She'd dismissed Poppy in order to do so, as this wasn't something she felt comfortable having a maid around to witness. Staring at her stomach, she ran her hand over it and wondered if there might be a baby growing in there. Certainly she and Edwin engaged in intimacies often enough it must be possible.

The question of a baby had arisen in her mind more than once, but often she pushed the idea off to the side, not wanting to worry about whether or not Edwin's passionate interest in her might alter once she was with child.

Perhaps that would be the true proof of his affections... if they waned after she provided him with an heir.

But could she wait that long? Falling more in love with him every day, wondering, yearning. And constantly testing, because she knew deep down she wouldn't be able to stop. She knew if she asked he would tell her what she wanted to hear, but how could she trust such a declaration? Only a freely given one was truly dependable.

The creak of the door behind her made her jump and she covered her breasts and mound with her hands, eyes flashing up to see her husband entering their bedchamber. It wasn't that he'd never seen her naked before of course, but she felt as though she'd been caught doing something illicit. Something private. He took two steps in and stopped, his gaze fixing upon her naked body. Color rose in her cheeks as she stared at him in the mirror, too frozen to spin around and face him.

She could see his eyes caressing her back, her legs, her bottom, the curves of her hourglass, and the long fall of hair which obscured her shoulders from his view. Then their eyes caught in the mirror and she could see him studying her position, the way her hand couldn't entirely cover the golden hairs of her mound, the flesh of her breasts which spilled out around the press of her arm.

"I was... I was just l-looking at... at... um, myself," Eleanor stuttered, feeling dreadfully exposed at being caught.

Edwin grinned at her wickedly, pulling off his jacket as he strode forward. Unlike some of the men of the *ton* he didn't often wear any garments so tightly fitted that a valet was actually necessary to help adorn and remove them. Not only was Nell's abashed face absolutely delightful, but there was a wicked excitement in catching his wife looking at her naked body. Quickly he palmed the little glass bottle he had brought upstairs with him before dropping the garment to the floor.

Coming up behind Eleanor he met her eyes in the mirror as he wrapped one arm around her body, pulling her soft backside against the hard ridge of his groin. Gently he kissed the back of her head, smelling the flowery perfume she wore in her hair.

"I can understand, as I enjoy looking at you as well," he said, wrapping his other arm around her although his hand remained closed around the glass bottle. His free hand stroked her soft skin as he surrounded her cream and gold body with his darker one. "Especially when you look like this."

Shivering, Eleanor watched in the mirror, fascinated, as one of Edwin's arms banded around her waist and the other explored her with gentle fingers. She'd never been able to watch from this angle before, see his hand as it cupped her breast and pinched at the pink nipple. Next to him she looked so soft and pale, so small, as if his entire body was encompassing her. When his hand slid further down and pushed hers aside so he could push his fingers through the golden curls at her mound and into the slick wetness below, she gasped and averted her gaze as she blushed.

Their eyes caught again, holding, as he slid two fingers into her wet heat, rubbing over the excited bud of her clitoris, and she moaned with the exquisite intimacy of it. The vulnerability. The hot need in Edwin's eyes as he watched her.

With an exertion of his willpower that almost felt like a physical wrench, Edwin pulled himself away. As much as he wanted to make love to his wife in front of the mirror—and made a note to himself to make that possible sometime—he had come up here with a plan. And also a reward for her for her recent good behavior.

"Go lie on the bed on your stomach, sweetheart," Edwin murmured into her ear, giving her a gentle push on her bottom to send her in the right direction.

Eleanor hesitated and then mentally shrugged and headed for the bed. Part of her had liked watching herself and Edwin in the mirror, another part of her just wanted to automatically dig in her feet about any order he gave no matter how innocuous, and the last part—which won—was curious about what he was going to do. Their nights were lessons in passion, in which she learned more about the male body than she'd ever considered possible, all the while Edwin learned new ways to pleasure her.

Lying on her stomach on the bed, Eleanor could hear the rustle of clothing as Edwin finished undressing himself, tossing the clothing negligently on the floor. She rolled her eyes. Before she'd become his wife she'd always thought Edwin must be a bit of a clothes horse, a demanding aristocrat who was always up to date on the latest fashions. It couldn't be further from the truth; she was quite sure that without Johnson, his fussy and demanding valet, Edwin would go out of the house looking like he didn't care at all. He relied entirely on Johnson for sartorial and fashionable matters (other than colors which he was quite vehement about, having no desire to be seen as a dandy), although now Johnson constantly conferred with her as well because he wished to have the mistress' opinion. As far as she could tell, Edwin didn't have one and he treated his garments with reckless indifference, causing Johnson to constantly wring his hands even as he set matters to right.

She often wondered if Edwin would even notice if Johnson dressed him as a dandy.

THE BED DIPPED beside her and she turned her head to see the gloriously naked body of her husband. Immediately her body hummed with anticipation and she turned her head back around, lest he catch a glimpse of the yearning emotion in her eyes. In bed was the only place she truly felt safe showing him how much she loved him, meeting passion with passion, but only in the heat of the moment when he was as intensely involved as her.

Dripping some of the oil onto his hands, Edwin rubbed them together, smiling at the slickness it produced and then placed his oiled hands onto his wife's shoulders and began to rub in the way Wesley had showed him. Wesley had used one of his amours for the demonstration, although of course he'd had her keep her clothing on while Edwin was in the room and hadn't used the oils, but he'd gotten the general idea.

"Ohh..." Eleanor's muscles tensed under his hands and then relaxed as his fingers pressed into her flesh. She groaned as he began kneading her shoulders and upper back, smoothing the oils over her skin so that his hands slipped and slid easily without catching or pulling on her flesh. "What is that?"

"Part of our wedding gift from Wesley," he said, marveling at how she softened beneath his hands. Very similar to the way she practically went boneless after a particularly intense climax. "He says these oils are used often in the East for medicinal and pleasurable purposes."

"Remind me to thank him," she murmured, closing her eyes and relaxing into the delightful sensations of Edwin's hands massaging her. Little knots of tension seemed to pop and release beneath his fingers, a feeling of wonderful lassitude spreading through her limbs as he began to work his way down her back.

It would be so easy to fall asleep... except the little coil of excitement that occurred whenever Edwin touched her.

Dripping more oil onto Eleanor's back, he admired the way her ivory skin gleamed in the candlelight. The oils slowly sank into her skin, necessitating him adding more to his hands and her flesh, but it continued to show as a glowing sheen. He smiled as he listened to her heartfelt groans and sighs of pleasure, his cock rising as it recognized the sounds he often heard from her in this bed, albeit for a very different reason.

Deciding to prolong their enjoyment, Edwin worked his way down her legs and her arms until Eleanor literally felt as limp as a boned fish. She was lost in a misty haze of relaxation and bliss, aware of Edwin's hands on her and yet feeling almost completely disassociated from them. It felt wonderful. The kind of care and pampering he was showing her made her feel as warm inside as she was outside; surely a man wouldn't do something like this, take his time the way Edwin was, unless it meant something? As far as she could see there was no return benefit for him. Of course these weren't concrete thoughts moving through her mind, more like fuzzy concepts; she was too far gone in her blissed out stated to be able to focus on anything.

By the time he finished rubbing oils all over his wife's back and limbs, Edwin was in such a keen state of arousal he seriously considered just oiling his hand and thrusting his cock through the slick surface to spill out all over her... but then he wondered what it would be like to make love to his wife when she was in such a submissively boneless state. It wasn't often he could describe Eleanor as anything like submissive. Gripping her hips, he pulled her up so she was kneeling before him, her body folded over her knees. She made a faint noise of protest until she realized he wasn't expecting her to move or do anything but lay how he had just placed her.

With her arms trailing before her, her body curled up, she looked like a heathen at prayer. Edwin grinned. He certainly planned on making her cry out to a deity.

Lining up his hard cock with her entrance he pushed upwards and in. Since the massage hadn't been entirely erotic she was wet but not overly so, making him work to fit his cock into her body. They both moaned—Edwin with relief as he sank into her and Eleanor with strange pleasure as she stretched to accommodate him, her sense still feeling as though they were scattered all about her. He had to move himself back and forth, thrusting a little deeper each time, to fully embed himself inside of her, the wetness of her tunnel growing as he slid his hands around to the unoiled front of her body and cupped her breasts.

With his oil-slick hands it was a completely different sensation as he pinched and rubbed at her nipples, one which made her insides tighten around him as the pleasure lanced through her. Her nipples were hardened to little points which he squeezed, but the oil made them pop out of his fingers and then he'd reach for them again. The constant renewing and relieving of pressure on her aching buds had Eleanor crying out, she would have writhed if she had more control over her muscles, but relaxed state of her body made it almost impossible for her to do more than raise her hips slightly to meet Edwin's hard thrusts.

Feeling Eleanor so passive beneath him was an unusual experience for Edwin, and while he definitely preferred her active involvement, he had to admit there was something immensely stirring about her lying so still beneath him as she moaned and shuddered. It allowed him complete control over her body, it was almost as good as if he'd tied her in place because she didn't seem to be able to move very much, allowing him to ravish her as he desired.

Sliding one hand down between her legs, he managed to wedge it into her tight crevice and rub her little pearl of pleasure between two slick fingers. Eleanor cried out as her orgasm caught her almost by surprise, boiling outwards from Edwin's clever fingers as his cock dragged over a spot deep inside of her that sent her reeling. She tightened around him as his thrusts came hard and fast, pummeling her pliable body until she felt him burst within her. The convulsing muscles of her tunnel rippled, milking him dry of his seed as he groaned and rocked, squeezing her breast so tightly that the slippery mound popped out of his hand.

For the first time, Eleanor lay completely passively as Edwin cleaned them both up, rubbing her down to remove the excess oil from her body as she smiled sleepily up at him.

Crawling into bed beside her, Edwin laid his lips against hers and kissed her deeply, enjoying the soft, loving attention he was receiving from her. He didn't know whether his volatile wife would keep up this sweetly obeisant demeanor tomorrow, but he intended to enjoy it while it lasted.

WATCHING his wife laugh as she galloped across the fields, putting the feisty chestnut mare he'd presented her with as a wedding present through her paces, Hugh thought he'd never been so happy. Irene in the county was nothing like Irene in London. Well, that wasn't quite true. She was still sweet and demure, polite, pleasing, but over the past few days he'd begun to catch glimpses of a freer Irene. One whose laugh chimed like bells, whose eyes sparkled with mischief, whose sly wit had surprised him more than once.

And her rampant curiosity was nothing like what he'd expected.

She wanted to explore everything, look at everything on the grounds of Stonehaven. There wasn't a room in the house she hadn't been in and thoroughly examined with him, asking questions about some of the pieces and artwork and the people in the portraits. They'd even explored the wine cellar, giggling like children who were doing something naughty. Irene's poking through a dusty, dark corner of the cellar had her coming up with a very old bottle of wine they'd decided to take out and try.

Hugh had spat it out immediately and then laughed so hard he hadn't been able to stand at Irene's nearly cross-eyed expression as she'd forced herself to swallow it. He'd laughed even harder when she'd given up the attempt and run around the corner of the house to try and keep him from seeing her spit it out. Of course he'd followed her.

And then reassured her that he didn't mind her unladylike behavior at all by pinning her against the rough stone and kissing her senseless. The kisses had helped to get the foul taste of the vinegary wine out of their mouths as well.

They were going to be spending the rest of the week exploring the lands around Stonehaven before moving on to their next destination on their honeymoon—his main seat in Westingdon. But this was the land he'd grown up on and he was eager to show her his favorite spots: the small glen where'd collected violets to give to his mother, the creek where he, Edwin, and Wesley had caught fish and cooked them on a spit over a fire, the small series of caves they'd used to play hide and seek. Although he thought he might omit the story about how he'd fooled Nell into following them in there so they could ditch her when she'd been following them around one time. Of course Edwin had gone back for her twenty minutes later, with Hugh and Wes guiltily following; she'd been hunkered down in one of the caves, crying her eyes out although she stopped the moment they appeared and pretended she'd been doing no such thing, and he'd never felt so bad in his life.

That had been the first time his father had taken a strap to his backside and not one of his best memories.

But he had plenty of other good memories about the caves, and he'd known he deserved that particular punishment, even at the time. He wanted to show them to Irene. Indeed, he found himself wanting to show her everything about his time here as a child.

"She's wonderful," said his wife, finally pulling her mare up beside him and nodding at the beautiful creature's tossing head. Hugh grinned at her. Rex, his stallion, was about two hands higher than the mare which she'd named Liberty so she had to tilt her head back to look up at him. Green eyes sparkled at him with pure pleasure and the color was high in her cheeks; little wisps of coppery hair had escaped her pins during her gallop and she looked incredibly beautiful. In fact it reminded him of how she looked in their bed. "Thank you so much for giving her to me."

"Well if we're going to go exploring then you need your own mount, as much as I might enjoy having you share mine." Hugh winked at her, enjoying the way her cheeks flushed even darker. Truthfully he was happy she now had her own mount, even though it meant she was no longer pressed up against him. It obviously gave her a great amount of joy, and she was a fantastic rider. He loved to watch her.

Despite the fact that she eagerly and passionately shared his bed, she still blushed whenever he flirted with her. It was a quality he found particularly endearing.

He was an extremely lucky man. Irene was even more intriguing to him out in the country where they could indulge in their shared interests, and despite her delicate looks he'd already discovered she was a bruising horsewoman and she enjoyed being outside much more than being cooped up in a house. Being away from the city—and perhaps being away from her mother was part of it—Irene had blossomed. And she was just as curious in the bedroom as she was around the house.

In fact just this morning they'd had an interlude which had been as erotic as it was frustrating for him, where he'd allowed his wife to explore his body with her eyes, fingers, and eventually her mouth. Although she hadn't taken it quite to the point where he might have liked it to go with her mouth before his control had finally snapped and he turned her onto her back, thrusting his almost angry looking manhood into her soft wetness. He'd given her as much time as he could bear to explore their differences and learn his body, her soft fingers brushing through his chest hair and over his nipples, seemingly entranced by the flat brown discs and the tiny nubs in the center. When she'd made her way, almost shyly, down to his groin he'd already been achingly hard and it was only the expression of curious awe on her face as she gently brushed her fingers up and down his shaft that had kept him from taking her right then and there.

Just thinking about it was already making it difficult for him to sit in his saddle considering the tightness of his riding breeches.

"Where would you like to go first?" he asked her, desperate to change his mind to other matters. Honeymoon or not he couldn't just drag her off to bed this morning. Again. "The flowers in the glen should be in bloom, it's the right time of year for them."

The smile he received in return was brilliant and so very pleased, he thought his heart might actually burst. Well, better his heart than the front of his breeches. "Then let's go there."

"Catch me if you can," he teased, before making a sharp turn and jolting Rex into a gallop.

He could hear the tinkling of Irene's laughter behind him and the pounding of hooves as she followed.

THE GLEN HUGH brought her to was more beautiful than Irene could have ever imagined. There were plenty of trees for shade in almost a perfect circle around a tiny meadow filled with violets. It was like a sea of purple and green at ankle height, and she desperately wished she could wade into them without crushing any of the beautiful, tiny flowers. That Hugh looked just as awed and delighted by the glen didn't quite surprise her, although at one time it might have.

Some men would never be able to look masculine while admiring a tiny violet, but Hugh was not one of them, despite his gorgeous blonde hair and grace of movement. With his broad shoulders and strong limbs, the slightly rugged state of his attire for riding which was so different from the impeccable gentleman he presented himself as in the evening, Hugh was decidedly quite manly and it didn't matter the venue or what he was doing.

"I used to come here every year at this time and gather flowers for my mother," he said, reaching down to cup a violet in his hand. "Violets are her favorite."

"They're one of mine too," Irene heard herself saying. Hugh looked up at grinned at her, making her heart thrum unevenly.

He plucked one tiny flower from the plant, walking towards her as she stared up at him. When he reached her, he tucked the violet into her hair, just above her ear. Since her mother was not there to lecture her on the importance of keeping her skin lily-white, and because she was already married so what did it matter anyway, Irene had gotten out of the habit of wearing a bonnet when she and Hugh went out. He certainly didn't seem to mind.

"The color suits you," he murmured, cupping her cheek in his hand and leaning down to feather a kiss over her lips.

Yearning surged inside of her and she leaned into him, putting her hands on his chest as she tilted her head back. He teased her lips with the lightness of his kiss, just brushing his over hers again and again as she went up onto her toes to try and catch him. As he purposefully kept her reaching, she couldn't help but giggle.

"Are you laughing at me?" he asked, putting his hands on her waist to steady her as she leaned against him, pulling his head back just enough to look into her green eyes which seemed even brighter out in the sunlight.

The sun had given her little freckles across her nose, which he decided he adored, and brought out golden highlights in her coppery hair. The violet was a stain of purple against the sunset background.

"Of course not!" Irene said, sounding surprised.

Hugh just laughed. He'd already learned she didn't always understand when she was being teased and it made his heart ache when he wondered what kind of childhood she must have had. So he took every chance he could to make up for it. Sliding his hands down her waist, he reached down and gripped her bottom before his lips descended again.

This time his kiss was much firmer, his lips parting hers as she opened for him to thrust his tongue into her willing mouth. Irene groaned.

Although she had become less intimidated by Hugh and her reactions to him, she still couldn't do anything about the physical disturbance he caused within her. The little flirtations, the teasing kisses, those she could handle. Then he was like a different, gentler man, the way she'd always imagined herself kissing Alex. But then Hugh would become something more wild, less contained, and she was always shocked to find herself responding so ardently.

The most frightening part was that she was beginning to enjoy the strangeness he created within her, as if there was a wildness inside of her that he called forth. Something untamed, uninhibited. It frightened her even as much as it excited her. Especially because when he did that, she completely forgot about Alex. Her entire body, her entire world, became about Hugh and what he was doing to her.

Surely that wasn't supposed to happen.

She was still confused about marital relations and the very large differences between what she had been told to expect and what she was actually experiencing. It made her long for a woman to confide in, but she didn't know her maid well—even if it hadn't been drilled into her by her mother to never trust the servants with personal secrets—and all the other women she might confide in were back in London. Yesterday she'd tried to write a letter to Eleanor, thinking perhaps her new sister might have some insight or understanding, but it was impossible to put her emotions and fears into words without sounding quite crazed. She'd ended up putting the letter in the fireplace rather than sending it.

No, she was on her own. And on her own meant trembling and needy in Hugh's arms as he tightened them around her, kissing her the way he did in their bedroom.

When he pulled his mouth away she was left gasping.

Hugh considered taking his wife down to the ground right there in the glen, but he didn't want to offend her sensibilities. Or risk having someone come looking for them, as it was almost time for luncheon. Although she was as passionate in the bedroom as any man could ask for, Irene still blushed when they made love in the light of day. It was too much to ask to have her do so outside. Not yet, at least.

"Perhaps we should continue on," he murmured, controlling himself as he brushed one last kiss over her swollen lips. "I will show you to the creek before we return to the house."

"If it pleases you." It was Irene's standard response, one which she had said many times to her mother, but with Hugh she found herself wanting to please him in order to see him smile. With her mother it had been to avoid an unpleasant scene.

"It does not please me," he said, pressing his thumb to her lips. "I would be much more pleased by a return to the house and our bed, but I wish to show you the creek and as we have already saddled the horses and ridden them out it would not be fair to return too soon." Irene blushed as he referenced their bed, confirming his modest wife was not yet ready for the outdoor activities he would best like to engage in currently.

"We do not have to go to the creek..." Her voice trailed off, and to his delight she truly did look rather torn.

"No, we will go to the creek," he said, releasing her. But he put his lips by her ear to whisper: "But after lunch I hope you will be in the mood for a nap." The little wink he gave her as he escorted her back to Liberty gave Irene no doubt as to exactly what he meant by 'nap' and the blush rose in her face again.

Hugh helped her up onto her saddle, settling her in, before he pulled himself up onto Rex. Watching his athletic ability as he swung up into the saddle always made Irene a little breathless. He was just so strong and sure of himself, in the saddle, as a man, and as a husband. Sometimes she wished she were like that.

"Do you think I might be able to ride Rex one day?" she asked, thinking she'd like to show Hugh how strong she could be in certain situations. "I would love to try his paces."

"Absolutely not," Hugh said in a tone that brooked no argument, it was almost harsh and she looked at him in surprise. "Rex behaves well enough for me but he is not a safe ride, especially for a lady in a side saddle."

Although his words were not particularly surprising or unkind, his tone was harsher than he'd ever used with her before. She was surprised to feel a little spark of rebellion deep inside her chest. Hugh knew she was a bruising rider, otherwise he never would have gotten her a spirited filly like Liberty.

"I've ridden stallions before," she argued. Hugh was so good at everything, she rather desperately wanted to show herself to be on his level. "In a side saddle."

"Other stallions, but not Rex," her husband said, his voice still stern although his expression had gentled as if he realized he had hurt her feelings by declaring her riding skills not up to his stallion. Sidling his horse closer he reached out with his hand; Irene reached back and took it although she was still feeling put out with him. "I don't know what I would do if anything happened to you, especially on my horse, Irene. I would never get over the guilt." He studied the disappointment clearly etched on her face. "Perhaps sometime you might ride double with me on Rex."

"It's not the same," Irene surprised herself by grumbling. Something about being married to Hugh must be stiffening her spine, because a month ago she never would have thought to argue with anyone, much less him. Then again she'd always been more bold in the country than she had ever felt in London, and she'd become comfortable with the fact that Hugh enjoyed hearing her thoughts even when they were contrary to what he wanted. It was a relief to be able to let them out, rather than keeping them bottled up like she'd always had to do at home.

Indeed, he just laughed and squeezed her hand, not at all distressed by her impertinence.

"No it's not, but it's the only way you will be allowed on Rex's back," he said firmly. Just the idea of her trying to ride the horse made his chest tighten in fear.

As he led the way to the creek, Irene watched his posture and the movement of his body as he rode the stallion. Although Rex was spirited and much heavier than Liberty, she was still convinced she could ride him given the chance.

She thought of Eleanor and wondered if Hugh's bold sister had ever ridden the stallion. Somehow she couldn't see the other woman being stymied by her brother's orders.

CHAPTER 8

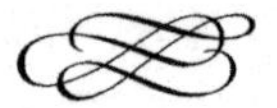

In the afternoon, the tables at Whites were half-filled with various gentlemen, some talking, drinking, smoking or some combination of the three, others reading newspapers, a few indulging in a late lunch. It was a gentleman's retreat, a haven away from the burdens of the world, and Edwin appreciated it as such. This particular afternoon he'd decided to reward himself for the hard work he'd been putting in on behalf of his father in London. Not just matters of the estates, but also the various political issues his father was interested in despite his abhorrence for actually coming to London and becoming involved in them. Instead he did this vicariously through Edwin, who appreciated the experience he was gaining even as he occasionally wished he didn't have the burden on his shoulders.

Since Eleanor was out at some afternoon tea, doing the social rounds and being his eyes and ears when it came to the latest reform bill (it was amazing how much information she was able to pick up through the wives and daughters of his peers once she knew what interested him), there had been nothing to entertain himself with at home. So he'd headed off to Whites, knowing Wesley and Alex were there almost every afternoon of the week. If Wesley was awake, that is. Despite Wesley's own responsibilities as Earl, somehow he managed to continue to live the life of a dissolute rake.

Edwin didn't begrudge him the pleasures, seeing as Wesley had spent so much time abroad. It was only natural he would revel in the freedom to enjoy London as Edwin and Hugh had for the past several years. He knew Wesley and Alex were becoming quite close; he rather enjoyed Lord Brooke's company himself and had passed more than one afternoon with the two over the past weeks. Especially since Hugh was away on his honeymoon, it was nice to have another man he could consider a closer friend at the endless round of evening social events.

The three of them together was more than enough to make the ladies swoon, even without Hugh's angelic looks to complement them. Lord Brooke cut as dashing a figure as Hugh did, even if he rarely smiled and often looked quite forbidding, Wesley still had the look of a pirate but the ladies seemed to find his tanned skin and lack of fashion to be just as intriguing as Alex's well-tailored clothes, and Edwin's dark good looks were always well presented by the clothing his valet dressed him in. Still, he had no interest in the fluttering sea of females they were often surrounded by in the evening and was grateful he had Eleanor constantly on his arm. He'd gotten into the habit of glaring at the men who asked her to dance, not because he thought they might have a chance at flirting with his wife—he knew he kept her well satisfied—but because it invariably left him without her as a shield from those amorous ladies of the *ton* who were not being attended to by Wesley and Alex.

But there was no point in dwelling on the stresses of the evening when he was at White's, that was the point of the club—a bastion against the women's social whirl. Currently he was enjoying listening to Wesley read aloud the latest letter from his mother, outlining the various antics of his ward which were giving her much grief.

"Therefore," Wesley rounded up, his hazel eyes sparkling with good humor, "I despair of ever marrying the wretched girl off. If you know of any gentleman who is willing to take a wife unseen, I beg of you to increase her dowry to whatever amount will incite him to take her off my hands."

The trio of men howled with laughter. Although Lord Brooke was only socially acquainted with the Dowager Countess of Spencer, even he knew what ends she must be driven to in order to make such a bald and rude statement. Edwin was beside himself at hearing of her troubles; she'd managed Wesley and his brothers with an iron fist—albeit a rather kindly one, especially when compared to their father—but this one slip of a miss barely out of the school room had her writing to Wesley twice a week now with complete exasperation and frustration. The young woman sounded like an unmanageable hoyden.

"Perhaps you should get yourself to Bath and take the chit in hand," Edwin said grinning. "But whatever you do, don't bring her back to London. I've had to blister Eleanor's bottom on a regular enough basis as is, there's no need to introduce her to any more bad influences."

Wesley laughed, but Alex gave a start and looked at him in surprise, the expression looking rather unusual on his stony face. "Blister her bottom..." he echoed, saying the words as if he was tasting them and was unsure of the flavor.

"My wife has a sad tendency to need... corrective treatment on a regular basis," Edwin said, not at all ashamed to admit it. Wesley already knew and there weren't any other gentleman close by enough to hear him speak of his wife in such indelicate terms. "Part of her father's understanding with me when I married her was that I would provide it."

Looking like he was torn between being appalled and intrigued, Alex leaned forward. "Are you... are you speaking of..."

Remembering his own amazement when he'd discovered Eleanor received the same kind of discipline from her father that he had from his own, Edwin grinned. "Spanking. Occasionally something harsher if she truly deserves it; I've only birched her once but I know her father did so on multiple occasions before she was presented."

"We witnessed it," Wesley said with a grin as Alex looked to him confirmation. There was a bit of shock in the lord's eyes. "Believe me, Nell richly deserves any discipline Edwin hands out to her."

"I have spanked her just for the pleasure of it on several occasions," Edwin confessed. "She enjoys it as much as I do. Of course she doesn't enjoy the punishments at all, but she's just as eager for conjugal bliss following them as I am."

"Truly?"

The expression on Alex's face was one Edwin had never seen before; indeed, Alex rarely showed very much emotion at all. Now he looked almost dazed, as if the world had tilted on its axis and he was seeing everything in a new light. Then again, this was not a conversation most gentleman would have except in the closest of company if then. The way spouses in the *ton* lived their lives was always behind closed doors and rarely discussed, because of the gossip it would create.

"Don't tell me you've never thought of turning *your* wife over your knee," Wesley said, his voice filled with amusement. Immediately Alex's face hardened, and Edwin shot his friend a glance. As far as he knew Wesley was the only one who dared bring up Lady Brooke to Alex. Not since Alex had liberally applied his fists to some wag who'd dared make a joke of roaming wives to the man a few months after he and Lady Grace had started living apart. As ever, Wesley ignored the warning looks he was receiving from his two friends. "She certainly deserves it."

Surprisingly, Alex didn't rebuke Wesley. Instead he looked almost thoughtful, although there was no definite change in his expression. Just a slight softening around the eyes as he sat quietly. Edwin could almost hear the gears turning and he wondered if Alex was giving the suggestion serious consideration. He almost asked what exactly had happened to estrange the couple, but he wasn't as daring as Wesley and he certainly didn't think he was close enough to Alex to merit the question.

"Perhaps," Alex said eventually. "I shall take it under consideration." Downing the last of the brandy he'd been drinking, he set the glass down on the table and gave his friends a slight smile. From Alex, that really just meant a slight upturn of the edges of his lips. "I must be off. I shall see you gentleman later."

After Edwin and Wesley had tendered their goodbyes and Alex had left, Edwin turned to his rakish friend. "Do you know what happened between him and Lady Grace? I've asked Nell but she doesn't seem to know any of the specifics."

Wesley shrugged, tipping his glass back and forth as he studied the amber colored liquor left in it. "Not much, just that after they returned from their honeymoon she kicked him out of her bedroom and wouldn't let him back in. Wouldn't even speak to him about it."

About a half hour later Edwin and Wesley parted ways, Edwin pondering Wesley's words. He could certainly imagine Eleanor trying to bar him from her bedroom out of pique; not that he'd ever tolerate it. But then he and Nell had a rather different relationship from many marriages within the *ton*, having known each other for so long. There was affection and understanding on both sides.

He grinned. Also his wife desired him just as much as he desired her. All he had to do was take Nell in his arms and kiss her for her to go up in flames, her soft body eagerly submitting to his. She might be furious with him afterwards, if they had been fighting beforehand or if he made them more than fashionably late for an event, but that didn't stop them from enjoying each other to the fullest. Just thinking about her made him feel full of masculine smugness.

Nell might run hot and cold on a daily basis with him, driving him to confusion, but one place she was always hot was in their bedchamber. Too bad he couldn't just keep both of them locked up in there.

THE BALL WAS A COMPLETE CRUSH, Eleanor thought with a tinge of annoyance as she was jostled yet again. She remembered at the beginning of the Season when she'd dreamed of being at a ball which could be described that way, sure it was the epitome of romance and she would be swept off her feet by multiple suitors. Instead she found it to be an annoyance.

A *hot* annoyance.

Snapping open her fan, she created a breeze for herself, flicking her eyes upwards at Edwin who was speaking at length about his father's interests out in the country. She was bored by the conversation, bored by the ball, and overheated on top of her boredom. Was this really what she had been dreaming about?

Perhaps it would have been more exciting if she had those swarms of suitors—certainly she had found her come-out ball to be rather enchanting—but now the only man she wanted to be swept away by was her husband. The thought was bringing less and less panic every day. While he certainly didn't go as far as to reveal any of his inner thoughts or feelings to her, she was able to watch him interact with the various ladies of the *ton* and even an inexperienced eye like hers could tell he had no lascivious interest in them. Certainly nothing she should get herself worked up over.

She'd become quite adept at people watching; not just noticing who was flirting, but also deciphering who meant it and who didn't. Some only flirted for show. Some in order to make someone else jealous. Some because it was second nature. Wesley seemed to be in the last grouping, although of course he also occasionally meant it when he flirted.

As if summoned by her thoughts, the man himself appeared at her side, looking decidedly roguish. Even in formal clothing he couldn't quite shake the look of a slightly dangerous savage; perhaps it was the residue of scruffy hair on his cheeks or the disheveled state of his cravat, although she privately thought it had more to do with the way he held himself. Wesley looked like a jungle cat, prowling the drawing rooms and balls of the *ton*. She'd actually overheard some of the dandies discussing the possibility of sunning themselves to attain the dark complexion he'd returned from India with, as if it was a new fashion fad.

"Good evening, sweetheart, don't tell me Edwin here is neglecting you again," he said, bowing low as he took her hand for a kiss. Now this was flirting for show and Eleanor grinned at him, fluttering her eyelashes at him for good measure.

"And if I inform you he is?" she asked, making a little moue with her mouth and trying to look mournful and attention-needy.

The grin Wesley gave her would probably send another woman to her knees, but sadly had no effect on her. Now if her husband looked at her that way then her heart would have started pounding because that kind of look was always an indication she was about to be dragged off to somewhere private—preferably, although not necessarily, with a reasonably comfortable flat surface. Leaning in, Wesley whispered in her ear. "Then I'll steal you away and make all your dreams come true."

Eleanor laughed delightedly, drawing Edwin's attention and he looked up to see her and Wesley exchange a conspiratorial look.

"Good evening, Wesley, have you met Lord Casper?"

"Sometime back, good evening Casper. Pleasure to see you again."

"Spencer." Although he was polite, Lord Casper had a slightly disapproving look on his face as if he had just sucked a lemon.

Ignoring the other man, Wesley plucked Eleanor's hand from Edwin's arm. "I'm just going to take Nell for a turn around the dance floor," he said as she rolled her eyes at him.

"Aren't you supposed to ask me first?" she complained as he whisked her away.

"Don't tell me you were enjoying sitting there and listening to that old bore," Wesley said with a wink as he pulled her into his arms just as the first strains of a waltz started. "We're too young for that, dear Nell."

"Edwin isn't?"

"Edwin's a good old soul. Much more responsible than me." He winked at her again, whirling her around a slower moving couple. Eleanor laughed, enjoying the sensation as Wesley directed her around the floor with ease, despite the large number of people congregated on it.

"Why did Lord Casper look at you like that?"

"Like what?"

"Like he tasted something unpleasant when he had to greet you."

This time it was Wesley who laughed. "Nell, you are a treat. Don't ever change."

"Aren't you going to tell me why?" she demanded, pinching his arm.

"Ouch! Stop it, you hoyden. Of course I'm not, it's not fit for your ears."

Eleanor gasped as she nearly stumbled over her feet, only saved by Wesley's strong arms around her. "You slept with his wife?!"

"What? Good God Nell, you aren't supposed to talk about things like that. And no. You must not have met the lady in question or you'd know she wasn't my type."

"Is there a woman alive who isn't?" she teased. "Alright then, if not his wife... his daughter? His niece? His mother?" Shaking his head after each question, Wesley chortled at that last one. Eleanor narrowed her eyes at him. "His ladybird?"

"You aren't supposed to know about such things, much less discuss them in public," he retorted, after nearly stumbling himself.

"I'm a wife, not an unmarried miss," she said, frowning at him. "Of course I know about mistresses. I have to." That last was said a little darkly and Wesley frowned.

"Nell... Edwin doesn't... he wouldn't..." Wesley searched for the right words. The little flash of vulnerability he'd seen in Eleanor's crystal gaze had unnerved him.

"You don't think so?" she asked, shooting a little glance over to where Edwin was standing, still talking to Lord Casper although they'd also been joined by Lord Brooke. But her tone wasn't harsh or disbelieving, if anything it was almost wistful, as if asking for confirmation.

"Of course not," Wesley said stoutly, for once his rakish winks and teasing humor had deserted him. "Nell, he'd never do that to you."

He could tell from her expression that she wanted to believe him but she wasn't entirely convinced. Unfortunately the song was ending and once they stopped moving it would be all too easy for others to overhear their conversation and to make the worst possible interpretations upon it.

While Wesley might not be very serious about a lot of things, that sad little wistful tone of Eleanor's wasn't something he could ignore. He'd never heard her talk in such a manner before and he didn't like it.

~

WATCHING his wife waltz in his friend's arms was surprisingly distracting. Edwin knew he had to remain on Lord Casper's good side, he was trying to recruit the man's vote after all, but Eleanor was looking stunningly gorgeous tonight. He much preferred having her on his arm than anywhere else, even if it was only Wesley. When she was dancing, Eleanor practically glowed, assisted by the gleaming yellow satin of the gown she was wearing. It made her look like candlelight, like an angel floating across the floor; she was so fresh and bright it almost hurt to look at her, but he couldn't look away. If she was dancing with anyone other than Wesley he wouldn't have been able to contain himself and would have ended the conversation with Casper to cut in, vote or not.

So when the other Lord began to make biting insinuations about Wesley's character and his probable pursuit of Eleanor, it was all Edwin could do to stay polite. Fortunately Alex joined them right at about that time, giving Edwin the opportunity to get his temper back in line. He knew full well where Lord Casper's bile was coming from —he'd been having a tempestuous affair with Lady St. Aubren and the lady had used Wesley to make the other lord jealous. Apparently it had worked.

But Edwin trusted Wesley implicitly and he knew there were no feelings like that between Wesley and Eleanor.

Still, when they returned he rather firmly pulled Eleanor into his side again, this time holding her there with an arm around her waist, hand splayed possessively over her hip. She looked up at him with an almost bemused expression and he desperately wished it wouldn't be completely out of bounds for him to kiss her right there and then.

Propriety had to be maintained, however, especially in front of a conservative moralist like Casper.

Fortunately Wesley's presence had the Lord taking his leave as soon as he'd bowed over Eleanor's hand, practically stalking away after giving Wesley the cut. Not that it bothered Wesley at all, of course, it would only enhance the reputation that he was garnering for himself. Edwin knew Wesley worked quite a bit more than he claimed, but he seemed to want to hide his responsible activities behind his reputation for being anything but. Perhaps a habit from when his father was alive.

Actually, Edwin wasn't quite sure where Wesley got his energy from. He was out all night, tending to his duties during the day, fairly active in Parliament... but then again he didn't have a wife to keep track of and occasionally chase after.

"Lady Hyde, how are you this evening?" Alex asked politely by way of greeting.

For a long moment Eleanor studied him, a slightly contemptuous frown on her face and Edwin frowned down at her, squeezing her side before she finally responded. "Very well thank you."

Wesley raised an eyebrow as Edwin's expression darkened. Eleanor could feel him beside her like a dark cloud. There was no excuse for being rude, especially to one of his friends, whether or not the man was unhappily married to her friend.

"Are you enjoying the ball?" Alex didn't look at all perturbed by her cold manner and her lack of reciprocated questioning.

"I was."

"Nell," Edwin growled. Rather than looking up at him she looked away, toward the dancers, fan fluttering furiously in front of her face as she studiously avoided Edwin's glare, Wesley's amusement and Lord Brooke's neutral expression. She knew she was being rude... but really! The man was married to her best friend and she knew their marriage was desperately unhappy, not only that but he was constantly seen with various cooing women on his arm.

Normally he was at least courteous enough about it to avoid Grace so she wasn't humiliated, but from having visited her friend the day before she knew Lord Brooke had practically been stalking his wife through the *ton's* events. He was the reason Grace had stayed home tonight. When Eleanor had visited her friend had been pacing the floor, nervous and overwrought.

"I can't eat... I can't sleep... He's just there, he's always *there*," Grace had said, wringing her hands. The dark circles beneath her eyes had been testament to her restless nights and Eleanor had been helpless to do anything but sit there and listen. "He just stands there, watching me, always with another woman on his arm... he doesn't care. Why should he? I've just barely managed to stay on the right side of the *ton*, only the high sticklers won't receive me, but I can go anywhere else... and he's going to ruin it for me, I know it. I can always feel everyone watching us, just waiting for one of us to do something. I swear they're all sending us both invitations, hoping we'll cause some kind of scandal at *their* party... I can't take it anymore Eleanor. I swore I wouldn't let that man effect my life but I just can't stay here in London any longer if he's here too, I *can't*."

Remembering Grace's distress, Eleanor had absolutely no compunction about her rude behavior to Lord Brooke. If it wasn't for him, Grace would be here right now, keeping her company, laughing, dancing, and happy. Instead she was at home, a ball of misery, and soon she might not even be in London.

"Yes?" she asked, keeping her voice distant and light, as if her heart wasn't pounding inside of her chest. Whatever punishment Edwin came up for her blatant rudeness, it would be worth it to show Lord Brooke that not every woman thought he was divine. She'd seen them flocking around him, teasing and flirting. The coldness of his gaze and the hard, unsmiling face (handsome or not) didn't seem to deter them at all. At this point everyone was used to Lord Brooke's somber expression and rarely thought anything of it.

The growl that came from deep in Edwin's chest sent a shudder through her, but she wasn't going to bend to his will on this, she thought fiercely. As her husband, he shouldn't ask it of her.

"My apologies for my wife's behavior," he said in a deep, angry voice to Lord Brooke. Eleanor's head whipped around, her eyes wide with indignation. How dare he speak for her! "I assure you she will be thoroughly... disciplined for her rudeness."

The little break in his speech made Eleanor gape at him, especially when Wesley chuckled. Did Wesley and Lord Brooke know? Did they understand... had Edwin been *telling them* about spanking her?

Humiliation swamped her, red heat rising in her face and now she couldn't look in the men's eyes for an entirely different reason.

"Don't be too hard on her," said Lord Brooke, his voice almost gentle. She peeked at him through her lashes, surprised. Even more so when she saw the expression on his face. Somehow he didn't look as hard and craggy, he looked almost... approving. "I know she's Grace's friend and I appreciate loyalty."

The dryness of his tone had her frowning. He appreciated loyalty? Then how did he explain his faithlessness to his marriage vows? He didn't want Edwin to be too hard on her—so he *did* know she'd earned herself a spanking. Or was he just speaking in general? Eleanor stared at him in confusion, opening her mouth and then closing it again, unsure of what she wanted to say.

For a very brief moment a smile flashed across Lord Brooke's face, making him look much younger and much more handsome. Then it was gone. She stared at him in some shock at the glimpse of a man the *ton* never saw.

"I'll keep your perspective in mind," Edwin said, although his voice was still too tightly controlled to be anything other than angry. "I think it's best we go now, Nell seems to be rather tired."

She wasn't, but she knew Edwin wasn't going to give her any more chance to misbehave. That was part of the punishment of course, taking her away from a ball he assumed she wanted to be at. If only he knew she'd much rather be at home with him.

Of course, she'd have preferred to be at home with him with her bottom unpunished, but she had a feeling that was no longer in the cards tonight.

CHAPTER 9

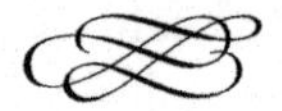

For once Edwin couldn't contain his anger until they'd gotten home. He managed to be civil enough to their hosts as they departed the ball, but as soon as they got into the carriage and the noise of travel made it impossible for the groom to hear him, he let vent his frustration with his wife.

"What happened in there?" he demanded, his voice low and harsh. "Why were you so rude to Lord Brooke?"

"Because he deserved it," Eleanor retorted, although she wasn't quite so certain of that anymore. His reaction hadn't been at all what she'd thought it would be, in fact he didn't seem nearly to be the kind of indifferent and uncaring brute Grace had made him out to be. Would someone like that tell Edwin to go easy on her? Commend her loyalty to her friend?

"Exactly what did he do to deserve your sharp tongue? He was nothing but polite to you when you were rude to him, and he even gave you a second chance to return his regard."

"He treats Grace horribly," Eleanor said, the only defense she had. "I saw her yesterday... she's an emotional wreck and it's all his fault!"

Edwin wanted to bang his head against the carriage wall; the flickering lights of the streetlamps allowed him to see glimpses of

Eleanor's face as they traveled. She was upset, he could see that and he knew she meant what she was saying, but he was also frustrated with her. Sometimes she could be so stubbornly immature when it came to relations between the sexes. That was something he was grateful for the majority of the time, but sometimes—like now—it was a hindrance to her understanding.

"It is rarely all one person's fault," he said angrily, wrapping his fingers around his cane so he didn't reach out and drag Eleanor across his lap. He itched to spank her but he didn't want to do so in a moving carriage. "Grace hasn't exactly been an exemplary wife. From what I can see she's been making Alex's life a misery ever since they married."

"You don't know how things are between them."

"Somehow I doubt you do either. There are always two sides to every story, Eleanor, and while your loyalty to Grace might be admirable, the truth of the matter is that blind loyalty often means you will find yourself on the wrong side of the equation. I can assure you Alex is just as upset with her behavior as she apparently is with his."

"He's had just as many lovers as her! More!"

"Why is it any of your business?" he countered.

"Because Grace is my friend."

"As her friend you should be her confidant and her support, but that does not mean you go about willy-nilly making judgments on people whom you haven't bothered to have a conversation with, much less get to know them on their own merits."

Biting her lip, Eleanor privately conceded Edwin had a point. It wouldn't have mattered what Lord Brooke said to her, she would have been rude to him anyway. But his responses to her rudeness had given her second thoughts about Grace's presentation of him already, and she was well aware Grace had never given her all of the details about their marriage. Also, she conceded, she was sensitive on the subject of men with wives having mistresses. Not that she would admit it to Edwin.

The long silence told Edwin his wife was finally thinking about what he had said. Thank goodness, he thought exasperatedly. Just because he liked Alex didn't mean he begrudged Eleanor her friend's company, even if he wished his wife's best friend had better morals and less lovers, but he wasn't going to allow her to be rude to a peer in public either. Especially not one he *did* consider a friend.

The rest of the carriage ride was spent in silence, but the waves of resentment emanating from Eleanor's direction had ceased. Instead he saw a thoughtful expression on her face as she looked out the window. Rather than forcing her to talk about it, Edwin let her process his arguments on her own. Pushing Nell was not the way to change her mind, she would just dig in stubbornly. And it's not as if this was a behavior he could spank out of her—although he certainly intended to spank her for her rudeness. His cock stirred at the thought.

Unfortunately he was going to have to wait until they were home before he could indulge in anything physical with her, whether it be punishment or pleasure. He wasn't going to rush her now that she was finally thinking things through instead of just reacting. Although even if she decided she still didn't like Lord Brooke, Edwin was absolutely not going to tolerate that kind of lack of decorum in public from his wife. At the very least, she could be civil.

Following Edwin upstairs, Eleanor did her best to drag her feet without actually seeming to drag her feet. She still couldn't decide whether she hated the way she responded to the punishment he meted out or if she was glad she managed to find some pleasure in it. It seemed singularly humiliating that she should become so aroused while being demeaned by a spanking—or worse—and yet she couldn't be entirely sorry her discipline was invariably followed by passion.

At least she knew her strange reaction was entirely due to her husband. She'd certainly never found any kind of enjoyment during the spankings and birchings she'd received from her father. So perhaps it wasn't that she responded to the punishment but to Edwin. That made it slightly more palatable. And more embarrassing.

Worse, she found herself rather embarrassed by her behavior this evening as well. The more she'd thought about Lord Brooke's reactions and his defense of her, the worse she'd felt about how she'd acted. Not only had she been deliberately rude to someone her husband obviously considered a friend, but she certainly hadn't furthered Grace's cause at all in Edwin's mind and probably not in Lord Brooke's either. And lately she'd been thinking perhaps it wouldn't be so bad to be in Edwin's good graces, to try and be the wife he wanted. Perhaps he would be more inclined to show his feelings towards her if she behaved.

At least that was a theory. One which would, hopefully, cut down on the number of disciplinary spankings she received from him and the humiliation of her reaction. Although, she thought as she blushed a little, she did enjoy it when he gave her a light spanking just to warm her bottom and heat up her body before making love to her.

But that was very different from the kind of spanking she knew she was about to receive.

Edwin preceded her into the room before turning and facing her; she could feel the color rising in her cheeks under his disapproving gaze. To her horror, her nipples tightened as he looked at her and she internally cursed her body's response. Reminding herself that she was here for punishment, not passion, didn't deter the arousal curling inside her stomach at all.

Then again, who could entirely blame her when the man she was looking upon was so devastatingly handsome in his evening attire? In the flicking light of the candles and fire Edwin looked even more like a fallen angel, his face partly shadowed, his dark hair and eyes seeming to drink in the light.

"Come here, Nell," he ordered, holding out his hand.

When she reached him, tilting her head back to look pleadingly into his eyes, he turned her around to face away from him and she could feel him pulling at the laces on the back of her dress. She started to tremble. Not because she was afraid, but because she so desperately wanting him to touch her. The feel of her clothing sliding off of her body always became erotic when Edwin was the one undressing her.

After she stepped out of the dress he tossed it to the side, treating her undergarments with the same lack of care until she was standing before him in nothing but her stockings and the blue ribbons holding them up. The same blue ribbons he'd bought her because they matched her eyes exactly. As he turned her around to face him again his eyes were hot with desire and she knew he'd noticed.

"Do you understand why I'm going to spank you tonight Eleanor?" he asked, cupping her chin in one hand and forcing her to look at him.

Surprisingly there didn't seem to be any fight in his wife tonight, instead she looked both resigned and almost relieved. As if she felt she deserved the punishment she was about to receive—which she did—and accepted that fact. While he enjoyed her spirit, he was glad to know he wasn't going to need to actually beat this lesson into her rebellious bottom; sometimes he was sure his wife was contrary just for the pleasure of it.

"Yes, I do," she said, looking up at him with what looked true contriteness in her sapphire eyes. "I'm sorry I was rude to Lord Brooke."

"You would have done better to apologize to him," Edwin said mildly, pleased at this change in Nell. Of course he didn't want her without her spirit, but he also didn't want her to think she could get away with bad or rude behavior, and it pleased him to know she wasn't so self-involved and spoiled that she couldn't recognize and change her ways when the situation merited it.

"I wasn't sorry yet," she said, a little waspishly, and he had to swallow a laugh. But Eleanor could see the twinkle in his eyes which meant she had amused him and she was glad of it. That meant he wasn't truly upset with her, although she knew it wouldn't make any difference as to her spanking.

"Then you will apologize the next time you see him?"

She sighed, but she knew it was the right thing to do. "Yes," she muttered, her eyes glancing away from his even though he kept her facing him. It was uncomfortable to look away for too long so she found herself back gazing into his deep brown eyes, searching hers as if he was looking for the secrets to her soul.

"Good," he said, and she bristled, which only amused him again. Still, he knew she wouldn't back out of apologizing just because he approved. That wasn't the kind of person Eleanor was.

Deciding he was done with the lecture, because having her standing in front of him in nothing but the ivory silk stockings clinging to her long legs, was killing him. He loved undressing her and seeing her body slowly revealed to him, and even more than that, he loved having her naked in front of him when he was fully clothed. It was about more than just her beauty, it was also about his domination over her... he never tired of having Eleanor submit to him. Some wives might do so just to placate their husbands or to make them happy, with Eleanor it was always a struggle and that made her final submission all the more special.

She would never do it for a man who didn't deserve it and he knew that.

Releasing his hold on her chin, feeling the loss of warmth against his palm, he sat down on the chair in front of her vanity, facing away from the other piece of furniture.

"Come here, Nell," he said again, patting his lap as he did so. Unlike before, when she had come slowly to his hand, this time she hesitated before moving towards him. It gave him time to admire her soft skin, the strawberry nipples which had already hardened into little buds, and the enticing golden cover of her mound. With her hair piled high like a lady's, the jewels he'd bought her still clasped around her neck, she looked like an erotic dream as she came towards him. His cock was already rock hard and she wasn't even across his lap yet.

As she lowered her upper body, using his thighs and the sides of the chair to brace herself, Edwin sat back and forced himself to watch without touching her. This was the first time she'd truly given herself over to discipline without a fight and he wanted to relish it. Of course she deserved it, but that didn't mean he couldn't enjoy it.

The way her back arched, tendrils of golden hair caressing the back of her slim neck as she moved, her body pale and creamy against his dark pants. For a moment her breasts pressed against his thigh and then they were gone as she tipped herself forward more, positioning herself so she could brace herself on the floor with her hands. Now that she couldn't see him, Edwin allowed himself a grin as he pulled her body towards his, nestling her soft stomach against his aching hardness.

"Because you were deliberately and unrepentantly rude at the ball, I think a count of twenty is fair," Edwin said.

He could feel his wife shift as if she wanted to say something but she didn't argue. Truthfully it was more than fair, especially as he didn't plan to be particularly hard on her—although he wouldn't describe his swings as soft either.

SMACK!

Eleanor let out a little yelp, her body tensing and relaxing as Edwin rubbed his hand over the spot he'd just hit. There hadn't been any warning and he'd caught her off guard. His hand rubbed at the sting and she couldn't tell if he was making it better or worse.

"Count them out for me, Nell."

"One," she said immediately, not wanting him to repeat a blow just because she hadn't counted it.

SMACK!

"Two."

SMACK!"

She gasped. "Three."

Part of the reason Edwin wanted to hear her count was because otherwise she wouldn't make much noise at the beginning. Eleanor had the kind of pride which made her hold in the soft gasps, the little cries that made his cock throb. But it was much harder for her to do so when she had to open her mouth and speak immediately after instead of clenching her jaw against her natural reaction.

He could hear her voice strain with the effort not to reveal how much the spanking hurt, even as he peppered her bottom hard and relentlessly, turning the creamy color a hot pink. Granted, this was certainly not the hardest punishment she'd taken, compared to the wooden spoon it was probably rather mild, but that didn't help her in the moment. Remembering how much worse the spoon had hurt didn't do anything to soothe the heat building as Edwin's hand came crashing down on her buttocks.

SMACK!

Whimper.

"Ten!"

Watching the color blossom on her ivory skin, watching it darken as her flesh jiggled after his hand impacted it, was something Edwin didn't think he would ever tire of. Eleanor aroused him with nothing more than her person, but he thoroughly enjoyed disciplining her; it added an extra something to their relationship, despite the passion he indulged in with her every night.

SMACK!

Yelp.

"Eleven!"

Her body rocked against his thigh as if she was trying to rub her clit on him. There was no doubt she was aroused, he could actually smell her wetness now as her bottom clenched and opened, legs closing and spreading. With his arm securely wrapped around her body, his hand on her stomach, he'd been able to feel her breathing turn to panting as she'd dealt with the confusing rush of pleasure and pain that a spanking like this induced.

Particularly harsh punishments, such as the spoon, created the same physical reaction of a sopping pussy, but he could tell she didn't enjoy it. Right now she seemed caught between finding the spanking pleasurable and having it be too painful for pleasure. Deciding he liked that added bit of humiliation to her punishment, because he knew she was unhappy that part of her enjoyed being disciplined, Edwin decided to keep her on the fine line.

He made sure to spread the last of her spanking out over her entire bottom, turning the surface of both cheeks a glowing pink, without over doing it and pushing her past the threshold into real pain. Perhaps physically it wasn't as great a punishment, but he knew mentally it was.

Standing her back on her feet in front of him, he made a show of pushing his fingers between her thighs and rubbing them between her wet lips. Eleanor moaned and put her hands over her face, unable to look at him as he drew his fingers away sopping wet.

"I don't know how much of a punishment a spanking is, if you enjoy it so much," he murmured.

"I don't enjoy it," Eleanor snapped back, glaring at him through her fingers.

It was a complete lie of course, her body had gotten hot and aroused while he'd spanked her, but it wasn't her fault. There was nothing she could do about it. She told herself it wasn't because of the spanking—of course it wasn't, she'd never had such a reaction when her father had disciplined her after all—it was because she was attracted to Edwin, because she loved him, and because she was aroused by him touching her.

She was even willing to admit to herself that she enjoyed being helpless across his lap, enjoyed having him caress her body when she couldn't touch him back... when he'd tied her up on their honeymoon she'd discovered she liked it. Since their return home he hadn't done it again, the closest she got was being across his lap where she couldn't lift her hands off the floor without feeling as though she was going to slide forward onto her head.

"Liar." Pulling his fingers from her glossy, wet curls, he showed her the sheen of liquid on the digits and she groaned, hiding her face behind her hands again.

Edwin laughed and stood, pulling her into his arms, ignoring her glare. It didn't bother him when Eleanor glared at him, in fact it just made him that much more determined to make her sigh and melt in his arms. Lowering his head he kissed her as she squirmed in his arms, mad enough at him for mocking her response to the punishment that she wanted to get away from him.

Not that he would allow it. She almost hated the shiver of excitement that went through her as his arms tightened, holding her in place. The fabric of his shirt rubbed against her breasts, which were already feeling exquisitely sensitive, and his thigh pressed between hers, sliding against her swollen clitoris in the most delicious way as he practically ravished her mouth. Moaning, Eleanor gave in, knowing from experience that she would eventually anyway.

She had enough experience with passion now that Edwin couldn't completely overwhelm her immediately, she could fight her responses, but eventually the need between her legs always won. Because she wanted him as much as he wanted her. Sometimes she wondered if part of her surrender was because she worried who he might turn to with his passions if she didn't, but she also knew it was mostly because she truly loved making love with him. If she didn't then she wouldn't care if he did this with someone else.

Clinging to him, she began to push his clothing off of him, undoing the buttons down the front of his shirt to get to his skin. Edwin loved that during the time they'd been married Eleanor had become more forward in what she wanted, that she'd started to learn how to touch him, how to drive him wild. Not that she'd needed to do much in the first place to make him out of his mind with lust for her, but he lost all control when she began to touch him with those tremulous, curious fingers of hers.

It didn't take very long for their combined efforts to shuck off the rest of his clothing and then he was tossing her up onto the bed, her stockings and garters still on but slipping. He liked the way she looked with nothing on but those delicate scraps, and as he moved into position between her legs he ran his hands up the silky material and then to the different, but no less soft and satiny, smooth skin of her thighs. Eleanor whimpered a little as he pushed his hands beneath her bottom, squeezing the pink cheeks, and her hips rocked upwards.

Lowering his head, he chuckled as he heard her moan when he planted a kiss on her hip rather than on the wet flesh of her womanhood. Her hands came down on his head, trying to push him lower, but he was enjoying teasing her too much. Kneading the stinging flesh of her bottom, he licked little circles over her hips, ignoring her pleas and almost frantic movements.

"Edwin... Edwin, *please...*" He was driving her crazy, his hands and mouth so close to where she ached to be touched. It felt like her lower body was on fire as he dragged his teeth over her hip bone, lightening flashing through her as she writhed for him. The heat in her buttocks, the squeezing of his hands reigniting the sting, only inflamed her further.

"Tell me what you want, Nell."

"You, I want you... touch me, Edwin!"

"I am touching you."

"Not there... Edwin, please!"

She groaned as he moved upwards instead of downwards, his mouth latching onto her nipple which was already puckered into a hard little bud. It soothed the needy desire in her breast but did nothing to assuage the hunger growing between her legs. Still, at least it was something and she arched her breast, clasping his head to her chest with her hands as she felt the head of his cock drag wetly along her inner thigh.

Remembering what her husband liked, Eleanor moved one hand down to the base of his skull, tugging gently at his hair there as she dug the nails of her other hand into his shoulder. She could hear him groan around the mouthful of breast flesh, a tremor going through his large body above hers as she scratched a line across his shoulders.

Quick as a whip, Edwin grabbed her arms and pushed them above her head, gathering her wrists together and holding them with one of his large hands. Eleanor protested, but her words were drowned by a heavy moan as he squeezed her breast with one hand, his mouth attacking her other nipple, and the head of his cock rubbed against the wet flesh of her pussy. She was helpless underneath him, squirming and needy and unable to use her hands to spur him to move faster.

Holding her down increased Edwin's arousal as well as hers. He loved to hear her voice become increasingly ragged, her breasts heaving beneath him as she panted for her, her arms twisting uselessly against his tight grip. Beneath him she bucked, her legs wrapping around the back of his thighs as she tried to pull him into it.

"What do you want, Nell?"

"You..." she whispered, lowering her eyelashes as she blushed. It was part of why he made her verbalize her desires, he loved the shy modesty she hadn't managed to completely shed. "I want you inside me."

"Look at me," he demanded.

Blue eyes clashed with dark as he began to push into her, enhancing the intimacy as he breached her body and her sheath encased the head of his cock like a silken fist. Perfect pink lips parted on a gasp as he spread her open, spearing her on his body, his elbows on either side of her head, hands entwined as he held hers pressed against the mattress, watching every flicker of pleasure and passion in her crystal blue eyes.

As he pulled out slightly and thrust deeper she let out a sharp cry, her legs tightening around him as her head fell back. He could feel her inner muscles squeeze him and then he was thrusting again, harder, faster... deeper. Eleanor's throat worked, her moans and cries increasing in volume and tempo as he took her. Lowering his mouth he sucked at the skin on her neck, right where it met the shoulder, and felt her ripple around him in response.

She arched against him, pulling him hard into her, her hips moving upwards to meet him as she abandoned herself to the passionate sensuality of their coupling. His movements became more forceful, his weight bearing down on her as she struggled against the hold of his hands, wanting to touch him... to wrap her arms around his neck. The fight only added to their ardor, their bodies rocking together in erotic rhythm.

"Edwin..." Eleanor writhed and tightened. "Oh God... Edwin..." He knew she was getting close when she began to sound like that, a kind of joyful frenzy in her voice, a desperation as if she worried she might not cross over the edge into ecstasy. "Oh please... Edwin... Harder..."

The burn in her bottom as it was pounded into the mattress mixed with the rapturous friction of his rod rubbing against her insides, his hard groin pressing against the swollen nub of her clitoris with every hard thrust. Eleanor had stopped struggling for the use of her hands, she was beyond caring whether or not she could touch him, and in the back of her mind she knew it excited him even more when she gave in on the fight.

His cock slammed into her, again and again, and she could feel herself come closer to glorious climax with every pummeling thrust. Just one more... it burned its way from her core up through her mouth as she screamed out her completion, her body bucking and tightening, massaging his cock as he moved even harder and faster, fucking her through the waves of sensation assaulting her. The thickening of his cock inside of her, the pulsing heat as his seed jetted into her body, his own shout of pleasure mingling with hers, sent her reeling down a corridor of passionate rapture until she thought she might actually burst from it.

When Edwin settled into the comfortable haven of her thighs, his hold on her hands gentling as his passion subsided, Eleanor couldn't stop the shivering gasps and jerks as aftershocks of pleasure rippled through her. Her husband murmured sweet compliments against her neck, nuzzling her, as she moaned and shuddered against him, her body slowly coming down from the incredible high of pleasure. Was it any wonder she'd fallen in love with the man, she thought a little dazedly.

"So beautiful," she heard him say as he kissed his way up her neck. Then he chuckled. "Oops."

"Oops?"

Releasing one of her hands, he stroked his fingers over the spot just between her shoulder and neck. "I may have left a mark."

"Edwin!" Eleanor's first instinct was to jump up and go look in the mirror, but it was impossible with the heavy weight of her husband on top of her. He only laughed as he felt her try to shove him off, putting his lips on hers in a passionate kiss. For a moment she resisted and then her lips parted, letting him in.

It was a slow, languorous kiss that had nothing to do with sex and everything to do with sweet emotion. The tenderness of his kiss nearly brought tears to her eyes and Eleanor found herself surrendering to it, the flash of anger she'd felt at discovering he'd given her a love-bite melting away as he kissed her so sweetly. She loved the way Edwin caressed and cuddled her after coupling, it always made her feel as though there must be something more there than mere lust or passion.

There had been a smugness about him, as well, as he'd made his little announcement. Was it possible he liked the idea of having his mark on her skin? But if so, was it a sign of possession or something more?

"I don't know what you're thinking so hard about, but stop it," Edwin said, pulling away from the kiss with an almost amused expression on his face. "I want your attention here, on me."

Without waiting for a reply he was kissing her again, his hands moving down her arms to her head, cradling it and massaging her scalp as his lips moved over hers. Letting go of her worries and doubts, for now, Eleanor sank into the moment and gave herself over to loving her husband.

CHAPTER 10

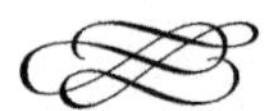

The next morning Eleanor woke up to an empty bed. It wasn't entirely surprising since she always needed more sleep than Edwin, especially after a night like the night before. He'd kept her up for hours. Even now she had a sore but satisfying ache between her legs. Unfortunately her bottom was still sore too but that couldn't be helped.

With a sigh, she forced herself out of bed and rang for the maid to help her dress and put up her hair. She had planned to visit Grace today, but she knew the visit was going to go very differently than she'd originally thought. While she still had a good deal of sympathy for her friend, her own impression of Lord Brooke last night said he was not the man Grace described. Of course Eleanor was seeing him from a completely different viewpoint, but she couldn't shake the idea she was missing something from the equation.

Perhaps Grace was missing something too.

"Good morning, my lady," said Poppy cheerfully as she bustled into the room. "His lordship is having breakfast and invites you to join him as soon as you're able."

"Thank you, Poppy," Eleanor said with a smile. It wouldn't surprise her to learn Edwin had been in his office doing work until she had rung for a maid, specifically so he could join her for breakfast. Little gestures like that made her think perhaps he did care for her, in the way she wanted him too. At the same time, she was afraid to read too much into them—after all, her father had done similar things for her mother when they were actually in residence together. The very next day, however, he might order her off to Bath or Stonehaven again. So Eleanor could not rely on those little gestures to tell the whole story. But she could certainly enjoy them. "I'll be visiting Lady Grace after breakfast. I think I'll wear the rose damask today."

"Yes, my lady," Poppy said, searching through the wardrobe for the requested dress as Eleanor stood and stretched.

"Ah Lady Hyde, please come in," Peters, Grace's butler said. He scanned over her head as if assuring himself there was no one behind her as she came in the door.

"Is everything alright, Peters?" she asked, a small frown on her face.

The normally stoic butler actually hesitated before answering her. "Her ladyship is not at home today, although she gave me special instruction you were to be the exception. We've had a number of callers come to the house the past couple of days." His voice lowered, despite the fact that there was no one to overhear. "It is my opinion most of them were only here to drop gossip in her ladyship's ear."

Eleanor's mouth tightened. She could just imagine the kind of gossip the *ton* would bring to Grace's house in hopes of eliciting a reaction. Thank goodness her friend had the loyal and stalwart Peters to help shield her from the supposedly morally upright but less savory members of their class. The butler had been protective of Grace for as long as he'd been in her employ and it appeared he'd become even more so—and not without cause.

"Thank you, Peters," she murmured as he showed her into the sitting room. It was decorated in cheerful yellows and pinks, not overly bright but enough that anyone in the room couldn't help but eventually feel a bit more hopeful and happy. She wondered if Peters had chosen this room on purpose so Grace would feel its effects.

Settling herself onto the cream sofa, Eleanor stared up at the familiar decorations on the wall; Grace's favorite flower paintings were scattered about the room, as well as some watercolors she'd done herself. Grace truly was a rather gifted artist, rather than just cultivating the talent because it was what young ladies were expected to do.

Fortunately she didn't have to wait long before Grace swept into the room, her usual cool demeanor looking rather fractured. The dark circles under her light eyes had deepened, making the blue of her eyes look almost feverishly bright, and her dark hair was slightly rumpled, as if she'd been touching it too much. Something Eleanor knew her friend only did when she was agitated. The deep violet of her dress normally looked quite well with Grace's dark hair and creamy skin, but today it only emphasized the bruised looking skin beneath her eyes.

"Grace," Eleanor said, by way of greeting, as she got to her feet.

"You have no idea what a relief it is to see you," Grace responded, before Eleanor could say anything more, coming forward and hugging Eleanor to her. The trembling in her friend's body unnerved Eleanor, as did the impression that Grace's bones were poking through her skin. It had been only a few days since they'd last seen each other and yet it felt like Grace had lost even more weight. Weight she could ill afford to lose. Grace laughed, but it was a brittle sound. "The vultures have been more relentless than ever the past few days. I miss one or two functions and suddenly everyone has a burning desire to see me at home."

"Thank goodness for Peters," Eleanor murmured.

A genuine smile broke out on Grace's face, bringing back her loveliness even as she looked more delicate than before. "Yes, thanks goodness for Peters. I don't know what I would have done without him. He's like Cerberus guarding Hades." She gestured around them a little wildly, as if to indicate that the house she was living in was the embodiment of Hell.

"Oh surely it can't be that bad."

"How would you like to be trapped in your house, unable to go out without facing public humiliation?" Grace asked, her voice snapping. She rubbed her hands over her face as Eleanor looked at her reproachfully. For all their occasional competition, they were rarely actually snappish with each other. "I'm sorry, Nell... I'm just tired and upset and I shouldn't take it out on you. I'm feeling rather... wild if you must know the truth. I truly think I must quit London and go out to the country. I'm ready to cede the field to Alex. He can have London, I don't care anymore."

"Grace... are you sure..." Eleanor paused, trying to think of how to phrase what she wanted to say. Somehow she didn't think Lord Brooke would want Grace to be suffering like this, or to be driven from the social scene she loved so much, but how could she say such a thing? "I met Lord Brooke last night," she finally said rather tentatively. "He didn't seem the type to... well..."

"Ah. So you spoke with him. He can be quite charming when he wants to be, can't he?" Grace closed her eyes, leaning back against the sofa. "Did he say anything about me?"

Curiously, Eleanor watched her friend, but with her eyes closed she couldn't tell what Grace was feeling at all. Those wonderfully expressive eyes were usually what gave away her emotions while her face was placid and neutral.

"He defended me to Edwin after I was rude to him," Eleanor said. "He said he admired my loyalty to you. Well, he said he appreciates loyalty."

"Ha," Grace said with a snort, her eyes snapping open, bright with anger. "I'm sure he does." Her mouth primed, tightened, and she looked away from Eleanor as if all too aware she was showing a wealth of bitterness and hurt and she didn't even want her best friend to see it.

"Grace... you've never really told me what happened between you and Alex..."

"It was too humiliating," Grace said in a quiet voice, the anger seeming to drain out of her as she looked down at her hands, twisting them in her lap. "That's why I never really told you."

Reaching out, Eleanor put her hands on top of Grace's. "Will you tell me now?"

Grace gave her a rueful smile. "You know I married Alex at the end of my first Season and I didn't particularly want to be married yet."

"I remember." She and Grace had both had similar sentiments when it came to enjoying the social whirl, even if they'd had different reasons. Unlike Eleanor, Grace had wanted to marry for love. Eventually. Once she'd enjoyed London to the fullest.

"It was arranged."

"I knew that too." It was why Eleanor had never blamed Grace for her behavior. She always thought Grace's father should have realized his daughter would rebel in one manner or another, although she'd thought on more than one occasion Grace had gone too far.

"My father saw me as nothing more than an item to barter," Grace said, holding her chin up in defiance of the worth her father had placed on her. "I was *useful* because I could get him something he wanted. I thought Alex at least cared for me... we weren't in love but there was... there was *potential*. I thought I could come to love him and he could come to love me. We have plenty of mutual interests. He was so attentive and charming... I enjoyed speaking with him and I found him to be quite exciting. After our wedding night and honeymoon I even thought I was falling in love with him."

"Then what happened?" Eleanor asked, completely enthralled. This was all new information to her, as she hadn't seen Grace until a month after she'd returned from her honeymoon and by that time her friend had already set up a separate household from her husband. She'd always assumed Grace had been dead set against the wedding from the beginning.

The bitter twist of Grace's mouth could have been interpreted as an attempt to smile. "I overheard a conversation he had with my father after we returned home. They were congratulating themselves on the deal they'd made with my marriage contract and their alliance.

Alex said one woman was as good as another for a wife, but at least with me he'd gotten something *useful* in the bargain. That's when I knew he didn't care who he'd married, but the alliance with my father had gotten both of them what they wanted. No one cared what I wanted or how I felt."

"Oh Grace..." Eleanor's heart ached for her friend. No wonder Grace had turned so brazen and scandalous. At least Eleanor still had hope Edwin might have emotions for her, she certainly knew he cared for her as a person.

"It doesn't matter," Grace said almost fiercely. "I don't care anymore." But it was obvious, to Eleanor at least, that Grace did still care. She was still hurting. No matter how many lovers she'd had since her husband, they had not healed the wound to her pride, her self-esteem, or her heart.

"Of course not," she said, anyway. Grace could keep her pride in front of Eleanor, that was something she could give her friend at least.

More than ever she could understand Grace's desire to leave London now that it was apparent Alex was staying put. She could understand Grace's animosity toward her husband. No matter how polite Alex had been last night that didn't mean he was right for Grace. Unfortunately his attitude was not uncommon amongst the *ton.* There would have been many women who would be willing to marry such a man for his title and money, but not Grace. While she might seem cold and hard on the outside, her inner core had always hidden a soft romantic.

"You want him to divorce you," she said suddenly, the revelation slamming into her. It explained so much. Grace could have chosen any other kind of rebellion against her father and her husband, but she'd deliberately chosen something to shame Alex, something which would make him want to set her aside. Something which would allow him to set her aside. It was very like Eleanor's original plan for dealing with Edwin, although the motivations were completely different.

"Yes." Grace gripped Eleanor's hand, giving her a sad little smile.

The dark smudges beneath her eyes looked more like bruises than ever. There was a vulnerability to her that Eleanor had never seen before. Then she shored it up again, regaining control over her features, shutting down her emotions behind a cold mask.

Eleanor wondered if that was what she would look like if she discovered Edwin didn't love her. If she would use those same defense mechanisms of shutting out the world and pushing away her emotions.

"I once thought he might divorce me and marry someone more willing," Grace said. She laughed softly and shook her head. "Of course, the most likely candidate is married now herself."

"Who?" Eleanor asked. She didn't really care but she welcomed the change of topic. Stepping around the conversational minefield surrounding Grace's marriage and the details she'd just confided to Eleanor was daunting.

"Your new sister-in-law, of course," Grace said, looking at Eleanor with something akin to real amusement. "I know Alex was at her wedding, surely you didn't miss that she's head over heels in love with the man."

"Irene?" Eleanor felt her jaw dropping. "And... your husband?... But... but..."

"Oh dear..." The amusement on Grace's face immediately faded. "Don't tell me it's a love match for Hugh? I'd heard it was arranged by your parents and hers."

"I'm not sure. I know he cares for her... he wouldn't have married her if he didn't feel something for her... but she didn't... she wouldn't..."

Grace laughed mirthlessly. "Oh she would. I was there when she and Alex saw each other for the first time after I married him. I saw her face. At the time I felt sorry for her. Two months later I felt sorry for myself."

"If you felt sorry for her, then why are you so mean to her?"

Soft pink lips hardened into a straight line again. "I don't want to talk about it."

Silence fell over the room as Eleanor tried to remember every interaction between Irene and Lord Brooke at Hugh's wedding that she'd witnessed, but she'd been so preoccupied with avoiding Edwin that she hadn't been watching anyone else. Of course, Irene had been rather quiet and subdued when she had joined Eleanor's company, but Eleanor had assumed her demeanor was due to the Baroness. That woman was enough to make anyone try to shrivel into themselves in an effort not to be noticed.

"Do you think she'll be unfaithful to Hugh?"

"It wouldn't matter if she wanted to be," Grace said with a shrug, her face was calm but that was belied by the nervous movements of her fingers within Eleanor's. "Alex never has affairs with women who are married." Still, there was a tension about her which said she wasn't as sure of her words as she sounded. Eleanor wondered if Grace was worried Irene would be the exception to the rule.

She'd become so used to the estrangement between Grace and her husband that her new curiosity had been almost startling. Now she wished she had never asked. The knowledge that Irene might—Eleanor was fervently hoping Grace was mistaken—be in love with Lord Brooke was something she wished she didn't know.

Should she warn Hugh?

Should she tell Edwin?

LAUGHING, Irene waded through the creek's bubbling waters as Hugh pretended to mistake her feet for fish, doing his best to catch them in his hands. Her handsome husband had divested himself of his coat and boots, his trousers were rolled up to display his calves and the damp fabric of his shirt clung to the muscled lines of his body. Sunlight glinted off of his golden hair and his white teeth flashed as he grinned, reaching out and trying to catch one of her feet, his fingers grazing her ankle. With a playful shriek, Irene ran back to the bank.

That one was too close and, truth be told, she didn't entirely trust him to let go if he *did* get a good hold on her. All she needed was to go toppling into the water and reveal she wasn't wearing a corset beneath her light cotton riding dress. With such a beautiful day, and knowing they were going riding again, she'd opted for less constrictive undergarments, and Hugh hadn't seemed to notice—he'd said she looked beautiful.

Perhaps he didn't notice the freckles on her nose. Or perhaps, she thought a little rebelliously, her mother was wrong and men didn't mind freckles as much as she claimed.

Little thoughts like that had been cropping up in Irene's mind quite often during her honeymoon. They'd made the transition from Stonehaven to the Stanley House and she couldn't remember a time when she'd been happier.

No—wait... of course she could. Or at least, almost as happy. Whenever Alex had been home; his presence had always protected her somewhat from her mother's harsh words. She might be happier here but of course it wasn't fair to compare the situations, because Hugh had the advantage since her mother was far, far away in London.

"Come back here," he demanded, standing with his fists planted on his hips, mock-glaring at her from the shallow water as she clambered back up onto the bank.

"No," she said impishly.

A slow smile spread across Hugh's face, replacing the pretend-forbidding look, a smile Irene recognized and her heart began to pound faster. "Are you saying I should come and get you?"

Instinctively she took a step back, licking her soft pink lips as she stared at him.

"No?"

"Oh, I think you are," her husband said silkily, his tone dark and dangerous in the kind of way that led to all sorts of sensual pleasures. Irene blinked at him before glancing around, as if worried someone else could hear what he was saying.

Hugh almost laughed. She had no idea how delectably tempting she looked, like a sweet nymph about to take flight. He was feeling decidedly satyr-like at the moment. There was nothing he would enjoy better than chasing his little innocent down and making love to her outdoors. Irene had been shocked when he'd first made love to her outside of their bed, catching her unawares in the drawing room where she'd been staring out the window wistfully the one day it had been raining. By the time he finished with her the wistful expression had been replaced with one replete with feminine satisfaction.

She was always shocked when he showed her something new. Shocked but curious, passionate and quick to learn.

Taking a step forward he felt his desire surge as she took another step back. Her hands were still clutched in her skirts, showing off her slim ankles and feet, sunlight had turned her hair into golden flame, and her breasts heaved beneath her dress. Even though he was at least fifteen feet away from her he could see the excitement rising in her emerald eyes, he knew her heart must be beating as quickly as his own.

"Are you going to run from me, wife?"

"Should I?" She teased, taking another step back and Hugh surged forward.

With another shriek, Irene turned and fled, giggling madly. Behind her she could hear Hugh's chuckles and his pounding footsteps, gaining rapidly on her.

The end of the chase was already a foregone conclusion. She tried to dodge aside, but his arms wrapped around her and he twisted, bringing her down on top of him, gentling her fall. Then he rolled on top of her, pinning her to the ground with his hands about her wrists, holding them on either side of her head, and his lower body pressed against hers.

Inside her chest her heart beat frantically against her rib cage as she gasped for breath, staring up into the hot need in Hugh's eyes. The blue was so bright it practically glowed as he stared down at her, the gentle man she married erased by the lusty pillaging rogue who had just caught his prize. Tingling awareness spun through her, the disturbing sensations she felt around him no longer felt so disturbing —they had become familiar and somehow exciting.

Lowering his lips to hers, Hugh ravaged her mouth. Normally he tried to be more gentle with her, but the chase had gotten his blood up and he kissed her hard and possessively. Beneath him Irene moaned and kissed him back, her legs spreading to cradle him more completely against her.

When his lips moved to kiss the side of her neck, Irene opened her eyes to see nothing but bright blue sky. The same color as Hugh's eyes. But instead of drowning in it, it reminded her of where they were.

"Hugh! We can't here. Let's go back to the house—Oh!" She gasped as his teeth nipped at her skin on her shoulder in a spot where he knew she was particularly sensitive.

"No," he said definitively. "I've been wanting to make love to you outside since the glen at Stonehaven… no one's going to be looking for us for hours and even if they did come looking for us they wouldn't know where to start."

"But it's improper," Irene protested. Of course the very impropriety of it was only making her more aroused. Hugh brought that out in her, a wildness she'd never suspected. A wildness which was becoming more and more focused on him. She moaned as he kept his hands on her wrists, ignoring her attempt to move them as he moved his mouth across the fluttering pulse in her neck.

"But darling, you so like it when I'm improper," he murmured into her ear as he transferred his hold on her wrists to one hand, just above her head, the other beginning to work at the tiny buttons down the front of her dress. "Like on Sunday when I put my mouth on your sweet pussy in the study. Or last night when I showed you how to put your mouth on me."

Irene whimpered at the reminder, his words fanning the flames of her arousal higher as he slid his hand into the top of her dress and squeezed her breast.

"No corset… I see I'm not the only one feeling improper today," he grinned wickedly down at her as he tweaked a nipple. Hot need lanced through her, straight to her core and Irene bucked beneath him.

"I didn't leave it off so you could do *this*," she protested, although she had already given up on trying to stop him.

"I don't particularly care why you did it, sweetheart."

Baring her breast to the warm sunlight, Hugh sucked her nipple into his mouth and felt his wife writhe beneath him. She was so damned responsive, it made it almost impossible for him to control himself. So damned responsive and so damned eager. Last night he'd nearly spent himself in his pants when she'd looked up at him with those big green eyes and asked if it was possible for her to pleasure him with her mouth the same way he pleasured her. He'd been only too happy to demonstrate exactly how possible it was, and over the moon when he'd warned her of his impending climax and she'd asked what he wanted her to do and then had willingly swallowed the entire load. The incredibly erotic dichotomy of his innocent wife sucking him, with her pure and prim mouth, and then swallowing his seed had made him so randy he'd barely needed another minute to recover before he'd had her on her back in their bed.

Now he had her on her back, in a field.

Pulling at her skirts he bared her legs to the world as well, fumbling at the front of his trousers as Irene moaned and clutched at him. She looked beautifully wanton in the sunlight, the rays sinking into her creamy skin, enhancing the adorable freckles on her nose, her breasts bared and framed by the fabric of her dress, nipples hard and upright. When he'd freed himself from the confines of his trousers he felt for her core and found her wet and ready.

The touch of Hugh's fingers against her flesh had Irene writhing. She was shocked at her reaction, considering their location, but she'd already learned Hugh was a master at sending her into unthinking and eager bliss. The gentle strokes of his fingers through her slick folds made her moan loudly as she stopped caring about whether or not someone might hear her or come upon them. The warmth of the sun on her skin was like a balm against her anxieties, her insides heating up as did her outside.

"Hugh, please," she begged as his fingers teased her, his mouth suckling at her nipple. The sensations coursing through her begged for relief and she was still new enough to love play that she wanted her satisfaction immediately. Hugh enjoyed keeping her on edge, listening to the edges of her voice growing more and more ragged until she completely lost control and would come screaming on his mouth, fingers or cock. "I need you inside me."

Biting gently on her nipple, he slipped one finger inside of her, probing deeply for that sweet, rough spot in her channel. Irene groaned—that hadn't been what she meant, and she knew he knew it. Still, it felt wonderful to have his finger pumping gently, even though it didn't stretch her the way she knew his organ would.

Switching to her other nipple with his mouth, Hugh stroked her pussy, pressing the heel of his palm against her clitoris. Smug success came as Irene's hands pulled at him, trying to drag him more fully on top of her.

"Please Hugh," she said with a whimper, almost a sob as her body tingled and flamed. "Please, please, please..."

Releasing her nipple from his mouth with a pop, Hugh stared down at her. The blue of his eyes had darkened with passion, no longer the color of the sky above them, they were the deep blue of the ocean. "Touch your breasts, sweetheart."

Shuddering, Irene cupped her breasts, pinching her nipples as she tried to find relief for the aching need throbbing inside of her. She loved it when Hugh told her what to do, how to make their love-making more passionate... at first she had always told herself it was because she was learning how to please Alex, but during the actual interludes of love-making with her husband, her childhood friend was the farthest thing from her mind. Indeed, her entire world was currently focused on Hugh and pleasing him, on tempting him to do what she wanted—needed—as she arched her back and offered up her breasts to him, twisting her nipples slightly and relishing the little bites of pain that only seemed to spur her pleasure to further heights.

The sight of his wife behaving so wantonly was a powerful aphrodisiac for Hugh. During their honeymoon he'd discovered an unknown penchant for controlling their love-making, probably because she was so responsive. No other woman he'd indulged with had ever been as eager as Irene. They had always laid back and expected him to do the work—which he hadn't minded at the time, but now he knew he could never get enough of Irene's particular brand of passion. Seeing her body become so aroused for him, her eagerness to obey him, to follow his commands until they were both lost in repletion.

Spreading her thighs wide with his hands, he looked down at the striking picture she made with her innocent face and her erotically writhing body. The lips of her quim were plump and ready for him, slick with moisture, the musky scent of her arousal filling the air around them like an exotic perfume. As she squeezed her breasts more tightly, the soft flesh spilling out between her fingers, Hugh couldn't take any more either.

Grasping her by the hips he buried himself in her in one hard thrust, Irene moaning wildly as her body lifted to meet him. Her sheath clasped him tightly, rippling around him, and she cried out as she almost came just from the heavenly sensation of her body stretching to accommodate his spear. She pinched her nipples even tighter, unaware that Hugh was watching her every move, she was so lost to the incredible pleasure.

With a groan of masculine satisfaction, Hugh began to pump into his wife, taking her hard and fast, the way he knew she wanted it but that he so often made her wait for. Irene had expected a slower pace, had expected to beg more, and so his sudden rhythmic pounding caught her off guard. Releasing her breasts she reached up to cling to his shoulders, sobbing with the sudden ecstasy as her body jerked and spasmed, her orgasm coming fast and unexpectedly.

It began small and grew as Hugh's body rubbed against hers, his groin sliding against her clitoris with every hard stroke of his cock, the shaft rubbing against the spot deep inside of her that never failed to send her up in flames.

"Hugh! *Please, Hugh...*"

She screamed, unable to process the incredible pleasure as her orgasm overflowed her, it had grown by leaps and bounds until her skin felt too small and too tight to contain it. Her nails ripped down

Hugh's chest, an automatic reaction as her body struggled to reassert control over itself, to stop the overwhelming pleasure as it began to verge on the border of pain rather than ecstasy. The sharp jabs of nails had Hugh's body arched backwards, his hips thrusting forward, eliciting another scream of passion from Irene.

Grasping her wrists again he held them down beside her head, still thrusting roughly into the swollen and dripping folds of her cunt, full of the power and pleasure of sending Irene to such heights that there were tears leaking from her unseeing eyes. She screamed again, her body struggling against his, as the intensity of her climax practically choked her. It was too much… it was heaven, it was hell, and she couldn't break free. The hold he had on her wrists, the useless struggle, only made her body react even more passionately, she was excited by the restraint and it sent her spinning.

Her world narrowed to the rubbing friction of his cock, the swollen pulse of her clitoris as his body slammed against it, the bursting rapture which bubbled and raced along her nerves. When he finally filled her to the brim and began to jerk and throb inside of her, Irene was sobbing from the incredible climax. Tears coursed freely down her cheeks as Hugh finally released her wrists and clasped her closely, her face buried in his chest as he filled her with his seed.

It had been so far beyond anything she'd experienced before that she didn't even know how to process the bliss, she couldn't do anything but sob, to the point where Hugh began to worry.

"Sweetheart," he murmured cradling her face in his hands, searching her face for some clue as to why she was reacting the way she was. He didn't think he had been that rough, but he knew he had lost control in a way he wasn't used to. "Did I hurt you? Are you alright?"

Irene hiccupped, trying to stifle the welling sobs, choke them back. She hated the look of concern on Hugh's face. Her body was still tingling from the abject ecstasy, Hugh hadn't done anything wrong at all, she just didn't know how to handle everything he had done right. "I'm fine," she said, hiccupping again as she let out another little sob. "I don't know why I'm crying. I'm more than fine... that was... that was indescribable."

"Yes it was," he said with a little laugh, still looking down at her in concern but seeming slightly reassured. He kissed her cheeks, kissing away the tears, and Irene laughed through them.

She loved the way he felt on top of her, so powerful, so concerned... her gentle giant, capable of reducing her to quivering moans and sobs, and yet so caring of her wellbeing. Covering his hands with her own, she turned her head to kiss his palm, the sobs and tears slowly gentling as he cuddled her and murmured words of praise for how beautiful, how wonderful she was. The words, his touch, it was soothing, healing balm to the little cracks and fissures she'd lived with her entire life.

THAT EVENING before dinner Irene was reading a letter she'd received from her father while Hugh took care of some of the estate business that needed tending to. Her father described the balls in London he and her mother attended before heading back to their home in the country. Thanks to Irene's marriage they now had plenty of money to cover the debts they had incurred and he described her mother's pleasure over the new jewelry he had purchased for her. Irene knew her father wanted her to be aware of the way her marriage had made their lives better and she was glad for it, especially because Hugh was a wonderful husband. Her body was sore in the most delightful way from their exertions earlier that day.

In fact, everything was wonderful with her world until she came to the last paragraph of the letter.

Before we left London I met with Lord Brooke at the club and he sent you his greetings and his hope to see you upon your return. He had been rather concerned over the fact that your marriage was arranged, I think, but informed me he had spoken with your husband at the wedding and was greatly reassured by their conversation.

Groaning, Irene set the letter down, feeling a sudden headache beginning in the back of her head. Too often she forgot about Alex of late. It made her feel dreadfully guilty whenever she realized she'd put him from her mind yet again, but lately she'd been feeling just as guilty whenever she was reminded of him. Was it possible to love two men at once? Because she knew her feelings for Hugh had grown leaps and bounds out here in the country where they were able to spend time together without the shyness her mother's hovering usually caused. The disturbing excitement had been tempered with warmth, a glow whenever he looked at her, and the increasing sense she would do whatever it took to make him happy.

In short, very similar feelings to those she'd always had for Alex, but enhanced by her body's response to Hugh.

Over dinner she distracted herself from her growing anxiety over her conflicting emotions when it came to the man she'd always loved and the man she was increasingly fearful she was coming to love, by arguing with Hugh about whether or not she should be allowed to ride Rex. The more she watched him on the magnificent stallion the more she wanted to prove she was enough of a horsewoman to handle him. Hugh's stubborn insistence that she not even be allowed to try felt like an insult, although she knew he didn't mean it that way.

"You could ride alongside me," she coaxed prettily, "and ensure that nothing goes wrong."

Sighing, Hugh took a fortifying sip of wine. Irene's soft voice and pleading eyes were extremely hard to say no to. "I don't have a horse his equal in my stable," he said. "If Rex bolted for some reason, I wouldn't be able to catch you."

"I wouldn't let him bolt."

"You may not have a choice. He's a much larger horse than you're used to."

She pouted, slightly hurt by his insistence. At the same time, the argument was making her feel more inclined towards Alex. After all, he'd always protected her but he'd never tried to control her the way Hugh currently was. Her husband's careful nurturing of her confidence had made her feel rebellious against her mother's strictures about her behavior and permitted conversation, now those feelings of rebellion were spreading to include her husband's limitations on her.

"I'm a good enough horsewoman to handle him," she insisted.

Hugh shook his head, setting down his foot well and truly for the first time in their marriage. "No, Irene. I don't want to hear any more about it. He's too big and too unruly for me to trust him with you."

Although Irene bowed her head in seeming submission, Hugh felt rather unnerved. Before her emerald eyes had been hidden from him, they'd looked remarkably like the rebellious sapphire eyes of his unruly sister—not at all the kind of expression he'd ever wanted to see on his wife's face.

CHAPTER 11

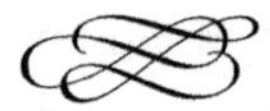

Edwin grinned as he read over the missive from Hugh, leaning back in his favorite chair in his study. The Season was mostly over, but Hugh and his bride would be returning to London for the remainder of it, having enjoyed a most pleasurable honeymoon. Of course Hugh didn't go into detail in the letter but it was obvious to Edwin how very pleased Hugh was with his new wife. Edwin was happy for him, he had been slightly worried considering Hugh didn't know Irene very well when they'd married yet had already been rather enamored of her. She was so quiet and reserved that Edwin had wondered whether or not Hugh really knew her.

At the time he'd preferred Eleanor's outspokenness, although of course his wife alternated between being very vocal and being very secretive. But he found he usually didn't mind, it kept him on his toes. Lately he wished she would just tell him what she wanted from him.

As if the thought had summoned her, his wife knocked and then swept into the study without waiting for him to answer. She was looking beautiful, as always, in a cream and pink morning gown, her hair piled in a fetching coiffure. Sometimes he thought he could sit and admire Eleanor's beauty for hours—if he could keep his baser desires from rising and causing his contemplation to turn to a more physical form of appreciation.

"I want to have another dinner," she said rather abruptly, without pausing for greeting. They hadn't hosted an event since the dinner she'd planned in which she'd served all the foods Edwin hated, after which she'd been soundly punished. Since then he hadn't suggested they host another and she hadn't mentioned it. The defiant tilt to her chin said she expected him to deny her request.

"Hugh and Irene will be home in a week," he replied rather casually, tossing her brother's letter on the desk. "We could have a dinner to celebrate their return."

"Hugh's coming home?" Eleanor's eyes brightened in excitement and then dimmed quite suddenly as her expression turned contemplative. "Yes... yes I think I would very much like to hold a dinner for them."

Edwin raised his eyebrows at her. Speaking of being secretive. He knew Nell well enough to know a statement like that indicated some kind of ulterior motivation. Knowing Nell, it wasn't always a motivation he would approve of. "Any particular reason why?"

The brilliant smile she gave him didn't fool him in the least. "Just looking forward to seeing Hugh again. And Irene of course. She and I didn't have a chance to spend much time together so of course I'm looking forward to getting to know my new sister better."

Studying her expression, he almost cracked a smile when she looked away, but he doubted whatever her secret motivation was, that it was something which would affect him. Perhaps she and Irene had discussed some feminine ah... confidences before the honeymoon and Eleanor wanted to speak with her new sister-in-law again. Either way, Edwin was content. Eleanor would get her dinner party and he would see what she did with her second chance.

"I'll write to Hugh and send it by courier with a selection of dates," he said, tapping his fingers along the arm of his chair before sitting up straight and reaching for a clean sheet of paper. He paused. "Don't invite Lady Brooke this time, please."

Although he didn't look up he could feel Eleanor's clear, crystal gaze on him. "Should I invite Lord Brooke?"

"As he's a childhood friend of Irene's and become a rather good friend of mine, I think that would be appropriate."

His wife made a small noise he couldn't interpret and decided to ignore. Something about the way she was standing made him think she wanted to say something snappish and likely to get her in trouble and he didn't particularly want to punish her today. Some days he was certainly more inclined to it than others, although he wouldn't hesitate to dole out the necessary punishment if he deemed it necessary. Hopefully ignoring her would keep it from being so.

"I'll want to invite Grace to the next one."

"That's fine," he responded absently, already beginning the salutation to Hugh. If this dinner party went off well then he had no reason to deny Eleanor something so simple.

Eleanor muttered something that sounded like "if she's still in London." By which he supposed her friend had indicated she might be leaving the city soon. It didn't make a difference either way to Edwin.

"Thank you for letting me throw the dinner party," she said, breaking through the silence with a loud, firm voice, demanding his attention. He glanced up to look her in the eye and found she was staring at him with the queerest expression on her face. One he hadn't seen before. "I appreciate it."

"I trust you've learned your lesson from the time before," he said with a little half-smile. "If you did not then I will not hesitate to ensure it does not happen a third time."

The way she shifted, obviously remembering both the pain and the accompanying passion, almost made him want to set aside the letter and begin something else entirely. But that would take quite a bit of time and he still had work to do; he'd taken a short break to read Hugh's letter and once he was done responding he needed to get back to it.

"I have no wish to antagonize you again," she said, sniffing as if affronted by the very idea.

"I'm glad to hear it." Edwin returned his attention to the letter, congratulating Hugh on his marital bliss and his own anticipation of the happy couple's return to the Season.

"I rather care for you, you know."

"I do."

There was something tense about Eleanor's silence which caught Edwin's attention again. He looked up. That strange expression was still on her face, as if she was waiting for him to say something more.

"I care for you too, Nell, you know that," he said with the grin he knew made the ladies flutter their fans. "Always have, ever since we were kids."

"Of course," she said, but her tone was neutral and he suddenly felt as if he was disappointing her again, but he didn't know why or what she wanted from him. Somehow she seemed even more perturbed than usual by the lack of whatever it was she wanted to hear from him, but it's not as if she ever gave him any damn *clue*. Eleanor shifted and looked away. "I'm going to go discuss dinner tonight with Cook."

"Very well," he said, lacking any other response. Eleanor swept out of the room almost as suddenly as she'd entered, taking quite a bit of the vitality and light from it with her. He felt as though something important had just happened but he didn't know what or why he even felt that way.

One thing he knew for sure was that Eleanor had been looking for something in particular and he didn't think he had provided it. He shook his head as he returned his attention to the letter. Women. Even the one he thought he knew best could baffle him on a regular basis. It was a sensation he was becoming accustomed to.

STOPPING by one of the windows to stare out onto the street, Eleanor didn't even have to try not to cry. Her insides felt numbed, like ice. It didn't even hurt that Edwin obviously still saw her as a woman he cared about because of his long relationship with her and not because he was in love with her. It couldn't hurt because she couldn't really feel anything at all. As if her heart was encased in cold, soothing ice. A barrier to keep out all the pain she would otherwise be feeling.

It had been hard enough to tell him she cared for him, to try and bare her feelings to him when she had no idea what his return would be, but he'd barely given her his attention much less reciprocated. Would it have really hurt him to take a moment or two to actually speak with her? To look at her as she spoke to him rather than dividing his attention between her and the letter to her brother? It wasn't as if Hugh was even there to compete with her for Edwin's attention, and yet he held it anyway.

Was she only important to Edwin as an extension of Hugh?

Hopelessness welled up in her only to slam against the wall of ice and melt away, but it was out there, just waiting to slam down on her. She could feel it, at a distance removed.

Her fingers splayed over her stomach. Her monthly courses were due, had been due for the past two days, and so far had not come. That was why she'd finally gotten up the courage to try and say something directly to Edwin, to try and spark a conversation about their feelings for one another. One which he'd basically brushed off. A sick feeling rose inside of her and she clung to the icy barricade which kept her safe.

If she was pregnant with his child, his heir, then perhaps the smartest thing to do would be to leave the city with Grace, if Grace left, and then she could have Edwin's heir without the constant emotional highs and lows that living in the same house as Edwin caused her. No one would be able to say she had denied Edwin his rights, the way they spoke of Grace. She would do her duty but avoid revealing her vulnerability to her husband. Because she knew he could easily shatter this new cold exterior, either directly or indirectly by his behavior. He could read her well enough she couldn't hide her feelings for him forever if they were residing in the same household.

The best thing to do would be to wait and see if she truly were with child and then escape the city with Grace. Escape this awful one-sided love that threatened to undo everything she'd ever wanted for herself in a marriage.

Escape her fate of turning into her mother.

THEY WERE GOING to be returning to London tomorrow and if Irene was going to ride Rex it had to be today. Once they were in London she knew it would be much harder to find the time and the opportunity to do so, and she didn't relish the idea of attempting her first ride on the big horse in the hustle and bustle of the city. Although she was sure she could handle him, eventually, she knew it was much safer in the country where there was less activity to spook and rile him. Even the most docile horses could have their patience tested in the city where there were so many other people and animals and carriages.

The honeymoon had been lovely, although she was becoming concerned over her growing feelings for Hugh. How could she be in love with two men at the same time? Yet as Hugh had shown her his favorite places on his lands and in the houses they stayed in, as she'd interacted with him every day and lay in his bed every night, her emotions had become more and more tangled. The sparkle in his blue eyes when he was being mischievous or playful set her at ease, the hunger on his face when she disrobed made her heart pound, and every day she worried a little more that the image of Alex's face in her mind seemed to be fading.

If Alex was her one true love then that shouldn't happen… but she didn't know how to explain it. Perhaps she was like Guinevere with Lancelot and Arthur. Only she couldn't imagine deserting Hugh to be with Alex, not completely. She enjoyed having him in her life too much.

Eventually she turned her attention to something much simpler—her desire to ride Rex. There were other emotions coiled up in her desire, of course. She wanted to show Hugh he was wrong and she could handle the horse, to prove her skills to both him and herself, combined with a burgeoning need to run wild and free on the stallion. Something simple and lovely that she would thoroughly enjoy before they returned to London, where Alex was… where her feelings would have been be examined more closely.

After directing the servants in the packing for their return to London, Irene had her maid dress her in a riding gown and snuck out to the stables. Hugh was as busy as her and she hadn't seen him all morning since they broke their fast so she wasn't too worried about him stopping her.

Surely once she showed him that she could handle Rex close to the house he would allow her to truly try the stallion's paces. Standing in front of the magnificent animal's stall she looked up and actually felt a touch of trepidation. He was much larger than he'd looked from Liberty's back.

Feeling as though someone was watching her, Irene glanced over her shoulder. Somehow she felt as though her mother was right there watching her with cold, censorious eyes.

"Hello beautiful," she whispered, turning her attention back to the horse. He whuffled and snorted, tossing his head a bit and she took a step back. Because it was the smart thing to do, not because she was afraid… at least that's what she told herself. When he calmed down again, eyeing her warily, she gathered her courage and reached out to try and touch his nose.

The horse struck, causing her to stumble backwards as she snatched her hand out of reach of its teeth. Landing heavily on her backside, Irene glared up at the magnificent creature as he whickered. It sounded like he was laughing at her.

Equal parts fear and rebellion, Irene stood up and brushed off her skirts, glaring at him. She was the best horsewoman she knew; she'd seen the way ladies of the *ton* "rode" in town—if it could even be called that. While she might not have been equal to them in style of dress or quality of jewels and fabrics, she was better than any of them at riding. It was a point of pride with her and she'd never come across a horse than she couldn't master.

Of course, it didn't occur to her that she'd never been presented with a horse beyond her skills, because no competent stable master would risk his position that way. Or that the grooms of this particular stable would have gone running to their master the moment they saw her attempting to approach Rex's stall. It was well known that the devil-horse was a one-man horse; they instinctively knew Hugh would not approve of his lady-wife getting anywhere near the unruly animal.

For a few minutes he'd been standing just outside the doorway to the stables, watching her, rather amused if aggravated that she'd obviously gone against his wishes. If she'd looked out the door she would have seen him, but her attention was all on Rex. She'd been approaching him intelligently at least, with patience and caution, and Hugh had been sure she'd realize the error of her ways without his interference. Unfortunately almost getting knocked onto her backside, while entertaining him, had only increased her resolve.

She looked akin to his sister as she approached the stall door again, despite the difference in their complexions and coloring, the stubborn expression on her face was pure Eleanor. Not what Hugh wanted to see, especially now that Rex was already riled up and Irene had passed the point of patience and calm contemplation. He was going to have to intervene before she did something stupid.

Irene almost screamed as an arm wrapped around her waist and swung her away from Rex's stall. The horse stamped his hoof and tossed his head as if in triumph. Spun around, breathless, she found herself looking up into the stern blue eyes of her husband.

Caught.

"What are you doing?" Her voice was shrill, high, as her hands pressed against his chest, trying to push him away. It was like pushing at a stone wall.

One blond eyebrow arched at her as his lips quirked, almost looking amused before the solemn mien of disapproval descended again. "What are *you* doing, sweetheart? I seem to specifically recall ordering you to stay away from Rex."

"But I'm a good horsewoman," she said, half-arguing, half-pleading. "You know I am. I just wanted to show you I can handle him."

"By sneaking around behind my back and approaching him alone?

You couldn't even get near enough to open his stall door, much less get a bit in his mouth or a saddle on his back." Hugh's eyes darkened as he looked down at his wife, not at all liking the rebellious tilt to her mouth. "You lost your temper just now and tried to approach him again, without even considering the fact that his temper is short as well. You could have been seriously injured, do you not realize that?"

The sparks in her eyes said she was unpleased with his assessment and that just made *his* temper come perilously close to the surface.

"Promise me you'll stay away from him."

"No!" The word was out of her mouth before she had time to think about it. It was the first time in a long time she had said the word, she was so used to acquiescing to whatever was asked of her. This new independence was both frightening and exhilarating. Hugh loomed over her and she pushed at him again, uselessly. He was almost scary looking and she could feel her heart pounding faster.

"Irene, promise me you will stay away from him. I won't have you putting yourself in danger." Holding her securely in place with one arm, he cupped her chin with his opposite hand and lifted her gaze to his so she could see how in earnest he was.

"But I want to ride him," she pleaded, opening her green eyes to their widest advantage. "I can handle him Hugh, I can!"

The muscle in his jaw tightened. "*No.* If you approach him again I will put you over my knee."

"Over your..." Irene's soft voice trailed off as she tried to comprehend what he was saying.

"Over my knee and spank you."

"You wouldn't!"

"I would," he said, a little grimly. The last thing Hugh wanted was a wife he had to constantly keep in line with a spanking, he'd gotten a certain thrill from being in such a powerful position when it came to his sister and the discipline he'd meted out to her while his father was teaching him how to handle a household, but he didn't need that thrill with Irene. He had chosen her because he wanted a docile wife who didn't require punishment, but he wouldn't hesitate to give it to her when the situation warranted it. He was of the opinion that it was best to nip any kind of rebellion in the bud immediately, rather than let it fester and allow her to think it would be tolerated. Especially in matters concerning her safety. "Promise me you won't go near him again or I'll give you a taste right now."

"You can't!"

The expression on Irene's face plainly said she didn't believe his threat. In the time she'd come to know Hugh she'd seen mostly his gentle side and his lustful side, she didn't realize it was because she'd never provoked the disciplinarian in him. Her mother had never spanked her—she'd never needed to. When Irene was seven years old, the Baroness had taken her below stairs to see one of the maids being punished with a cane. For what transgression Irene didn't know, all she remembered was the screams and howls, the horrifying bright red welts across the girl's skin, the sobbing, the pleading, and her mother's cold voice in her ear—'If you ever misbehave, Irene, then I will spank you just like that.'

She absolutely did not believe gentle Hugh could do something so awful to her.

"You wouldn't."

"I will."

Unfortunately for her, Hugh was quickly realizing his wife was going to require a demonstration. Not something he was eager to give. With a few long strides he had them over by the bales of hay and he had Irene bent over a stack of two before she could do more than gasp. It was just high enough her toes were barely touching the ground, he didn't need to do more than flip up her skirts and place his hand in the small of her back to keep both the fabric and her pinned in place.

The moment he had her skirts up he suddenly understood what Edwin and Wesley had meant when they'd told him that disciplining his sister was going to be unlike disciplining his wife. When he'd spanked Eleanor he'd seen quite a bit of her private areas, but he'd never thought of them as particularly interesting. He'd assumed that when it came to disciplinary measures that it would be the same with any female.

But he had his usual immediate reaction to his wife's skirts being flipped up, exposing her creamy bottom and the soft pink of her quim, framed by coppery curls.

"Hugh, please! Don't!" Irene's voice came out high, shrill, panicked.

He ignored her plea, it was too late. On top of that, he was fascinated by the revelation of his cock hardening as he prepared to introduce his wife to discipline, and by the excitement that rose in him as he raised his hand.

SMACK!

Irene screamed, much more loudly than the pain warranted it. Because Hugh had experience in such matters he realized that immediately and so felt no guilt about ignoring what he considered an over-dramatization of her distress. It didn't occur to him that she was screaming as much in fear as she was in reaction to the actual slap of his hand against her bottom. It took her a moment to dazedly realize the strike hadn't hurt nearly as much as she had expected before another one landed on her other cheek.

SLAP!

This time she just yelped, her fingers digging into the hay. She was confused. Frightened. Still surprised that he was using his hand. Was some awful instrument still to come?

SMACK! SMACK! SMACK!

Since she was obviously such a novice to this kind of experience, Hugh peppered her creamy cheeks with short, sharp smacks that would sting and burn for the afternoon but no longer. He would turn her bottom a warm pink. The experienced disciplinarian in him went to work while the new husband in him watched, fascinated, as his wife's flesh jiggled and bounced under the slap of his hand. His cock pressed against the front of his breeches as he warmed her bottom, almost appalling him with his eager response to her soft cries.

As the spanking continued the stinging pain began to increase and now Irene really did begin to cry, having gotten over her shock and feeling her tender skin begin to burn.

"Hugh! Stop! Please! I'll be good, I won't go near Rex again, please stop! I promise, I'll listen to you!"

Her legs kicked as she begged and pleaded, but Hugh didn't stop, even though she sounded quite sincere, because he'd just noticed something else equally fascinating.

As her limbs kicked and parted, he caught a glimpse of shiny pink wetness. Leaning closer as he smacked her bottom again and again, he smelled the musky sweetness of her arousal, saw the honey now slicking her soft folds. His wife was aroused as well.

The last flurry of spanks had her squealing and crying out, legs kicking, body bucking... but his hand held her firmly in place until he was done. When it ceased Irene tensed for a moment, waiting for another spank to land, and then her muscles loosed and she slumped onto the hay, sniffling and feeling very sorry for herself. While she hadn't screamed or wailed the way the maid in her memory had, there was no doubt her husband was a cruel and heartless monster for using her so ill.

She was ashamed of herself for starting to think she might have feelings for both him and Alex. Alex would never have treated her—or anyone else this way. Irene was almost beside herself that Hugh had carried out a punishment that even her mother had never actually used on her.

But what truly shocked her was when she felt his hands on either side of her bottom, parting her, and then his hot wet mouth planted itself on her most intimate area. Her body shuddered and bucked as hot pleasure sliced through her, almost paralyzing in its intensity.

"Hugh... noooooooo..." She moaned in utter humiliation as familiar sensations flared to life in her core. During their honeymoon she'd become used to her breathlessness, her racing pulse... they hadn't seemed disturbing in quite some time. Now they were more disturbing than ever because of the very inappropriateness of the situation. Hugh had just brutally beaten her, she was bent over a hay bale in their stables, and yet her body was responding to him as eagerly as if they were in the privacy of their bed chamber and he had just spent the past half hour kissing her instead of spanking her.

Once again Hugh ignored the plaintive cry coming from his wife. The slick wetness of her pussy was calling to him, the sweetness of her coating his tongue as he licked and sucked at her sensitive flesh. She might be telling him no, but she was making no move to stop him and the eager movements of her body were screaming *yes.* With one hand he unlaced the front of his breeches as he licked her slit from stem to stern, his other hand braced against the hot pink flesh of her bottom. It seemed to sear his hand with the heat and awed him all over again at how erotic he'd found disciplining his wife to be.

Irene cried out as she felt her husband's mouth move and then he was shoving into her, so hard and thick she could barely take him all at once and her body trembled as her insides clenched, struggling to accommodate him. The front of her skirts cushioned her against the scratchy hay as he began to push in and out of her, harder than he'd ever taken her before as her helpless position made it impossible for her to move with him or against him... all she could do was lay across the hay as he impaled her over and over again with his rampant cock.

The force of his body bounced against her bottom, her pink cheeks jiggling and clenching as he took her from behind. Hands on the soft flesh, he squeezed and kneaded it, reigniting the burn from her spanking as he plowed her. The mingle of pain and pleasure had Irene's muscles tightening involuntarily, convulsing as she struggled to deal with this new interplay of sensations. Her fingers dug into the hay as she sobbed for breath, her insides now burning as much as her bottom was, all of it feeling delicious rather than painful.

She felt as if she was unraveling under the sensuous assault; Hugh's cock rubbing against her insides, his hands unmercifully squeezing her flesh, and the edge of the hay bale pressing insistently against the spot which craved it most.

"Please... Hugh... oh please..." Her voice was ragged with desire, she writhed as he thrust forward and buried himself in her.

"Promise me Irene," he ordered, slowing his pace as he felt her body tighten in anticipation of climax. He retained just enough control over his raging passion to hold back, to wait until he'd gotten what he wanted from her before he gave into the wildness threatening to break out of him. "Promise me you won't go near Rex again."

She wailed as he squeezed her bottom, her legs trying to kick as she came so close to falling over into the well of pleasure but couldn't quite get there. It was like hanging on the edge by her fingers without being able to let go. She needed Hugh to give her the last little inch so the stone would crumble and she could free fall in the rapture churning below.

"Promise me, Irene."

"I promise!"

It was wrung from her with punishment and pleasure, with a desperate need for release and the stinging burn of her chastised buttocks... but it was a promise and that was all Hugh needed to hear. Releasing the barely leashed reins of his control, he leaned forward and grasped her hips, ravishing her helpless body from behind. His hard stomach bounced off of her cheeks, renewing the sensation of being spanked as she screamed his name in ecstasy, her inner walls spasming around his marauding cock.

Groaning, he rode her hard and fast until she was sobbing from the overstimulation of her sensitive flesh, and then he buried himself inside of her one last time. The hot spurts of his seed, the throbbing of his rod inside of her, left Irene shuddering and spent, her throat hoarse from all the tears during the spanking and the subsequent cries of her ecstasy.

Almost tenderly, Hugh withdrew from his wife, kissed each of her bottom cheeks which were still a rosy pink, and then stood her up and gathered her in his arms. Irene burst into tears, overwhelmed by all the emotions and physical sensations warring inside of her. She clung to him, sobbing and he stroked her hair and back, enjoying the feel of her taking comfort from him.

But it only lasted until she realized what she was doing—taking comfort from her tormentor. From her husband who had betrayed her trust, who had made her think he was something he wasn't. In doing so, he'd made her promise to stay away from Rex. Well it didn't matter now, she didn't want to impress him anymore anyway. She didn't care what he thought. Whatever feelings she had for him were false, because they were given to a kind, gentle man who would never abuse her like that.

Shoving away from him, she glared at the bemused expression on his face. Hugh looked as handsomely angelic as ever. She looked like a hissing cat. Her hair was completely disheveled, her dress wrinkled and hanging askew, her eyes and face red and blotchy from her crying jag. Her green eyes were spitting sparks, brighter than the most highly polished emeralds.

"You're a monster!" She bit out at him and then turned and ran, heading for the house.

Sighing, Hugh let her go. He knew he could catch her and chase her, but she had a lot to process. That was obviously the first time she'd been physically disciplined—or spanked at least since he'd seen the bruises her mother had left on her just from a hard grip—and having it followed with unexpected pleasure was sure to leave her confused. Eleanor had always hissed words of hate at him following a punishment session as well. It was to be expected.

What he hadn't expected, at all, was his arousal or hers.

Turning back into the stables, straightening his own clothing, he decided he might as well give Rex a nice long grooming. It would help calm the horse and himself as well, besides giving Irene time to herself.

If her reaction was anything to go by, hopefully she would come to the realization that in the future she should do her best to avoid another disciplinary session.

Even if the thought of never spanking her again did cause a little pang of regret in his chest.

UPON REACHING THE BEDROOM, Irene threw herself on the bed and burst into tears again. She hadn't known where else in the house to go, even though Hugh had just as much right to enter this room as she had. More than her. There wasn't a single bit of space that was just hers other than her vanity in here, but she couldn't sit on the stool there because of her poor bottom.

"My lady? Are you alright?" The worried voice of her maid, Flora, penetrated through the haze of misery. The stern lectures her mother had driven into her head about never revealing too much to the servants were shattered by Irene's response to a sympathetic and worried voice.

Lifting red rimmed eyes and tear-streaked cheeks to the worried gaze of her maid, Irene shook her head. "My husband is a monster."

"Viscount Petersham?! No, my Lady... please tell me what happened," Flora begged. She'd never seen her mistress in such distress, not even during the years when the poor thing had put up with the awful treatment of her mother, the Baroness. Biting her lip, the maid worried about the proprieties and then decided to break her own training. In her short time in the Viscount's household she'd noticed that the family had a preference for servants who were cheerful and respectful, but there was an obvious amount of care which went both ways between the classes. Sitting on the bed, she made soothing noises as she stroked Irene's back and hair, grooming it with her fingers and getting it back into some semblance of order.

"He... he *beat* me."

"Oh dearie... where? I have some salve that might help," Flora said sympathetically, hiding her shock. The Viscount didn't seem the type from what she'd seen, but then vicious men could easily hide themselves behind a facade. Obviously the period of goodwill between master and mistress was over and she was sorry to see it go, although she knew both she and Irene were well versed in placating others. The Baroness had seen to that. She had begun to hope for better, for both of them... perhaps if the Viscount was only occasionally brutal, things wouldn't be so bad.

"On... on..." Letting out another heart rending sob, Irene patted her bottom.

A little line appeared down the center of Flora's forehead. "Anywhere else, my lady?"

Irene shook her head, not looking at her maid as she let out another sob.

For herself, Flora felt a sense of relief. She knew from experience that a bottom, although it could be painful, would heal quite easily and could actually take quite a bit more ill-treatment than other parts of the body. Still, she should check and make sure her mistress had not been completely ill-used, although if she had made it up to the bedroom on her own two feet then surely the damage couldn't be so bad.

"May I see, my Lady?" she asked, turning and tentatively lifting the hem of Irene's skirt. With another little whimper, Irene nodded, huddling into her arms to avoid looking at Flora's face as her maid saw her shame.

"Oh Miss...." To Irene's shock, her maid laughed with relief. "You had me going there! You won't need the salve at all."

"What?! But... but... he *brutalized* me." Irene jumped up and ran over to the mirror as Flora watched, some sympathy as well as some contempt in the maid's eyes. Lifting her skirts, Irene turned her back to the large mirror, looking over her shoulder and then gaping as she saw what Flora had seen.

A shapely bottom, very pink to be sure... but nothing else. No welts. No bruises. It wasn't even a very dark pink. In fact, it was the same pink Irene's face was now turning as she wondered why something that had hurt so badly... but then had it hurt that badly? She'd endured true pain when she'd fallen out of a tree when she was younger and sprained her wrist. It hadn't even hurt as badly as that.

"A man has a right to discipline his wife, my Lady," Flora said, having remembered herself and reverting back to Irene's new honorific. There was quite a bit of sympathy in her voice, she realized Irene had never been spanked that she knew of. No doubt it had been a bit of a shock to the young woman. While the Baroness was often cruel and vicious, she hadn't needed such measures to keep her daughter in line because she'd kept her constantly cowed. Now Irene was coming out of her shell and she would need someone to set boundaries for her. But Flora also knew how much a spanking could hurt, especially when it was unexpected. "Now that you know what to expect, next time won't be so bad."

"Next time..." Irene shook her head and dropped her skirts, turning to face Flora and ask the question now burning in her mind.

"My mother... she showed me a maid being spanked once, she had... it looked so *painful*... Malvin was doing it..." The butler who ran the household on her father's estate, although he'd been hired by the Baroness and reported to her rather than to the Baron.

"If it was Malvin then you saw a caning, not a spanking," Flora said, shivering a little. She remembered Malvin's form of discipline all too well. "He has a liking for the cane, he does."

"You...?"

Flora pursed her lips and nodded her head. "I druther a spanking any day."

Putting her hands over her bottom, which was still a little sore although she already could barely feel the after effects unless she actually pressed against the rounded curves, she couldn't imagine a punishment how much something worse would feel. The spanking she'd just received had hurt enough as it was. To know Flora had endured something even more painful…

"That's awful."

"Yes, my Lady," Flora said. She paused and then decided she'd already stepped so far beyond the bounds of her usual duties, she might as well give a last little warning. Lord knew the young woman's mother had never seen fit to give the poor thing any useful advice. "I'd be careful around the Viscount, my Lady. He seems a good sort, but he still has the right to discipline you as he sees fit."

"Thank you, Flora," Irene said through numb lips. She gave herself a little shake. "Can you help me out of my dress? I think I'd like to lay down for a bit."

Truly she just wanted time to think, and if Hugh did come searching for her then at least she could feign sleep. For a moment she'd felt conflicted, realizing that perhaps her husband was not quite the monster she'd painted him to be immediately following the spanking. Then she reminded herself that she shouldn't be feeling relief about that, it shouldn't matter. Her whole reason for marrying him without a fuss, other than the help it gave her family, was to learn how to please a man so she could become Alex's mistress.

It didn't matter what Hugh thought of her or whether he allowed her to ride his horse. From now on she would only focus on two things, getting him an heir and cultivating Alex for after she'd done her duty to Hugh. Just like the other ladies of the *ton* in arranged marriages, she'd been foolish to think that hers might be any different. A man with feelings for her would never treat her so, Alex would never treat her or any other woman in such a manner... Hugh was unworthy of the false feelings he'd managed to engender in her with his facade of gentleness and caring.

Slipping into the bed, Irene hardened her heart against him, glad they were to return to London soon. Perhaps it had been for the best that his true colors had not been revealed till now. She had greatly enjoyed learning how to please a man and soon a man deserving of such pleasure would reap the reward.

CHAPTER 12

Eleanor wasn't pregnant and she didn't know whether she was happy or sad about it. As usual, with anything to do with Edwin, her feelings were incredibly conflicted. Part of her was saddened, because she had enjoyed the idea of carrying Edwin's child and having a part of him irrevocably tied to her. Another part was frustrated because now she didn't feel as though she could leave with Grace, not without becoming the kind of scandal Grace had invited upon herself, and Eleanor knew neither her father nor her husband would bear that quietly the way Lord Brooke had. The worst part was, she was relieved. Relieved she had a reason to stay with Edwin. Relieved to have her plan to leave his presence stymied.

Relieved to still be trapped with him.

Logically she knew she was being ruled by instinct now rather than logic. Emotion rather than intelligence. Her brain knew she was sinking closer and closer to the abyss of misery her mother lived in. Her heart didn't care, wanting to wring every last bit of happiness she could out of her life and her husband before the rug was pulled out from under her.

In the meantime she distracted herself by organizing the dinner which would welcome Hugh and his new wife home. After her discussion with Grace, who had begun venturing out of the house for exclusive teas and at-homes, although she'd retreated from Lady Carrington's ball last night when Lord Brooke had appeared around midnight, Eleanor was very curious to know how her brother's honeymoon had gone.

HUGH HELPED his wife out of the carriage in front of his London house, trying not to look as impatient and frustrated as he felt. Ever since he'd spanked her Irene had become cold rather than warm—although last night he'd managed to heat her up once they'd gone to bed. He supposed he should have expected that she wouldn't return to her normal self immediately, but it hadn't made for a very pleasant carriage ride. Eventually he'd given up on making conversation in the face of her single word answers.

It was good to be back in the city. The first thing he wanted to do, after making sure that Irene was settled into the household and introduced to the staff, was meet with his father and then his friends. His lips twitched downwards as Irene swanned by him, barely even glancing at him as she headed straight up the steps to the doorway, forcing him to step quickly after her to catch up.

The introduction of Irene to the household went fairly well, although she barely glanced at him once she met the Housekeeper, Mrs. Lewiston. Obviously eager to show the new mistress around, the two of them went off together. Although Hugh had hoped to show Irene around the London house, he realized that to force his company on her might do more harm than good at this point.

Grumbling under his breath he let Marling, the butler, know he was going out before grabbing his coat and hat and making a tactical retreat.

AN HOUR later he found himself in Edwin's billiard room, rapidly losing his second game of pool. Unfortunately his father had gone with his mother to Bath almost as soon as Hugh had left on his honeymoon, and unusually his father was still *there.* The household was mostly closed up, although he had been presented with a packet of letters and work his father wished for him to tend to now that Hugh was back in the capital. He'd only given it a quick look through but it seemed as though Lord Harrington was taking a page from the Earl of Clarendon's book. Like Edwin's father, he wanted to spend some time in the country and was giving his son the responsibilities of tending to affairs in town.

"You seem more agitated than I would have thought," Edwin said, raising his eyebrows in Hugh's direction as he missed yet another easy shot. "Honeymoon not as wonderful as you made it sound in your last letter?"

In the absence of his father, Hugh needed someone to unload his burdens onto and Edwin was the next best thing. Even if he hadn't been married much longer than Hugh himself.

"It was, all the way up until the day before," he said gruffly, watching as Edwin moved to bend over the table in his usual graceful way. Normally they were well matched at billiards; today he was giving Edwin barely any sport at all. "She tried to sneak out and ride Rex."

Edwin laughed as he stood up, the ball he'd aimed for sinking neatly into a corner pocket. "That sounds like something Eleanor would try to do."

"Yes." Hugh scowled. He *still* didn't understand what had made Irene try to do such a stupid thing, especially after he'd warned her not to. "I had already warned her to stay away from him and she refused to promise not to try and go near him again, so I told her I would blister her bottom if she did." He sighed. "She didn't seem to believe me and she became... well I ended up giving her a small spanking."

His attention captured, Edwin leaned on his cue, listening to Hugh with a look of almost disbelief on his face. After all, he knew very well

Hugh hadn't wanted a wife like Eleanor, one who would need constant discipline, but he could tell from Hugh's expression that his friend had enjoyed the experience more than he'd ever thought he would. Yet things hadn't turned out well anyway.

"And now she won't talk to me. Barely looks at me. It's driving me up the wall. She's not like Eleanor… I keep wondering if I did the right thing."

"Well of course you did," Edwin said immediately. "Rex is… well even I don't want to try to ride Rex. It has nothing to do with how good a rider I am, he's the kind of horse who will only allow one person to ride him. I hate to think what would happen to him if something were to happen to *you.* She'll get over being spanked, she *wouldn't* get over whatever Rex would do to her if she actually attempted to ride him."

"True," said Hugh, feeling marginally better. With Irene acting as though he truly was the monster she'd named him, and no immediate support in the form of his father or friends, he had started to feel as though he'd over reacted. Edwin's immediate approval of his actions helped to bolster his confidence. He watched as Edwin turned back to the task at hand—soundly trouncing Hugh at billiards.

They played a few more turns in silence, other than the wooden clack of the balls slamming into each other and the slightly muted thuds as they bounced off the sides of the table.

"I don't know what to do to get back into her good graces," Hugh confessed as the game neared its end. "She was just truly starting to come out of her shell in the country and as soon as she showed some real spirit, I punished her for it."

"Stop trying to get back into her good graces at all," Edwin advised, lining himself up for his next shot. "Do you think I pander to Nell after she's done something she needs to be disciplined for? The more you act like you think *you* did something wrong, the more she will. She'll eventually realize you were disciplining her over a matter of safety, not anything else."

As Hugh mulled that over, Edwin's butler knocked and announced the arrival of Lord Brooke and the Earl of Spencer. While he was glad to see Wesley, Hugh felt a bit more ambivalent about Lord Brooke's presence, especially considering the man's brotherly protective attitude about Irene and her current demeanor towards her husband. Fortunately, upon their arrival, the conversation switched over. Wesley had another letter from his mother to share about his ward, his dark eyes sparkling as he outlined the recent escapades of the young lady.

It was obvious the Countess was coming to the end of her rope in regards to Wesley's ward, she was practically demanding her son come and take the young woman in hand.

"I'm not sure what she thinks I'll be able to do that she won't," said Wesley as he folded the letter back up following his recitation. "It's not as if I have any experience in raising a lady."

"But you do have quite a bit of experience with ladies," Edwin riposted, causing all of them to laugh. He and Hugh had given up the table to Wesley and Lord Brooke and were enjoying snifters of brandy while they watched the two play.

"Perhaps she thinks you'll be able to provide a more ah... stringent discipline?" Lord Brooke said, brushing an auburn lock of hair out of his face. His lips twitched into almost the facsimile of an amused smile.

"Perhaps," said Wesley easily. "If she's as wild as mother describes the chit could probably use a sound spanking. Mother was never very good at playing the disciplinarian, not that she ever needed to. Somehow she always had us toeing the line without it... I can't imagine why she's having trouble with a schoolroom miss."

Edwin sighed. "Unfortunately even strict discipline doesn't guarantee immediate good behavior. Eleanor can go for days being absolutely perfect and then she'll do something that makes me think she must *want* to be spanked." He grinned, his eyes getting a bit of a faraway look in them. "Not that it bothers me to do so, but she seems just as infuriated by it every time. Even if she enjoys it as much as I do, she doesn't want to admit to it."

"Less information please," Hugh murmured with a little wince. Hearing about his sister's discipline didn't bother him. Knowing the intimacies of her relationship with his best friend was asking a bit much, however.

Wesley guffawed a laugh and even Lord Brooke looked rather amused, although the expression was all in his eyes. Edwin gave him a long-suffering look. "Just pretend I'm talking about someone other than your sister."

"I try, and then I get angry thinking you'd dishonor my sister by doing *that* with another woman," Hugh said dryly, making Wesley laugh again.

"He's got you there."

"Says the man who's slept with half the bored wives of the *ton.*"

"Not half… I haven't had nearly the time for that."

Lord Brooke shook his head. "Give him the time and he may make the full round." The man's voice sounded disapproving, Hugh noted with surprise. But Wesley didn't take offense.

"I'm not that bad. Actually, I'm rather discerning. I've no desire to end up on the dueling field with an angry husband… women start expecting things when you make them widows." He shook his head almost sadly, as if mourning those ladies he couldn't approach due to overprotective husbands. "I prefer to deal with those who have no expectations."

"As long as you stay away from *my* wife, you know I have no quarrel with you," Lord Brooke said, almost absently as he studied the table. Both Edwin and Hugh studied him with interest, but Wesley just shrugged; it was apparently something he'd heard before and of no interest to him.

"Even if I had an interest in the lady, I wouldn't do that." Wesley grinned at his friend. "Despite how beautiful she is. But mostly because I have no desire to die at dawn."

"You're that good a shot?" Hugh asked Lord Brooke with some interest. After all, if Irene went complaining to the man and he didn't bother to hear out Hugh's side of the story, he might well be facing him early one morning. Wesley, Edwin, and Hugh were fairly evenly matched when it came to shooting, and they were all considered crack shots. If Wesley thought Alex was better…

The man shrugged.

"He is," Wesley said cheerfully. "Not that you'll ever hear him brag about it."

Delightful. Hugh sighed. Hopefully if Irene did take it into her head to complain to her unofficial big brother, Wesley would be able to hold the man off long enough to allow Hugh to explain. It seemed the two of them had formed a fairly solid friendship, especially if Wesley were comfortable talking with Lord Brooke about his wife. Everyone in the *ton* knew you did so at your own peril.

THE INVITATIONS HAD GONE OUT and responses were already coming back in. Eleanor wished her parents could be at the dinner welcoming Irene and Hugh back, but both of them were still in Bath. Actually she was rather surprised her father at least wasn't back in London by now; he'd never before spent this much time away from the city with her mother. Granted, from what Edwin had told her there wasn't anything pressing being discussed on the political front currently, but she still hadn't expected her father to spend so much time dancing attendance on her mother. She hoped he wasn't feeling ill—after all, an extended stay in Bath with her mother could be cover for his need for the healing waters of the small city if he was sickly.

She made a mental note to write a letter to her mother. It had been awhile since she'd last written anyway.

Turning her attention back to the responses, she counted them out and smiled. Nearly everyone she had invited was coming. Including Lord Brooke. She made a little face because she didn't particularly want to see him again, even if she was curious about why he was still in the city. At least she would be able to see how he and her new sister-in-law interacted.

Not that she could do anything if it turned out Grace was right and Irene was in love with the man. But perhaps she could warn Hugh. Or help to keep Irene and Lord Brooke apart until Irene and Hugh's relationship could be solidified.

Then again, knowing her brother, he would be just as happy retreating to the countryside with his wife and staying out of the city entirely. Although he enjoyed occasional city life, he was much happier on the estates with his horses and dogs, interacting with the tenants and occasionally getting his hands dirty. A little dirt had never bothered her either, when she was younger, she remembered almost wistfully. Now she could barely conceive of getting on her knees and grubbing in the mud—after all, her dresses would be ruined... but she could still go riding and walking.

The Season in London was exciting, but part of her was yearning for the pure bright sunshine of the countryside, the lazier days, the calmer pursuits. The endless round of balls and parties were exciting and beautiful, but they were also exhausting and occasionally painful. Especially if the gentlemen asking her to dance were not very adept on the dance floor.

This dinner was going to be one of the quieter and more exclusive events, which suited Eleanor just fine. She'd been working hard on gathering the necessary foods and decorations to make it a lavish and elegant affair. It seemed all of her hard work was going to pay off.

If only things were going so well with her marriage.

Despite numerous hints that she'd made to her husband over the past couple of weeks about her feelings for him, feelings which went beyond mere affection, passion, or a prolonged attachment left over from childhood friendship, he had said nothing in return. Indeed, there had been times when he'd seemed almost confused by her attempts at sparking a conversation in such a vein. He didn't thwart such declarations, but neither could his responses be called encouraging.

Yet he continued to lave passion on her nightly, he danced attendance on her at every event, and he'd recently bought her the most stunning diamond bracelet for no reason at all. If only she could be sure of the sentiment behind his actions... instead she was elated and downtrodden by turns. Jealous whenever he danced with another woman, despite knowing it was a social necessity. Furious whenever one of his reputed former mistresses dared to approach him, even though he always received their greetings coldly and swiftly sent them on their way without her interference or insistence. Thrilled when he refused to quit her side, miserable when he relinquished her to another's care while he continued his conversation with whatever Lord he was speaking. Even more miserable when she noticed he didn't seem to suffer the same throes of jealousy wracking her.

If only he'd come out and say how he truly felt about her, then she would be either the happiest woman alive or the most miserable, but at least she'd be able to move forward.

"My lady?" Mrs. Hester came into the room, interrupting Eleanor's thoughts as if she'd sensed their turn towards the melancholy. Somehow the older woman often seemed to make timely interruptions when Eleanor was depressing herself, as if her position as housekeeper had somehow sensitized her to knowing when something was amiss in the household.

"Yes, Mrs. Hester?" Eleanor said, putting down the list of responses that had been made. She was only waiting on one or two more.

"There's a problem with the linens—it seems the mice have gotten into them and ruined about half of them. We can order more but they may not be quite the same make. Cook says the recent crop of strawberries isn't nearly high enough quality for the tarts you wanted, he thinks they'll do better as jam, but that leaves us without a dessert..." The housekeeper rattled on as Eleanor forced herself to pay attention to the various problems about the household.

The linens weren't a major emergency, she could just change the color scheme for the dinner if she didn't have the time or inclination to purchase new ones in the lovely cream color she'd initially chosen. However the lack of decent strawberries made her frown. She'd so wanted to make up her last dinner's food choices to Edwin by incorporating some of his favorites into this one. Tarts might not be considered the most elegant of foodstuffs, but they were one of Edwin's favorites and Cook did a marvelous job of making them more fanciful by adding chocolate and cream toppings.

Would he even notice the amount of effort she'd put into this dinner? The attention she'd put towards the menu? As much attention as she'd put towards the last dinner but in a completely different way. Even the colors she'd put together were the ones she'd noticed he'd complimented the most in her dress or when they'd seen them at others' events.

Would he notice? Would he care?

"My lady?" Mrs. Hester asked hesitantly and Eleanor shook herself.

"Yes, Mrs. Hester, I'm sorry, my mind wandered. Let's start with the linens. What other options do we have here in the house?" Forcing herself to concentrate, Eleanor turned her attention back to making her dinner a success rather than thinking about the possible reward if she actually managed it.

The two of them walked down as they discussed their options.

To Irene's dismay, like the manors they'd stayed in on their honeymoon, the house in Mayfair had also been prepared with only one bedroom. She had been utterly humiliated the last night of their honeymoon when she'd discovered that, while she might want to shut Hugh out emotionally, she had been all too easily swept away physically. Considering the layout of the townhouse, it would have been no trouble to prepare the mistress' bedroom, but the room was cold and there were no linens on the bed; whereas Hugh's room had obviously been made up to be comfortable for both of them. Some of her furniture from her parent's house had even been moved in, and the room was more than spacious enough to accommodate all of it.

In some ways it warmed her heart to see how he had moved aside his own things to make way for hers, but she hardened herself against her softening of emotion. Now that she knew his gentle kindness was just a foil for another side to him. She was still amazed there was no mark or even lingering soreness in her backside, which made her wonder if perhaps she had overdrawn the situation… after all, it's not like he had marked her the way she'd seen Malvin caning that poor maid...

But then she reminded herself that the spanking wasn't the point anyway. The point was she loved Alex, and Hugh had almost made her forget her love for Alex—or at least question it. Alex, who was the perfect gentleman. A true white knight who would never treat a lady so. Just look at how he tolerated his shrewish wife's transgressions. Irene was sure that if Lady Grace wasn't such a harpy then Alex would never have the need for mistresses—although she reminded herself she was glad of such a need. Otherwise there would be no hope for her.

She wasn't even sure if she cared about ensuring Hugh's line of descent anymore either. After all, Lady Brooke hadn't born Alex any heirs and she moved about easily enough in Society. Only the highest-steppers declined to invite her company. If Irene had Alex's company then what did she care for others?

Chewing on her lower lip, she peeked out the window into the streets of London. They didn't hold half the beauty of the country-side, but it was where she had to be to see Alex and that made it worth the sacrifice. Out in the country there was nothing but Hugh and his dismissal of her chilly demeanor, his demanding lips, his practiced caresses... she had succumbed to his passion, telling herself a good wife would submit to her husband's desires, but the truth was she'd enjoyed herself as much as she ever had. It didn't seem to matter she'd been determined not to be engaged; at some point her passion and her primed senses had overcome her mind and left her aching and gasping in Hugh's arms.

He'd seemed almost amused by her coldness after that.

With a sigh, Irene quit the bedroom and went downstairs to check their correspondence. She was sorting through invitations by level of importance, desperately trying to remember all of the instruction her mother had given her, when Hugh appeared in the drawing room. He was quiet enough that Irene didn't hear him approach at first and he was able to admire how the beauty of the room framed the glorious appearance of his wife. The deep evergreen of the trim and the velvet drapes with their golden cord and the gold, cream, and deep mint of the walls suited her admirably. She was like a flame in a forest, the sunlight coming in through the windows sinking into her hair and turning it into a fiery mass of copper and light.

When he actually entered the room she caught a glimpse of him from the corner of her eye and immediately sat up straight. Considering how tall he was, it didn't matter how straight she sat on the elegant couch, it was never going to be enough to make her feel anything other than vulnerable.

"Good afternoon, darling," he said amiably as he strode forward, settling himself on the couch next to her with an air of lazy self-assurance.

Irene eyed him warily. There was something different about him. Ever since he'd spanked her he'd been rather solicitous of her, he'd watched her as if expecting she might spark up and flare at him all over again. Now he seemed relaxed again. Supremely confident in a way that made her insides tingle. As if it didn't matter he'd put her over a hay bale and beaten her.

Remembering sparked her temper, but Irene was a past master at reigning herself in. Especially when she had no idea of the consequences.

"Good afternoon," she said coolly, although it was hard to keep her voice even when he was sitting so close to her. She couldn't move to the side either, not without it seeming like a retreat and she already knew how much Hugh enjoyed the chase. Heat flamed in her cheeks as she determinedly pretended to ignore his nearness, affecting that she didn't remember his fondness for passion in the middle of the day on inappropriate pieces of furniture. Like the spindly couch they were currently seated upon.

Fingers stroked her shoulder and her breath caught. Deciding the best defense was a good offense, she shoved two elegantly scripted invitations at him. "Next Wednesday we've been invited to two major balls, Lady Felsingham's and Lady Durgess'. Which do you think we should attend?"

Inwardly Hugh sighed, social niceties were not what he wished to discuss with his wife, but he also realized that such events were important and their presence at one or the other would make a statement. Especially as they were newly arrived back to the Season. Irene was not experienced at the social whirl, before he'd begun his courtship of her she hadn't received many coveted invitations, and without her mother or his to guide her, it was his responsibility to help.

Hm. He made a mental note to ask Eleanor to go over these things with her as soon as possible. Much better his sister than forcing Irene to go to her mother for help, especially as the Baroness' social agenda might not be the same as his family's.

Studying the two invitations he smiled. At least he knew what to do with this one. "Lord Felsingham is a particular intimate of my father's. We'll start the evening at Lady Durgess', stay long enough to pay our respects and show you off before finishing the evening at the Felsinghams."

"We can do both?" Irene asked, a little startled. Her family had never had to deal with the issue of deciding between two important events.

"Most of the *ton* will," said Hugh, tossing the invitations back onto the table as he leaned back against the sofa, spreading his arms out and stretching his legs forward. He took up so much space it was impossible to ignore him physically, although Irene was still doing her best to. "The only thing that will differ will be where they start and where they end."

"Oh."

"I'll see if my sister is up for a visit from you tomorrow, if you like," Hugh said casually. "If we could attend as many events with her and Edwin as possible I'd enjoy that."

As much as she wanted to show she was capable, Irene could recognize when she was being tossed a much-needed favor. Hugh was allowing her to maintain her pride by making the request to spend time with his friend, rather than outright saying his sister would have a better idea of how to maneuver the social whirl and could advise Irene on how to handle it. She felt a rather grudging gratitude towards him for both his tact and the offer.

"That sounds lovely," she said, setting the invitations down. She couldn't quite hide her relief. "I've already responded to Eleanor for the dinner she's having tomorrow night and we have Lady Cowper's ball on Saturday. There isn't anything else being held that evening."

"There wouldn't be," Hugh murmured. Lady Cowper was one of the grande dames of the *ton*. If anyone else had dared to plan an event at the same time as one of her ladyship's balls they would have already changed the date once her invitations went out. Even the men most assiduously avoiding the marriage mart would make an appearance at Lady Cowper's before retreating to their more usual haunts later in the evening. He coughed and then raised his voice again. "I'll send a note to Eleanor tomorrow morning."

"Thank you," Irene murmured. Her voice had gone cool again, as if she'd remembered she was angry at him.

Deciding to follow Edwin's advice, Hugh ignored it. While his instinct was to stay and try and placate her, instead he stood and looked down into her startled eyes. Obviously she'd expected him to continue his attempts to return to her good graces. Cupping her chin with one hand he swiftly stole a kiss before she could react.

"I'll be in my study," he said, ignoring the confusion and hint of outrage in her eyes over the stolen kiss which she hadn't even had the chance to thwart. "Dinner is at seven?"

"Yes," she said, her tone rather clipped, but confusion swam in her eyes. Before she could jerk her head away he dropped his hand, gave her a slight bow and quit the room, feeling—for the first time in the past few days—as if he'd scored a victory.

CHAPTER 13

Striding through the house in search of his wife, Edwin couldn't wipe the frown from his face. Wesley had pulled him aside before leaving for a quick word in private, intimating he'd had a conversation with Eleanor where she'd indicated there was a real possibility he might have a mistress. The very idea had shocked him. How on earth could shåe think that? Even if hadn't cared what Hugh's reaction might be upon hearing such a thing, he was in her bed every night, most mornings, and often hunting her down at other odd times during the day. While he might have been considered one of the wolves of the ton before his marriage, even he didn't have the stamina to be at her night and day as well as indulging with another woman. Then again considering how often he did avail himself of her, and her level of inexperience, perhaps she didn't realize men weren't readily recharged for such activities.

Around her it didn't seem to be much of a problem, but she might not realize she was a unique case for him.

Well he'd be more than happy to show her. His hand slid into his pocket, fingering the little trinkets he'd taken with him from his study. Another part of his wedding gift from Wesley, one which he was eager to share with Eleanor. While he hadn't fantasized about such things before, he'd found his fantasies had become increasingly dark and decadent now that he had Eleanor in his bed every night and occasionally across his lap. The urge to imprint himself on her body, until she was assured of his passionate desire for her and only her, was almost overwhelming.

He didn't at all like the idea of his beautiful, rebellious Eleanor thinking he had a piece on the side, especially not when she already had such bad influences in her life as Lady Grace. The last thing he needed was Nell deciding to take a page out of her friend's book. Not something he'd worried about before now, considering how passionate their marriage was, but if she was worrying over his constancy…

Edwin was more than happy to reassure her.

"There you are," he exclaimed when he finally came upon her and Mrs. Hester in one of the back storerooms. It was certainly not one of the first places he'd looked and it had taken questioning one of the undermaids to finally discover her direction.

She looked up at him, a touch of dust on her cheek, marring the cream of her skin and making the rest of her beauty stand out in contrast.

"Should I not be here?" she asked, a little tartly, taken aback by his slightly exasperated tones.

It wasn't unusual for Edwin to search her out during the day, but if he couldn't find her right away then he usually waited until he happened upon her later. This was certainly the first time he'd searched her out while she was obviously busy with household matters.

"I have something I'd like to discuss with you," he said, which wasn't really an answer. The truth was that realizing Eleanor didn't trust him, realizing she thought he had betrayed his marriage vows when the truth was no other woman stirred him anymore, had rattled him. He was an active kind of man and he wanted to set matters to right and he wanted to do so *right now.*

A little crease appeared on her forehead but she nodded. Glancing around at the linens in front of her and Mrs. Hester, Eleanor tapped the pile they'd been considering. "Have a footman take these down to the dining room please, Mrs. Hester. I'll come and look at the colors in the candlelight later this evening."

"Very good my lady," Mrs. Hester said, giving Edwin a little wink when Eleanor's back was turned.

He grinned at his housekeeper. Now obviously *she* knew which way the wind turned when it came to his respect and desire for his wife. When Eleanor reached him he wiped the smudge of dust from her cheek with his thumb before turning and leading her out of the storeroom, heading towards their bedroom.

Feeling rather anxious about the strange expression on Edwin's face and his unusual demeanor, Eleanor tried to slow her steps. "Edwin, what's going on? What's wrong?"

The sidelong look he gave her as he wrapped his arm around her waist, pulling her to his side and hurrying her along, down the stairs towards the wing with their bedroom, was nothing short of predatory. The caress of his fingers on her hip made her heart rate double. She might have harangued him for interrupting her preparations for the dinner if she thought it would do any good, but she'd long since learned that trying to derail Edwin from amorous intentions resulted in nothing but a quick spanking into compliance. By which time she was always as hot and needy as he was.

"Really? Now?" She couldn't stop the curve of her lips into amusement, even as she tried to give him a hard look.

"Always."

The almost savage tone of his voice, as if he was making a vow, startled her and she peered up at him in surprise, which nearly caused her to stumble. Stifling a curse, Edwin caught her and then swept her up into his arms, making her squeak as one wrapped around her waist and the other tucked under her knees. "Oh!"

"You were taking too long," he said wickedly as his stride lengthened, hurrying them down the hall towards the bedroom.

Giggling, Eleanor wrapped one arm around his shoulders for balance, her other hand beginning to pluck apart the intricate knot of his cravat. "I didn't realize you were so impatient."

"For you and only you."

The sentiment surprised her into silence, which he didn't notice because he was too busy pushing open the door to their bedroom. His valet was in there, fussily attending to his wardrobe.

"Out," Edwin ordered. Johnson took one look at the couple and immediately vanished into the closet and out that way. Chuckling beneath his breath at the slightly scandalized look on Johnson's face—he always had been a bit of a stickler for the proprieties—Edwin set his wife down on the bed, climbing on top of her without even taking off any of their clothes.

"Edwin!" Eleanor yelped as he tore the front of her dress down, the sound of ripping fabric filling the air.

"Yes, dear?" He kissed the side of her neck as he tossed away the front panel of her dress, ignoring her outraged eyes.

"I liked this dress!"

"I'll buy you a new one."

Lowering his mouth to hers, he ignored the muffled sounds of fury, pinioning her beneath his large body and kissing her into submission. Eleanor knew she should be furious, but she had to admit that part of her was enjoying this primitive and eager display from her husband, even though she didn't know exactly what had caused it. Excitement was flaring up inside of her, physically and emotionally. Especially since he hadn't even seen the plans for the dinner she was basically specially putting together for him, even if it was ostensibly for Hugh and Irene. She didn't know where this sudden need of his was coming from, but she wasn't going to argue with it either. When hot passion flowed between them it was easy to forget her doubts and insecurities, to feel the promise in his hands and mouth, the overwhelming demand of his body.

Feeling Eleanor's body slowly submitting beneath his inflamed Edwin. He was going to take full advantage of it. Literally tearing the last of her dress from her as she wriggled beneath him, he unlaced the rest of his cravat and wound it about her hands. Eleanor moaned as she felt what he was doing, excited by his sexual dominance over her and the enhanced vulnerability which came from being bound. She couldn't help but be excited by the passion pulsing from him as he ripped through her clothing like it was nothing.

"Beautiful, Eleanor," he murmured as he hovered above her, securing her bound wrists to the headboard of their bed. She was laid out like a banquet beneath him. Pulling the remains of her dress from underneath her, he tossed them to the floor before swiftly tearing through the delicate fabric of her chemise and drawers. She'd stopped wearing a corset around the house a few weeks ago, only putting one on if she was going out because of Edwin's penchant for indulging himself at any time of day. "You are the most beautiful woman I've ever seen."

Leaning back, he stared down admiringly at her naked form. With her arms above her head, her breasts were thrust upwards and her little pink nipples were tightly puckered, tempting his fingers and mouth. The soft plane of her stomach led down to the thatch of golden curls, slightly parted so her legs could settle around his, just the slightest shell of glistening pink showing through. Her eyes glowed with happiness at the compliment. The way he was looking at her set her lower body throbbing with need.

Large hands rested on her thighs and then traveled upwards, sliding over her hips and up the sides of her stomach as she writhed and let out a little moan, wanting him to touch her so much more intimately. She sighed with pleasure as he cupped her breasts, gently squeezing them. Sometimes Edwin could be so tender; emotionally she appreciated the sentiment, but her body craved something harsher. These gentle caresses were a tease igniting and kindling the flame within her, but would have no power to quench it.

"Edwin... harder..." The breathy plea made his hands clench and Eleanor moaned her approval.

Chuckling, he rubbed his thumbs over her sensitive nipples, her thighs tightening around his kneeling legs. He was teasing her with his body, keeping her splayed and open, vulnerable and naked, while he was fully clothed and fully in control.

Greedily she watched him as he released her breasts, obviously hoping he was done toying with her. Instead he reached into his pocket.

"What do you want, Nell?"

"You."

She arched her back, thrusting her breasts up and relishing the look of hunger on his face as his eyes fell from hers and down to the pink tipped mounds. It hadn't taken her very long to learn how very *much* Edwin liked to see her squirming and offering herself up to him. When his gaze returned to her face, she darted her tongue out to lick her lips, an invitation to come and kiss her.

"I want you too." Dark eyes met light, earnest and unyielding. "You and only you, in my bed. I don't have a mistress, Nell, and I don't intend on taking one."

Red heat that had nothing to do with passion flamed in her face. "I didn't... I mean..."

"Mmmm, little liar," he purred as he removed his hand from his pocket. The singularly wicked look on his face didn't do anything to relieve the butterflies jumping in her stomach. Eleanor's insides clenched as she realized Edwin was going to punish her for doubting him. Her bottom tingled in anticipation, but she hadn't yet realized her tender cheeks were not yet his target. "Wesley told me you didn't believe him when he tried to reassure you. Maybe you'll believe me."

"That rat!"

Edwin laughed, cupping her right breast and pinching the nipple. A flash of silver showed as he dropped the tiny instrument from his pocket. Watching curiously, Eleanor wrinkled her forehead as he opened it and then let it slowly close around her nipple.

"Ow... Ouch! Edwin stop, take it off, it *hurts!*" The tiny vise pinched her nipple and she squirmed, trying to shake it off and finding her attempt did nothing other than jiggle the flesh and enhanced the sharp burn. She whimpered and took deep breaths, automatically breathing through the pain the way she'd learned how to when she'd been bent over the arm of her father's chair for discipline. It was in a different area, but after a few deep breaths the sharp bite of the pain dulled to a more manageable throbbing pressure.

"They're called nipple clips, according to Wesley," Edwin said almost conversationally as he hefted her left breast, pinching the nipple to full hardness between his fingers.

"Edwin please... noooooooo..."

Even though she protested as he secured the other clip, yelping at the sharp initial pinch, part of her was relieved that her body was now symmetrical with the throbbing pressure and pain. Looking down at her poor little nipples, which were quickly darkening in color in their tight confinement, she felt rather shocked. She hadn't thought Edwin could do anything further to surprise her, even in the bedroom where she knew he had a great amount of experience, but this wasn't something she could have ever imagined. To know these came from *Wesley*... they must have been something he'd picked up on his travels but she knew she'd never be able to look their friend in the face again. Not without knowing *he* knew...

"Beautiful," Edwin said, his cock throbbing inside of his breeches. Part of the reason he'd remained clothed was to force himself to move slower, knowing how difficult it was for him to stay in control once both he and Eleanor were naked. Without such a hindrance he'd already have his cock buried inside her luscious body. His fingers delved into the wet heat that his body was aching for, feeling the heavy coating of cream the pain of the clips had coaxed from her. "You like this, Nell..."

"It hurts," she protested.

"Ah, but sometimes you like it when it hurts, or you wouldn't get so delightfully wet when I spank you." Lowering his head, Edwin flicked out his tongue experimentally to lave it across the tip of her nipple.

Eleanor's reaction was explosive as her body jerked; pleasure and pain jolting through her. The tight grip of the clip had made the tiny nub a thousand times more sensitive and it throbbed and burned as Edwin toyed with it. His hands cupped her breasts from beneath, kneading the soft flesh as he began to torment her with his fingers and mouth.

Just like with a spanking or even a more severe punishment,

Eleanor's body didn't care that she didn't want to enjoy it. Tingles of hot need assailed her as little jagged edges of pain nipped at the heels of her pleasure. Her legs parted even further, tempting him with the flash of the sweet pink shell of her pussy, begging him to satisfy her. Tugging at the binding he'd made out of his cravat only made her writhe even more as her fingers tingled with the need to touch him.

"How does it feel now?" he asked, squeezing and brushing his lips over her nipple again.

"It hurts..."

"Where?"

Eleanor moaned and tried to close her thighs. It hurt everywhere. Hurt with how badly she needed him, her body actually feeling as though it was going to explode if he didn't stroke and soothe it immediately. The pressure on her nipples was never ending, keeping her insides clenching in a steady rhythm as she pulsed and ached.

He could tell Eleanor was practically melting inside her own skin, her eyes were completely glazed, as if peering at a clear sky through cloudy glass. The hard little tips of her nipples were turning a reddish color and he knew he was going to need to take the clips off soon, but he was reveling in watching her lose control... in knowing the sensitive parts of her body were going to be sore for days. She wouldn't be able to get dressed without thinking of him as cloth brushed against her breasts.

"Where does it hurt, Nell?" he murmured, his voice almost hypnotic as he squeezed her breasts again. Beneath him her hips lifted, searching for purchase, but he was finding it surprisingly difficult to release his hold on her soft flesh in order to disrobe.

"My pussy, Edwin... it hurts in my pussy... please I *need* you..." Her voice was almost broken and it finally broke him.

With a low groan he released her breasts, trusting in the clips to keep her throbbing as he hastily pulled off his own clothing, tossing it to the floor in crumpled heaps his valet could have fits over later. Seeing the darkening color of her nipples, he decided to take the clips off now. Wesley had warned him doing so would not actually relieve the sensations for Eleanor, it would only change them.

The gasping cry she gave as he released the pressure on both of her nipples at once bore out Wesley's instructions.

"Ouch! Edwin that burns!"

Rubbing his hand over one of her aching nipples, he sucked the other one into his mouth, adding pleasure to the swirling pain that had burgeoned as the clips were released. It felt like her pulse was pounding in her ears and through her body, more strongly than ever, her nipples throbbing in time with it. She moaned as she felt the blunt head of his cock tease the outer folds of her pussy, her back arching up as Edwin moved his head back and forth between her nipples, suckling them between his lips until the sharpness of the pain had subsided.

When he finally began to push inside of her, she was nearly mindless with the pleasure and hot need. Her body opened for him, tight muscles rippling as he filled her wet sheath, and her back arched, thrusting her breasts upwards. The taut nipples retained the deep red color they'd achieved, hard little buds rubbing against his chest. As they met the wiry hairs on his body, scraping against them, Eleanor shivered and moaned.

The line between pleasure and pain had blurred, leaving her in Edwin's hands to send either way. Remembering one of the pictures in the Kama Sutra book Wesley had given him, Edwin grasped each of Eleanor's ankles and rested them on his shoulders, bending her nearly in half. They both groaned as his cock slid deeper than ever inside of her, bumping up against the back of tunnel and nudging her womb. She could feel the muscles in her legs straining as Edwin leaned forward.

The position made it incredibly easy for him to reach down and grip the rounded cheeks of her bottom, lust flaming through him as he looked down at her and deliberately pulled halfway out of her body and then thrust back in hard. The high keening sound Eleanor made as her breasts jiggled from the force of the thrust went straight to Edwin's cock. Gripping handfuls of her soft bottom, he dug his fingers in as he began a steady rhythmic pounding of her open pussy. Looking down he could see the way his cock was splitting her open, the pink lips tightly stretched around his straining rod which was coated with her glossy cream.

His wife whispered his name over and over again, as if she couldn't think to say anything else, writhing and arching as he rode her. With her ankles around his ears, it was the deepest penetration he'd ever achieved and he felt as though he was claiming every last inch of her, branding her with himself. He wanted her to feel the lingering effects of his loving for days afterwards, to wipe away every last doubt she might have about his constancy.

The chanting of his name grew louder and louder as Eleanor neared her climax, his thrusts following the speed and intensity of her voice. He could feel his balls tightening just as she began to shriek, her eyes closing as the intense ecstasy flowed over her, fireworks bursting behind her eyelids as the explosion rocked her core and spread outwards like lightening along a rod. She could feel it through her stomach and sore nipples, up her legs and arms, until every inch of her body was throbbing and tingling with the orgasmic rapture. The inside of her body clenched over and over again, muscles tightening in such a way it was like she was trying to suck Edwin's cock deeper into her body.

Hot cum splashed against her womb as he groaned and his seed pulsed into her. His cock expanded, throbbing against her walls as they tried to tighten around him, their bodies' reactions dueling for supremacy. Eleanor's legs slipped down, allowing Edwin to slump on top of her, and she thrashed as the new position pressed his body against the swollen nub of her clitoris, sending a second wave of overwhelming pleasure through her already sensitized body.

She was practically insensate by the time Edwin unwound the cravat from her hands. A damp cloth swiped between her legs, setting off another chain reaction. Then warmth surrounded her, cuddling her. Hard, strong arms drew her against the long, muscled body of her husband, nestling her head into his shoulder so they were facing each other and he could envelop her completely.

"I have no need for a mistress when I have you, sweet Nell," he murmured as he kissed her forehead, caressing her shoulders and hair. The little loving touches were enough to make her eyes spark with tears, even as she felt herself sinking into much needed oblivion under his touch.

Edwin would have been happy to spend all afternoon holding his wife while she napped in his arms, but his valet came in to quietly pull him away. Lord Hartford had come to call, and unfortunately the man had urgent business which needed to be attended to immediately. Reluctantly he pulled away from Eleanor and allowed Johnson to redress him, ignoring the man's muttered comments about the clothing that had been left on the floor.

Pressing another kiss to Eleanor's forehead, careful not to disturb her slumber, he sighed and went back to work.

THE MAID WOKE ELEANOR, leaving her feeling strangely disappointed when she realized Edwin was no longer in bed with her. She knew it wasn't entirely fair of her to feel abandoned, she vaguely remembered Johnson coming into their room which meant someone had come to see Edwin, but she still would have preferred to wake with Edwin there.

"I brought you some tea, my lady." The maid bustled around, gathering up the shredded dress Edwin had so eagerly ripped apart and doing her best to hide her shock. Garbed in her dressing gown, Eleanor couldn't help the little smile playing on her lips as she remembered her husband's passion.

Her nipples were still sore and hard, making her lean forward a little so the fabric of the dressing gown didn't brush against them. The area between her legs tingled with the aftermath of their loving.

Today had felt... different. As if Edwin had wanted to prove something to her. Something emotional.

But, casting her mind back to everything he had said, she felt the same vague disappointment she always did. There had been no words of love, only of desire and passion. He did not have a mistress, which caused her much relief and joy, but that didn't mean he loved her. It only meant he desired her and she satisfied his needs. What if she stopped satisfying his needs?

Eleanor nibbled her lower lip wondering if she dared deny him. When she had her courses he still wanted to sleep in the same bed as her and was remarkably affectionate, but that was only a matter of days. What if he was denied for longer? Would he remain faithful if his wife was denying him his marital rights?

The only reason she could think of that Edwin would tolerate such a situation would be if he truly loved her. What other reason would a man such as he, with his high passions, remain faithful when his needs were not being met?

Of course, Eleanor had no illusions about her ability to deny Edwin when he was with her. He knew exactly how to touch her, to tease her, and he insisted on sleeping in the same bed every night whether or not she had her courses. She loved sleeping in his arms, having his warmth beside her. Which meant she would have to leave his presence for a while and see what happened.

Bath! She could visit her parents in Bath! Edwin had already planned to visit his parents after the Season was over, she could go see hers and tell him she would join him later. If she left before the Season was over it would cause some comment but most would probably assume she was with child. It wouldn't matter they were wrong. Still, she couldn't travel such a distance on her own. Perhaps she could find a traveling companion and then leave as soon as possible, whether or not the Season was over. Unfortunately her brother probably wouldn't want to leave the city so soon after his return.

But Grace wanted to leave London.

"I need to dress," she said to the maid, setting down her teacup only half finished. "The lavender and cream jaconet, please."

To Eleanor's surprise, when she arrived at Lady Grace's townhouse, her friend was having an at-home. Peters looked both concerned and disapproving when he informed Eleanor there were several visitors. Fortunately the parlor wasn't overly full; Lord Conyngham, Grace's escort to Eleanor's last dinner was there, as were several other men with rakish reputations, and several ladies who were tittering and flirting with the men. Eleanor recognized them all as the young, bored matrons who had already born their husbands an heir and a spare and so were basically free to enjoy their own pursuits.

Only Grace had been able to shake off that requirement, although it did exclude her from some very select events. Still, she certainly seemed to think the trade was well worth it.

Putting a social smile on her face, Eleanor gracefully joined the gathering. Grace welcomed her with every evidence of happiness. Although the dark blue eyes were still shadowed and there were still slight circles under them, overall Grace looked healthier than she had the last few times Eleanor had seen her friend. Beside her on the couch, Conyngham was lounging comfortably, as if he felt perfectly at home in Grace's parlor.

The next hour passed quickly as Eleanor chatted and flirted, in a rather detached sort of way. Although the gathered rakes had quickly attached themselves to her, seeing her as new blood, it didn't take them long to figure out that she meant her carefully couched refusals and they moved back to easier prey. Gossip circulating amongst the *ton* had indicated Lord Hyde had turned in his wolfish reputation for one of a shockingly loyal husband, and apparently his wife was cut from the same cloth—even if she was spending her afternoons at the scandalous Lady Brooke's.

They didn't realize the distance in her demeanor was partly because she'd found her nipples were incredibly sensitive even hours after Edwin had used the clips on her. Even the slightest brush of fabric had her tingling. And the area between her legs was still sore in the most delicious way. But she kept her smile on her face and interacted as naturally as she could, not even realizing that the slight distance her distraction created only intrigued the men even more.

Slowly the crowd trickled out until only Grace, Eleanor, and Lord Conyngham were left.

"Give me a moment, Nell," Grace said, smiling as she excused herself to see the young Lord on his way.

"Lady Hyde, once again, a pleasure," Lord Conyngham said, a merry twinkle in his eye. Eleanor found herself smiling back at him automatically, a sincere smile to match his own.

"Lord Conyngham."

No wonder Grace enjoyed the young lord's company lately, Eleanor mused. He had similar looks to Lord Brooke, both had the same height and breadth of shoulder, although Brooke's hair was more auburn, but the biggest difference was that Conyngham always had a smile on his face. The rake was dangerous not because he was an obvious predator, but because he could lure a woman in with his smiles and friendly charm before she even noticed he was seducing her. While she hadn't been able to speak much with him during her dinner, she now knew he was possessed of a quick and ready wit, although he was never cruel with it that she'd seen thus far, and an obvious admiration for Grace's spirit and disdain for the *ton*'s protocols.

In short, personality wise, he was practically the complete opposite of Lord Brooke who was quite serious and very proper. Although she suspected that beneath his stony exterior, Lord Brooke might be harboring a much kinder and more open-minded person than anyone suspected. After all, he did let Grace do as she pleased whereas another man would have already divorced her or taken... other measures to force her to his will. Grace could have very easily found herself locked away in the countryside.

Eleanor wondered whether it was benevolence or something else on Lord Brooke's part that he allowed his wife to behave as she did.

"Hello darling, do you have time to stay? I'd hoped for a few moments alone," said Grace as she re-entered the parlor and came to sit next to Eleanor on the couch. Her eyes were sparkling and the smile on her face was the first Eleanor had seen in a long time. She was glad for it, she was, it was just that she had hoped Grace would be willing to quit the city with her. If her friend was happy again then perhaps she wouldn't be.

Had Lord Brooke left London?

"No," said Grace, a vague look of anxiety passing over her face before it was replaced by defiance. Eleanor started guiltily, she hadn't even realized she'd spoken out loud. "He's still in the city... but Rupert came by a few days ago and we had a long talk and he talked me into going out with him. We went to Lady Poplar's soiree and of course Alex wasn't there."

"Of course," Eleanor echoed, trying to hide her shock. She'd realized Rupert Conyngham would have entrance to some of the less, ah, proper gatherings of the darker echelons of Society, but she hadn't expected Grace to ever go to any of them. Normally Grace kept to the more acceptable outings.

"I know what you're thinking," Grace said with a sigh, her hands balling in her lap. She looked down at them and then shrugged and looked back at Eleanor, her expression resigned. "But I miss going out. It was so lovely to go somewhere and not have Alex show up... although Rupert is trying to convince me to return to my usual events as well. He pointed out that it's not as though Alex actually approaches me."

There was something in Grace's voice which made Eleanor wonder if Grace wished her husband would approach. Although Grace went out on another man's arm, she was sure she'd seen Lord Brooke with other women on his arm—or in them on the dance floor —when she had seen him in the evenings. Did Grace still harbor some kind of feelings for the man? Did it hurt her to see him with those women?

Goodness... that would explain so much.

"True... although I can't imagine you enjoy seeing him," Eleanor hedged. She didn't want to dissuade her friend from the activities she loved, but Eleanor's life would be so much easier if Grace agreed to go to Bath with her.

"No." Those dark blue eyes suddenly got a very faraway look as she answered softly. "No I don't."

"Are you still thinking about leaving London?"

Grace hesitated, brushing a strand of raven-wing hair off of her face. Pink lips pursed. "I don't know. I don't feel quite as... trapped as I did before." A slight blush suffused her cheeks. "Knowing Rupert is willing to escort me about, whether or not Alex is there, is a great help, especially as he can find events where I can enjoy myself without worrying Alex will suddenly appear."

"I see."

Something in Eleanor's voice must have given her away because Grace looked at her curiously. "Is everything alright?"

"I've been considering a visit to my mother in Bath," Eleanor said.

"Before the end of the Season?" Grace's eyebrows rose in true surprise. "I thought your highest ambition was a Season in London."

"That's also when I thought I would be spending the Season being courted," said Eleanor a little sourly.

But Grace only laughed at her. "You're the envy of half the ladies of the *ton*, Eleanor. Both married and unmarried. You have a husband who spurns the invitations of any number of women, indulges you with jewelry, and dances attendance on you at whatever event you decide to attend. The goal of any Season is to procure a marriage, and yours is a particularly successful one. What on earth do you have to complain about?"

"I don't know," Eleanor said a bit waspishly. Having Grace point out all the things Eleanor should be grateful for in her marriage only made her more irritable. The problem was that she truly *wasn't* satisfied with all those things. She wanted Edwin to treat her the way he had been, of course, but she also wanted to know she had his heart. But it seemed like the wrong topic to bring up with Grace, who, unlike Eleanor, had always wanted to marry for love and whose own marriage was such a travesty. After hearing her friend's story, Eleanor wasn't going to rub bitter salt in the wound.

To her surprise, Grace placed a gentle hand upon Eleanor's. "Don't mind me dear," she said with a trilling little laugh which belied her own hurt. "Alex did all those things before I discovered he had married to make a deal with my father. I, more than anyone, know that sometimes what looks like perfection is hollow on the inside."

When Eleanor left Grace's she felt more turmoil than ever. Her friend's marriage was a perfect example of a woman assuming one thing only to find out she was wrong. Which is exactly why Eleanor didn't want to assume Edwin's feelings towards her, she wanted to know. The dratted man didn't seem inclined to just declare himself and while his actions were certainly indicative, they were not conclusive.

So she would just keep testing. The sooner she could get out of the city and away from him for a bit, to see what he would do, the better. Perhaps he would remain faithful... perhaps she would discover that his expressed desire for her and only her was nothing more than locational. Since Grace was no longer an option she would just have to find someone else.

CHAPTER 14

The dinner celebrating Hugh and Irene's return from their honeymoon was a wild success. Everyone agreed the food was delicious, the decorations elegant and sumptuous, and the conversation was surprisingly lively. This was due, in part, to the number of Hugh's friends who were unmarried rakes and Eleanor's preferred female friends amongst the *ton* who were not at all shy about voicing their opinions. Since the older generations were all absent from the city, Eleanor had invited only the younger sets and so the dinner had a very youthful vibrancy about the tableside.

Even Irene was able to shed some of her coldness towards Hugh, the shyness she'd retained while she was an unmarried miss, and engaged in a lively debate about horseflesh with him and some of his compatriots at one end of the table. Needless to say, his friends were more than impressed with her knowledge of their beloved horses and more than one of them silently cursed Hugh for finding her first. Then again, Irene had never been so bold as to express such unladylike opinions on such an unladylike subject before her honeymoon with Hugh.

Unfortunately for her, Alex was an entire table length away, because Eleanor had kept Grace's warnings in mind. Of course if

Irene had known what he was thinking she would not have been encouraged. Seeing how vibrant and almost outspoken his childhood friend was behaving, Alex was entirely reassured Hugh was a good match for her. It was obvious she'd gained in confidence already.

For himself, Hugh was relieved to be able to pick up some of the easy banter he and Irene had originally had. He hoped it was a sign of things to come. She was obviously having trouble keeping up her cold shoulder in a group setting, especially on a topic she was well versed in and they had discussed many times together in the past weeks when they were on the estates.

After the dinner Edwin took Eleanor up to their bedroom and showed her just how very much he appreciated having a dinner tailored to him rather than against him.

Lady Cowper's ball was the definition of a crush. Dressed in a deep green organza to highlight her hair and creamy skin, Irene fanned herself with a matching green and gold fan, knowing her fair skin was probably growing increasingly red and blotchy due to the heat. Her mother had warned her of the effect often enough that she could actually feel when it was beginning to happen, her skin overheating and reacting.

Eleanor and she were traversing the crowd together, fortunately for Irene since her sister-in-law was much better acquainted with the members of the *haut ton* than Irene was. She was able to keep Irene on track and prevent her from embarrassing herself. Now that she was Hugh's wife, suddenly quite a few more people wanted to speak with her, many of whom she'd only met once and barely remembered. When she had been a plain, nearly destitute Baron's daughter they hadn't had any interest in her.

The men had disappeared to the card room almost an hour after they had arrived. Hugh had asked Irene if she wanted him to stay with her, but she'd practically pushed him in the direction of the room. It was too difficult to maintain her mien of ill-will towards him. The man acted as if he'd decided he'd done nothing wrong. And he was far too adept at the little touches and caresses which roused her body, making it impossible for her to be entirely icy with him once they'd retired for the night. Passion awakened and claimed her all too easily under her husband's influence.

Spotting Alex leaving the card room, Irene's heart leapt. At Eleanor's dinner she'd never had the chance to speak with him alone, only a few words when he'd arrived and left and with Hugh by her side the entire time. It had been impossible to discover whether or not Alex had a new lady love since she'd been on her honeymoon.

Strangely the thought didn't bother her as much as it had in the past. She dismissed the lack of jealousy as being completely reasonable, considering she had been engaging in the marital act with her husband during that time. Since she had been in another man's bed it would have been completely illogical for her to be jealous that Alex had someone in his.

"I'm feeling a need for some fresh air, I'm going to ask Lord Brooke to take me out," she murmured in Eleanor's ear.

As she eagerly stepped away, heading for the tall and rather forbidding figure, she missed the sharp look her sister-in-law gave her retreating back.

The crowd around Alex swirled, as if the people near him were trying to retreat from his hooded gaze but didn't have the room to actually do so. A few women had edged closer, but it was a rare person who would approach Lord Brooke in a social setting unless he met their eyes and gave a clear indication of whether or not he'd welcome their conversation. Irene was one of those rare people of course.

She was so excited to be able to speak with him, she didn't even notice the whispers that sprang up as soon as Alex smiled at her. One woman fanned herself as if feeling faint. There were very few among the *ton* who had ever seen Lord Brooke smile and the effect was dazzling. Of course, the women who noticed were immediately shooting dagger looks at Irene, but she didn't see them.

"Irene, how are you this evening? Hugh mentioned you were out here with Eleanor." Alex's dark eyes tracked above her head as if looking for her chaperone.

Irene frowned. She wasn't a young miss who needed a chaperone anymore and she certainly didn't want Alex to see her that way. "Yes, but it's become such a crush... I was hoping to get some fresh air if I could find someone to accompany me?"

"As my lady wishes," he said, holding out his arm in an conciliatory manner.

As they swept away through the ballroom, Eleanor watched them, the faintest hint of a frown on her brow.

"Childhood friends, aren't they?" asked Lady Windham, noticing Eleanor's distraction. She patted Eleanor's arm reassuringly. "Lord Brooke never dallies with married ladies, no matter how much they importune him." The easy smile that spread across her beautiful face had only a trace of regret in it. "I have ample reason to know."

Eleanor's eyes widened as she turned her attention to the beauty. In her early thirties, the woman had been married for more than ten years and born her husband three children. She supposed she shouldn't be surprised the woman was sampling the rakes of the *ton,* but she hadn't expected her to speak so plainly. Then again, now that Eleanor had joined the ranks of the wedded and bedded she found women were much more forthcoming with all sorts of information she hadn't been privy to as a young miss.

"Your husband's friend, Spencer, on the other hand," Lady Windham's smile changed, becoming more seductive and she was practically purring. "I hear he's much less discriminating. I don't suppose you could give me an introduction?"

As if Wesley needed help with assignations. Besides which, he had a strange tendency to cleave to one mistress at a time and as far as she knew he was still wrapped up in his affair with Lady Lilienfield. On the other hand, it was up to him to deny or accept Lady Windham's proposition and she could build up some good will from the Countess by providing an introduction.

"If you wish," Eleanor said, turning her attention back to the conversation going on around them. "Although I can't guarantee anything more than that."

"No need," said Lady Windham smugly, obviously secure in the power of her charms, which were admittedly considerable.

Although Eleanor's attention seemed as though it had returned to the inside of the ballroom, she was keeping an eye on the door to the terrace, Grace's words about Irene and Alex echoing in her mind. Alex's preferences notwithstanding, if they hadn't returned to the ballroom within ten minutes, Eleanor was going to go looking for her brother.

~

"WHAT A BEAUTIFUL NIGHT IT IS," Irene said, sighing with relief as they stepped out on the terrace. It was indeed cooler outside, although not nearly as private as she'd hoped. More than one couple was strolling about the terrace and lit pathways down into the garden, and more than one was secreted away in the shadows.

"For the city," Alex replied, giving the obvious comparison as he began to lead her down the stairs to the lit pathways below.

Smiling, Irene couldn't help but wonder at the warmth she felt when she was with Alex. Soft, comforting warmth... nothing like the tingling jumpiness she felt around Hugh. If it were Hugh leading her down into a garden with many darkened nooks her stomach would have been bouncing with anticipation. With Alex she just felt comfortable. Safe. She felt those things with Hugh as well, but it was different.

If only she could put her finger on exactly how and why.

"I was surprised to see you still here," she confessed. "I thought by the time we returned from our honeymoon you might have retreated back to the countryside."

"I have no current plans to return to my estate," he said amiably enough. "Not until I finish what I came to the city to do."

"What did you come to the city to do?"

Smiling again, his head tipped down towards hers in the moonlight, he tapped the fingers of his free hand under her chin. The way he used to when they were children and he was teasing her. "Well, pet, one thing was to see my childhood friend married and get to know her husband."

"Oh..." Irene floundered. She didn't quite know how to respond to that. While she loved the idea she was responsible for his return, that didn't explain why he was still here. Or why he'd want to get to know her husband. Irene definitely did not want Hugh and Alex to become friends, she would much prefer they were kept far away from each other.

While her mother had explained the "way" things were done within Society when it came to extramarital affairs, Irene was astute enough to realize Alex's sense of honor would not include having a friend's wife as his mistress. No matter that Irene had known him first.

"Were there any other reasons?" she asked, hoping to distract him away from the part she didn't want him thinking about.

"A few," he said non-committedly, but Irene knew him well enough to see how he withdrew rather than giving her a real answer. She didn't like being closed out. Not at all.

Coquettishly, she shifted closer to him as they walked, snuggling her side against his. Strangely she didn't feel the same excitement she did when Hugh's arm brushed her breast or when she was pressed against Hugh. No sense of anticipation, no breathless pounding of her heart or tingling between her legs. Irene ignored her body's response. This was Alex, after all, the man she'd loved all her life. Perhaps she just didn't respond that way to him yet because they hadn't been intimate.

To her surprise he frowned down at her. "Are you alright, pet?"

"I'm feeling a bit chilly now that you mention it," she said, tilting her head so the moonlight could catch her fluttering eyelashes and pouting lips. Tilting her head the way she would for a kiss as he stopped to face her, pressing herself close to him. Warmth suffused her but... none of the expected heat. The lack of it, as well as Alex's apparent confusion as to her intentions—not that they had been great, she had only wanted to plant the idea in his head but the fact he didn't seem to be getting the message was making her more frustrated and more brazen than she would have normally been. She was also frustrated feeling as though she had to convince her own body that Alex was who she wanted, that the position of Alex's mistress was one she desired.

"What are you doing Irene?" Alex's obvious confusion, her strange reluctance, and the desire to prove to herself that Hugh didn't actually hold her affections, combined into a dangerous determination as she grasped the collar of Alex's jacket. She was no longer thinking about how clearly visible they were in the moonlight, her emotions were wildly out of check and all she could think about was proving to herself and to Alex that she was destined to become his mistress and they could be happy and in love and together—as together as Society would allow them to be.

WITH A SENSE OF RELIEF, Eleanor watched her brother exit the card room and obviously ask one of the footmen standing nearby for his wife's direction. Everyone in the room knew Lord Brooke had escorted Lady Harrington to the terrace; it was already the talk of the *ton* because Lord Brooke never escorted married ladies anywhere even remotely questionable. Despite the acknowledged childhood friendship it was still a juicy enough piece of gossip to cause comment. She watched as Hugh headed towards the terrace, his easy stride giving the *ton* the verdict that he was going to join his wife and his friend in getting some air.

Nothing at all scandalous.

And she didn't even have to search him out or worry about Grace's warnings. If Irene had, indeed, had ulterior motives for asking Lord Brooke to accompany her for some air, Hugh would put an end to them. She hadn't had to intervene at all.

Her stomach tightened as her own husband followed Hugh in exiting the card room only a minute later. Edwin's dark gaze scanned the room, obviously looking for someone. A woman stepped up to him; from behind Eleanor couldn't recognize her but she saw Edwin bow and kiss her hand. Once again jealousy wracked her, but there was nothing she could do. If the woman was propositioning him she knew he would say no.

Because he had Eleanor in his bed that night, at his beck and call, passionate and eager. Once again she wondered whether she should continue with her plan to go to Bath. She still had yet to find a traveling companion and she hated the idea that Edwin might be with another woman in her absence. On the other hand, it seemed like the risk she had to take in order to know his heart.

Watching him finish his conversation with the woman and brush past her, his eyes lighting on her and his smile broadening when she saw her, she felt the inevitable tug to stay by his side. Always.

But she couldn't risk her heart without knowing his. She'd spent her entire life doing whatever she could to prevent ending up in her mother's situation, she wouldn't give that up now.

"Irene!"

She found herself forcefully thrust away from Alex as two different and distinct voices said her name. One was appalled and shocked, that was Alex. The other was appalled and furious, and the immediate weakening of her knees and swirling of her senses told her exactly who the other voice belonged to.

The moonlight showed the absolute fury in Hugh's face, it was written in every line of his stance. Next to her Alex was practically vibrating in affront.

Everything had spun so wildly out of control so quickly... Irene's heart was pounding as she thought over the last few minutes and tried to understand herself. What had she been thinking? Had she been thinking at all?

Alex's quick eyes took in what Irene was too shaken to notice and Hugh was too angry to see; the gathering, curious crowd.

"She's faint," he said loudly, his voice carrying. The glance he gave to Hugh was a tiny warning that unless he wanted a serious social scandal, he needed to go along with the cover being provided. "Here, you'll need to carry her."

The man she loved passed her off to her husband before Irene could protest. Her knees buckled and she did indeed feel faint when she looked up into Hugh's eyes. In the moonlight they seemed much darker than usual; his features shadowed and unforgiving. Something inside of her clenched.

Then he was sweeping her up in his arms and she became aware of the voices around them. Groaning in mortification, she buried her face in his shoulder, wrapping her arms around his neck as if she could hide away from the entire world. Herself included.

"I'll have your carriage summoned," she heard Alex say, his voice clipped and tense.

As he carried her from the garden Hugh was forced to answer questions from the others who were strolling. His wife was fine, just overwhelmed by the crush and a stroll with Lord Brooke hadn't been enough to help, he was taking her home. Sympathetic murmurs arose. It was well known Viscount Harrington's wife was shy and retiring, such a crush as Lady Cowper's ball and her new position... no wonder she was overwhelmed.

The constant whimpers and tiny moans from Irene, as well as her clinging to her husband's neck, only affirmed the story. No one knew she was moaning and whimpering as much from embarrassment and anxiety over the repercussions of her actions, as well as the shattering of her plans, or that she was clinging to Hugh because she couldn't face anyone, much less him.

To her shock, when Hugh gently placed her in the carriage and sat beside her, Alex climbed in after him.

Covering her face with her hands, Irene turned to the side of the carriage so she didn't have to look at either man. The ride to Harrington House was made in silence.

~

HUGH COULDN'T DESCRIBE his feelings as he helped his wife out of the carriage and they headed into the house, Lord Brooke bringing up the rear. While he had no reason to distrust Lord Brooke, and it was blatantly obvious the man had a care both for his marriage and Irene's reputation, the fit of fury that had engulfed him at seeing his wife in another man's arms had been overwhelming. And that didn't even begin to describe his feelings when he'd realized Irene had been the instigator.

Why?

To pay him back for the spanking? To lash out?

She could have hurt her reputation far greater than she could have hurt his, however, and how could she have known he would go looking for her at that moment if she wanted to hurt him personally?

Gripping her by the arm, he led them to the study. The short nods he'd given the staff upon his entrance to the house had kept them at bay. It was obvious something was going on that he didn't want any of them to be a part of. Thankfully Lord Brooke followed.

"Sit." Hugh released Irene's arm so she could sit in the seat in front of his desk. A chair which had seen many a disciplinary session in fact; it was the same one Eleanor had frequently found herself bent over for her various transgressions. The chair itself was as comfortable as ever, but the wide, cushy armrests had a much darker use. One Irene hadn't been introduced to yet. Hugh leaned against the desk directly in front of her, basically looming. Since she was seated she felt even smaller than usual with him hovering over her like that.

"Viscount Petersham," Alex said from behind her. The tension growing between Irene and Hugh changed as Hugh focused his attention behind her where Alex was standing. She felt abject relief that her friend had not abandoned her. The moment she'd stopped trying to figure out how exactly she'd gotten into the position she had with Alex and starting thinking about what Hugh might do once they were home, she'd known deep down that she was in for another spanking.

Worse, some part of her felt as though she deserved it. She had basically thrown herself at Alex, which had not been her intention... and Hugh had seen them. The implacable look on his face didn't entirely obscure the hurt and disappointment in his sapphire eyes. Irene knew it was due to her. Still, she didn't want it. She worried how much more severe a punishment for her scandalous behavior might be compared to the spanking she'd had before. Were Hugh's true colors about to be revealed? Would he beat her bloody with some horrible instrument?

Not with her white knight about. As always, she knew Alex would protect her and she took comfort in that security.

"I just want you to know that... the interlude in the garden wasn't what it looked like." Alex blew out a breath. "I'm not... entirely sure what it was..."

"I do believe you may have been caught in the crosshairs of a marital dispute, Lord Brooke," Hugh said. His voice was cold but civil as he faced the other man. Irene peeked up at him, keeping her head bowed, doing her best not to draw attention to herself.

"I apologize for my part in it nonetheless," Alex said firmly. It was obvious he didn't want to cause any trouble with Hugh for his own part, which Irene appreciated. Hugh could make it very difficult for her and Alex to continue their friendship if he took a dislike to the man.

"I'm not inclined to blame you," Hugh replied. His gaze dropped to Irene and hardened. Clenching her hands in her lap, she focused on them and decided to stop peeking up at him. What she saw only made her more anxious. "I do appreciate your efforts to nullify the issue for the gossip mongers. It seemed to work. They won't be speaking about anything other than my wife's 'delicacy,' which could have any number of reasons." There was only the slightest emphasis on the way he said 'my wife.' "I assume you accompanied us to hear Irene's explanation for her behavior."

Since he didn't reply, Irene assumed he nodded. Anxiety welled up inside of her again.

"I don't have an explanation," she burst out, glaring up at Hugh as if it was all his fault. "I don't know... It was just the night. And the moonlight. And the excitement. I wasn't thinking... I don't know..." She ran out of breath, panting raggedly.

The bright blue eyes of her husband caught and held her, measuring her defiance and finding her wanting. The rebelliousness seemed to drain out of her under his steady gaze.

"Well whether there's an explanation or not, there *will* be repercussions," Hugh said finally. His voice was low, controlled. Looking up at Alex he nodded his head. "Lord Brooke, I apologize for my wife's behavior. You can be assured it will not be repeated in the future. I think she and I need to... speak alone now if you don't mind."

"No!" Wild panic filled Irene as she tried to push away from Hugh, but the chair was too heavy a piece of furniture for her to be able to move. She twisted, clutching at the broad arm, ready to crawl over it if need be, catching a look of intense surprise on Alex's face. "You can't leave me here with him, he'll *beat* me."

CHAPTER 15

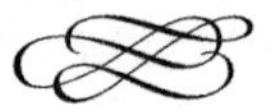

The reaction Irene received from the men was not at all what she expected. Alex frowned and looked at Hugh, as if asking for confirmation, Hugh's expression went from shocked to insulted to a kind of angry glare. The arms braced across his chest tightened. He didn't looked at Alex once and he didn't look at all guilty.

"I have never once in my life beaten a woman."

"You beat me just last week!"

"I *spanked* you, Irene. A well-deserved spanking you were warned you were going to receive if you approached Rex, and you did it anyway."

"That just proves you're the kind of man who would beat his wife given the chance!" Irene looked pleadingly up at Alex, her stalwart defender, the man who'd never failed to save her. He'd been her white knight all her life, it was why she'd fallen in love with him, why she'd followed her mother's dictate and agreed to any means of being with him after he'd married even though it meant marrying another man.

The fury growing in Hugh's eyes had almost set them ablaze, she was sure she needed Alex's protection more than ever. Yet he looked like he was hesitating.

He glanced at Hugh, obviously hesitant to intervene.

"Tell him Alex! You'd never spank a woman."

The man of her dreams let all of his breath out on a huff as he looked down at her. "Honestly Irene, it's becoming more of a temptation every day."

Her jaw dropped. It was the last thing in the world she'd expected him to say. Alex, wonderful and chivalrous Alex, Alex whom she'd loved all her life... he would beat a woman?

The crestfallen look on her face made it clear to both men that Alex had shattered some kind of belief or illusion she had about him. The kind of look a child had when they first realized life wasn't fair and not everything they wished for would come true.

Something about this entire situation had sparked an emotion akin to jealousy in Hugh's breast. He'd come to realize that Irene put her childhood friend on a pedestal, one which had just taken a severe blow. Perhaps the same kind of pedestal she'd put him on before he'd spanked her. It irked him to think Lord Brooke might retain his pedestal, but considering some of the conversations he'd had with Edwin and Wesley pertaining to Lord Brooke's interest in domestic discipline as well as the few hints Lord Brooke himself had dropped, he thought he had a solution to that.

"Lord Brooke, perhaps under the circumstances you might wish to stay as my wife and I have our discussion," Hugh said dryly, his eyes locked onto Irene's face to catch every nuance of her reaction. "That way you can assure yourself she is not being *beaten* and I can give you some instruction on the proper way to spank a deserving wife. You did seem to have some interest the last time we discussed the issue."

There was only a moment of silence. "That would be much appreciated, Viscount Petersham. Thank you."

"Hugh, please."

"And you may call me Alex."

Irene felt as though her world had tilted on its axis; she was actually dizzy from the events taking place right before her eyes. The view she'd always had of Alex had come crashing down around her with just a few simple words. Not only was he not going to save her from

Hugh, he *approved* of Hugh spanking her. He was going to learn how to do so himself.

Licking her dry lips, her hands clenched so tightly on her lap that her knuckles were white, she pled with him. "Alex… don't… please…"

"Irene," he said gently, starting to kneel down to look her more easily in the face before he glanced at Hugh. When her husband nodded his permission, Alex went down on one knee and took one of her cold little hands in his. "Your behavior tonight… it went past improper. I don't know what you were thinking. You shouldn't have spoken to your husband the way you did when he asked. Or accused him of something he hasn't done. There are men in the *ton* who do beat their wives, leave them black and blue. I've become friends with Edwin, Wesley, and Hugh and I know none of them are like that, they are all honorable men who are honor-bound to care for their wives. That means disciplining you when you've done something wrong, and tonight..."

The gentle tone he was using was one she'd heard all her life, but the words were all wrong. Her champion had quit the field, leaving her alone. Averting her gaze, she snatched her hand back from him. She heard his sigh as he stood.

"Irene, do you know why you're being punished?" Hugh asked, his voice low and implacable. She hated that it sent a shiver through her which had nothing to do with fear or anger. How could her lower body be tingling at a time like this?!

"Yes," she said sullenly.

Because somehow she'd lost complete control of herself and behaved like a loose woman, throwing herself at Alex. That hadn't been what she'd meant to do. It hadn't. Not tonight anyway. She was so angry with herself, angry at Hugh, angry at Alex, angry at everyone who had helped to put her in this awful situation.

"Ensuring she understands she's being spanked for a reason is important," Hugh said in an almost lecturing tone to Alex. Her cheeks flared with heat and began to burn with embarrassment; she kept her gaze at their pant legs, not wanting to look at either of them. "You must confirm she understands why she's being punished otherwise there's no lesson being learned. Irene, *why* am I going to be spanking you tonight?"

She knew she should have been seething, but hearing Alex murmuring his understanding of Hugh's instruction took the spark right out of her. There was going to be no saving her from what she had done. Alex had obviously been made uncomfortable by her actions, her plans were in ruins around her and she wasn't even sure she cared because the perfect man hadn't turned out to be what she thought he was.

"Because I behaved improperly at Lady Cowper's," she responded dully, her shoulders slumping.

Cupping her chin under his hand, Hugh forced her to look at him. He didn't like the lack of spirit he saw in her eyes but he knew he still needed to discipline her. There was no point in telling her there would be consequences for her actions if he didn't bother to follow through.

"Yes. Although there won't be a scandal thanks to Lord Brooke's quick thinking, but do you understand how badly your little scene could have come off to everyone? Especially since we've just returned from our honeymoon. You could have shamed yourself, me, Lord Brooke, our families… the *ton* would have talked about nothing else for weeks."

A lone tear rolled down Irene's face. As soon as Hugh had interrupted them and she'd realized how brazen she'd been, how clear the pathway they were standing on was, and how close she came to bringing two men to blows over her she'd felt horrible.

"I'm sorry," she whispered. "I truly didn't intend… I mean… I didn't… I'm sorry."

"I'm glad to hear you say that." Hugh kissed her forehead and let her face drop again. "Stand up and lean over the arm of the chair." His voice was still gentle but stern, the kindness had leached out of it.

Keeping her eyes averted, not wanting to see the expression on Alex's face—even if she now realized he wasn't the man of her dreams, he was still her childhood friend and it was humiliating to have him witnessing this—she complied. The arm of the chair was surprisingly soft against her hips and stomach, cradling them, although it pushed her bottom high in the air. Turning her face towards the back of the chair, she curled her arms around her head, doing her best to pretend she wasn't bent over, awaiting a spanking.

"If you'd like a chair like this, I can send you the direction of the maker," Hugh said, and she knew he was talking to Alex again. "This one was purchased by my father. It's comfortable to sit in but the arms are wider than usual, which helps when you're about to be punished." He chuckled. "I should know, although I was in this position a lot less often than my sister. I'll try to go over the same things my father did with me; Eleanor gave me plenty of practice growing up."

Even though she'd originally wanted to close her ears, Irene couldn't help but be engrossed by this astounding information. Strong, fiery Eleanor had been spanked? A lot? How did she remain so… so…

"Does Edwin have a chair like this?"

"No, he prefers an over the knee approach," Hugh said. "He says it's more intimate at which point I usually bow out of the conversation." Alex chuckled.

It took everything Irene had not to stifle a gasp. To her, Edwin and Eleanor had seemed like the perfect couple. So obviously attentive to each other, so obviously well-fitted. To hear that Edwin spanked his wife, that Eleanor allowed it… the entire way she saw the world was changing tonight. It was almost enough to distract her from being bent over the arm of a chair in front of her husband and her oldest friend.

She felt almost dazed, reviewing everything she'd ever seen between her sister-in-law and her husband in her head, ignoring Hugh as he told Alex to stay where he was since it was a good viewing location. A moment later she would be thankful for the positioning as Hugh lifted her skirts, obviously intent on spanking her bare bottom. From Alex's position he was able to see the upper curves of her buttocks and what Hugh was doing, but the rest of her private areas remained the purview of her husband.

The entire situation felt surreal, as if she was dreaming or as if she had become detached from her body. How could such a thing truly be happening after all? That Alex not only proved himself to be unworthy of the love and devotion she'd always attributed to him, but that he would encourage Hugh to spank her and think to learn from it.

"Spread your legs Irene," Hugh ordered, resting his hand on the exposed upper curve of her buttock rather possessively. "This position makes it harder for her to clench against the slaps, which makes them more effective. If you ever have to use a paddle or tawse or even a birch then it makes it harder for her to injure herself accidentally." Feeling his wife tensing under at the mention of such instruments, Hugh rubbed her bottom. He was feeling decidedly jealous about Lord Brooke—Alex—seeing Irene in such a state but it was more important his wife understand he was not a monster for disciplining her. Even more so, it was important she understood her childhood friend approved of Hugh's methods and would not save her from them.

He still wasn't sure if Irene had truly meant to kiss Lord Brooke, the way it had seemed to his eyes, or what she had been doing or thinking, but he was determined she realize her friend was certainly not "better" than Hugh, as she seemed to imply by her assertion that Lord Brooke would never spank a woman.

"My personal preference is for nothing more severe than a spanking," he said calmly, feeling the slight relaxation that occurred under his hand when he said so. "However, some transgressions require greater consequences. I certainly had more than one instance of practicing with both a tawse and the birch with my sister."

"Do you keep one of each on hand?" Alex asked, shocking Irene. A quiver went through her. He actually sounded interested.

"I have a tawse of course, and a paddle." Both were in a cabinet across the room; he'd been on the receiving end of both as a young lad. The tawse was about 2 feet long, a strap of stiffened well-worn leather; the paddle was a large circular wooden instrument which would thwack resoundingly against the entire cheek of a buttock. "A birch is best fresh so I don't keep one on hand. My father did, but that was due to Eleanor's constant need for it rather than his preference. I never thought it would be something I might require."

None of this was helping Irene, although she was still having trouble believing that this was actually happening. Hugh could feel her buttocks attempting to clench over and over again, obviously in trepidation over the litany of punishments she might receive. He hoped after hearing the options she would choose to demonstrate more restraint in the future, in all things.

"Hmmm." The contemplative and slightly far away expression on Lord Brooke's face was interesting. Hugh took heart observing Alex's complete disinterest in Irene's exposed bottom, even if he didn't have a very good view of it. It seemed like he was thinking about some other female. Possibly his estranged wife?

But he needed to focus on his own wife now. His cock had been standing at attention since he'd turned up her skirts, it was all he could do not to rub his hand all over her luscious bottom and dip his fingers down into her quim which he could see was clearly dewed with arousal. Just as had happened the first time he'd disciplined her, her body was reacting in an unexpected manner.

"Irene. I'm going to spank you now. And you're going to count each one as I do so. If you miss any they will not count towards the total. Do you understand?"

"Yes," she whispered, feeling lightheaded. The hand on her bottom was rather gentle and yet… how could Hugh do this to her?

How could Alex allow him to?

SMACK!

The painful, smarting blow to her bottom made her yelp, bringing her back to the harsh reality that no matter how surreal the situation might feel it *was* really happening.

"Irene, you have to count."

"One." The word was blurted out and she felt a shocking surge of gratitude Hugh had reminded her to count rather than making her start over. It was a revelation to realize she felt gratitude rather than anger at what he was doing, but it was as if her fury had been wiped away by resignation and the realization that she had no support from her white knight.

SMACK!

"Two!"

The word almost choked her as she heard Alex suck in a breath, reminding her that this punishment was being witnessed by a man she'd thought would save her from it.

SMACK!

"Three!"

Counting gave her something to do as Hugh alternated between her cheeks, igniting a slow burn which grew in between the sharp sting whenever his palm impacted against her flesh. Every smack seemed to hurt more and more as he covered her bottom with his palm, turning every inch of creamy flesh a bright pink that slowly began to darken towards red. Tears smarted in her eyes, her fingers clutched at the cushion on the bottom of the chair.

"Eighteen!"

SMACK!

His hand landed on the spot where her thigh met her bottom, the immediate pain was sharper and much more intense than she'd experienced so far and she let out a gasping yelp. Several tears dripped down her cheeks but she was too busy squeezing the chair's cushion in a reflexive grip so as not to reach back and attempt to cover her bottom to wipe them away.

Fingers stroked the sore spot he'd just smacked. "Irene, this is the last time I will remind you."

It took her a moment to realize what he was talking about and then she frantically tried to remember what the last number she had said was.

"Nineteen."

SMACK! His hand landed on the sit spot of her other leg.

"TWENTY!"

She moaned as he put his hand on her bottom, gently touching the flaming skin. Was it over? Slumped over the arm of the chair she felt the tears well up and spill over.

"Sometimes, especially for a lengthy punishment, it's best to allow a few moments for recovery and to let the initial sting sink in," Hugh explained, reminding her of Alex's presence yet again. It was amazing how easy it was for her to forget he was there and each reminder brought a new wave of humiliation.

Especially because now, as Hugh caressed the hot skin of her bottom, she could feel the strange tingling between her legs announcing her inexplicable reaction. A kind of despair followed her embarrassment. How could her body react the same way as it did when Hugh kissed and caressed her?

"We're halfway through, sweetheart," Hugh said almost comfortingly, rubbing his hand on the small of her back, which was exposed and untouched. She did take comfort from his tone and touch, even as she whimpered at hearing her ordeal wasn't over yet.

There was forgiveness in the way he spoke to her, even as he prepared for the second part of her punishment. Forgiveness she craved. Unlike the incident with Rex, she'd known from the beginning that she had done something wrong. She'd hated the way Hugh had looked at her when he'd come upon her and Alex in the garden, the way he'd looked at her when he'd asked for an explanation and she hadn't been able to give him one. This spanking felt merited and she felt strangely safer, despite Hugh's talk of paddles and other instruments of torture, she believed him when he said he preferred a spanking.

And now that she knew a spanking didn't necessarily mean a frightening cane which would result in evil looking welts and broken skin, the terror that had accompanied her first spanking had completely dissipated. It didn't make the spanking hurt any less, but it meant she wasn't shaking in fear of what was to come, she just had to endure what was happening.

"Spread your legs again, Irene," he said gently but implacably. As she'd rested her legs had drifted back together, her bottom clenching as her body attempted to assimilate the burning pain of her punishment. A shudder went through her body as she complied, exposing her glistening pussy again. The coppery curls around her pink lips were dark with moisture, make his cock throb in response. "This will be twenty-one. Don't forget to count."

SMACK!

"Twenty-one."

In some ways Hugh knew it might be more effective if he were to enforce the counting without reminding her, but he wanted to encourage her cooperation and submission to the necessary discipline. Since she seemed to be doing so, he intended on making it as easy as possible on her—as easy as he could anyway. He correctly interpreted her acceptance of the punishment as indication of her feelings of guilt as well as her realization Alex wasn't going to protect her from it.

SMACK!

"Twenty-two."

For this second round Hugh had moderated the strength of his slaps, not wanting to overwhelm her now that her skin was already dark pink and smarting. He was spreading the spanking out over the entire expanse of her bottom, doing his best to cover every last inch of her creamy skin. From his position at the desk, Lord Brooke was watching with a kind of scientific fascination. The kind of fascination Hugh had felt whenever he'd witnessed or participated in one of Eleanor's punishments; not at all sexual, but rather a kind of astonishment and the desire to see the results.

All in all it was a very reassuring experience for Hugh. Time and again Alex had shown nothing more than a brotherly interest in Irene. He was still concerned about Irene's actions towards Alex, but her submission to the punishment helped to allay some of those concerns.

SMACK!

"Thirty" sob "four."

Irene's legs kicked out every so often and he would lightly smack the back of her thigh to get her back into place. The blows were so light he didn't even have to explain to her that they weren't part of her punishment, she would just let out a pathetic little whimpering sound and move herself back into position. This was a much more controlled and less passionate punishment than her last one, on both their parts, and yet it didn't dim Hugh's erotic interest in the least.

The way her flesh jiggled, the hot temperature of her skin, the swollen lips of her pussy and the sweet slickness of her sex all combined to excite him immensely. Alex's presence helped him to hold his impulses in check, otherwise he might be testing the level of wetness between Irene's lips in between smacks to her bottom, which had turned a bright cherry red under his hand.

SMACK!

"FORTY!"

There was a measure of triumph and relief in Irene's voice as she counted out the last of her punishment. Her quivering body slumped, small sobs wracking her frame. She didn't even hear Hugh asking Alex for some privacy as her husband lifted her up from her position bent over the chair and wrapped her in his arms. Although her skirts had fallen back down they didn't provide much cushion as he cradled her on his lap, her face tucked into his shoulder.

The sudden comfort only made her cry harder. It felt so nice to be cuddled and soothed, to hear Hugh's deep voice telling her what a good girl she'd been and how proud of her he was for admitting her wrong doing and taking her discipline. She clung to him, whimpering every time her bottom shifted and pressed against his hard thighs and even harder cock.

It was obvious he'd become aroused during her discipline. She hated that the area between her legs tingled incessantly now the actual spanking was over. The respite only allowed her to focus on the very different burning in her core, a needy burn, the heat nearly as hot as the fiery surface of her bottom.

"I'm sorry," she whispered. "I truly am."

"I know, sweetheart," Hugh said, kissing the top of her head. While he might not understand why she'd put herself in such a compromising position with Lord Brooke, he truly believed she regretted her actions even before her punishment. The 'why' of the incident still bothered him, but he was enjoying their current closeness—especially after her coldness since her last spanking—too much to bring it up.

Perhaps that coldness partially explained her desire to find some affection with a trusted childhood friend. The theory helped to quell Hugh's jealousy somewhat, especially since Irene was currently curled up in *his* lap and seeking comfort from him.

Once her crying had subsided Hugh sent her up to their room. "I'll join you there shortly," he said, giving her another kiss on her forehead before gently pushing her out into the hall.

Lord Brooke stood there, obviously intrigued by the obvious closeness being exhibited between Irene and Hugh despite the fact she was obviously walking gingerly due to her burning backside. "Good night, Irene."

"Good night, Alex," said a much subdued Irene, not looking at him as she passed by. There was a slight coolness to her manner, as if to save her pride or possibly due to Alex's lack of support for her. His usual stony expression covered any reaction he might have had to her diffidence.

Both he and Hugh watched as she slowly walked away and disappeared around the corner. Although Hugh desperately wanted to join her immediately in their bedroom, he also recognized he needed to see Lord Brooke on his way.

"Is she going to be alright?" Alex asked, his frowning features showing his concern as he peered after the subdued redhead.

"Very," said Hugh. A small smile quirked his lips. "I was adamant Edwin not go into too much detail about his relationship with my sister, but both he and Wesley assured me that spanking a wife is a very different matter than spanking my sister and I've found that to be true. It incites an entirely different kind of reaction and I can guarantee that before she goes to sleep tonight Irene will be *very* well."

"I believe they hinted something similar to me," murmured Alex with a faint smile, looking reassured. "I appreciate your discretion."

"As I do yours." Hugh hesitated but he had to ask. "Do you know what happened tonight?"

For a moment Alex seemed to struggle with himself, emotions flickering across his face. It was an unprecedented display as far as Hugh could tell.

"Much as I hate to admit it, I think my wife might have been right about something."

"Lady Grace?"

"Ah. Of course you're acquainted with her, being Eleanor's brother." Alex leaned back against the wall, closing his eyes for a moment as if gathering himself. The resignation that settled upon his hard features made Hugh feel rather sorry for him. While Hugh had never particularly liked Grace, he hadn't disliked her either. He'd never really had an opinion on her marriage, although he'd always been surprised at the fact that her affairs didn't incite stronger condemnation from Society at large. "Grace once told me Irene idolized me. She seemed rather jealous and spiteful at the time, I thought she was just making things up to be angry with me. She wanted me to be less friendly, which of course I was unwilling to do as I've always taken care of Irene the way an older brother would."

"Hm."

"Grace said Irene's feelings for me went beyond the kind of relationship I felt we had." Alex shook his head, as if he trying to shake the new revelation from himself. He looked at Hugh, his eyes apologetic. "I certainly never thought Grace's accusations had any basis in reality, but tonight... Irene seemed determined to try and push past our usual interactions. But I could swear she wasn't, isn't, attracted to me. We just don't have that kind of connection."

"But she does idolize you," Hugh said with a sigh. "I think that much is clear. She expected you to side with her and to save her from... well, me."

"I think inviting me to stay and learn from your methods was probably the best approach you could have taken," Alex said. The look they exchanged was full of male sympathy for each other's positions. "Although I appreciate how difficult it must have been for you."

"If it means she doesn't continue to look at you like you're her hero and I'm a villain, then it will have been worth it," said Hugh dryly. He was still feeling a bit affronted he'd been cast in such a role, although logically he supposed he could understand it.

"I'm quite sure she no longer sees me in such a light." The sad resignation on Alex's face was back and Hugh felt a pang of sympathy for him. Considering the low esteem his wife obviously held him in, Irene's adoration and friendship had probably meant quite a bit to him.

"She won't hold it against you forever," he said consolingly.

"I certainly hope not." Alex sighed as he stood up straight. "I already have one female in my life who is all too skilled at holding a grudge, I don't relish the idea of having another. I should be off, so you can ah, conclude your evening."

Smiling, Hugh led him to the door before heading immediately upstairs towards the bedroom. He didn't want to leave his wife too long to her own devices.

FLORA HELPED IRENE TO UNDRESS, exclaiming over the reddened area of Irene's bottom. It was obvious this punishment had been much more prolonged than the one she'd received before.

"He didn't use anything other than his hand," Irene said, almost wonderingly as she looked over her shoulder in the mirror. Flora had put her in a nightgown, which she now had hiked up to her waist so she could examine the damage. Her buttocks very closely resembled a heart in both shape and color, the skin felt tight and hot to the touch.

"Doesn't look like he needed to," Flora muttered under her breath as she bustled around, putting away Irene's evening gown and jewelry.

"Alex didn't seem to think there was anything wrong with it." That was something she was still having trouble assimilating. Did it mean Alex wasn't the man she thought he was? Or did it mean there was truly nothing shocking about Hugh spanking her?

Running her fingers over the fiery patch of skin, she hissed a little. It stung when she touched it and only ached a bit when she didn't. The sensation reminded her of when she'd once stood out in the sun for too long and her skin had burned red and hot to the touch, an effect that had lingered for days and left her more freckled than ever. Her mother had not been pleased.

What would her mother say about Hugh's disciplinary methods? Flora seemed cautious but not entirely surprised. Eleanor was apparently subject to the same methods and had been her entire life. That had been a revelation on more than one level. Perhaps her sister-in-law could give Irene some insight into Irene's turmoiled emotions and the strange reactions her body had to such stimulation. But how could she admit, even to a sister-in-law, that she was inexplicably aroused by such a dreadful act?

Still, she was visiting Eleanor tomorrow to engage her help on deciphering the social rounds and accepting invitations. Perhaps she could somehow bring up some of her questions? Nibbling her lip, Irene studied her bottom. It would mean subjecting herself to more embarrassment, but truly what could be more mortifying than the experiences she'd already had this evening? From beginning to finish it had been a debacle.

The door opened and Hugh strode in, still fully clothed in his evening dress. The sapphire of his waistcoat brought out the blue of his eyes, even in the candlelight, as they scanned the room. Blushing, Irene dropped the hem of her nightgown and turned, her hands automatically moving to cup the burning swells of her bottom as if to hide them from view. She knew very well that the shade of red her skin had achieved was visible through the thin fabric of her gown.

Fortunately Hugh wasn't looking at her right away, he was looking at Flora. "Out."

The maid bobbed a curtsy and fled, shooting a sympathetic and what she probably imagined was an encouraging look over her shoulder to Irene. Then his attention turned to Irene, his lips curving in an anticipatory smile that made her heart begin to pound. It was so unfair how he could affect her like this when she should be angry at him for the state of her poor bottom, but the truth was she was tingling all over. The throbbing of her bottom seemed to beat in time with her treacherous pulse as Hugh yanked off his cravat and began to remove his coat.

Shuffling her feet, Irene stared at the floor, all too aware that underneath her nightgown her nipples were stiff and eager. Lord help her, she *wanted* to engage in marital relations. Had secretly hoped Hugh would follow her up her to help her quench the need she'd become all too aware of once her punishment was over. Cupping her hands over her bottom, she could feel the heat of her skin through the thin fabric.

Then Hugh was standing in front of her, completely and gloriously nude. She stared at his broad chest with its golden covering of hair, the broad planes of his muscles, the impressive breadth of his shoulders. Licking her lips, she shifted her weight back and forth as she waited to find out what he would do.

There was no question he wanted her, his cock was practically pressing against his stomach, but she felt ashamed of her desire for him. Despite how brazen she'd become over their honeymoon, she couldn't make the first move in this situation, she just couldn't.

"Here, let me help you with this," her husband murmured, stepping forward and putting his hands on her hips, grasping handfuls of fabric. He lifted the nightgown over her head, leaving her naked in front of him.

Peeking up at him, she tucked her hands behind her back again to press her cooler palms against her bottom and he groaned and wrapped his arms around her. Her head instinctively flew back as his lips descended and she whimpered as he kissed her. The long length of his body was crushed against her softness as his arms tightened. One hand slid down to grip her bottom, exploring the hot flesh her own hands weren't covering and she moaned, opening her mouth to his questing tongue.

The feel of her hot skin against his palm and her soft body writhing against his shredded the last of Hugh's control and he spun around with Irene still in his arms. She was so light and small, he lifted her easily while thoroughly kissing her. He couldn't get enough of her mouth, the taste of her; he devoured her as he moved them to the bed, laying her down gently on it before he climbed on top of her.

Irene whimpered again as her bottom bounced gently against the covers; despite how soft the bedding normally felt, now it was as if it were abrading her sensitive skin. But she found such irritations were easily swept away as Hugh's body came down on hers, insistently parting her legs. The need that had been growing inside of her flared higher, she was almost overwhelmed by the growing pleasure inside her core which was wiping away the painful part of the punishment.

His hands were gentle as he caressed her breasts, her sides, her thighs… she moaned as he grasped her legs and jerked her body downwards, dragging her backside over the sheets while simultaneously bringing her wet slit in contact with his rigid manhood. Reaching up she clung to his shoulders as he brought himself to her entrance. Neither of them were inclined to draw out the initial intimacies, their desires had already been advanced by Irene's spanking and then the wait between her punishment and their coming together.

The channel of her body was slippery and wet as he pushed in, her muscles clenching around him to draw him deeper and they both groaned with relief and excitement as Hugh sank into her. Feeling his wife's frantic squirming beneath him as she rubbed her swollen folds against the hard flatness of his groin, Hugh released the last reins of his control and gave himself over to his urge to claim and conquer. The remnants of his jealousy reared, fueling his hard, pounding thrusts into her body. He drank in her whimpers of pleasure and pain as the friction of his cock burned her wonderfully and the throbbing pulse of her bottom increased with every sinking thrust. Irene clung to him, sobbing his name whenever his mouth left hers as the pleasure of his rod sliding in and out of her came to a head.

Grasping her hips, his long fingers curved around to press against the hot flesh of her chastened cheeks and Irene screamed with ecstasy as the mingled pain and pleasure sent her soaring. This was not the playful, gentle loving of their honeymoon or even the creative, exciting sexual exploration; this was hot, passionate need blended with erotic pain that set her nerves sizzling and her mind shattering under the overwhelming mix. It was not the kind of banquet one could sup on every night, but it fulfilled a need, a craving, that dwelled deep in both their bodies.

The spurts of seed Hugh planted deep inside of Irene as she writhed beneath him in a painfully pleasurable climax helped to calm his demons. He rocked against her, filling her womb in the most primal way a man can claim a woman. As she whimpered and moaned beneath him, her own movements slowing as the gentle grind of her husband's body against hers, she felt surprisingly content. At least, until her bottom was pressed against the sheets again, a spurt of flame flickering through her.

Almost tenderly, Hugh rolled off of her and pulled her back against him so she was snuggled up to his front. One hand cupped her breast, the other arm was under her head and wrapped around her possessively. After a few moments of squirming into a relatively comfortable position considering the state of her buttocks, Irene relaxed in her husband's arms and sank into an exhausted slumber.

CHAPTER 16

It would have taken a much less astute and observant person than Eleanor to realize her sister-in-law had received some measure of discipline the night before. Of course, it helped that Eleanor was also intimately acquainted with the signs of such activities. Irene's expression, whenever she wasn't concentrating on smiling or remaining neutral, was pensive and distant as if her mind was somewhere else entirely. Since she had requested Eleanor's help with the current conversation at hand, Eleanor knew it wasn't because Irene was disinterested in the topic. And, of course, there was the way Irene moved and oh so carefully sat. Even now, despite the fact she was on the most comfortably cushioned chair in the drawing room, Irene was sitting rather gingerly.

In deference to Irene's pride, Eleanor didn't call attention to her sister-in-law's obvious affliction other than to ensure she sat in the most comfortable chair.

"Now, you'll want to attend Lady Stewart's tea but you should skip her ball."

"Because Lady Morningwood's having a ball that night as well?"

"Yes, and because while Lady Stewart's teas are perfectly acceptable, her parties tend to cater to a... ah... more focused crowd. Her card room is always much more lively than her dance floor."

"Oh... I see."

The somewhat dismayed look on Irene's face as she realized just how lost she was when it came to knowing the intricacies of maneuvering successfully around the *ton* made Eleanor's heart ache a little. Seriously, what had the young woman's mother trained her in? Or had she just steered Irene around for her own benefit without ever thinking of what she should learn for when she was on her own?

Unfortunately Eleanor could picture the scenario all too easily. No matter; she had found she rather enjoyed Irene's company. Even when she was obviously slightly agitated and distracted she had a much more restful presence than Grace. It was too bad the two women didn't get along, she had a feeling they would be good influences on each other. Irene was a little too concerned with propriety and Grace truly wasn't quite enough.

"Don't worry," Eleanor said sympathetically, reaching over to pat Irene's hand. "This Season is almost over and it truly won't take you very long to pick up on the little nuances which define which invitations you and Hugh should accept. You're a very quick study."

"I suppose I have to be," said Irene rather glumly. Despite her fiery red hair she truly didn't seem to have much spirit at all that Eleanor could see. Then again she supposed many women among the *ton* would seem lacking in spirit compared to her and Grace. "Perhaps Hugh will want to stay out in the country next Season."

"No, no, no," Eleanor scolded gently. "I'm sure my brother would love to do just that, but it's your responsibility to ensure he attends to his social duties. Of course, you won't have to come to the events that are always held before the Season truly starts anymore since you're not trying to make a match of it, but important business is done during these balls. It won't be so bad, I promise. You can always come to me for advice about anything."

"Thank you so much, I truly don't know what I would have done without you."

"You would have managed," Eleanor said kindly. She was rather touched by the sincere gratitude in Irene's eyes. Although she'd worried a little bit about her bold phrasing, it was obvious Irene was accustomed to being directed and felt much more comfortable with someone else handling the reins. It would take careful handling to help her build up her confidence without being obvious about it.

Irene hadn't seemed to be so shyly submissive the night before at Lady Cowper's, so Eleanor supposed Hugh had done something during their honeymoon to help her come out of her shell a bit. She seemed to have retreated back into it, but Eleanor was sure that probably had something to do with the tender state of her bottom and obviously being in over her head.

"I do have one question," Irene mumbled, her voice so low and words so jumbled she was almost incoherent. Her vibrant green eyes were focused on the invitations she was clutching tightly in her lap, the pile she and Eleanor had sorted for her to respond with affirmative.

"Yes?" Eleanor leaned closer, her voice soft and encouraging. Her new position allowed her to see the flaming pink of Irene's cheeks, a color which clashed horribly with her red hair and yet was really rather fetching.

Being cast in a position of responsibility was rather new and exciting for Eleanor. She had found she quite enjoyed being the knowledgeable one and helping her sister-in-law.

"Last night... Hugh... he said..." Irene's cheeks were slowly becoming blotchy with intense reds and pinks that trickled from her face down to her neck. It was with a sudden jolt that Eleanor realized Irene's question had nothing to do with social engagements. With great bravery, Irene gathered herself and her words came out in a whispered rush, eyes flicking to the closed doors as if afraid someone might walk in while she spoke. "Hugh said he's spanked you before and that LordHydespanksyounowtoo."

The sudden silence that reigned in the room made Irene's panting sound extremely loud. She was staring at the floor while Eleanor found herself studying the ceiling, her own cheeks feeling rather flushed now.

"I'm sorry," Irene whispered. "I shouldn't have brought it up."

"I'm not angry," Eleanor said, reluctantly looking at her sister-in-law, but Irene's emerald eyes were riveted to the floor. "I just don't quite know what to say... Yes. I've received my fair share of spankings from both my father and Hugh, and now from Edwin." Although she kept her voice as calm and even as she could, she could still feel a hot blush rising. This wasn't a topic of conversation normally discussed—her own mother hadn't wanted to hear any details of Eleanor's punishments and she hadn't even tried to tell Grace.

"Really? I just... I can't imagine you letting anyone..." Irene finally looked up at her again, her expression rather shocked.

"I don't recall I ever had a choice," Eleanor said, somewhat bemused. This was not at all an appropriate conversation, but considering Irene had overcome her usual sense of propriety to bring it up she felt as though she should indulge her a little further. "My father spanked both of us on a regular basis and I supposed I was always a bit used to it because of that. With Edwin… I admit, one time I ran from him but once he caught me I regretted it."

"No one's ever... I'd never..." Irene's eyes and voice dropped again. "Not until Hugh. He's spanked me twice now. I don't know... I don't know how I should feel or..." Her voice trickled off.

A surge of sympathy engulfed Eleanor. Poor Irene. At least Eleanor had always known what the consequences of her bad behavior was, Irene still seemed to be assimilating the idea that Hugh might take his hand to her backside. Then again, from what she'd seen last night she couldn't deny her sister-in-law might have deserved it.

Perhaps Irene might like some space from Hugh to think things through...

"You know... Irene... I've been considering taking a trip out to the country and I need a companion to go with me. Perhaps you would be interested?" Traveling with her sister-in-law would certainly satisfy propriety. "I thought I might go to Bath to visit my mother."

"You won't be traveling with Lord Hyde?"

"No." Eleanor's calm expression became slightly more intense as

Irene looked at her with some confusion and a kind of dawning curiosity. "I would like to spend some time away from my husband at this juncture."

"Oh..." The idea appealed immensely. Achieving distance from both Hugh and Alex so she could sort out her feelings away from Society and in the calm of the country sounded wonderful. "I think... I think that sounds lovely. When?"

"It's only a few weeks until the Season is over and then Edwin plans to visit his parents, I'm sure Hugh will be returning to his estates at the same time."

A few weeks seemed like an interminable amount of time from where Irene was sitting, but she also knew that with all the social events it would pass quickly enough. Hope sprang up in her breast. Some time in Eleanor's company where she could perhaps gather the courage to speak more explicitly with her sister-in-law, away from Hugh and Alex so she could think, away from the bustle of the city... it sounded perfect.

"I would like that very much."

WHILE THE EVENING before had not quite gone as Hugh had intended, he couldn't deny he'd enjoyed parts of it immensely. Still, the disquiet that Irene had sparked at Lady Cowper's ball hadn't quite died down, despite the fact that she had seemed very much back to her old self before leaving to see his sister. They'd had a perfectly amiable breakfast with each other, without any of the coldness she'd displayed towards him after her first spanking.

Yet he knew he'd been much harsher with her than he had the first time. She'd certainly been sitting gingerly enough at the dining table.

Women. Who could figure?

Well, possibly the man sprawled bonelessly in an armchair in front of him. With no cravat, the top of his shirt unbuttoned and wearing a very rumpled jacket, Wesley was looking more than a little worse for the wear. Not that many ladies would agree with Hugh's assessment, he had to admit. They'd find his devil-may-care dress and scruffy face immensely intriguing, just as they did his piratical looks and roguish charm. It wasn't a tactic Hugh had ever used when he'd been cutting a swath through the accommodating ladies of the *ton*, but he could stand witness it worked very well for the Earl of Spencer.

No, Wesley could read women quite well, his current trouble came from a man.

"So Lord Windham wasn't quite as accommodating as you'd been led to believe?" Hugh asked, his lips quirking even though he had found he no longer found quite as much amusement in an irate husband. Still, it was Wesley and he knew his friend wouldn't presume to step where he'd be unwelcome.

"Not accommodating at all, in fact," Wesley said with a groan, his fingers lightly tracing over the swollen spot on this cheek which was already starting to darken and bruise. "I'd barely even gotten the woman alone to see if we'd even suit before he came crashing in."

"I thought you were currently involved with Lady Lilienfield," Hugh murmured. Not that he was entirely surprised Wesley had gone looking for a fresh conquest, he'd always been rather hard to keep entertained. It would take quite a woman to keep Wesley interested.

Wesley shrugged in response to Hugh's implied question. "Both she and I agreed the attraction had run its course. I gave her a suitably appreciative gift and I'd just begun looking for something to enjoy myself with for the last bit of the Season. Didn't realize it'd be so bloody hard."

"If Lord Windham demands satisfaction you know I'm happy to offer myself as your second, as would Edwin."

"For that matter I suspect Alex would be as well, but I seriously doubt it will come to that. Windham's a hothead but it was patently obvious Lady Windham and I didn't do more than exchange a few kisses... I've been considering ending my Season early."

"Really?" Hugh looked at his friend in surprise. Now that Wesley had returned to England and come back out into Society following his father's death, he hadn't thought anything would make his friend retreat again.

"Oh not over this," Wesley said with a negligent wave of his hand. He yawned, looking very much like a lazy lion contemplating bestirring himself. "Although giving the Windhams some distance is a distinct benefit. No, my mother wrote me again. She's threatening if I don't come and help her with my ward then she's going to come to *me*, ward in tow I assume, and do her best to interfere in my life by match-making."

A palpable hit, Hugh thought, hiding a grin. Although Wesley might be a rake and a rogue and play at being an irresponsible lordling with not a care in the world, Hugh was well aware Wesley was quite responsible about his estates and finances, as well as the business endeavors he's become involved in during his travels, and he could never be harsh to his mother. The Countess had obviously realized her son was finding it much easier to deny her requests and pleas at a distance. If she were to arrive wherever Wesley was and insist on trotting him out to all manner of debutantes, he'd feel forced to humor her.

While the late Earl had been forceful and demanding, it was the Countess who knew how to tug at her sons' heartstrings. Which was why Wesley's brothers had applied to him for support for their desired futures and why Wesley had informed his mother of his support for their wishes by letter. He'd gotten a scathing written reply but that was preferable to the Countess descending in person.

"What did your ward do this time?" Hugh was genuinely curious as Wesley had thoroughly entertained him with the letters from the Countess he'd missed while he'd been away on his honeymoon. Every letter had a new descriptive for her: blue-stocking, hoyden, unmanageable impudence, etc. From what Hugh could tell the girl was even more spirited than Eleanor had been; he didn't envy the Countess or Wesley their tasks.

"Ah," Wesley said, pulling the letter in question from his coat with a flourish and a grin. "I knew you'd ask. Apparently she's now become a brazen hussy."

"Oh my."

"Indeed. My mother says, and I quote, '*The ungrateful brat told me in quite strident tones that she did not appreciate my 'meddling' as she called it. I took the opportunity to remind her that no man wants to marry a young woman who rides astride, as it is remarkably scandalous, especially in public, and the sooner she is wed the sooner she will have her own household and would no longer have to abide my meddling. I thought perhaps such a description would encourage her to curb her behavior at least until I can get her wed and off my hands. Well! The brazen hussy is now throwing herself at the various gentleman we meet, some of them with the worst reputations and who are known fortune hunters, and I'm quite sure she's now not only going to ruin our good name and my reputation, but herself as well. I will not have it be said that any ward under my care was ruined. Wesley, I implore you, if you do not make your way to Bath to assist me within the next month then I will make my way to you.'* She goes on and on."

Finally able to let loose his laughter, Hugh was practically doubled over with mirth. With each letter the Countess of Spencer sent her tone became more irate and her language much less elegant. He'd never thought to hear her utter the term "brazen hussy," and the high-pitched imitation Wesley used to read aloud her words only added to the entertainment value of such a recitation.

Even Wesley was smiling, able to recognize the humor in the situation and in his mother's letter. Since he hadn't met the wench, he didn't feel particularly beholden to finding her a husband or taking care of her, he'd thought he could reliably leave that in his mother's hands. The reality of having a ward was not something which had in any way affected his life, other than entertainment value whenever he'd received another letter from the Countess. But obviously the situation needed to be taken in hand. With his considerable charms, and a strong hand if necessary, he doubted it would take him very much time to make the chit behave well enough to lift the burden from his mother and get her married off so he wouldn't have to deal with her anymore at all. Of course he'd have to make sure she had a suitable husband, despite his mother's obvious frustrations with the wench he knew she would expect him to assist in making a match she could brag of.

Really the letter had come at quite an opportune time.

"So I suppose you'll be off to Bath soon then?" Hugh said as his amusement died down to chuckling. "What will the ladies of London do without you?"

"Hopefully learn to be more discerning about their husbands' inclinations," Wesley said dryly. "And yes, I'm planning to leave within the week. It seems too good an opportunity not to take advantage of, especially since I no longer have anything keeping me here."

"Other than my scintillating company, of course."

"Of course. Although I might find it a dashed bit more scintillating if you'd feed me."

Laughing, Hugh rang for the maid and asked her to put together lunch. Idly he looked at the clock. He'd expected Irene back by now.

"Now then… how are your brothers doing? Have you heard from them recently or only your mother?"

The two friends chatted through lunch, not gossiping of course although a word or two of the latest *on dits* may have indeed been passed along. As they finished their repast, the conversation had segued into business, seeing as Hugh had asked Wesley to start helping him with his investments. While his estates were prosperous enough, both he and Edwin had seen the benefits of diversifying their interests. Most of the *ton* looked down on anything having to do with business, but Wesley had made his fortune at it while he'd been away. All three friends were now financially involved in various endeavors and making quite a bit of money doing it. As long as they didn't discuss with Society at large where they were making their money then it would just be assumed they weren't doing anything out of the ordinary.

Fortunately Wesley had learned quite a bit about making sound investments and so did quite a bit of advising for both Hugh and Edwin who were still learning the ropes. They were debating the wisdom of investing in a certain railroad line when the butler announced Lord Hyde.

"Brandy? Cigar?" Hugh greeted Edwin. "Thank you for bringing Irene home, although you didn't need to."

"Irene?" Edwin frowned at him as he sat down.

"She was with Eleanor all morning," Hugh said, the slightest hint of a frown marring his brow. What on earth could those two still be talking about? "I assumed that since you were here, she had returned with you."

For a long moment Edwin just stared at him, snifter of brandy in hand, his dark eyes inscrutable.

"I'm afraid Irene concluded her visit with Eleanor hours ago," he said very slowly, the gears of his mind obviously turning. "Perhaps she had some shopping to do."

A muscle in Hugh's jaw clenched tight, as did his knuckles around his own snifter. He took a long draw on the cigar in his other hand, allowing his lungs to fill up with the fragrant smoke before blowing it back out again. The action calmed him. Somewhat.

"Of course," Hugh said, forcing a smile to his face. Somehow he felt incredibly reluctant to share the recent trials of his marriage with his friends, although they were both studying him intently, having gotten the wind something was up. Wesley consistently slept with other men's wives and Edwin would never have to worry about Eleanor betraying him with someone else. How could they possibly understand?

Although explaining his concerns to his friends was the least of his worries; the largest looming in his mind was wondering exactly where his wife was and what she was doing. And, possibly, who she was doing it with.

THE OSTRICH FEATHERS LOOKED LUDICROUS. They sprouted from the garish blue turban like weeds in the middle of a flower garden. But Irene knew was not what her mother wanted to hear, so she mouthed the appropriate compliments on what the Baroness claimed was the "latest fashion." After taking her leave from Eleanor, Irene had found herself reluctant to go home and face her husband immediately, feeling a bit guilty about her agreement to go to Bath with Eleanor without even consulting him.

She was torn between the conviction that she should be angry with him as he was a monster who beat her, and the strange awareness that there was something wrong with her conclusion. Not just because Alex had not supported her, although that was part of it. While she no longer thought of him as a knight in shining armor, she was having trouble with the idea he didn't care about her or that he wouldn't protect her if he thought she needed protection.

Which led to the obvious conclusion that he didn't think she needed protection from Hugh. In fact he seemed to want to be more like Hugh; he hadn't just been there to watch over the spanking and ensure she was unharmed, he'd asked questions and listened attentively to the answers. Alex wanted to emulate Hugh.

And what of her feelings for Alex? Somehow they seemed to have changed... or maybe just her perception of them had. Alex was as handsome as ever, as charming, warm with her where he hadn't been with other ladies, and yet kissing him had felt *wrong*. Compared to what she thought would happen. She'd thought kissing him would be even better than kissing Hugh—more exciting, the culmination of all the fantasies she'd had since she was a young girl. Instead, he'd just still been Alex. Warm, safe, and without any of the sparks or arousal that accompanied her kisses with Hugh.

That might have been because he'd been trying to push her away, but there had been a moment when her lips had first touched his that he'd frozen in place. The lack of fireworks had been both surprising and disappointing.

Yet, even after spanking her, she responded to Hugh.

Although she'd wanted to ask Eleanor some questions about love and marital relations, she just didn't feel comfortable discussing such things with her when the marriage in question was her brother's. There were no other ladies in London she was particularly close with and only one who knew anything about her feelings for Alex. Which was how she'd ended up finding her way to her parents' house in town.

They were still renting, but they'd moved to a much more fashionable part of town following Irene's marriage. The house was lovely, although privately Irene thought it was far larger than her parents needed considering they were the only ones occupying it. Still, her mother was obviously very happy with the move, as well as the new wardrobe and fripperies she was currently showcasing to her daughter.

It was the first time in years Irene could actually remember her mother looking at her with anything like approval.

"I wore this one last week," the Baroness said, showing Irene a gown of deep green cambric, edged with gold lace. It would have been quite beautiful if it hadn't been so ostentatiously ruffled and trimmed. "Even Lady Jersey stopped to remark upon it."

"It's beautiful, mother," Irene said quietly.

"Yes well," her mother said, sitting down on her bed with the air of one who was completely exhausted. Not surprising since she'd spent the past several hours showing Irene one new item after another. Irene wasn't tired at all, not physically at least, although her head felt rather bruised. While she hadn't had the opportunity to bring up her marriage or her questions yet, the thoughts spinning round and round her head had never stopped. "Your marriage did turn out to do us quite a bit of good, didn't it?" For a moment her mother stopped and really looked at Irene, a little frown wrinkling the center of her brow. "You aren't here to stay for any length of time are you? It really wouldn't do to be seen having some kind of difficulties with your husband so soon after your return to the city."

Looking at her mother, Irene wondered why she'd come to her parents' house in the first place. It seemed as if she were constantly making the wrong decisions lately. Had she really thought to find any comfort or helpful words of wisdom from her mother? And yet... where else would she have been able to go?

If nothing else, at least she'd gained a few hours of space from her husband and her new home to just sit and think. But there was nothing for her here.

"No mother," she said quietly, her hands neatly folded in her lap like the demure young miss her mother had taught her to be. "Hugh and I are quite well."

"Good," her mother said stoutly, casting a covetous gaze over the pile of fabric that had been heaped onto the bed. "Just keep him happy, Irene. Your father and I will be most displeased if you do not."

The calm resignation that settled over her stomach made her feel rather detached; numbed in a way her chilly demeanor had never quite been able to achieve. There was no shelter or succor for her here, that much had been made obvious to her.

"Come now, let's go have some tea," her mother said, standing and brushing her skirts off. "There will be several ladies coming by to visit. I didn't know that you would be here but since you are you might as well be of some use to me."

By which Irene knew her mother meant Irene's new social status, not Irene herself. "Yes mother."

She suddenly wondered if her mother had really ever intended Irene be able to find happiness as Alex's mistress or if she just had said whatever she'd needed to in order to induce Irene to marry Hugh. Strangely the thought didn't hurt her at all, it just circled around her head with all of the others.

IT WAS late afternoon when Irene returned home. To her surprise, Harrington House felt even more like home than it had when she'd left that morning. Perhaps it was due to the fact that her parents were no longer in the house they'd been in every other time she'd come to town with them. While she still felt as though their small estate out in the country was her true home, here in London Harrington House was the closest thing she had to a real home. Even if she hadn't been here for very long.

That feeling of settled comfort was only amplified by the smiling greeting from the butler, who opened the door as she approached. Irene smiled back at him, feeling a kind of weary relief. While she might be unsure of her feelings towards her husband and while she might be nursing both her pride and the kind of heartache that came from broken dreams, at least here she didn't have to deal with her mother.

Stripping off her gloves, Irene moved down the hallway, heading to the morning room which overlooked the small garden in back. It was her favorite room in the house and had been from the moment she'd first been given the tour.

Unfortunately she only made it halfway down the hall before the door to her husband's study, which had been open a mere inch, suddenly pulled open all the way and she found herself facing a rather irate looking Hugh. He'd left the door open apurpose so he could hear when his wayward wife returned home. The suddenness of his appearance made her jump backwards a pace, her face flying up to look at his and his expression made her want to stumble back a little farther.

"Where have you been?" he snapped out.

Irene blinked. "Where…"

"This afternoon, where have you been all afternoon?" he asked, striding forward to loom over her as her neck tilted backwards to keep her gaze on his. He reached out and grabbed a hold of her upper arms, his touch surprisingly gentle as he ran his hands down to her elbows. It was only his hold on her that kept her from trying to step away. "Where did you go after visiting Eleanor?"

"To see my mother."

"Why?" He glared at her suspiciously, not entirely sure whether or not he believed her. After all, her mother was a harridan, why would Irene want to spend so much time there?

"Because I wanted to."

"Did you go anywhere else?"

"No… Hugh what is going on?" Exasperation made its way into her voice as she stared up at him, utterly confused. "Has something happened?"

"Other than my wife disappearing for hours without anyone knowing where she is or what she's doing?"

"I was at the house my parents are renting, having tea with my mother. I didn't realize I couldn't visit her without asking your permission," Irene said a little snappishly, the spirit that had begun to break free on their honeymoon rearing its head. After an afternoon of chit chat and smiling gamely as her mother had shown her off like her father would a prize bull, Irene was feeling decidedly temperamental.

"Well especially after last night perhaps I'd like to know where my wife is," Hugh snapped back, his hands tightening a bit on her arms.

Tears sprang up into Irene's eyes, of both frustration and guilt. As if she would have gone to Alex today after what had happened last night. As if she'd go to any other man. Yet she couldn't blame Hugh for his suspicions... but that didn't make her feel any better.

"Well then let me *inform* you, husband, that when the Season ends I will be making a trip out to Bath with your *sister*. She would like some space and time from her husband and so would I."

"Eleanor what?" Edwin was suddenly out in the hallway, dark eyes blazing as he came up behind Hugh. "My wife is going where?"

"Oh dear..." Irene whispered. Couldn't she do anything right? Eleanor had said she hadn't mentioned the trip to her husband yet, that she wasn't sure how Edwin would react to her wanting to go on a trip without him. While Irene hadn't quite understood why Eleanor would want space from her husband, who obviously doted on her even if he did spank her, she hadn't disclosed her reasons to Eleanor either. Irene had felt the same way; she hadn't meant to just blurt her intentions out to Hugh.

Just as she hadn't meant to throw herself at Alex last night.

It seemed no matter what she tried to do, she always ended up doing the wrong thing. Her mother was happy with her, but she was the only one. Lord Hyde looked furious, Eleanor would surely be unhappy with her even though it had been an accident, Alex had been unhappy with her last night, and even though she thought she and Hugh had patched things up after Alex had left last night, now he was angry all over again.

Irene's upbringing had not prepared her for standing on her own nor for being able to express herself. Once her true self had begun to emerge, thanks to Hugh's careful nurturing and obvious approval, it was as if a dam had burst and she didn't have the requisite controls to temper herself. She'd never required a way to lessen her responses because she'd always been kept so confined and completely closed off, no response had been acceptable other than the one her mother demanded. In many ways she had been kept as a child, her actions and words directed by her mother.

Not that she understood any of this completely yet, but she was starting to realize she didn't know how to handle herself without following her mother's edicts to be silent and accommodating. She didn't know how to be herself without making a mess of everything. Her entire life was falling apart around her, every good new beginning unraveling, and it was all her own fault for being so thoughtless and uncontrolled.

Tears welled up in her emerald eyes and her face crumpled. Hugh acted instinctively, pulling her into his arms as she clung to his coat and began to sob. He didn't entirely understand why she was so upset, but he knew her tears were sincere and something more was amiss than he knew of.

"I-I-I-I-I'm so-so-soooorryyy," she sobbed into his shoulder.

"Dammit all, did she say Eleanor and she are going to Bath?" Edwin came up beside him, his words snapping out like a whip.

Clinging harder to Hugh's front, Irene's sobs increased, as did the shivering going up and down her spine.

"Leave her alone, Edwin," Hugh said with a glare, protectively shifting Irene slightly to the side so he was subtly between the two of them. "If you want to know what's going on, go interrogate your own wife."

"I think I'll do just that."

Perhaps if he hadn't had his own hands full, Hugh would have felt a bit sorrier for his sister, but right now he was a bit occupied with Irene. Eleanor could take care of herself—and would. He could only imagine what hare-brained idea she might have gotten into her head and why she would want to drag Irene along with it.

"I think I'll be taking my leave as well," Wesley said, edging by him. The twinkle in his eye said he was more amused than anything else by the tumult going on around him. Hugh almost growled. "If Eleanor does indeed desire to go to Bath then perhaps she and Edwin will go with me. Shall we make a group of it?"

"I don't think so," Hugh said. He had too much business to take care of in town to leave before the Season was over, not to mention he and Irene needed to stay in the public eye to dispel any possible rumors or scandal after her behavior at Lady Cowper's. A retreat to the country only days afterwards would fan the flames of gossip. "Irene and I will stay in town and then return to Westingdon in a few weeks when the Season is over."

The shaking female body in his arms shivered again but she didn't protest. Which allowed Hugh to keep his temper firmly leashed.

"Then I'd best catch up to Edwin so I may offer my invitation. Good day, Viscountess."

Whatever Irene said in response was muffled by Hugh's jacket. As Wesley strode away down the hall, Hugh turned his wife and picked her up in his arms. The heavy shaking sobs had finally ceased but he could tell she was still crying, her little panting breaths making the inside of his chest tight. His immediate response was to slay whatever dragons were plaguing her, but he hadn't the slightest idea what they might be.

Carrying her into his study, he kicked the door shut behind them and settled them down onto a rather large and comfortable chair. Stroking her hair he cradled her in his arms and murmured to her that everything would be alright, he would take care of her, and all other sorts of soothing comforts until her body finally relaxed against him.

"I'm so, so sorry," she said again finally, her voice small and almost broken.

Hugh kissed the top of her head where her coppery hair met the pale slope of her forehead, shifting her in his lap so he could wrap his arms more firmly around her body. He had to admit that while he didn't enjoy listening to her cry the way she had, he had certainly enjoyed knowing she trusted him enough to turn to him, wanted him enough to nestle against him.

"What's wrong, sweetheart?" he asked gently, feathering light kisses over her forehead and hair.

She didn't know if it was because she'd kept everything bottled up for so long or perhaps because she just no longer had the fortitude to keep it all to herself, but everything came spilling out at once. The feelings she'd had for Alex since childhood, the beating she'd witnessed their butler giving a maid, the devastation she'd felt when Alex had married someone else, her mother's description of *ton* marriages, the guilt she'd felt over marrying Hugh when she had feelings for another, the confusion she'd felt on their honeymoon when her feelings toward him began to change and she started to wonder if it was possible to be in love with two men, her horror and fury at the spanking, her further confusion when she'd realized it hadn't been as bad as she'd thought...

All the way up to the events of the night before when she'd wanted to confirm her feelings for Alex and had only ended up more frustrated and confused than ever when the tingling and excitement that occurred whenever she was with Hugh didn't happen with Alex. The shock she'd felt at the loss of her hero, the realization that perhaps spanking her didn't make Hugh a monster...

Every thought, every emotion, it all came pouring out until her throat was sore and dry from talking. Several times during her long monologue Hugh's arms had tightened around her or he'd stiffened beneath her, once or twice he'd shifted and she'd thought he would interrupt her but he didn't.

When she came to the end of it all she was left panting a little, still curled up against him, too afraid to look up at see his face. Worried she had hurt him. She couldn't find any energy to worry about herself; the lengthy confession had left her too wrung out, as if all the tension of her entire body had drained out and left her limp as a rag doll. Even if he caned her now, she wasn't sure she'd be able to react to it.

For long moments they sat there in silence, Irene waiting, Hugh contemplating as his fingers absently stroked against her. She drank in the feel of his gentle touch.

"How do you feel about me now?" he finally asked.

It was the question Irene had wanted space from him to think over the answer, but it turned out she hadn't needed space from him to figure it out. All she'd needed to do was talk through everything and now she knew.

"I think I'm in love with you," she admitted quietly, watching her finger as it traced over the trim of his jacket lapel. "I thought I loved Alex... but it was the love of childhood. Of a young girl who needed a champion and romanced it, nourished it with fantasies after he'd left. It never occurred to me that he might not be what I'd built him up to be in my head or that his motivations might be something other than love. Although, of course I do think he loves me and I him, but it's different. I just didn't know there were different kinds of love between men and women who are not family. I love him, care for him and want him to be happy... but he's not the man I fell in love with. That man was nothing but a dream. You're real. I feel as safe with you as I did with him but I also feel excited... passionate... stronger." She hesitated. "But I understand if you do not believe me and I do not expect you to reciprocate of course, I know our marriage was arranged and that was not part of the bargain... but if you think you could perhaps... in time..."

"Oh, you silly little thing," Hugh said, tipping her back so he could look into her eyes. They were veined with red, the lids pink and swollen like her lips from crying, her skin was blotchy red, pink, and white and all of it clashed horribly with her hair. Yet he thought she was incredibly beautiful. "I wouldn't have married you if I didn't care for you, no matter what land was included in your dowry. I thought you would be the perfect submissive, docile wife. The more I saw of you on our honeymoon, the more I came to care for you."

He kissed her eyelids, her lashes fluttering against him as she made a low sound in her throat.

"I love the woman who raced me across the fields, who teased me in the creek, who didn't care if I came to dinner smelling of horse and dogs."

He kissed her nose.

Irene looked up at him with solemn green eyes, almost disbelieving.

"I loved that you attempted to approach Rex even though I was furious you didn't back away once he snapped at you."

Now she really looked disbelieving and Hugh laughed. "But I wasn't docile or submissive."

"Compared to my sister you are," Hugh said with a chuckle as he leaned forward and brushed his lips across hers. "That's what I wanted. But I don't think it would matter even if you weren't... I was enamored of you almost from the start and it didn't take me long to fall in love with you."

"But you spanked me!" It was a concept she was still struggling with.

"In order to keep you safe." Something dark flashed in his eyes and he gripped her a little tighter. "If you insist on putting yourself in danger or testing out your emotions on other men again then you can damn well be sure I'll do it again."

"No other men," Irene said earnestly, putting her hand on his jaw and feeling the tension slowly lesson. "Not because I do not like being spanked—although I certainly do *not*—but because I do not need or want any other man but you. I was foolish and naive over my feelings for Alex, but at least it taught me that what I feel for you is different and special."

"Good," he said possessively. This time his kiss was anything but light or gentle and Irene let herself sink into it, her lips clinging to his. "Although I'm not entirely sure I believe you do not like being spanked. Last night you seemed to—"

He was interrupted by a sharp poke in the chest and the narrowing of his wife's eyes. "Enjoying what we do *after* does not make it hurt any less during, you brute."

Rubbing the sore spot she'd just jabbed her finger into, Hugh grinned down at her. "I suppose brute is better than monster."

Irene laughed and he chuckled. Strange to say that for both of them the past twenty-four hours had been extremely trying, and yet now they were glad of it, for without those trials they would not have made their confessions to each other. For the first time Irene looked up into Hugh's eyes and realized the warmth she saw in them was love for her... and the emotions welling in her belly and chest was her love for him.

They spent the rest of the afternoon until supper like that, curled together. She told him, in much more detail, about what her childhood had been like and her mother's edicts, some of which made him snort with laughter. He reassured her that she absolutely did not have to follow the majority of them, just the ones which would keep her safe. The ones meant to keep her from causing a scandal she could break, but only with him. In fact, he got a few ideas from the list, specifically about dragging her off to a darkened corner at the next ball they attended.

Fortunately for the sensibilities of the housekeeper, she interrupted them to announce supper before Hugh could begin to act on practicing any of those ideas.

CHAPTER 17

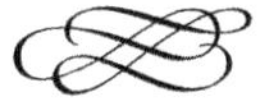

The roiling emotions inside of Edwin jangled together like discordant notes, smashing into each other within his chest and causing his head to pound. Irene's words circled around his head, pecking at his insides. Eleanor wanted space? From him? The fact that his wife was evidently planning a trip to Bath to see her parents without even speaking to him about it was something he could all too easily believe.

The question was why.

Although their marriage had been hasty, he'd been under the impression she'd become reconciled to that. She had been furious when she'd realized he wouldn't allow her to misbehave any more than her father would have, and that he'd use the same measures to keep her in line, but she'd seemed to have accepted that as well. Especially since she had the most amazingly passionate reaction to him following any discipline.

So what had happened? And why hadn't she spoken to him about it?

He suddenly wondered if she would have told him beforehand or just slipped away with Irene, leaving a note or some such behind. Somehow that seemed very Eleanor. Rash, impulsive even in her planned escapades, putting off the consequences until the last possible minute. Did the silly chit truly not think he'd be after her the moment he discovered her gone?

Over and over his fist clenched on top of his knee as he was jolted along in the carriage. When they reached the townhouse he was out before the groom could open the door, waving off the astonished man without even looking at him. The door to the house opened before he reached it and he barreled through.

"Lady Hyde," he snapped out Banks. "Where is she?"

"I believe Lady Hyde is in library, my lord," said the man with a look of surprise on his face. After all, he'd never seen Lord Hyde in quite such a state before, although the look of frustration was becoming more well-known to the staff ever since Lady Hyde had taken up residence. The butler gently closed the door as Lord Hyde stalked off down the hallway, thinking to himself that the parlor maids would have ample opportunity for gossip after this.

Eleanor was indeed in the library and Edwin paused in the doorway, taken aback for a moment by the picture of domestic bliss she presented. She was perched on one of the window benches, her knees drawn up to rest her book upon, wearing a soft blue dress which made her look both younger and more innocent than he knew her to be. Still, the sight of her softened him somewhat, enough so that when she glanced up, sensing his presence, she didn't immediately realize something was amiss.

"You're home," she said smiling as she put her book aside and stood to greet him. As always, her heart beat a little faster when she saw her handsome husband. "How is Hugh?"

"Hugh is fine. How was your visit with Irene?" His voice was soft, dangerous, and Eleanor stopped walking toward him, taking a moment to really look at him. There was something slightly disheveled about his appearance, his cravat was just a little off center, his jacket not pulled quite right and his hair looked as if he'd run his hand through it multiple times. The expression on his face was of contained emotion, his jaw tight with it.

Instincts said to run, but she already knew where that got her.

"Very productive," she said carefully, watching as his eyes flashed. Her breath caught in her throat. Did he know? Had Irene said something to him after promising not to? "She's a quick learner, by next Season she shouldn't have any trouble sorting through which events she and Hugh should attend."

"I see," Edwin said softly. The menace in his tone made her spine stiffen, especially as he strode forward, circling around her like a predator examining a particularly tasty treat. Ignoring his prowling as best she could, Eleanor did not deign to turn with him as he circled behind her.

"Is there something wrong?" she asked lightly, still unsure whether or not he actually knew anything. If he didn't then she surely wasn't going to give him any hints. For all she knew this was just another side to Edwin being amorous, although her bottom was already tingling instinctively, as if trying to warn her.

"I don't know," Edwin said coming up on her other side, he'd circled much closer. Close enough that she had to tip her head back to look up at him. "Is something wrong, Eleanor?"

"N-no..." Inwardly she cursed herself for stammering.

"Are you feeling quite well?"

"Yes."

He paused, studying her. "Missing your parents?"

Eleanor sucked in a breath. *He knew.* The guilt flashed across her face and his eyes flared, seeing the confirmation. She took an involuntary step back and he followed.

"I hear we're taking a trip to Bath."

Immediately Eleanor's chin lifted. While she might have been surprised and momentarily cowed, it was not her natural state. So her plan had been discovered before she was ready for it, it didn't change what she wanted. Besides, perhaps he would give some hint as to his feelings for her in his reaction. After all, her father was always shipping her mother off to Bath or the estates whenever he could. If Edwin was amiable to her trip and only angry she hadn't spoken with him about it first then that could be rather indicative, couldn't it?

"I was planning a trip to Bath to see my parents and asked Irene if she would care to accompany me, if that's what you're referring to."

Edwin shifted closer, staring her down. Their bodies were only inches apart, her breasts a deep breath away from brushing his chest, but Eleanor refused to back down. Her roiling emotions were threaded through with sensual excitement. Why was it that angering Edwin was so desperately thrilling to her? Or was it just that she liked knowing she affected him?

Recklessly she tilted her chin up even more haughtily. "I don't recall inviting *you* however."

"Why not?"

"Why not what?"

"Why am I not invited?"

There was something incredibly invigorating about arguing with Edwin this way, their tones similar to the spats they had when they were younger but with the stakes and emotions so much higher. With him standing so close to her, his dark eyes flashing dangerously, her chest was feeling tighter and tighter. She desperately wanted to back away but she refused to back down. It felt akin to poking a tiger with a stick and wondering how long the beast was going to allow such a thing.

Eleanor licked her lips and saw her husband's eyes drop down to watch her tongue. The room felt heavy with tension that had to break at some point and she had no idea which direction it was going to crack in.

"Perhaps I wish some time away from you."

Something like hurt flickered across Edwin's face and Eleanor felt wretched. She did wish time away from Edwin, to think and to talk to her mother, to see what he would do with that time, to give him enough space to test his interest in her... but she didn't wish to hurt him.

"Why?" he asked softly, raising his hand to brush the backs of his fingers over cheek. A shiver went through her at his touch. "I thought we were getting along well enough."

Well enough, she thought, a little despairingly. That summed up their relationship. She had fallen in love with him and had no idea if he was in love with her or if he was just indulging her the way he thought he was supposed to. Many *ton* marriages could be described as the couple getting on 'well enough' while the husband had his mistresses and the wife had her lovers. Eleanor couldn't imagine letting another man touch her the way Edwin did and the idea of him touching another woman in that way made her sick. She knew he'd had lovers before her of course, but that didn't bother her as much because he hadn't been *hers* then. Just the thought of him taking a lover now made the inside of her chest ache as if her heart might shatter into pieces.

The need to know what direction their marriage would go in was overwhelming to her. She knew her need to separate herself from him wasn't entirely rational, that—like the other tests she'd set—this one might not give her the definitive answer she needed... but it didn't seem to matter what she said to prompt him, he never responded verbally with any assurances of love. Just of affection, caring... the kind of emotions one might have for a friend or a woman he'd known all his life.

Hearing Grace talk about Irene's long-time infatuation with Lord Brooke had made Eleanor wonder if Edwin felt the same way but had married her anyway to make their families happy. She knew very well that her father had arranged the match. Would Edwin have denied her father anything?

It was in her nature to test limits and boundaries, but she'd never tested anything so important as her husband's feelings for her.

For her, well enough was just not good enough.

"I don't have to explain myself to you," she said, although the truth was she couldn't think of an explanation that sounded at all reasonable and didn't give away her own feelings towards him. Edwin already had enough weapons to use against her, she didn't need to hand him another.

Studying the closed expression on his wife's face, the hint of resignation and sadness in her clear blue eyes, Edwin felt a rising panic. He realized that in many ways he'd taken Eleanor quite for granted since their marriage, despite knowing it hadn't been her choice. While she had run hot and cold in her behavior with him, he'd never worried the coldness might actually become so dire that she might leave him, especially since he could always count on her hot passion in the bedroom no matter how she behaved during the day. It had frustrated him, but never worried him.

Now he was beginning to worry.

He'd thought he could read Eleanor, that he knew her well enough from their long acquaintance not to be truly shocked by anything she did, but hearing Irene say they were going on a trip to get space from their husbands had knocked his notions completely sideways. He didn't want her to go away without him, he hadn't considered it and the idea of being separated from her filled him with a longing he knew he'd never admit. What could be her possible motivation? If she had wanted to run to her parents without him after the first time he'd disciplined her then he could have understood that, but she hadn't.

So why now? Why this silent yearning in her eyes, this lingering sadness and unhappy tilt to her beautiful lips?

It was making Edwin feel quite frantic and the immediate thought of one of the usual symptoms of unhappy *ton* marriages popped into his head. After all, this marriage had not been Eleanor's choice, even if he thought she had accepted it and come to enjoy it even.

"Is it another man?" he asked harshly, his insides feeling strangely tight and heavy.

Eleanor's eyes widened, and she stepped back; he immediately reached out and gripped her arms, fighting the urge to haul her against him. The most incredible rush of possessive jealousy roared inside him, shocking him to his core. He'd never felt such a way in his entire life and despite the shock on her face, her silence was killing him.

"Is it?"

The rage on Edwin's face fascinated Eleanor; she could feel his hands tightening on her arms, his body shaking with thinly leashed emotion. When she'd set out to bait the tiger she'd never imagined such a reaction. Part of her leaped in joy, another part worried that his rage was only because he didn't want someone touching what was his—especially before he'd gotten an heir—not because it had anything to do with her.

"Eleanor." The way he growled her name, so dangerously threatening, had her shaking her head.

"No..."

"Good. There won't be, Nell, not for you. Not ever." The wild look in his eyes almost had her backing away again except he hauled her close and kissed her before she could. His lips were like a brand on her mouth, his tongue pushing in to taste and ravage her; she felt breathless from the tight band of his arms around her body, whimpering as she felt her ribs actually creak from the pressure.

This was not the reaction she'd expected.

But she loved it. His possessiveness thrilled her. When the kiss ended and he picked her up over his shoulder she didn't even do anything more than squeal his name, her hands clutching at his jacket as he carried her off to their bedroom, one hand wrapped around her legs, the other resting on her upturned bottom.

He wasn't sure he believed her. While Eleanor was usually a very truthful person, she'd taken so long to answer, he wasn't entirely sure she was only telling him what he wanted to hear. The revelation that he didn't know what was going on inside her beautiful head tore at him. The thought that their marriage might turn into the usual *ton* arrangement made him want to lock her away and never let her out of his sight. He was having trouble convincing himself such a tactic would not be feasible.

When he reached the bedroom they shared every night he didn't set her down until he reached the bed, stripping her with ruthless efficiency as he kissed her breathless, not giving her a chance to protest. Although she didn't seem inclined to do so anyway, which was barely enough to soothe his rampaging emotions.

Lately he'd taken to carrying spare cravats in his pockets, one that was kept soft and unstarched, so he could bind his wife's wrists at a whim. As soon as he had her undressed he pulled the length of fabric from his pocket and wrapped it around her wrists.

"But you're still clothed," Eleanor protested, although her eyes were sparkling. Passion was making her glow again, it had wiped away her sadness which he was pleased to see...

Although he knew those sapphire depths weren't going to be sparkling for long.

Not answering her, Edwin scooped her up and tossed her into the center of the bed, crawling up quickly to straddle his legs over her middle and hold her in place as he secured her wrists to the headboard. It was a position she'd been in more than once. He loved to have her helpless at his hands and mouth, to tease her until she was writhing and begging him for completion. Now it allowed him to relax, to gain some self-control back over himself.

Because Nell wasn't going anywhere.

Pulling another spare cravat from his pocket—Johnson would have a fit if he knew Edwin's intentions for it, he really must find some better alternatives, Edwin pushed it into his wife's mouth and secured it around her head. Shock rendered her immobile only for a moment and then it was a struggle to tie the thing in place.

When he was finished his beautiful was rumpled, her hair sticking out in more than one direction as the gag and struggle had mussed it horribly, and her blue eyes were promising retribution. No doubt those high shrieking sounds were her screaming invective at him, but for the most part the noise was muffled and nothing was discernible. Edwin glared down at her and pinched her nipples sharply.

A short sharp yelp and then she fell silent behind the gag, glaring up at him with flushed cheeks.

"I have some arrangements to make apparently. We'll be leaving for Bath tomorrow with Wesley." Every sentence was said crisply, as if he was biting out the words. "So you will get part of your wish. I sincerely doubt Hugh and Irene will be joining us... he was almost as displeased to hear of her plans as I was to overhear their conversation." Eyeing her, Edwin could see her anger at being stripped, restrained, and gagged had been tempered by confusion and wariness.

Unable to resist, he leaned down and kissed her forehead, ignoring the renewal of her muffled shrieks and yells.

Having her, for all intents and purposes, wrapped up and at his mercy had gone a long way to tempering the tumult of emotions jumping through him. She wasn't going anywhere without him. Scooping up her clothes, he ignored the sounds coming from his bed as he tossed the clothes into her dressing room and then locked the doors to both rooms so she couldn't re-dress herself even if she did somehow manage to get loose, and then locked the door behind as he exited.

Down the hall he saw a footman whom he beckoned closer. "Don't let anyone in this room until I return. Ignore anything you hear."

"Yes my lord," the man said, looking only slightly confused. He glanced at the door and then at Edwin and then looked away.

Satisfied his wife was going nowhere without him, Edwin headed to his study to write a quick note to Wesley and then to find Mrs. Hester to tell her to begin the process of closing up the London house. After Bath they would head out to the country; the Season was almost over anyway and out in the country he and Eleanor would have a chance to spend more time together. London was not conducive to patching up a relationship, with the constant social demands and hectic pace of the city.

Then he could figure out what had gone wrong and how he could fix it.

FUMING, Eleanor jerked uselessly at her bonds for the umpteenth time. She'd managed to work herself up into a sitting position against the headboard so she didn't feel quite so incredibly helpless. At least when her husband deigned to return she wouldn't be lying out like a pagan sacrifice for him.

Still, she couldn't deny that as angry as she was to be tied up, gagged and left naked on their bed—for hours it seemed like!—there was something incredibly arousing about it all as well. It gave her plenty of time to think. From what her husband had said Irene hadn't knowingly betrayed her plan, which made Eleanor feel better about her sister-in-law. Especially since she'd asked her not to tell Edwin. Of course she would have had to tell her husband eventually but she'd still been trying to decide on the best way... somehow just disappearing didn't seem like the best idea. But she really hadn't known how he was going to react.

Edwin *really* didn't like the idea of her leaving town without him. He'd also seemed incredibly upset about the idea of her with another man. Both things seemed significant. The first especially so as she could only base her ideas on love off of what she'd seen with other couples—most notably her own parents when her mother was constantly wishing to be by her father's side and her father was constantly sending her away. Since their relationship was the one she'd sworn never to emulate, Edwin's anger over her intent to send herself away was rather heart-warming.

Was it possible to be furious and delighted at the same time?

She wouldn't have thought so, but that was how she felt. In fact, if he hadn't gagged her she would have been a lot less furious and quite a bit more amused. Well, once she'd had time to cool down after her initial rage—and time was something he was giving her plenty of. She scowled. So much time, in fact, she was quite sure she'd be able to work her temper back up if he left her alone for much longer.

At least she was going to get her trip to Bath. More than anything she longed for a coze with her mother. Surely her mother would have words of advice for her. Eleanor regretted not having confided in her before, but she hadn't realized how damned confusing it could be trying to decipher a man's actions and determine his feelings.

Looking down at her hands, Eleanor scowled. She could remove her gag if she really wanted to. With time and patience she would even be able to untie her hands. But she kept putting it off because she wasn't sure when Edwin was returning or what state he would return in.

A spanking seemed like a foregone conclusion but she didn't want to make it worse than it had to be and undoing his work seemed like a good way to do just that. On the other hand, part of her wanted to be standing and facing him when he came in. But remaining helpless and in her current state might sway him towards less punishment. Especially if he came back still angry.

She was still considering the quandary when the door banged open and she jumped in surprise. It slammed behind Edwin as he began stalking towards the bed, controlled energy in his every movement. Eleanor decided she was glad she hadn't untied herself. The way he was eyeing her as he shucked off his jacket and cravat, undoing the top buttons of his shirt and rolling up his sleeves, said he was still on edge.

Sitting curled up by the headboard, naked with her nipples hardening under his eyes, mussed hair and flushed cheeks, gagged and wrists bound, Edwin thought his wife made an extremely enticing picture. Almost amusing, how docile she managed to look when he was intimately aware she was anything but.

"We'll be traveling with Wesley tomorrow," Edwin said, his eyes trained on her, traveling up and down the portions of her he could see. The way her legs were curled he could only catch the barest glimpses of the gold and pink of her core, the curve of her breast, a peek at a nipple. It was extremely enticing. "And you are not to leave my sight before then."

Eleanor made a noise behind her gag which he ignored as he finished rolling up his sleeves. Going over to her dressing table, he opened the drawer on the left and heard her muffled moan behind him. A small smile curved his lips as he turned to face her, the wooden hairbrush with its large flat back in his hand. The expression on her face had changed to both beseeching and irritated.

Striding over to the bed, Edwin grasped one of her kicking ankles and began to pull her down the bed slowly so she didn't hurt her arms as she struggled against him.

"If you don't stop resisting I'm going to add another ten strokes to your count," he warned her as her free foot came a little too near his face.

His wife made a little humphing noise but she stopped trying to kick him and let him pull her body down so she was lying flat on her back. Edwin flipped her over and placed the hairbrush down on the bed so he could wedge some pillows under her body until her creamy bottom was pointed towards the ceiling the way he liked it. Picking up the brush again, he tapped her on the back of the thigh with it.

"Spread your legs."

After a momentary wiggle, as if she wanted to resist but knew it would only cause her more trouble, Eleanor did as he asked. Reflexively, Edwin held his breath as her thighs parted, followed by the outer lips of her pussy to reveal the glistening pink interior. As usual, his wife was aroused even if she was furious with him.

"Good girl." His voice was tight with lust, just like the front of his breeches. Raising the brush, he brought the hard wood down on one plump cheek.

CRACK!

The flesh jiggled as Eleanor let out a muffled squeal. It occurred to Edwin that he hadn't removed the gag, which he had intended to do because normally he enjoyed listening to the various noises Nell made when she was receiving a spanking, as well as doling out extra punishment when she cursed or threatened him, but with a shrug he decided to leave it on. For someone as vocal as Eleanor it would serve as an extra punishment, being unable to express herself.

SMACK!

The brush came down on her other cheek, matching it to the first; they now both had bright red marks in the center.

THWACK!

Edwin set to her punishment with fervor, although he remained firmly in control of himself which was why he'd taken so long about coming back to discipline his wife. He hadn't been sure of his control before and he certainly wasn't going to try and punish Eleanor when he was feeling so undisciplined himself. Now, after having made the arrangements to go to Bath and then his estates, he was feeling much calmer and in a much more suitable frame of mind to chastise her soundly.

Creamy cheeks jiggled and turned hot pink under the steady assault of the brush as Eleanor wailed and begged behind her gag. She was well disciplined though; her legs didn't kick up very often and she always hastily returned them to their original place—if she didn't do so quickly enough then she got a short tap on the back of her thigh which smarted horribly. Edwin could see her pussy plumping and becoming even juicier despite her tears and the quickly reddening state of her bottom.

Even though her bottom was on fire and Edwin was still raining down blows onto the tender flesh, Eleanor couldn't quite bring herself to be sorry for her actions. The possessiveness, the heightened and uncontrolled emotions it had stirred up in her husband were too important to her. Although the throbbing, stinging, burning skin of her buttocks were making her feel *almost* regretful that she felt the need to keep pushing him rather than just accepting what their relationship was for the moment and putting off discerning the truth of his feelings for later.

The hairbrush bit into her flesh yet again, right on her sit spot and she jerked as the hot pain flared. For the first time she was glad of the gag, she could scream and cry as much as she wanted and the sound was muffled enough that she didn't have to worry about anyone other than Edwin hearing her. Just like the ropes around her wrists which took away her choices, it also gave her a freedom she hadn't had before... there was only one choice left and so there was nothing to do but revel in it.

With Eleanor's pert bottom glowing, Edwin placed his hand over the hot skin and nearly groaned with appreciation. As much as his wife decidedly deserved her punishments, he couldn't deny the effect they had on him as well. He was never sure whether or not he sometimes wanted her to do something to deserve something much more severe than a light, erotic spanking, just because he did love to see her creamy skin turned bright pink and red. The muffled cries from behind her gag made his cock jerk with each one and as he dug his fingers into the soft, tender flesh and heard her mewl, it did so again.

Letting her lay there for a moment, crying freely now that the spanking was over, Edwin began to pull off his own clothing. He struggled a bit, his own eagerness hindering him, and by the time he was completely naked Eleanor's soft crying had considerably diminished. Fetching a clean handkerchief from their bedside table, he turned his wife over onto her back.

Immediately she squealed and pushed her bottom upwards, her feet firmly planted on the bed, to keep her weight off of her poor, aching nates. Edwin chuckled as he used the handkerchief to clear the remnants of her tears from her face, ignoring the glare she gave him and the jerking of her head which indicated she wanted him to take the gag off now.

"It occurs to me, my dear, that there might be quite a few benefits to leaving your gag on," Edwin said, almost conversationally as he straddled her waist, settling his weight down—not so it was fully on her, but so it was more difficult for her to keep her bottom off of the bed. Cupping her breasts, he began to fondle them, his cock bobbing above her soft skin and practically between the two mounds. Eleanor glared at him and jerked her head again, a slight frisson of pain crossing her expression as she lost the fight to keep her bottom off the bed, her leg muscles burning with the effort. Smiling lasciviously, Edwin pinched her nipples between his forefingers and thumbs, rolling the little nubbins back and forth. "For instance, there's no tempting me with your sweet words to hurry things along... I can take as long as I want..."

Flashes of pleasure slid through the throbbing waves of pain from her spanking as Edwin began to fondle and pinch at her nipples with a kind of perverse glee. Eleanor had certainly learned what things to say in order to make Edwin lose control, she knew how much he liked to listen to her beg, but now she couldn't even do that. All she could do was writhe and press her thighs together, trying to quell the rising heat in her core as her husband squeezed the soft flesh of her breasts, tugged and pinched and rolled her nipples, and teased her until she thought she might actually explode.

It was utter torment, to have her body so highly aroused without any kind of relief and no end in sight. Edwin seemed fascinated by her responses as the pleading sounds behind her gag grew in pitch and frequency, tears actually beginning to leak from her eyes again as the acute need to orgasm grew and grew and grew. Her nipples were becoming highly sensitive under his tugging fingers, her pussy felt so swollen, and she could actually feel fluid leaking down from her slit and to the bed beneath her, her juices were flowing so freely.

Every writhing movement reminded her of her spanking as the burn flared and sparked, yet it did nothing to quell the pleasure and ache growing inside of her, it only added to the tumult of sensations until she could barely tell where one began and another ended.

"You know...." Edwin mused, pressing her breasts around the length of his cock and finding both the sensation and the visual to be rather stimulating. "I think I could very easily use those oils Wesley gave us to make your breasts just as slick and inviting as your pussy... why I could spend myself right here and never touch your sweet little quim at all."

The very idea made Eleanor mew and writhe frantically, her blue eyes feverish and pleading. He grinned at her, enjoying the stark erotic need he'd awakened in her body. The idea of using her breasts to find his gratification appealed to him greatly, but it was an experiment to be made at another time. Once he'd had the thought, he just wanted to see what kind of effect it had on her.

Not that Nell didn't deserve a bit of extra punishment really, but more than anything he wanted to exhaust her to make her more malleable. Really was there anything more malleable than a female wrung out from sensual pleasures? He could tell from the expression on her face and the look in her eyes that she was more aroused than he'd ever seen her before. Pleading blue eyes gazed up at him, without a hint of any emotion other than desperate need, her wriggling movements and thrashing legs told him all he needed to know about the state of her desires.

Deciding he'd enjoyed her breasts for long enough, he smiled down at his wife as she almost sobbed with relief when he began moving down her body. The smell of her arousal filled his nose almost as soon as he knelt between her legs. She was sopping wet, the golden hair around her pink lips dark with it, her inner folds soaked with cream.

Almost as soon as Edwin placed his mouth on her honeyed opening, Eleanor screamed and her body arched against his sucking lips, a violent climax ripping through her. It was all the pent up energy from the spanking and Edwin's extended tormenting of her breasts and nipples rushing out in one glorious burst.

Smiling, Edwin pushed her thighs wider apart and began licking up her cream, laving his tongue over those soft folds as Eleanor's culmination began to recede, leaving her panting and satisfying the overwhelming need consuming her. She moaned some more, wriggling fretfully as he continued to lick and suck at her tender petals which felt incredibly sensitive in the aftermath of her orgasm.

Sliding his hands beneath her, Edwin wedged her legs apart with his shoulders and cupped the hot glutes of her bottom in his hands, squeezing gently. The mix of pleasure and pain he was creating in her core had Eleanor arching and moaning. It was bliss, it was torment, and she was helpless to resist whatever Edwin wanted to do to her.

When his lips moved to suckle at the tiny scrap of flesh at the apex of her slit, Eleanor cried out as she came again, almost before she was ready to. Edwin's skillful handling of her body left her at his mercy, her hips moving in rhythm against his mouth as he squeezed and kneaded the tender flesh of her buttocks. Pain flashed through the waves of pleasure, sending her higher, and her head thrashed back and forth with the utter rapture of it.

As he finally allowed her to descend from the pinnacle again, Eleanor was moaning from the rush of sensations. Her netherlips felt incredibly sensitive in the aftermath of two climaxes. When Edwin began to lick up and down her slit again she wanted to protest, his tongue now felt as though it was rasping against the sensitive surfaces, but no matter how she twisted he was relentless.

She felt almost dismayed as tension began to coil in her belly again; her muscles already felt weak and watery from all she had been through. If she hadn't been gagged she'd be begging him to mount her, to end it, because she knew he certainly wouldn't stop until he'd been satisfied as well and she didn't know how much more she could take. Every inch of her body felt like it was buzzing, she could swear she heard a ringing in her ears like a bell that droned on incessantly, and yet still Edwin licked and pleasured her.

The sensations were almost too much to bear and she found herself crying out in protest behind the gag, tears sparking in her eyes as the pleasure began to veer towards painful. She fought against the rising tide, trying to turn her thoughts to anything other than Edwin's questing tongue. Then she felt him release one of her buttocks and fingers pressed against the opening of her pussy, spreading her as he sheathed them in her tunnel. The stretch of her inner muscles left her gasping as her body moved instinctively, involuntarily, heightening the needy pleasure.

Watching the dismay on her face, Edwin searched out the one spot deep inside of her. He knew when his fingertips rubbed over it because she moaned in denial. A fine glow covered her skin, not quite sweat, but a bit of moisture from her exertions as he toyed with her body. She didn't have the strength to fight him successfully, but she was resisting his ministrations.

Unfortunately she couldn't completely resist the dictates of her body, and as his fingers stroked and pumped, his mouth closed around her clitoris again and his tongue rubbed and licked it in time with his fingers and Eleanor screamed behind her gag, tears stinging her eyes as she was forced into a third orgasm. This time it felt as if fireworks were actually exploding inside of her body, as painful as they were pleasurable.

Her body was wracked with spasms, shaking her and leaving her breathless as she tightened and convulsed around Edwin's probing fingers. The wet slickness of her tunnel made it easy for him to slide his fingers back and forth despite the tightening muscles.

When the crescendo of passion finally reached its culmination and began its denouement, Edwin allowed his tired jaw a rest and pulled his fingers from her body. Eyes half-lidded, his wife lay sprawled out before him, her limbs limp as she moaned lightly behind the gag. Between her legs he could see the damp patch on the bed linens where her juices had overflown in her ecstasy and pure male smugness spread through him in a satisfying wave.

Now it was time to satisfy another part of his body.

Eleanor moaned a weak protest, barely audible behind the cravat tied around her head, as Edwin pulled her legs upwards and draped them over his arms, her knees settling into the crook of his elbows. She was dimly aware she was entirely at his mercy with her hands tied, her watery muscles too weak to resist and her pussy open and vulnerable to his advancing cock. The feel of his hot rod of flesh pushing into her sopping opening had her quivering.

The sensation was akin to an orgasm although only pleasure shuddered through her, there was no spasming of muscles that accompanied a true climax. Her over sensitized nerves buzzed and tingled as he pushed deeper, an occasional convulsion of her sheath making both of them moan. He filled her up, so hot and hard inside of her, her body so sensitive, that she thought she might truly faint from the pure rapture of it.

His hands reaching down to hold her hips, bending her lower body so that her thighs splayed wide so as to not bend her in two, Edwin began to pump hard and fast into his wife's soft, unresisting warmth. Moaning non-stop, Eleanor shuddered and quivered beneath him, her entire world dwindling down to the pounding cock stroking her so deliciously. Resistance had melted away, the pleasure was so exquisitely intense it almost registered as pain; she no longer had the energy or strength to try and fight off the sensations.

Instead she settled into them, floated on them, immersed herself until she was in a place that felt like heaven. It wasn't like anything she'd ever felt before, and as Edwin's cock pounded into her she went flying.

~

THE FEEL of his wife's body spasming around him, milking him, set Edwin off and he pumped what felt like buckets of cum into her squeezing sheath. Groaning, he let her legs slip down as he lay on top of her, half of his weight on his forearms as she wrung his body of every last drop of fluid. He was in such a state of heavy satiation it took him a moment to notice Eleanor wasn't moving beneath him.

Frantically he pulled the gag off of her, shaking her as he pressed his fingers to her throat where her pulse beat strong a steady. She let out a little moan and her eyelids fluttered.

Smiling, Edwin laughed at himself as he fell onto his back beside her. His goal had been to utterly exhaust her and then he panicked when he did. Sighing, he propped himself up beside her and undid the bindings about her wrists, rubbing them gently where they were marked pink from her movements.

After doing his best to clean them up, he tucked her into the bed and rang for some food. Although he didn't think she would wake up, if she did then she would have no reason to leave the room. Not that she'd be able to, since he planned on tying her to the bed again before he retired for the night as well.

CHAPTER 18

The gentle rocking of the carriage made Eleanor wince even though Edwin had thoughtfully provided her with a cushion to sit on. Not only was her bottom sore from the spanking she'd gotten the night before, but the area between her legs was still incredibly sensitive to the touch. Fortunately she was alone in the carriage other than her maid and Poppy had fallen asleep a quarter of an hour ago, leaving Eleanor to her thoughts and allowing her to cease hiding her discomfort. Not that Poppy would think any less of her, but Eleanor did have her pride.

The men had decided to ride for this portion of the trip, something Eleanor would have normally joined them in doing if it hadn't been for the sore and sensitive state of her lower half. Still, at least the carriage Edwin used for long trips was extremely comfortable. Truth be told, she still wasn't sure she wanted to spend any length of time in conversation with her husband at the moment. She could barely look at him without turning the same crimson red as the cushion she was currently sitting on.

That morning she'd woken up ravenously hungry, incredibly sore, and with her wrists still secured to the headboard while her husband was wrapped around her. When she'd tried to wriggle away she'd ended up awakening him. He'd untied her and checked over her entire body, to ensure she'd suffered no true ill effects from the night before. Other than soreness and the usual lingering pain from a spanking she'd been just fine, but for some reason she couldn't stop being embarrassed over her behavior.

Not the behavior that had goaded him into spanking her. No, the ease with which he'd taken her body and pleasured her relentlessly and thoroughly. Somehow the vulnerability she'd felt at the time had transferred itself to her this morning.

Although Wesley's sly comments when Eleanor climbed into the carriage hadn't helped. Nor had the twinkle in Edwin's eye as he'd refused to answer the other man's questions.

Sighing, Eleanor looked out the window at the passing countryside. If she leaned far enough to the left she could see ahead of the carriage on the road where two accomplished and rather dashing horsemen were leading the way.

"So THEY'RE GOING to stay out the remainder of the Season?"

Wesley chuckled, shifting on his horse as it minced its steps over a rut in the road. "They were practically glowing at each other over the breakfast table. I've never seen Hugh so disgustingly happy. I have to say, I found the Viscountess much more attractive with a true smile on her face."

"How long do you think it will last?" Edwin wondered.

Although Hugh had only confided the barest details to Wesley, he and Edwin were more than observant and bright enough to put together most of the story. Edwin felt rather sorry for Alex, who had obviously been as oblivious as Hugh to Irene's intentions.

"I don't know," Wesley said with a careless shrug. "I will say there was something different about the way Irene spoke and behaved. Nothing overt, but just something that made me feel like she was thinking more... like she'd grown up a little bit overnight. She always struck me as rather child-like, even though she's older than Nell, this morning she didn't."

"Interesting."

Personally, Edwin had his doubts about Irene now that she'd shown some of her true colors. But he also hadn't spent very much time with her and as long as she made Hugh happy then he supposed he should be happy.

"You seem rather judgmental for a man who's having to take his own wife from London out of fear she might run away without you," Wesley observed, but there was no bite to his words. Indeed they were said almost cheerfully.

Edwin still growled. He knew his friend was amused by what he had taken to calling "marital obsessions." But then Wesley had never met a woman he couldn't let go of and when he did think of marriage at all he always assumed he'd make the usual *ton* marriage to a girl of good breeding who would bear him an heir and be responsible for his social duties while he enjoyed himself with his mistresses on the side. He didn't understand either of his friend's all-absorbing interest in their wives.

THE HOUSE EDWIN had rented for them was in the most fashionable part of Bath. It was also quite a bit smaller than Hyde House in London, but Eleanor supposed that was to be expected. After all, it had been procured on rather short notice, and they weren't going to be staying long. Only until the end of the Season, at which point they'd go to visit Edwin's parents. She looked forward to seeing Lord and Lady Clarendon, although it still startled her to realize they were now her parents-in-law. After her wedding she'd received the nicest letter from Lady Clarendon, welcoming her to the family and expressing her delight to have Eleanor as a daughter-in-law, as well as an invitation to visit them at the Manse whenever she pleased.

Wandering into the small parlor, which was decorated in a muted pinks and yellows with accents of blue, Eleanor admired the furnishings. She could be very comfortable here for a few weeks, and she had to admit she was rather relieved to be out of London. It wasn't until they'd arrived that she realized how tense she'd been in the city; she felt much more relaxed now.

"Sweetheart!" Eleanor's mother burst into the parlor, the butler trailing behind her looking rather embarrassed he hadn't been able to hold back the Countess.

Smiling as she hugged her mother, Eleanor waved him away. With a little bow of his head, the man closed the door to give them some privacy.

Wrapped up in her mother's arms, Eleanor felt herself unwind even more. She knew her father thought her mother had spoiled her dreadfully, and perhaps she had, but they'd formed a very close bond as Eleanor had approached womanhood. When she'd been younger they hadn't been close at all because Eleanor had been interested in more boyish pursuits; which was only to be expected since she'd always trailed after Hugh and his friends. Once they'd gone off to school and Eleanor had grown up a bit, under her mother's influence she'd found that she rather liked being a girl as well.

"You look lovely," her mother said, pulling away. There were tears in her eyes and Eleanor found her own eyes were feeling rather watery as well. "It's so delightful to have you here in Bath with me again. Is there an... ah... ulterior reason for your leave-taking the city before the end of the Season?" Arching her eyebrow, her mother glanced down at Eleanor's stomach.

She blushed.

"No I'm not... that is..." Eleanor took a deep breath. "I wanted to come visit you in Bath, although I was going to wait until the Season was over, but I hadn't discussed it with Edwin yet and he found out... well, we had a bit of a row and he decided we would both come and since Wesley was already coming out to Bath to see his mother, it just seemed convenient."

"Ah yes... his ward..." Something like amusement tempered with worry crossed her mother's face, little wrinkles crinkling at the corners of her eyes. "Well it's good he's here to take *that* situation in hand, the Countess needs all the support he can proffer." Taking Eleanor's hand, her mother smiled and led her toward the couch. "Come dear, sit so we can have a good coze. I've missed you so, I want to hear everything about what you've been up to."

"Let me just ring for some tea."

After giving the maid instructions for tea and scones, Eleanor went to join her mother on the couch, hissing slightly as she sat a little too abruptly, having forgotten the sore state of her bottom.

Eyeing her, her mother raised her all-knowing eyebrow again. "A bit of a row with Edwin, you said?"

"Yes," Eleanor responded a bit grumpily. She'd expected her mother to be affronted on her behalf, not amused. Then again, her mother had always allowed her father to handle any disciplinary measures, so she supposed it didn't bother her that Eleanor's husband might employ the same ones.

A small smile played on her mother's beautiful face. Eleanor almost smiled herself, seeing it. If she aged half as well as her mother she'd be quite happy.

"You know, I've found over the years that it's much better—and much less painful—to avoid rows with one's husband," her mother said, in the same calm manner that she'd often imparted words of wisdom to her daughter. "It's quite possible to work around getting what you wish without a show of outward defiance."

Rather aghast, Eleanor stared at her mother, wondering if she was implying what Eleanor thought she was. "Painful? Papa... he spanked you too?"

"More than once dear, although I've learned to give him as little opportunity as possible."

The tea arrived at that moment, stymying Eleanor's outrage on behalf of her mother. Although they looked quite a bit alike, it had always been obvious to Eleanor she was made of hardier stuff. Her mother was delicate, almost ethereal at times. Was this why she never protested when Eleanor's father sent her away? As much as Eleanor loved her father, she had never been able to countenance his treatment and neglect of her mother. Knowing he enforced his edicts to her with the same harsh measures he'd used on Eleanor herself incensed her.

Once the maid had left she poured the tea, trying to get a better grip on her emotions. She didn't want to distress her mother after all, but she was going to have words with her father the next time she saw him.

"You know, I was very happy with the match your father made for you," her mother said, delicately sipping from her cup as Eleanor stirred sugar into hers. She smiled warmly. "I've received quite a few letters from friends in London congratulating me on my daughter's grace and manner."

"I'm glad to hear it, but why do you give Edwin the credit for it?" Eleanor asked a little sullenly.

Her mother just laughed. "Because, dear heart, I could see as clearly as anyone else what you were headed for if someone didn't curb your behavior. I knew Edwin would be good for you; the men you were encouraging weren't nearly strong enough for you. Edwin's very much like your father, I knew you'd be happy with him once you accepted him as your husband."

"You wanted me to marry someone like papa?" Shock suffused Eleanor to the point where she nearly dropped her teacup onto her lap. The liquid sloshed but fortunately didn't make it over the edge. How could her mother want that for her? She knew her mother was in love with her father, but surely she couldn't have wanted the same for Eleanor, considering how she suffered from the lack of her husband's love.

Her mother blinked at her. "Well, of course. You wouldn't be happy with a weak man, you needed someone who was your equal. Of course Edwin's an honorable man, I knew he'd take care of you and respect you."

"I don't understand." Eleanor's hands were trembling so badly she had to set down her teacup before she spilled the hot liquid all over herself. This conversation was nothing like she'd expected and she felt as if she was missing some key knowledge, something that would make it all make sense. "You always told me love was the most important thing."

"It is, but Edwin's always loved you."

"Like a little sister!"

"When you were younger, but when I saw the way he looked at you at your ball and the way he danced with you..."

"That's just passion or desire, isn't it?"

"Well passion and desire is part of love." Rather concerned, her mother set down her tea cup and gathered Eleanor's hands in her own. They felt warm and comforting against her chilled skin; she hadn't even realized she was chilled until she felt the temperature of her mother's by comparison. "Dear heart, I know Edwin had a bit of a reputation, but it's often said reformed rakes make the best husbands. They've sampled all they need to of the buffet, enough to know what they want to settle down with and enough to differentiate between lust and love."

"But he never *says* he loves me," Eleanor muttered. That had been her largest sticking point. Shouldn't love be acknowledged? Assuming its existence seemed like a short road to heartbreak.

"That is a problem, but I'm sure he'll come around eventually. After all, how could he not love you?" Her mother smiled and squeezed her hands. "Men sometimes have trouble acknowledging their emotions, especially the first time they have to express them. I can count on my fingers the number of times your father has told me he loves me, but that doesn't make his emotion any less real."

"But he's always sending you away, Eleanor's shock was back.

Her father told her mother he loved her? Her father who was always in London while she and her mother were in Bath or the countryside? While she could accept her father could spank her mother and still love her, after all he spanked his children and still loved them, how on earth could those long distances be justified? Especially since it was obvious how sad it made their mother whenever they were separated? How could that be love?

"Oh dear..." The dismay on her mother's face matched Eleanor's own as she realized what her daughter had interpreted as an expression of disinterest. The older woman shook her head. "Sweetheart... It's not that your father *wants* us to be separated so often."

"Then why does he do it? It makes you so sad to be away from him; he was always sending us away or leaving us and not allowing us to come to London."

"For a while you were too young to go to London with us, and neither of us wanted to leave you alone with just a nanny or governess. I can't even imagine the shambles of a house we might have come back to," her mother said with a smile, releasing Eleanor's hands and picking up her tea cup again. "Then, once you were old enough... well I do enjoy London, but I have a decided preference for Society in Brighton or Bath. It's slower and not as demanding. I also have a bit of a problem with my lungs and London is so very dirty. The longer I stay there the more it effects my health. It worries your father so when I begin to cough or have trouble breathing, he gets rather frantic actually. But of course he has to be in London because he's so involved in the political scene. Although I think I've convinced him to begin passing a lot of that responsibility off to someone else. He'll still have to return to Parliament to vote of course, but he's getting older as well and he's enjoying our stay here in Bath, he needs to lessen the amount of stress on himself."

Bright happiness shone in her mother's eyes and Eleanor suddenly felt very small and confused. The explanation was turning her world on its head, casting a different kind of light on all the incidents she's witnessed throughout the years. Her father's impatience with her mother whenever she tried to remain in the city long, her mother's pale face and wane looks which she had always thought were due to being sent away rather than realizing it was the cause, and the fact that her mother currently looked as though she was glowing with health.

"Of course I pined for him when we were separated, but that's to be expected. He came and visited as often as he could, although I wouldn't let him overexert himself." Her mother sighed. "It hasn't been easy, I admit, but now Hugh is taking over so much of the responsibilities in London it will certainly be *easier.*" Her mother gave her a rather rueful look. "I wish you'd told me before what you thought about your father always being in London. I would have explained."

"Talking about him always made you so sad when you were separated, I didn't want to bring him up."

"Well I'm glad we've had this little chat," her mother said smiling as Eleanor picked up her tea again now that her hands weren't quite so shaky. She still felt as if she'd been blown sideways by a stiff wind, but at least her physical reactions were back under her control.

"Me too," said Eleanor rather wonderingly. Her mother had given her quite a bit to think about.

ALTHOUGH HE'D BEEN loath to leave Eleanor at home by herself, Edwin had been reassured when her mother had arrived and he'd gone with Wesley to greet Lord Harrington. They'd all gone to a gentleman's club to have a drink and chat until Wesley felt he needed to go and greet his mother, leaving Edwin alone with his father-in-law. Since most of Society was in London the club room was lightly sprinkled with other patrons, most of whom were much older and had already taken their leave from the Season if they had attended at all. Edwin and Wesley's presence had brought down the average age drastically, and even Lord Harrington had contributed to the effort.

As such, it seemed like the perfect place for Edwin to receive some masculine advice. His own father was more studious than anything else and he'd often gone to Hugh's father for advice on more mundane matters like women, boxing, swords, and really everything that labeled him as a Corinthian. It only seemed natural he would seek out the older man's advice now, especially as he was married to the man's daughter and hadn't had a chance to talk to Hugh. Who else would know her better?

"So I believe I may be guilty of taking her for granted a bit," he confessed, after having explained the quarrel that had brought them to Bath in the first place, although of course he didn't go into the more sordid details.

Lord Harrington chuckled. "Worst thing you can do to a woman, son. Especially a woman like my daughter, she's not the type to stand mildly by and wait for you to take notice."

"I'm just not quite sure what she wants." Edwin stared broodily at the drink in his hand. "I don't ignore her. I give her presents. I pay her more attention than most men do their wives at balls. But she runs hot and cold... although I never thought she'd tried to leave without telling me. I know she wants *something* from me, I just don't know what."

"Do you think she was really trying to leave?" Lord Harrington wondered. "Or just test you? My Eleanor does like to test her boundaries."

"It certainly felt like a test, although I'm not sure I passed," he grumped in response. The older man hid a smile. Edwin's black scowl went rather well with his dark good looks, if there had been any women in the room they would have been swooning over his rather Gothic demeanor. Personally Lord Harrington thought it was rather good for Edwin, from what he'd seen many things in life had come rather easily to the young man—including his marriage to Eleanor—it would do him good to work for it. It was obvious Edwin did want to work for it.

"I rather think you must have, if you got her to Bath without incident," Lord Harrington said rather dryly.

"That's true," Edwin said, his expression lightening somewhat. "I just... she's driving me wild. The idea of her not wanting to be around me... I can't..."

"The best way to be sure of a woman is to have her fall in love with you. Eleanor's been halfway there all her life, just get her the rest of the way there."

It was almost too simple to be brilliant, but brilliant it was.

Somehow, the entirety of his marriage, Edwin had never really considered love. Like he had Eleanor, he'd taken his emotions for granted, accepting what was on the surface without examining them too closely. It hadn't mattered to him why he constantly wanted his wife's presence, despite the fact she sometimes welcomed him and sometimes gave him the cold shoulder, he'd only known that he wanted it. He'd never considered why he danced attendance on her at balls, not that he'd ever cared about whether or not he was being unfashionable, he'd only known he didn't want her receiving too much attention from the rakes and roués of the *ton* without them knowing he was watching over her.

Of course he was in love with Eleanor, it was why he no longer cared to attract any other women. He admired them of course, he wasn't blind, but no matter how beautiful or sultry or desirable, the woman he desired above all else was Eleanor. All he wanted was to make her happy and to spend the rest of his life with her.

Because he loved her.

So all he had to do was make sure she felt the same way about him.

"Lord Harrington, I do believe you're right."

Rolling his eyes, the older man shook his head at the silly grin that was plastered across Edwin's face. "Of course I am."

EPILOGUE

Not entirely surprisingly, when Wesley was giving the direction to the house his mother was residing in, it was not far from Lord Harrington's house in the most fashionable part of town. What he hadn't expected was to discover that the front drawing room was not filled with her friends having tea and chattering loudly enough to send a man running for a stiff drink. Normally his mother was an incredible social butterfly, it was highly unusual for her to not be "at-home" or at the very least to not have at least one or two friends over to have a coze with.

The open door to the empty room made him surprisingly uncomfortable as the butler took his greatcoat with a judgmental sniff. Wesley hid a grin. Good old Manfred. He'd been the butler for the Countess for as long as Wesley could remember and a stuffier, more upright example of the breed Wesley had never met. Old age hadn't made Manfred's eyes any less sharp and they took in every wrinkle in Wesley's shirt, the less than perfect knot of his cravat, the mud on his boots and the unfashionable length of his hair. It gave Wesley a sense of normalcy that his mother's lack of visitors had unbalanced.

"Thank you, Manfred," he said politely as the butler folded Wesley greatcoat over his arm. The older man just sniffed, amusing Wesley even more. Who cared if he was the Earl now? Manfred obviously still saw him as the little rapscallion who had tracked muddy footprints through the entire manor when he was eight. "Where is my mother?"

"Her ladyship is feeling unwell and is in her bedchamber."

"Is she ill?" Wesley asked, pausing on his way to the stairs. She certainly hadn't indicated any such thing in her most recent letter.

The butler sniffed again, his dark eyes censuring. "I believe the responsibilities and trials of attempting to control *your ward* have had an adverse effect on her ladyship's health."

By which Wesley was given to understand that Manfred disapproved of both the ward and Wesley leaving her in his mother's care. The man practically worshiped the Countess, and considering his own prudish and proper sensibilities would certainly have been just as appalled by the antics his mother had described in her letters as his mother was. Possibly more so. For a moment Wesley almost felt sorry for the chit.

"Where is my ward?"

"Confined to her bedroom," Manfred said darkly.

"I see."

He didn't see, not entirely, but he knew he would. Taking the stairs two at a time he found the third door on the right, which Manfred had indicated was his mother's, and knocked.

"Come in."

The room was surprisingly dark, with just a few candles burning next to the bedside. It was decorated in soft greens, which was his mother's favorite color, and was filled with the kind of delicately carved wooden furniture she preferred and which always made him feel like he was about to break by touching it. His mother was laying on her bed, fully dressed, her maid sitting in the chair next to the window, knitting.

"Wesley," his mother said, sitting up and smiling.

"Are you alright mother?" he asked, coming closer so he could see her better in the dim lighting of the room. The curtains were almost completely drawn, only letting in enough light for the maid to knit by, and the candlelight didn't give him much to go by from a distance. "Manfred said you were feeling unwell."

"A megrim," she said, pushing herself to her feet and holding out her arms. "But I feel much better just for seeing you."

Gently wrapping his mother up in his arms, Wesley felt rather shocked at how small and fragile she felt. He hadn't traveled immediately to see her when he'd returned home, which he should have done, but she'd been on the estates and he'd always hated that house. It had been easier to wait till the end of the Season, especially since she hadn't approved of his support for his brothers' plans. When he'd left to go traveling, against his father's wishes, he'd been taller than his mother of course and more muscular... but now it felt almost as if she'd shrunken in his absence.

When she pulled away, her face tipped up to him, he could see the lines which hadn't been there before, the glints of grey in her mahogany hair and guilt flooded in. He should have gone to see her immediately, whether or not he hated Spencer Place. He shouldn't have left her alone with a young, hoydenish woman to handle on her own, even if she was better suited to guiding a young female. She'd never been very good at disciplining anyone, and he should have realized from her letters that she truly was overwhelmed and not just exasperated.

"Oh Wesley," she looked up at him in dismay, her fingers reaching up to his neckline. "Your hair!"

He couldn't help it, he burst out laughing.

THE HOUSE WAS in an utter uproar. After a chat with his mother in which he accepted her invitation to stay for dinner and fended off her demands he trim his hair immediately—he rather liked having hair longer than fashionable, and most of the ladies didn't object—he'd gone to introduce himself to his ward. Unfortunately, "confined to her bedroom" she was not.

She was missing, it appeared, and no one had seen her leave or even seen her walking around the house. But somehow the chit had snuck out.

Furious, especially after seeing how worn out his mother was from dealing with the hoyden's antics, Wesley had ordered his mother not be informed of this latest debacle until they located the little brat. At which point *he* would deal with her. For a moment he almost regretted they weren't at Spencer place, for he knew very well there was a large leather tawse there as well as a wooden paddle, either of which would come in handy right now.

When it became clear she wasn't anywhere in the house, he sent out what servants could be spared to look for her in the streets. Manfred supplied him with his greatcoat and then he went out looking for her as well, even though he didn't know what she looked like he was overwhelmed with the need to feel as though he was doing something. He'd always been an active youngster and he'd grown into an active man. It just wasn't in his nature to sit idly by.

Armed with a brief description, not that it would do him much good since she apparently had brown hair, brown eyes, a pleasing face, and figure and no one had any idea of what she was wearing, Wesley strode down the street.

He'd barely gotten halfway down the block when a woman burst through a crowd of young men who were walking in front of him and ran directly into his chest.

"Oof."

His first thought was that she squished rather nicely against him. Soft bosoms pressed against his chest before she bounced off. Looking down he realized he had a rather nice view of them as well. Somebody's mistress no doubt, no respectable woman would wear such a low-cut dress during this hour of the day.

"Oh I'm so sorry, I beg your pardon!"

Reluctantly removing his gaze from her rather spectacular bosom, he looked up to catch just a glimpse of her face before she continued to rush past him. He was left with an impression of a brunette with rather mussed hair glinting with hints of gold and copper in the sunlight, wide hazel eyes framed with long lashes, and soft pink lips that just begged to be kissed. For just a moment his ire was forgotten as he turned to admire her backside as she hurried down the street.

It wasn't until she darted up the stairs to a house and immediately went in without knocking that he realized she'd just entered his mother's house.

Hell and damnation!

Apparently he'd just met his ward. His incredibly attractive ward. Who squished very nicely against him and was dressed like a doxy.

Bloody hell.

~

ABOUT THE AUTHOR

Golden Angel is a *USA Today* best-selling author and self-described bibliophile with a "kinky" bent who loves to write stories for the characters in her head. If she didn't get them out, she's pretty sure she'd go just a little crazy.

She is happily married, old enough to know better but still too young to care, and a big fan of happily-ever-afters, strong heroes and heroines, and sizzling chemistry.

She believes the world is a better place when there's a little magic in it.

www.goldenangelromance.com

BB bookbub.com/authors/golden-angel
g goodreads.com/goldeniangel
f facebook.com/GoldenAngelAuthor
instagram.com/goldeniangel

OTHER TITLES BY GOLDEN ANGEL

HISTORICAL SPANKING ROMANCE

Domestic Discipline Quartet

Birching His Bride

Dealing With Discipline

Punishing His Ward

Claiming His Wife

The Domestic Discipline Quartet Box Set

Bridal Discipline Series

Philip's Rules

Gabrielle's Discipline

Lydia's Penance

Benedict's Commands

Arabella's Taming

Pride and Punishment Box Set

Commands and Consequences Box Set

Deception and Discipline

A Season for Treason

A Season for Scandal

Bridgewater Brides

Their Harlot Bride

Standalone

Marriage Training

CONTEMPORARY BDSM ROMANCE

Venus Rising Series (MFM Romance)

The Venus School

Venus Aspiring

Venus Desiring

Venus Transcendent

Venus Wedding

Venus Rising Box Set

Stronghold Doms Series

The Sassy Submissive

Taming the Tease

Mastering Lexie

Pieces of Stronghold

Breaking the Chain

Bound to the Past

Stripping the Sub

Tempting the Domme

Hardcore Vanilla

Steamy Stocking Stuffers

Entering Stronghold Box Set

Nights at Stronghold Box Set

Stronghold: Closing Time Box Set

Masters of Marquis Series

Bondage Buddies

Master Chef

Dungeons & Doms Series

Dungeon Master

Dungeon Daddy

Dungeon Showdown (Coming 2022)

Poker Loser Trilogy

Forced Bet

Back in the Game

Winning Hand

Poker Loser Trilogy Bundle (3 books in 1!)

SCI-FI ROMANCE

Tsenturion Masters Series with Lee Savino

Alien Captive

Alien Tribute

SHIFTER ROMANCE

Big Bad Bunnies Series

Chasing His Bunny

Chasing His Squirrel

Chasing His Puma

Chasing His Polar Bear

Chasing His Honey Badger

Chasing Her Lion

Night of the Wild Stags

Chasing Tail Box Set

Chasing Tail... Again Box Set